Saved by the Colonel

Book 4
in the *Al Sharika* series

by

Richard Sexton

Saved by the Colonel

Book 4 in the *Al Sharika* series

ISBN 97817385680-3-1

"Not so innocent, Sir. The driver reversed back over her. Then sped away."

Jonathan, MI-6 driver

"Royal Counties Bank? Nest of Spies and Vipers."

Colonel Muammar Ghaddafi,

Brotherly Leader,

Great Socialist Peoples' Libyan Jamahiriya

Table of Contents

Chapter 1

A Move to London

"Jess?"

"What?"

"You remember we said we'd stay here in New York at least until you got a promotion to Attending Physician?"

"Of course. As I remember, it was my idea."

"Er, right. You've been a Resident for, what? Three years, now?"

"Roughly, yes. What's your point?"

"Well, we also said that our parents would want to get involved in planning and organising our wedding – so that means it will need to be in England."

"Sure. Is this going to take long, Patrick? I need to go back to the hospital. I've got a patient who isn't responding to treatment and I don't know why."

Patrick sighed. He loved Jess more than he ever thought it was possible to love another human being. But her devotion to medicine was both enchanting and annoying, in equal measure. They met in Vanuatu when she was a newly-qualified doctor. Ever since, he'd admired her determination, imagination and willingness to try anything to improve the lives of her patients. He proposed to her during a brief period of holiday when they were both in the UK. She accepted with alacrity in the full knowledge that he was departing for some years to New York and she had only just landed a new job in the UK. After a year, she'd taken extra exams to be eligible for a job at the Mount Sinai Hospital in Manhattan. She flew out to join him when the job came through.

"Ok. We'll leave it until you get back. I want to talk about a UK visit to get married and have a bit of a honeymoon - make an honest woman of you!"

That generated a smile, at least. "I'd like that. I'd better go."

"How long will you be? We can have dinner together."

"I have no clue, Patrick. As usual. The man might pull through; he might linger for days or crash in the next few hours. The hardest part is I have to talk to some relatives to see what they want to do."

"Ok. I know that's hard. Good luck. Love you."

She favoured him with a grim smile and reached for her coat on the hook by the door. "Bye."

Patrick's own injuries were mending well. He'd been kidnapped from this very apartment by Fawaz Damra, New York head of *Al Sharika*. Years before, in Vanuatu, that terrorist organisation had tried to recruit him to siphon money into their global movement. But he had resisted and done his best to reveal their activities to the authorities. Neither blackmail nor intimidation worked on him. Instead, he had become a problem, threatening their operations. They attempted twice to kill him during his posting to the Middle East. Then again while on leave in England and yet again a year ago right here in New York.

To his surprise, Damra was not only an Imam at the local mosque, but also a Karate Black Belt. *Al Sharika's* instructions to Damra had been to make Patrick's death as slow and painful as possible. This would reflect the deal of trouble he had caused them. The F.B.I. raided the Brooklyn warehouse where he was being held in time to rescue him from drowning in the murky waters of New York harbour. But not in time to save him from a prolonged physical beating beforehand.

A number of urgent surgical procedures had saved his life and an intensive programme of physiotherapy had restored most of his mobility.

Moving from continent to continent had not shaken off the organisation's determination to end Patrick's life. Would they keep trying for ever? Right now, the danger was his burden alone. But he wanted to marry Dr Jessica, now his fiancée. It would not be fair to her, for ever to be on the lookout for assassination attempts and death threats. If he was to be a responsible husband and life partner, he needed to be around for the foreseeable future. He had already subjected her to enough emotional trauma for one lifetime.

-----//-----

Much later, he reheated food for them, poured glasses of wine and wisely kept quiet until Jess herself broached the topic. She drained her wine glass and pushed it towards him for a refill.

"I needed that. It was touch and go, today. That man I told you about has started to respond – I do believe we've pulled him back. But his relatives…" She shook her head. "Of course it's an emotional time for them, but I have rarely met a more heartless lot."

"What do you mean?"

"First, they were squabbling about who had the right to dictate the amount of life-prolonging treatment we give. Then who would get his car if he died. And then they asked me to 'put him out of his misery'."

"You mean euthanasia?"

She nodded. "I told them as firmly as I could that the practice isn't legal here. Not only that, but, in my view, provided he showed some response to all the meds we're pumping in, then we'd fight to get him well again."

"How did they react to that?"

"Two walked out. They had a complete sense of humour failure."

"And those who stayed?"

"There was one who stayed – his brother. He thanked me and asked if he could wait while I did what I could."

"Shame about the others. Did you think about the patient having to go home to face them as well as his brother?"

Jess nodded. She wiped her hands across her eyes, as though scraping away the memory.

"You wanted to talk about getting married."

This was Patrick's moment. He'd rehearsed how to start the conversation but hadn't settled on a good opening line. Better to just say it.

"Um, we got the timing right for your twelve month house rental in Chislehurst before getting your job here. You said promotion to Attending Physician was workable in around four years if all went well. We both want to get married, so… I wanted to suggest we set our parents off making some of the arrangements."

"It's a lovely idea, Patrick. I know this is what we planned, but the closer we get to being able to do it, the more daunting it is. There's so much to line up. It's not only getting holiday at the same time, but booking the wedding ceremony; the reception; finding somewhere to stay; flights, hiring a car. And a dress! Oh, God – my mother will want to hire a dress designer – I don't want that. I want to make it myself. How are we going to do it all?"

"We'll get through it, Jess – together. It's how we are going to do everything."

She threw her arms around him and gave him the biggest squeeze. She muttered something into his neck.

"Sorry? I couldn't hear that…"

"I said, 'You are the soppiest person sometimes'."

"Sorry about that. There was something else I wanted to say which has been weighing on my mind for a long time."

She pulled back and fixed him with what he had come to know as 'The Look'.

"What?"

"These *Al Sharika* people I've told you about."

"Go on."

"You know they tried to force me to help them steal money and do money-laundering things." She nodded. "They gave that up when I wouldn't play ball and have been trying to kill me ever since I left Vanuatu. I am beginning to think they will never stop trying. Everywhere I go I run into people who are part of their network. You never met him, but I used to have a colleague here named Charley. He was passing inside information to Fawaz Damra. I played a part in the bank finding out that it was him. That was why Damra came after me."

"Are you trying to tell me that you have a burning need to put right any wrongdoing you come across?"

As usual, Jess had diagnosed the problem while he flailed away, jumbled thoughts tumbling out of his head in no discernible order.

"Well, I suppose so – yes. It's…"

"Yes..?"

Patrick swallowed. This was it. "I'm worried that I am putting a burden on you which isn't fair. I mean, what normal woman actually wants to marry a chap who keeps getting into trouble? I could end up dead, leaving you with, I dunno – kids, a mortgage, who knows what else?"

Jess smiled at him and moved in for another, longer hug. "Maybe I'm not a normal woman – did you ever think of that? And, hey, who said anything about kids?"

He gulped. This wasn't a relationship area he'd planned on getting into – not right now, anyway. He realised she was shaking. This time, he pulled back.

"Are you ok? What's the matter?

Jess was trying to stifle her laughter. "Your face. You should have seen it!"

He knew he was easy to tease. Several people, usually girls, had told him so. But he found it hard to say in words exactly what he meant when it came to delicate or emotional topics. He took after his father in that respect, always sounding too earnest at best and clumsy at worst. He'd said the wrong thing to Jess several times during their relationship and had to work hard to gain forgiveness. His best friend from Bahrain, Barney, asserted that the best attitude to girlfriends was, 'Treat 'em mean and keep 'em keen'. But Patrick didn't think Barney honestly believed that and also, he reckoned that mantra more resembled how Jess treated him.

He judged that Jess was teasing about having kids, this time. He felt safe to join her in embarrassed laughter.

"Look, Patrick. I know these *Sharika* people are dangerous. Remember I was almost kidnapped by them – on my first day in New York, too – but even if they don't give up, we can't live our lives worrying about them all the time. And I'm not giving you up. So that's that. Ok?"

He nodded. Lots of words swirled in his head, but the lump in his throat prevented any of them making it into the open air.

"Sorry I put you on the spot, talking about kids. There will be time for kids one day, if we are lucky. All the while we are executing Plan A, I'm staying on the Pill. And we ought to get married first, don't forget."

Patrick hoped that hugging Jess tightly would convey the meaning he'd like to have said in words, but still couldn't. She was the most extraordinary, wonderful human being.

-----//-----

Part way through the next week, Patrick's boss, Hank, called him in.

"Patrick? Got a minute?"

"Sure, Hank. What's up?"

"Coupl'a things. London asked me to let you go back there on secondment for six months or so. They hired McKinseys to figure out how to improve their client profitability and they want to have some client coverage models to work from."

"They want to know what I do?"

"Something like that. Whatever it is, they wanna bottle it and sell it around the division."

Patrick smiled. "It isn't hard, I don't think. I listen to what people say, make some conclusions and introduce them to something which helps."

"Sounds like you were a consultant in a past life. The way they put it, you'd be flying to London on Sunday afternoons on the 'Redeye', reporting to Head Office as soon as the car can get through London traffic. Then leaving early on Fridays to arrive back here late on Friday nights. Would that be alright with your lady?"

Patrick frowned. "That's one issue. But who would look after my clients while I'm away? I expect this will impact my potential bonus this year, too."

"Spoken like an investment banker. Don't forget we struggled through a lot of months when you were horizontal in a hospital bed, moaning and groaning. Whose fault was that?"

Hank had a point. They'd managed without him for a prolonged period when he was stuck in a hospital bed, with no hope of travelling around the country, thanks to Fawaz Damra. At least he now had two dozen or so contacts in every bank with whom he could keep in touch on the telephone.

"I guess it could work. I'll have a chat to Jess tonight. Did they say when they want me to start?"

"End of the month."

"You said there were a couple of things..?"

"Yeah. There's a slot opening in London for financial institution coverage of the Middle East – your old stomping ground. You might want to have a think about doing that. Then you can turn it down and come back here."

Patrick grinned at him. The immediate lure of promotion and more money flared in his head. The truth of the matter was that he was well-positioned for the post. He knew the region, spoke some Arabic, knew some of the players, too. But this wasn't what he'd talked about with Jess.

Patrick returned to his desk, deep in thought. Him going to London might work to their advantage, given what he'd told Jess he planned for their marriage.

She was already in their apartment when he got home.

"Hey there. Something smells good."

"I've warmed up that ragu sauce I made yesterday. You want pasta with it?"

"Sure. Do we have any parmesan?"

"We do. Go wash your hands and change. Oh, and I think there's a bottle of red by the table."

Over the years since they met, Patrick had persuaded Jess that the addition of garlic to dishes helped the taste. It was 'good for the blood' and not as anti-social as she had assumed. Her initial sneers at the herb's medicinal properties evaporated when she found learned studies listing benefits as wide-ranging as lowering blood pressure, reducing inflammation and curing Athletes'

Foot. It caused her to reverse her first position of negativity to becoming something of a devotee. But he reckoned she still wasn't sure about how it tasted. He reasoned that she regarded it as a medicinal supplement which could get you a seat on the train in the morning.

Sitting in the 'fridge overnight had improved the sauce to a great extent. The flavours of its ingredients had softened and melted together. He knew she'd added chicken livers – a tip passed to him by old man Staubitz, owner of the wonderful butcher's shop close by in Brooklyn.

When they sat together, clinked glasses and began to eat, he found himself quite taken over by the depth of flavour.

"Oh, Jess. This is glorious. Could you pass the black pepper?"

She obliged. They ate in silence for a minute or two. Patrick laid down his fork and sipped his wine again.

"Remember what we started talking about with weddings and timings and everything?"

"Mmmmmph." An especially long strand of linguine was making a bid for freedom. It slapped against her nose on the way to its final fate leaving a thin, brown dribble. She laughed and dabbed at it with a piece of kitchen roll.

Now and again, Patrick found himself taking a mental snapshot of a situation he would treasure in his memory for ever. This was one of those occasions. Even wearing a faded T-shirt and jeans, her hair in what she'd claim to be a 'mess', Jess' clumsiness with the pasta and sauce was utterly endearing.

"Hank told me today that Head Office wants me to commute to London every week for about six months to work on some project. His idea is that I'll return on Friday nights to be here for most of the weekend."

"So if our Mums and Dads begin wedding preparations now, they might even have most of them done by the time the project is over?"

Patrick nodded. "That's right. I have no real idea what is necessary, or how they'd split up the work, but I'm sure they'd love to do it."

"You can be there to answer their questions and brief me when you get back every week."

Patrick started to protest ignorance of the process by saying, 'I don't know because I've never been married before'. But that wasn't true. He got as far as, "I don't know because I've…" and finished, lamely, "…not, um, found out what has to happen."

He had never explained to Jess how he had helped Mary-Rose Mattiesson escape from Saudi Arabia. He had got her into the British Consulate, gone through a marriage ceremony so she could have a British passport and then divorced Mary-Rose by post when she was safely out of the country.

He ought to tell her. But not today.

"Don't look so worried, Patrick. The parents managed to get married, so they have experience of it and know what's involved. When I said you could answer their questions, it would be for things like what colour of flowers we'll want, the menu for the wedding reception – stuff like that."

Patrick's face straight away radiated alarm. "Jess, I have no idea! I'm sure any flowers will be fine – won't they?"

"Patrick Field! You are the limit! Of course it matters." She sighed and clattered her fork onto her plate. "I'll write you a briefing list. And your job will be to report any arrangements to me. Like dress decisions..?"

She had a way of somehow underlining words and phrases by the tone in which she said them. Maybe it helped when doctoring. In this case, he remembered, when he'd shared his idea, her immediate horror that Mrs Smithson would try to cajole a dress designer to make something unique for her only daughter. He'd have to pretend to be an 'intelligent post office'.

-----//-----

Royal Counties Bank's personnel department made the decision. Patrick would fly to London from New York every Sunday afternoon. He'd work in the Head Office with McKinsey and Co, the consultants designing the project, going back to Jess in New York on Fridays. Hank told him two things about what he'd be doing.

The first was a little joke.

"Consultants? Give 'em a watch and they'll tell you the time."

The second was rather more useful, Patrick thought.

"Think of this as a brain-sucking exercise. Take the next few days to analyse what you do and why you think it is successful. Will it work in other parts of the world? That kind of thing. Ok?"

"Alright. I can do that. Should I tell my clients that I'll be away for a bit?"

"Uh, uh. Tell Maddy to field the calls by saying you are not around right now, but will answer them as soon as you can."

"But I won't be here."

"That's right. What's your point?"

"I'll be in London."

"Same question."

Wait. Did this mean Hank expected Patrick to keep up with his clients in America *and* take part in the UK Project?

"I'm not sure how effective I can be if I'm thousands of miles away in a different time zone."

"You'll figure it out. Remember: your bonus is at stake."

Hank's phone rang. Patrick needed a large coffee and some time to think.

Chapter 2
Falling out of Love

Patrick began his reflection. He started by writing a list of all the things he liked about his job. This technique was recommended to him by no less a figure than Hank's boss, Jerome Jackson III. That was the left-hand column and it stretched for two pages. Then he entered some things on the right which he disliked. There didn't seem to be many. But there were a couple of quite serious ones.

Chief among these was his worry that there wasn't anything else left for him in investment banking. He smiled to himself as the sentiment expressed by Walt Disney's character King Louie came to mind. In 'I wanna be like you' from the 1967 film The Jungle Book, King Louie had pretty much summed up his feelings. Like Louie, self-proclaimed 'King of the Swingers', he'd 'reached the top and had to stop'. Sure, he could take on more responsibility, learn new products, do bigger deals, attend more cocktail parties and travel more. But would he need things always to be 'bigger' and 'larger' to achieve the rewarding buzz? What good was he doing in the world, crafting financial solutions for banks? Did it help humanity?

No answer came immediately to mind. 'This is a bit philosophical, a bit 'mumbo-jumbo' and far too introspective', he thought.

He looked again at the left-hand column, but this time with a more jaundiced eye. It was true that he liked 'meeting new people'. And 'using his experience to help people'. There were other entries in the same vein. But they could all be describing a social worker. Or a policeman. Or a nurse. What individual skills and aptitudes did he have which could make a difference in the world as a whole? In short, what good was he doing as an investment banker?

Another important entry in the Dislikes column was that so many of his co-workers seemed to have a flexible attitude to morality. He didn't want to risk infection with this malaise. Did that go hand-in-hand with the job? A recent example swam out of his memory and bubbled up to the top.

He'd returned from a trip bringing an interest rate mismatch problem in one of his client banks which they wanted him to solve. As was his habit, he'd arranged a short meeting with a couple of the product specialists, so-called 'professionals'. Together they might craft a solution and earn money for Royal Counties Bank.

At the start of the meeting, he outlined the problem. Someone made a suggestion which he knew to be against State Laws. He declared it illegal and asked for more suggestions. Everyone stared. He asked again and somebody said that the legality of what they'd proposed was irrelevant. It was up to the customer bank to spot that. Their only point was that the first suggestion would earn them the most money.

Patrick knew that the Royal Counties Bank he'd joined in the mid-1970s would never propose something to a customer knowing it to be illegal. This investment banking division was only interested in doing more deals at increasing profits. Loyalty to the customer? Pah…

In a blinding flash of insight, he realised he had fallen out of love with his career.

For a few minutes, he sat, stunned at this revelation. His brain had seized up and couldn't progress past his chaotic conclusion. What else could he do? How could he support Jess? On its face, that was a stupid thought in itself. She earned plenty as a doctor and could support him with ease. But he'd promised Mr Smithson – Malcolm – that he'd look after his daughter.

Supposing she became disabled? Or had an accident. Or fell out of love with medicine? Ok – that wasn't likely, but still. He wanted to be able to look after her.

What else could he do? This was all too confusing and going too fast for him to process. First, he ought to make up his mind that he had indeed lost interest in his current job. And he'd write a list of the skills he had. In case another opportunity came along - so he'd be ready.

He started on a clean page, writing skills in the left-hand column. Later he'd try to enter skills which he didn't have on the other side.

-----//-----

During each week working in London, Patrick would live with his parents in Petts Wood. It was only a short train journey from there into the City. There were plenty of trains even at the ridiculously early hour when he would start work. He expected his mother would be delighted at the chance to look after him again and he looked forward to her cooking.

The bank sent a car to collect him from his New York apartment. When the buzzer sounded, he gave Jess an extra long hug. Now the moment had arrived, he knew he was going to miss her. They wouldn't have those quiet moments of blissful togetherness just before they fell asleep. Her hair wouldn't tickle his nose early in the morning.

"I'd better go. See you on Friday."

She didn't want to let go of his hand. This was harder than they'd expected. She sniffed.

"Ok. Safe flight. Love you."

He didn't remember hauling his bag down to the lobby, or the ride out to La Guardia airport. Or even checking in with a fist full of ticket stubs. He was on auto-pilot. His first real recollection was settling back in his seat with tears running down his face as the pilot began to taxi to the runway.

'This is like it was for me leaving Vanuatu', he thought. 'I doubt I will ever go back there. But I'm seeing Jess in five days' time. Why am I crying?'

Business class wasn't crowded. But he kept mopping away the tears in case a stewardess should appear to check on seatbelts or something. He'd have to pretend a speck of dust had got into his eye.

Take-off was uneventful and they climbed to cruising altitude. Shortly after the pilot turned off the seatbelt sign, another passenger came to sit in the seat beside him.

"Hi, there. The name's Grant. It was too crowded back there. You don't mind, do you?"

"No, no. It's fine, I'm sure. Um …Patrick."

They shook hands.

"Have you been here on a work trip?"

"No. I live in New York. I'm visiting England for a short time."

"Huh. Well you sure don't sound American. I'm from Missouri."

"Ah, yes. The 'Show-me' State."

"You know about that..? Well, I'll be... Bet you don't know where the name comes from."

"Wasn't it after a senator who was so down-to-earth that he claimed mere argument and fancy words wouldn't convince him?"

"Yep. That's one version. Willard Vandiver was his name. That's the polite story. Another is some Missouri miners travelled to Colorado when the locals went on strike back at the start of the century. They were so dumb, they didn't know much about mining, so people said you'll have to 'show 'em' everything."

"Who knows what the truth is, eh? Now do excuse me. I want to close my eyes for a bit."

Actually, if he had told the complete truth, Patrick would have said, 'I need to get my emotions under control as I'm away from my fiancée for a while. I am missing her already.' But even in a society which over-shares as a matter of habit, he wasn't ready to say all that.

"Sure, buddy. No problem. You'll have to forgive me. I like talking to people, you know? Actually, it helps in my business. I work in recruitment – what folks call 'head-hunting'."

Now, that changed things.

Patrick began paying attention to his new seat mate. He postponed Operation Control Emotions. If this guy was any good, and taking trans-Atlantic plane trips suggested he operated at the upper end of the job spectrum, then it might be worthwhile exploring other openings with him.

"That's interesting, Grant. As it happens, I am at something of a career crossroads myself. What industry do you look after?"

"Finance and construction. It's a complete accident, 'cos they're different as all get out. I started in construction, but I keep running into bankers looking for something worthwhile to do."

Patrick tried, without success, not to laugh.

Grant's face fell. "I'm serious. It does happen. You wouldn't believe how many people end up working in banks 'cos they didn't know what to do after college. It takes a few years to work that out."

"I'm sorry. I wasn't being rude. But you may have described me to a 'T'."

"No kidding? You work in a bank?"

"Royal Counties Bank. I'm in the Wall Street office at the moment, but I've just been seconded to London head office for a project."

"They wanna see how it's done, I guess?"

Patrick nodded.

"It's like you were in my boss's office when he told me."

Now Grant's face creased up into a grin.

"Well, then. This is seren… something, isn't it?"

"Serendipity?"

"Yeah. That."

They began talking. Patrick was so happy he'd prepared those lists Jerome Jackson III had recommended. He was able to regurgitate them to Grant's satisfaction and he even finished with, "So, I'm wondering what it's all for. Is there some activity I can do, better than other people, which actually makes a difference in the world?"

Grant had been making notes in a tiny notebook from which he'd extracted an even smaller gold propelling pencil.

"Is money important to you?"

"Up to a point. I'd like to be 'comfortably off'. By that I mean I could see a sofa in a shop and buy it without having to save for months. Or pay off a credit card debt over a year. An annual holiday somewhere sunny would be nice, but it wouldn't have to be expensive."

"Uh huh. And schools for the kids? You Brits have them private schools which cost as much as an annual salary."

"Hmmn. I see your point. Jess and I haven't had the 'kids' discussion yet."

"Here's my card. Give me a call after work one day. I have something in mind."

"You do? Alright. I'll show you the best pub in London. Do you know Leadenhall Market?"

"Heard of it. It's got a fish monger and a game butcher and a place that sells boxes of caviar."

Patrick smiled. Those shops were present in the market, it was true, but he had the Lamb public house in mind. And pints of Youngs beer.

-----//-----

Patrick reported for duty at the Head Office building in Lombard Street. Traffic from Heathrow had been bad, so it was now almost ten o'clock in the morning. One of the team secretaries came down to fetch him.

"How are you feeling? It's grim, isn't it, having to come straight to work after a long flight?"

"Not too bad at the moment, thanks. We'll see how I am doing come three o'clock."

"Come up and meet the team. You are the only man."

"I am? Gosh. There's a surprise."

Two of the women turned out to be far more senior than Patrick. He didn't know either Annabelle or Diana as they were both from the investment bank in London. The fourth member, Judy, was quite a bit younger than him and had worked in one of the European departments. There were also half a dozen men from McKinsey and

Company, the consultants who were running the project.

It was quite noticeable to Patrick, even within the first hour, that his female colleagues had lots of friendly banter going. Each had their allotted tasks which they pursued with diligence. But quite often, one would exchange a few light words with another. If somebody fancied a drink, they'd enquire of the others before disappearing to buy one. But no such mood existed among the consultants. It was almost as if they were in perpetual competition with each other. Each desperate not to converse in case they let slip some detail which another could use to his advantage.

Patrick had been set to work outlining what he felt he did which was different to his colleagues back in the New York office. It was a considerable relief that he'd thought this through in some detail before departing. By twelve thirty, he had produced a page and a half of typewritten guidance.

His little team of four then broke off, together, for lunch.

"In my view, we deserve a pub lunch today. Is that ok with you, Patrick?"

"Oh yes. But I'm not sure how well my brain cell will manage this afternoon – it's not had much sleep recently."

"We'll keep you awake," Diana winked. "Let's come back around three and we can go through what you prepared."

Chapter 3
The London Project

The three women had all chipped in for his lunch, refusing to let him pay for any food or drinks. "We're breaking you in gently," said Annabelle. "So you can be 'one of the girls'."

Patrick wasn't sure how he felt about that, but told himself he ought to adopt a collegiate attitude. It would be churlish to refuse such a welcome. He accepted, with grace.

Back in the office, Diana looked around and said, "Let's meet in the conference room in five minutes. Ok?"

Everyone agreed.

When they were all settled, Diana turned to Patrick. "I expect you've given some thought to the methods your New York colleagues use and how you do things in a different way?"

He nodded. "I have."

She went on. "Both Annabelle and I have come from product areas in the investment bank so we don't manage relationships, anyway. But Judy has been a relationship manager for European banks for some years and is very clear on what goes on here."

Judy chipped in. "It's all pretty reactive. People wait for their main contact to call and ask for something."

"But your approach isn't the same, is it, Patrick?" Diana finished.

"That's true. I've thought about this quite a bit and there's nothing complicated about it, I reckon. It's as much a credit assessment as a gathering of opportunities."

Judy produced a note book. "We'll have to make some slides, but I'll just take notes for now."

"All I've been doing is to spend a lot of time with each bank – I mean several days per visit, meeting everyone from the Chairman to the Doorman. I figure that if they all have roughly the same idea of the direction of the bank, it's likely to do well. Some of my best deals came from discussions with rather junior people who told the truth about what they saw. It's amazing what a coffee and a doughnut can reveal!"

"Wait – did you say, '*several days*'?" asked Judy.

"I did." He replied. "Maybe it says more about me than anything. I find that if I can fill my head with everything about a single institution at a time, then I ask better questions – relevant questions. It makes it easier to tie things together when people answer."

"I see that," Diana put in, "But it's too expensive, staying in a hotel for such a long time for a single counterparty." The others nodded.

Patrick knew this was the conventional wisdom. Royal Counties Bank expected calling officers to fill up their schedules with as many clients as possible in as short a time as they could manage. He remembered having a little alarm in his pocket which vibrated after half an hour when first he began managing bank relationships. It was his reminder to wind up that meeting and speed onwards to the next. But he'd discovered he was not effective doing it that way.

"I'm not sure how to convince our bosses of this, but all I can say is that it seems to be better to have half a dozen relaxed meetings in the same building. Bouncing around a town shaking hands with people, and little more, does not make them feel wanted. I also try to pick off key people outside the bank for coffees or lunch or dinner. They will tell you all you need to know. And it does save on taxi fares. There is time to explore what they need – whether they know it or not!"

"Tell us about the credit assessment part," Annabelle wanted to know.

"I guess some of it is subjective," Patrick started. "If you wander the corridors and sit in department after department, including processing areas, you get a feeling for where the bank places emphasis. You learn what's important to it. I find talking to junior people can be quite revealing." He paused.

"Go on," Diana encouraged. "I don't understand why that would help - they aren't decision-makers."

"I agree. They aren't. But they tell you a lot about the way a bank does business. Are they any good, for starters. I unearthed a securitisation opportunity in Louisiana by buying coffee for a clerk in their credit card processing operation."

"Hang on," interrupted Judy. "Let me get this down. What was the securitisation deal?"

Patrick explained. He had presented it as a way of the troubled bank reducing its capital needs by moving assets off its balance sheet but retaining most of their earning power.

Annabelle piped up, "We heard about that. But wasn't there some fraudulent trading in the bonds which financed the transaction?"

"Something like that. The SEC and FBI got involved. There were some money-laundering attempts at buying shares in the bank before the deal was public. It turned out that one of my colleagues was feeding confidential information to the Bad Guys. He got shot."

They all looked at him, horrified.

"Sorry. American expression. He was 'let go' - although there was quite a bit of naughtiness surrounding the deal where gunfire was involved." He sniffed.

"Do you want to tell us about that?" Annabelle asked. She put her hand on his arm.

"It's not relevant, in my view, but my fiancée was caught up in it. They were trying to get at me, of course." He looked around at them all. "That's a story for one evening when we share a bottle of wine."

The grilling proceeded in much the same fashion for another hour. Judy had half-filled her notebook, taking down what she thought were the main points of Patrick's method.

"Now - we should do a Mind Map," Annabelle announced. "Why don't you all take some of Judy's notes, read them and then shout out a summarising word for the most recent bit you read."

"Me too?"

"Of course, Patrick," she added. "It's all in your head and we need to extract the important parts."

They took turns shouting out words. Annabelle wrote them on a flip chart, tearing off each completed page as she went. She stuck them on the wall with BluTack. As the pace of new words from the others reduced, she had a chance to review what she'd written. She drew lines between some words and ringed others she thought most important.

At last, having wound down like an exhausted clockwork mechanism, there were no more words to be had. The flow stopped. Annabelle had covered three sheets with her squiggly writing.

"A spider's web of ideas," quipped Patrick. "It's hard to believe all that was in my head only an hour ago."

"I'll get coffee." Diana said. "I reckon we all need it. Anybody want sugar?"

"Ooh, let me," said Patrick. "I know where there's a great coffee shop around the corner."

"Alright – but I'm paying." This went against the grain for him, but Patrick quashed his old-fashioned attitude and subsided. He accepted the £20 note she held out. They gave him their orders and he trotted out of the department, looking forward to a breath of fresh air.

When he returned, bearing a papier-maché tray holding four tall coffees, Annabelle had started work on a fourth sheet. She had lined up some of the words in columnar fashion.

"Which is my coffee?" she asked. Patrick passed them around. "Ok. While you were out, Patrick, we've started organising these. There are some important action words. We've grouped them according to when you use them and their importance."

His eyes roamed over the sheet. It felt odd. His relationship management technique was now represented by a mere series of words.

"What are you thinking, Patrick?" Judy asked after letting him peruse the sheets for a while.

He shook his head. "It looks so …professional and disconnected. It's strange, seeing it expressed like this."

"We're going to summarise it on to a series of slides and then come up with a single word to incorporate everything." They all looked at Diana. "It will be the Central Premise."

-----//-----

At this point, Diana called over one of the McKinsey people.

"We've been through Patrick's general process. We've extracted the important actions and thoughts and are about to create some slides to present to the rest of the team tomorrow. Could you cast your eye over what we've done?"

"Sure. What time is it?"

"It's four o'clock," Patrick said.

"Damn. Look, this will have to be brief. Ok?"

They all nodded. Patrick saw the others were smiling at the man's answer. Annabelle took him through the sheets they'd constructed together. He nodded in acknowledgement but made no other comment. When he had gone, Judy told him that all McKinsey people set their watches at least half an hour fast. That way, even if they overrun in meetings, they wouldn't be so late for their next one. Patrick shook his head. 'Two wrongs didn't make a right', he thought.

It turned out that the supposed words of wisdom the McKinsey fellow had to impart were not so original after all. They were to sort through the terms extracted from everything Patrick had written and highlight the most important ones. These would become sub-headings or, in this case, slide titles for the presentation. They'd almost done this already by splitting the words into columns. All four shouted out their preferred force ranking and Annabelle tried to keep up, scribbling on another flip chart.

"Could I have a first crack at the slides?" Judy asked.

"Knock yourself out." Diana said. She knew it was important for one team member to construct a 'straw man' ready for the others to pull apart in search of the best result. Judy was the youngest and most junior, but was the only other dedicated relationship manager. She'd likely do the best job anyway.

"Would it be ok with you folks if I made a few calls …to my US clients? I don't want them to think I have abandoned them."

"We know how that goes. You don't want any of your colleagues making a move on your best clients, eh?" smiled Diana. She winked at him. "Dog eat dog."

"Something like that. Thanks."

In fact, Patrick's first call was to Jess at the hospital. He expected she'd be on duty, but he hoped to catch her in her office. She was on the wards, though, and he left a voicemail. Next, he tried a couple of the junior dealers in customer banks. He got them to brief him on the major financial market events that morning. That way, he wouldn't be so exposed talking to higher-ups later on. He moved on to more senior treasury folks and one or two senior management who were not yet 'at lunch'. After an hour, nothing significant had emerged, but he'd achieved his aim of keeping in touch with them.

-----//-----

The team spent the following morning agreeing and redrafting the slides they had been tasked to prepare. The most senior of the women was to present this package to the divisional director at the end of the week. Annabelle assured Patrick she understood all that he'd said.

He believed her. She had no ingrained belief to unlearn about the proper ways to conduct relationship management. As she had said herself, she was a product specialist, interested in selling product. Nothing more, nothing less. Annabelle reckoned all that Patrick had told them sounded logical. Moreover, he had proved it worked. It was hard to argue against good results.

Now the slides were complete, he was free to circulate among his new and old London colleagues. Among them was Elias Al Masri, the Egyptian who had interviewed him for his job in Bahrain a few years before.

"Elias – *kheif harlech*?"

"*Kheif harlech inter*? I see the Arabic specialist hasn't lost his touch."

Patrick chuckled. "I can't help liking the region, even if I kept getting into trouble there."

"I was thinking about you the other day, as a matter of fact. Are you busy for lunch?"

"Not any more. It looks like my part in this London project may be over. I'm not sure what else I can add. Lunch sounds great. But it should be my treat."

They argued good-naturedly about who should pay. But Patrick clocked the important message he was conveying: Al Masri wanted to speak with him somewhere out of earshot from the office.

They chose a fish restaurant a short walk away. Al Masri ordered a bottle of Sancerre. He waited until Patrick sank his teeth into the starter plate of scallops.

"I'm looking for a rain-maker in the region. Someone who can make contacts or who has contacts already at the highest levels in the important institutions. The person might bring Wall Street to Jeddah, if you follow me. Do you know anyone who might find that challenge interesting?"

The scallops smelt of the sea and were very fresh. The chef had cooked them fast in brown butter and served them with half a lemon, some pepper and several slices of wholemeal bread. Patrick's taste buds were doing star jumps of appreciation.

He stopped chewing and swirled a little of the chilled wine around his mouth. It was a perfect pairing. And he could see why Al Masri thought he too might be a perfect pairing for this job. As the Americans might say, he was a 'shoo-in'.

"I might. Can you expand a little on what you would expect? What freedoms this person might have?"

Al Masri's eyes formed tiny creases. He saw that the fish was nibbling at his bait.

"I have persuaded the Board that some of the institutions there have enough sophistication to utilise investment banking products. I'm thinking structured solutions which Royal Counties Bank provides elsewhere but which we have not deployed in the Middle East. And nor has anyone else – yet."

"Do they understand there are still some …how to put it? Political roilings?"

The eye creases Patrick had noted before disappeared.

"Perhaps. Perhaps not."

"So it would be fair to suggest the sky is the limit – at least to begin with?"

"I have already applied for increased country exposure limits. The person will need to structure products which use as little as possible of those limits."

Patrick nodded. "There must be some low-hanging fruit – some quick wins we can take before others wake up to the opportunity."

He saw that the eye creases had returned. It could be because Al Masri had begun to sample the scallops. But Patrick didn't think that was the real reason.

"Would it be helpful," he asked, "If I put a few thoughts on paper for you? You know – to frame the sorts of things the successful applicant might try?"

Now Al Masri actually smiled. "As you Americans say, 'That would be optimal'."

-----//-----

He shook hands with Elias Al Masri on the steps of Head Office.

"I have a couple of errands to run. Thanks for lunch. I'll get you those thoughts by tomorrow."

Then he remembered Penny Baxter, his MI-6 handler. He dug out her business card from his wallet.

"Baxter."

"Hi, Penny. It's Patrick. I've flown all the way to London to say hello."

"Well, let me see. Which 'Patrick' might this be? I'll run through the list."

"I'm the one who keeps getting shot at or drowned or abandoned in the desert."

She had the grace to snigger. "I was thinking about you, actually, this morning. Christopher was asking me where you are. Remember him?"

How could Patrick forget Penny's introduction to her boss, Sir Christopher Sherrif, at her favourite wine bar? He recalled his embarrassment at not knowing that the 'FCO' was actually the Foreign Office. Also how impressed he'd been to learn that Sir Christopher had been called to a meeting by the Foreign Secretary, Lord Carrington, when he left the wine bar.

"I do. What made him think of me?"

"He didn't say. But he did want to know if I'd heard from you lately."

"Is this a good thing, Penny? Remembering he's head of MI-6, I'm not sure it is. What did you say?"

"I said you were 'between jobs'. Which is accurate, isn't it?"

"Mmmn. Kind of. I'm on temporary attachment here in London. The bank thinks other relationship managers ought to copy my techniques." He paused. Peals of girlish mirth echoed from the handset.

"Penny?"

She recovered herself. "Sorry, Patrick. I didn't mean to laugh, but, well, you have to. Right?"

"I don't know what you mean. I told them there isn't anything special about what I do. My secret is to spend a fair bit of time with each bank and ask questions of everyone I run into." He sensed she was dabbing her eyes with a handkerchief. He could hear muffled sighs and stifled snorts of amusement. "What's so funny?"

"I have this vision of you striding around on a stage, tie over your shoulder, waving your arms and shouting about sales techniques."

"That's not what I do. I use more of the 'personal' touch."

That set her off again.

"Look, are you free after work this week?" Penny got herself under control and agreed that she could fit him into her busy social schedule. Patrick persuaded her to come to the Lamb public house again, in

Leadenhall Market. They met outside and went upstairs to the non-smoking bar.

-----//-----

"I'm hoping that Jess and I can get married soon – we would like to make it this year."

"Congratulations, Patrick. I'm very happy for you. Dr Jessica has clearly taken leave of her senses."

They clinked glasses as Patrick smirked at her reply. "We are asking our parents to start some of the administrative processes while we are still in New York. Actually, I offered to do some while I'm here in London, on a temporary basis, but Jess didn't seem too keen on the idea."

"I can't imagine why, Patrick."

He shook his head. "There are many things in life which seem so obvious to everyone else but which escape me completely. Like why the type and colour of flowers at the church matters."

Penny adopted a faux-horrified look, dropping her jaw and clasping both cheeks in her hands. But she quickly smiled again and said, "It's more of a 'girl thing'. But believe me, you'd better wise up to such matters pretty fast, else you'll have a very angry wife to deal with."

"Why do I not find this encouraging? On second thoughts, don't answer that. There are two things I wanted to say to you. The first is, simply, when we've set a day and location, we would both like you to attend our wedding. Can you come?"

"Oh, yes. I'd be delighted." Penny always looked happy and now her face radiated pleasure.

"If you'd like to bring a 'Plus One', that would be great."

She winked at him. "I'll let you know. And do be sure to tell me if there is a theme. I wouldn't want to look out of place. What was the other thing?"

"Ah yes. I'm hoping …well, actually, 'hoping' isn't the right word. Um, I might be in line for a spot of promotion after this London project finishes."

"Yes..?"

"The thing is…" He looked out of the windows as though seeking inspiration to find the right words. "I'm finding investment banking a wee bit boring."

The corners of her mouth twitched. "Now, I wasn't expected you to say that. The last few years have been full of surprises and excitement, wouldn't you say? And now you claim you are getting bored?"

"It's more of a moral question, Penny. What good am I actually doing in the world? I move money around; help finance projects, fix bank balance sheets. But how do these things improve society?"

"I would say that having a conscience is a bit of a handicap working as an investment banker. Is that your problem?"

He shook his head. "I am sure it ought to be possible to work in the industry with a fully-operational conscience. No, my problem is more basic. I've fallen out of love with what I do."

Penny thought for a few moments. "So... are you going to look around for something else?"

Patrick nodded. "But before talking in earnest to anyone, I'd better give it a lot of thought. You know – avoid a frying pan into fire situation? I need to figure out what I actually like doing and what might capture my interest for the foreseeable future. Any advice for me?"

That prompted a chuckle. And she took a long pull at her pint of beer.

"Patrick, I'm the very last person you ought to be asking for career advice. Well, you can ask, of course, but don't for heaven's sake follow what I say."

"You are too modest. I've got an idea or two already and, as it happens, I sat beside a head hunter on the plane over here. I thought we'd have a chat. He said a lot of his clients seem to have the exact same problem. He also covers the construction industry, and spends his time transferring people from one to the other."

"Construction? Do you know anything about building?"

"Well, no. But I'm sure they need someone who can do adding up and doesn't mind attacks by international terrorists from time to time."

To his surprise, that intended witticism didn't raise even half a smile.

"*Al Sharika* won't give up, you know, Patrick. They're …more influential than I had thought."

Penny went all serious after that.

Chapter 4
Safe Keeping Receipts

Patrick felt he had somehow soured the mood. He had tried to be amusing, saying he didn't mind if international terrorists attacked him now and again, but Penny didn't find anything funny about that. They talked a little longer, but she remembered some important reading work waiting for her at home. She finished her drink and said goodbye.

Sitting there, nursing the rest of his pint, he worried that once again, he had somehow said the wrong thing to a woman. Was he by nature clumsy? This happened now and again with Jess. It felt awful to have hurt her. But now he had done it to Penny too. Patrick sighed. He'd have to learn one day how to avoid doing it.

He remembered that head-hunters often chose here, upstairs at the Lamb, to meet their clients. It was usually quiet and lacked the raucous conviviality of the downstairs bar. He looked around. Now the thought had occurred to him, he could see several pairs of people sitting around in what he took to be different stages of the recruitment process. If you met someone for the first time and wanted very much to be on your best behaviour, you might wear your smartest suit and tie. You'd sit and pay attention. Two of the pairs were like that. Neither was sitting in a comfortable way, despite the social setting chosen to encourage relaxation.

One other pair Patrick reckoned had met before. They were now discussing actual opportunities. The difference was that both sat forward on their chairs, heads close beside each other to hear what was being said *sotto voce*. These were important, secret and confidential matters being imparted.

He began remembering what his fellow passenger, head-hunter Grant, had said on their flight about placing bankers into construction companies. Could such a move be possible for him? Now in his late thirties, any career adviser would point him towards his first Big Job. It should be something in

which he could make a mark on society –
before vaulting higher into something even
bigger. Patrick had acquired almost all his
experience abroad – in the South West
Pacific, in the Middle East and in America.
Yes. The more he thought about it, the more
he reckoned the time was right.

-----//-----

The next day, Patrick took advantage of
a coffee break to dial Grant's number.

"Hi, Grant, this is Patrick Field. We met
on the flight…"

"Sure, I remember, Patrick," Grant
interrupted. "How's it goin'?"

"Not too bad, thank you. I've given
more thought to our chat on the 'plane.
Could I explore opportunities with you? I
think I'm ready to make a move."

"You think?"

Patrick chuckled, betraying some
nerves. Grant had caught him out right away.
He had to remember the man was American.
He needed to be positive.

"I'm ready, Grant. Definitely ready."

"Great. I'll hook you up with my
colleague, Lars. Lars Heglund. He's
Norwegian."

"Oh. Right. Do you think he will be able to look after me better than you can?"

"Surely. He's been our highest earner for the last six …no, eight months. So he's in a better position than me to take care of someone of your calibre."

"Ok. Flattery will get you everywhere, eh?"

"Excuse me?"

It would seem British witticism was wasted with Grant. If this Lars chap was their highest earner, presumably that meant he'd placed more people in higher positions than any of Grant's colleagues. So that was good – wasn't it?

"Never mind. Can you put me through to him?"

"He's with a client right now. I'll have him call you. What's the best number to get you?"

Patrick repeated his contact details and suggested the best time slots when an incoming call of this nature wouldn't arouse suspicion.

-----//-----

Lars Heglund did return his call. They agreed a time and place later that week to meet. Patrick found him to be tall, with a slight stoop but broad-shouldered with thinning blond hair and a luxuriant moustache. This hirsute barrier did nothing to reduce the volume of his speech, though. His voice was very loud and his accent typically brash American – not the well-mannered Skandinavian Patrick had expected. During the day, Lars worked at the head-hunting firm, sourcing and placing senior executives in the construction market. He hinted that he did other work during the evenings. "I'll share that with you one day," he thundered in his version of a stage whisper.

The firm was also active in the financial market. Despite Lars' efforts and the occasional big-ticket landings by Grant, total commissions from both sectors were either flat-lining or declining. The two owners of the firm, Dave and Justin, were desperate to boost revenues, he reported.

It was on Patrick's second meeting with Lars that, some two pints into their discussion, the latter decided Patrick was trust-worthy enough for him to share his night time activities.

"I'm an inventor. I see a problem and the idea for a new product falls into my head."

Patrick was agog. He didn't remember ever meeting an inventor before.

"I did all the science courses at University of Colorado, but I didn't bother to stay for graduation. I had what I needed," boasted Lars. He went on to report he'd approached Dave (describing him as 'Mr Intergalactic salesman') and Justin, ('former engineer') suggesting they should join him in a separate venture alongside the head-hunting company. They'd pursue his composite building product idea as a second income stream on the back of their current business.

Patrick reasoned that Dave and Justin must have looked at their firm's rate of burning through cash and declining revenues and so were open to Lars' ideas. He could see that each found them appealing for different reasons. Lars talked big numbers, sweeping his hands in generous arcs when he described the market demand he claimed existed.

He possessed that knack of making the listener believe his words, no matter how improbable the project sounded in the cold light of day. You would feel guilty if doubts crept into your mind after he'd left. Could you get funding? Was it true that people would rush to buy and how on earth would you manage such an enormous, global business? Most in the UK, whose career prospects had plateaued, were assailed over and over with news of recent college graduates raising twenty million dollars to fund some hare-brained internet Dot Com technique. For such onlookers, the combination of disgust and envy at the extraordinary luck of Johnnies Come Lately, Lars' tales were particularly attractive.

They must have concluded this could be 'It', Patrick realised. Dave would picture himself flying between continents to lecture wide-eyed admiring audiences with slide shows - 'our first processing plant' - 'our fleet of distributing trucks'; his office decorated with a world map dotted with red markers denoting company locations.

The factory and manufacturing techniques will have piqued Justin's interest and his engineering brain. Although the processes Lars described with such determined passion and colour were outside his experience, he'd be able at least to follow most of them. He would know where to find younger engineers whose recent education and up to date specialisms would enable them to design or source the machinery necessary.

"So I formed 'LaDaJ Ltd' with Dave and Justin," Lars went on. "I needed a separate company to run out of the headhunting office to begin with. I told Dave to draw up a business plan and work out what skills to hire, commission market research and raise initial funding. You know – all that stuff you bankers like."

Lars' contribution to this process was to prepare a short list of people to include a banker, ("That's where you come in, Patrick"), someone to design a steel mill, logistics and marketing experts and someone knowledgeable in the composite materials arena.

"When Grant suggested you, I had you checked out. I liked what I saw and gave the word."

"Another pint?"

"Don't mind if I do," Lars reckoned, wiping beery foam from his bushy upper lip.

-----//-----

"I want to get the new gang together," Lars said when Patrick sat down again, trying not to bump the table and spill their brimming glasses. "Can you attend a meeting next Saturday at our office? Also there's someone I'd like you to meet in London. Have you heard of SKRs? 'Safe Keeping Receipts'?"

"I may have done. But I don't know much about them. Aren't they used in money laundering?" Patrick recalled Penny had warned him that use of SKRs was often a sign that a money transaction was fraudulent. It was because it was easy to circumvent them, leaving the unwitting dupe without funds or his securities.

"I know a partner at PwC who deals in them all the time. He can explain them to you."

"Well, I guess that would be useful. I suppose if I'm to be the banker in your proposed setup, I'd better understand them."

"Great. His name is Roger Hammerson. I'll fix it right away. And how 'bout this Saturday?"

"Oh, yes, sure. I guess so. Um, if it's the same Hammerson in PwC, I might know him already. But I'd better call my fiancée in New York to check she hasn't organised anything for Saturday."

-----//-----

Later on, Patrick telephoned Jess.

"Oh, great – I'm so pleased I caught you at home. You weren't asleep were you?"

"I was only dozing. I've got too much on my mind." Jess yawned. "It's time for me to get up, anyway. How's London?"

"It's quite exciting, actually. I met a head-hunter on the 'plane over here and he fixed me up with one of his colleagues. He reckons he can place me in a new company. He's asked me to attend a meeting this Saturday at their head office. So I wouldn't be able to come home this weekend. Would that be ok?"

"Hmmn. This had better be a good opportunity, then. No nooky for you for a while! How are you going to make it up to me?"

Patrick chuckled. "By doing everything you ever wanted me to do when I come home."

"That's a promise, mister. I accept the deal. All the ironing; hoovering, washing up…"

"Hey – no fair. I didn't mean that sort of 'everything'."

They sniggered together. Jess knew very well what he meant and was giving him a hard time.

"I'll have to invite my boyfriend around for the weekend, then – if I'm not on call."

"I'll kill him when I get back – so he'd better look after you until then."

Jess laughed. "I'd better go. You are so fortunate to have met me. Good luck, Patrick."

"Thanks. Love you."

-----//-----

The next day, Patrick was hard at work with Judy, drafting more slides for their presentation to Royal Counties Bank's senior management. A secretary came to interrupt.

"Sorry to butt in – there's a call for you, Patrick."

"Who is it?"

"Someone from PwC." She referred to her notepad. "A Roger Hammerson."

"Ah." Patrick tried hard not to look guilty – in case Judy thought he was seeing a head-hunter. "Er …could you take his number and say I'll call him back in about an hour?"

The secretary left them alone and didn't return, so Patrick assumed the secretary had passed the message along and Hammerson would wait for him to call.

Judy was looking at him with a strange look on her face.

"What?"

"I didn't know you were an accountant – are PwC hiring, then?"

Patrick was certain he looked as guilty as sin.

"An old friend. I knew him in Vanuatu. Haven't seen him for yonks…"

"Hmmn. An 'old friend' whose telephone number you don't know?"

"He's moved… Anyway, what makes you think I want another job?"

"Well, *we* all do." Judy batted her eyes at him. "Haven't you noticed how bad the atmosphere is around here?"

In truth, Patrick hadn't.

"Er, I haven't. But then, I work in New York. We don't tend to pay much attention to other people's feelings there."

He wasn't sure that Judy believed him, but perhaps it didn't matter. Of course, he really was looking for another job. But not in quite the straightforward way she surmised.

He did his best not to keep looking at his watch. At last, the hour ticked by and he excused himself and went to find the secretary to get Roger Hammerson's number. He found a quiet corner to make his call.

"Ah, yes, Patrick. Lars said we should get together. I understand you've been working in America for Royal Counties Bank?"

"That's right. I'm in their investment banking division. It's good to talk with you again - Vanuatu was a long time ago. I've been to lots of places since then. Lars said to me that he wants to use Safe Keeping Receipts to fund his …'our' project. And that you can talk me through their intricacies?"

"By all means. They aren't …how to put it? They aren't exactly, 'mainstream', I would say."

"I've only heard of them before in connection with money-laundering, but I haven't come across them myself." Patrick hoped his little laugh didn't sound nervous. After all, he was talking to a partner in one of the biggest accounting firms in the world.

To his surprise, Roger Hammerson gave a little laugh too before continuing. "As a matter of fact, I have a meeting later this afternoon with one of the key players in a transaction I'm putting together. We can catch up a little then. Would you care to join us?"

Patrick did. He excused himself from further slide preparation, mumbling something about a 'customer meeting'. He hot-footed it over to the PwC office in Villiers Street, beside Charing Cross Station.

He signed in at the firm's reception and someone showed him upstairs and straight into Roger's office.

"Well, this is a coincidence! It's great that we should run into each other again," Roger said, beaming far more than the occasion warranted. After all, they'd never been pally in Vanuatu – they just knew each other through work.

"It's nice to see a familiar face. What a small world." Patrick responded. Even as he said that, he remembered stumbling upon Hammerson having a furtive meeting in a dark restaurant car park. It was with Bashir Saleh, who ran the sovereign wealth fund of Libya. Both displayed embarrassment to be seen together and Patrick had suspected they were up to no good. He also recalled the delight of his colleague Gilles, the foreign exchange dealer. Giles earned a lot of money from the many large transactions he did on Saleh's behalf. Patrick and another colleague, Kim had been quite sure their branch was being used for extensive money-laundering. But because they thought the Chief Manager was in on it, they reported the transactions instead to the British Government. And that was how Patrick came to be contacted by an MI-6 agent, Penny Baxter.

"Look, my client, Captain John will be along soon. Do you want a tea? Coffee or something?"

Patrick accepted. But became much less keen when Roger pumped viscous black liquid from the top of a vacuum flask. Patrick's exploratory sip confirmed this had been a bad idea. He added three sugars to disguise the taste. It didn't help.

"Ok, I'll run through the basics first, then.

Sometimes, wealthy people don't want actual legal charges on their assets. They might only need the money for a short time or they need it in a hurry. They think it's too much trouble to register legal charges on, say, a forest, in the case of the Captain. It will take six weeks or more to file the papers with the land registry – or what passes for a land registry there. So they give the documents of title to a bank. The bank issues a receipt that they have the asset in 'safe-keeping'. Some other banks are prepared to advance funds against that safe-keeping receipt. Simple."

Patrick furrowed his brow. "But there isn't anything to stop the individual asking for release of the document of title – is there?"

"Well, no, but why would they do that? After all, they have their funding. I agree they should bring the receipt back to the issuing bank. But they might have lost the piece of paper and the bank will know them as customers of long-standing."

"Um, theoretically, couldn't the customer get his docs back and go to another bank for another SKR?"

Roger thought for a moment. "I suppose so. But that isn't how it works."

"Hmmn. This isn't …er, regulated is it?"

"No. Oh – here's Captain John, I think."

A secretary had appeared outside the glass door. She tapped and came straight in. "Roger – Captain John telephoned. He said he is going to be late. Is it alright or should I reschedule him?"

Hammerson looked at Patrick and raised an eyebrow.

Patrick said, "I'd better leave you to it, Roger. I don't think I'd add anything. You do whatever you'd prefer. Maybe we can have another chat soon?"

Hammerson turned to the secretary. "Tell him I'll wait here until six o'clock if he can still make it. Otherwise book him in as soon as you can."

They shook hands.

"See you again, Patrick. We should have a coffee to catch up anyway."

"Thanks. I'll give your secretary a call when I've worked out my diary for next week."

-----//-----

Using a car from the Royal Counties Bank pool, Patrick drove over to the head-hunting offices that Saturday as promised. The meeting was held early in the afternoon. There were sandwiches, coffee and fruit juices – much like every other corporate team-building Patrick had ever attended. So far, so normal.

There was little time for awkward greetings. Justin invited everyone to start the meeting, fill their plates and to eat as they sat around the table. He requested each to introduce themselves with a 30 second pitch to the others. Justin, Dave and Lars began – Lars put up a flip chart with some complex corporate structures on it and spent two minutes bragging about his past deals. Justin reined him in and the fellow subsided with ill grace. The rest took turns: there was a process scientist; a self-proclaimed logistics specialist; a materials scientist; a computer programmer, a marketing executive who was also an accountant and who'd spent years in the Army …and Patrick. Sensing that it would be his current investment banking role and expertise which would be needed for this enterprise, Patrick skipped through his first twenty years but detailed a couple of his larger and more complex recent transactions. He wasn't surprised when everyone looked a little blank. He was utterly lost when most of the others summarised their talents in what they probably considered layman's terms.

Lars got out his flip chart again. There was a brief pause to pour more coffees. Out of habit, Patrick copied down the illustrations of corporate names or processes in boxes. Some were linked by lines, arrows and sometimes ownership percentages. It was starting to look somewhat complex. 'Almost Maxwellian', he smiled to himself. He recalled the corporate web of cross ownership crafted by the Czechoslovak-born British publisher, Robert Maxwell. It is now thought it was a device to shield ultimate ownership from the tax authorities.

He spotted a connection between a Cayman Islands company and another in the Netherlands Antilles which added up to 100%, but there were two intermediate companies in Holland and Belgium. Surely it would be simpler to have the Cayman HQ owning the Antilles subsidiary directly, he asked. Lars explained that corporate taxation in Holland is 7%, so more of the group profits can be available to shareholders. Lars folded the page over to curtail questions and drew more boxes and arrows on a fresh sheet.

This incomplete explanation begged lots of questions in Patrick's mind: which shareholders? Us? Or someone else? Tax efficiency is all very well. But what does the Belgian link add to the process other than yet another lot of annual accounting and registration fees? And there was something else nagging at his memory. Glancing back at his scribbled notes, Patrick could see that earlier, Lars had said the Netherlands Antilles company owned the Cayman Islands entity. But that can't be right. It was the other way around on the diagram, no? Maybe he misheard. He put an asterisk in his notes and refocussed as Lars plunged onwards outlining his dream of an Industrial Box in which all the technologies are inter-related and ecologically responsible. Besides having the knack of believability, Lars would habitually talk over others. With his loud, Texan accent, he would immediately command the room's attention.

The only other person making notes was the Marketing/accountant. When Lars stopped for a cigarette break, Patrick went over and stuck out his hand.

"I'm finding this quite hard to follow. My name's Patrick Field."

"Gerald – Jerry Green," the Marketing Man amended. "Me too. Have you always worked for Royal Counties Bank?"

Patrick smiled and suggested that if you cut him in half, you'd read 'Royal Counties Bank Ltd' printed around his torso, much like in sticks of Brighton rock. "They collected me from my mother as soon as I was weaned." Actually, Patrick had joined the parent clearing bank when he was sixteen as a temporary job before going to university, armed with his A level qualifications (taken early) and had never meant to stay. But he had quickly been placed into a stock arbitrage department which appealed to his nascent appetite for risk. He could spot price differentials for mining stocks quoted on different stock exchanges. And so had stayed at the bank, even when transferred to other departments. Some jobs and some parts of all jobs would be tedious, but it was usually possible to find interesting and rewarding elements in most. The imaginative freedom allowed, indeed required in some investment banking sectors was most appealing to him.

What Patrick didn't like about his current employer was the increased emphasis on selling the bank's products to clients, whether they were the best answer or not. The doctrine of serving the customer, drummed into him throughout his formative years, was much diminished here, if it remained at all. He felt he was 'going through the motions' every day. His heart wasn't really in it. Patrick was ready for a change of career, he explained.

"What about you, Jerry?" Jerry too had been a grammar school boy and joined a large car manufacturer straight from school. One morning he'd wandered into an Army

Careers office, learned about the possibilities for sport and different lines of career progression and found the sense of structure attractive. He signed up on the spot.

There had been lots (and lots) of service abroad, some of it glossed over with practiced ease. Patrick didn't find that off-putting, somehow. There was an air of solidity about the fellow - hard to express without making him sound boring, but boring he was not. It appeared some of the foreign service had been in places which were quite unstable, politically. He dropped in references to the United Nations and battle planning, which were intriguing. This man was very interesting below the surface, Patrick concluded. How Jerry had ended up in a major steel manufacturer after the Army wasn't clear, but Patrick determined to try to meet up for a beer sometime. He'd tackle Jerry after the meeting.

Justin called them all back to the table. The following hour covered money matters. How could it be raised? The concept of what Lars called 'OPM' ('Other Peoples' Money') was to be deployed wherever possible. Deftly, Lars put Patrick on the spot: "Can you explain for us how we can start this process, Patrick?"

Ah, the wisdom of hindsight! Only now could Patrick look back and recognise the simple technique by which he and the others were being manipulated. Lars had known that Patrick would not wish to appear foolish or indecisive in front of the rest. Never before had he been asked to present without a chance to research or brief himself on the topic to be aired. But he remembered that this audience knew much less about financing than him and was hardly likely to quiz him on details. The easiest method would be to talk to investors with money and sell them shares in the project. But that might sound too obvious. He thought he'd try out the Safe-Keeping Receipts technique. Penny Baxter's warning from long ago about money-laundering echoed in his head, but maybe SKRs sounded racy enough to interest his potential new colleagues.

"It is possible that we will trip over an investor with deep pockets," he began. "But in case we don't, Lars says he can put us in touch with individuals who are asset-rich but cash poor. A little-known technique for raising sometimes considerable sums for investment is the use of Safe-Keeping Receipts. It parallels a well-used method in interbank markets of borrowing against government bonds which you hold. Banks can raise some 90% of the value of a government bond from other banks to buy more government bonds. They then borrow against these as well, and can perform this action over and over for several layers. The benefit is that they receive income from a much larger holding. Performing the action three times provides income from about three and a half times the original holding from which they pay the borrowing cost and then pocket the difference."

He saw that attention around the table was wandering and so returned to Safe-Keeping Receipts.

"That was the RePo market – 'Sale and Repurchase'. Let's call these Receipts I described 'SKR's. When someone owns say, a large area of forest, they make reasonable money from sales of the timber. But if they lodge the ownership documents in a bank which participates in this market and requests the bank to issue an SKR for the value, then other banks may be prepared to lend against that SKR. The owner can then earn more income on top. It's a bit like having a second mortgage on your house so you can build an extension."

Before anyone could say anything more, Lars jumped in to take over the presentation. He had achieved his aim. All of a sudden, others around the table felt greater 'buy-in' to his ideas. This international investment banker had added veracity to the dreamscape laid out by Lars. Patrick sat back in his chair with a confusion of feelings. Partly he felt a sense of achievement that he had risen to the challenge in front of all these others he'd never met before. Mostly and more strongly, though, came the uncomfortable sense that he had been a performing monkey, dancing when the trainer made him do it. He knew next to nothing about so-called SKRs. He had never dealt with them before and had only the briefest of introductions by the PwC Partner, Roger Hammerson. Now he had established himself as the group's fount of knowledge on funding.

He pushed this shifting feeling to the back of his mind, telling himself that it was good to step out of his comfort zone. This is how real entrepreneurs felt when they opened up new markets with new products and would reap the rewards in due course.

Lars was still booming away at the front, showing how the second-hand steel mill would be modified to create a new board which would be strong and fireproof. They would use it to replace whatever conventional sheets they started with for the composite building product. He was asking the logistics man how many trucks could arrive and be unloaded per hour as they brought waste material from many different industries to make these new wonder boards. Justin chipped in that this was a lot for everyone to absorb. He thought everyone should go away to research their individual areas of responsibility for a week.

"We could meet again next Saturday," he suggested.

Feeling slightly numb, Patrick thumbed his Filo-fax and wrote in the entry.

They all said goodbyes and headed downstairs to the car park. He cornered Jerry by the door.

"My brain is throbbing with all that. I'm going home to sit in a dark room to think it through."

"There were some challenging areas," conceded Jerry. "Fancy a soothing coffee somewhere nearby?"

Patrick was delighted. "I can't right now, but could we meet in London next week?"

They agreed on Tuesday after lunch at the Starbucks on Villiers Street, a little way up from Embankment Tube Station. That was easy for Patrick to get to. He would try to meet with Roger Hammerson further up the street around 4pm. It was away from his normal circle of business acquaintances in Canary Wharf or the City.

Chapter 5
Squash

Patrick arrived at Starbucks a few minutes early and peered through the window to see if Jerry was inside. It was still quite busy at 2:25pm. Workers lingered over the remains of their sandwich lunches and a couple of obvious office romances didn't want to let go of each other's fingers.

He straightened up and was startled by Jerry's sudden appearance right beside him. "Oh – there you are. Bang on time. Shall we go in?"

Patrick led the way and they stepped down from the steep street into the fragrant bonhomie of Starbucks. Earlier bank postings abroad had awakened Patrick's liking for coffee. He knew well what bean types he liked most and how he wanted them prepared. He noted with pleasure that today's 'House' blend was Verona, a dark-roasted blend from 100% Arabica beans.

"Tall Americano; Black; Extra shot, In, please," he said to the barista. "What'll you have, Jerry? My treat." To his surprise, Jerry was looking a little perplexed - alarmed, even.

"Erm …just a Nescafe, thanks."

"They don't sell Nescafe! Look, do you want black or white coffee?"

Jerry had been scanning the menu. "How about a Latte?"

"You know that's almost all milk, right? With a shot of coffee… It only just counts as coffee, you know."

Jerry assured him that would be more than adequate, so Patrick added a Latte to his order. It was a close-run thing - there was the temptation to ask for a blueberry muffin to go with his coffee, but Jerry shook his head when Patrick offered food as well. So he didn't either. He told himself it would have been mere greed on his part, prompted by nervousness. Jerry went to sit at a table while Patrick paid for the drinks.

When they were ready, he carried them to the back of the café where Jerry had selected a small table near the toilets but with a view of the front door. "Is this ok, here,

Jerry?" he asked. "I mean, there's a couch over there where we would be more comfortable…?"

"Old habits," countered Jerry, archly. And changed the subject.

They chatted for about an hour, going over Saturday's presentation. It was pretty clear that the only project in the whole presentation which sounded workable was the invention of a new building system. Neither man knew anything about construction, but the common-sense physics of the structural panel seemed a logical development. They could see themselves explaining it to a disbelieving investor. Patrick even felt confident enough with this taciturn man to confide his discomfort about Lars tricking him into magicking up an outline of how to finance all these fantastical projects. "Me too," said Jerry. "It sounded flaky, but what do I know?"

"As a matter of fact, I'm having a meeting with PwC up the road in fifteen minutes or so to discuss it further. I might be able to elucidate afterwards?" Patrick ventured. They exchanged business cards. Jerry's was very plain - 'Gerald R. Green -

Interim Management' with a mobile phone number and private email address.

"I look forward to it," smiled Jerry. "Thanks for the coffee. You haven't convinced me it's any better than Nescafe, though."

Patrick went left, up the street. Jerry went down towards the Tube station. Patrick had about ten minutes to compose his thoughts, sign in at the PwC Reception and make his way to Roger Hammerson's office on the 12th floor. As the early rush of commuters carried him along the street heading for Charing Cross Station, he spotted an odd figure crossing the road and entering Gordon's Wine Bar. The man walked with a rolling gait, leading with his considerable stomach. His rather magnificent full-set beard was proportional to his torso. The fellow's shirt was open half way down his chest. He resembled a modern-day pirate captain – he even wore knee-length boots. The sights you saw in London these days, Patrick thought. Fancy dress? An actor?

He paused behind one of the pillars of the portico in front of PwC. He was now right opposite the bar with its dark purple timber façade. He looked more closely at it. Faded gold lettering announced that patrons might avail themselves of 'Wine by the Glass'; they could choose 'Wine from the Wood' and finish themselves off later with 'Malaga Madeira'. Truly an old-fashioned City-style drinking tavern for banking staff from a simpler age. Those who didn't have to concentrate much in the afternoons before staggering towards the railway station on the way home. Unlike the floor to ceiling glass and steel coffee shops and hairdressing salons nearby, Gordon's dusty windows did not permit a view of the interior. Patrick couldn't tell whether the pirate was pausing for some refreshment before continuing his journey or meeting someone there.

He consulted his watch. No more idle musing. Time to head in.

Reception had a pre-printed badge for him and waved towards the lift. "12th floor, right?" Patrick checked.

The smartly-dressed receptionist smiled and nodded. "I'll call to say you are on your way."

Another smart young woman from the same mould stepped forward as the lift door opened. "Roger is expecting you, Mr Field. This way, please."

She showed him into a conference room with a long, highly polished table and a dozen leather chairs. By the wall was a side-table with vacuum flasks of hot water and coffee and a big plate of expensive-looking biscuits. Roger Hammerson sat at the end, barricaded in by a couple of stacks of papers and files. He looked up.

"Ah, Patrick. Come on in. I'm going through some documents for our next transaction and could use your help on a couple of aspects. Tea? Coffee?"

Patrick demurred. The taste echoes of that wonderful Americano were too good to spoil with whatever PwC put in their coffee jugs. Remembering the hideous black liquid served to him during his previous visit, he wondered if they used burned acorns… "Could I just have some water, please?"

The 12th floor receptionist had stayed to take any orders for drinks and now hurried away. The glass door swung shut behind her with silent remorsefulness.

They shook hands. "What's the structure?" Patrick asked, thinking it right to get straight into detail. Partners in accounting firms this big and reputable didn't have spare time for pleasantries.

"You were going to meet my client, Captain John Santos, when you came before, but he postponed. He controls a couple of thousand acres of Malaysian rainforest. Exploiting it is going to take longer than he wants and so he has agreed to go to his bank in Manilla to deposit the deeds and get an SKR. He wasn't expecting to have to travel there so soon, though, as he has other business in London and in Europe. It's I.B.P., he tells me. That's one problem."

Patrick nodded. It wasn't his area of responsibility, but there was a branch of International Bank of the Philippines in London, not far from Leadenhall Market. It could be that Roger didn't know that.

"The other is that Lars wants him to put up the seed money for LaDaJ and he's a bit short of ready cash right now. Do you have any ideas?"

Patrick thought for a moment. The return of the receptionist with a glass and bottles of still and sparkling water on a tray gave him a few extra seconds. "I know a branch of IBP near Leadenhall Market. One of my former trainees went there when she left Royal Counties Bank. I expect they could help him – at least to raise the seed money. Where are the land deeds at the moment?"

"They're already in the Manilla Head Office, physically, in his deposit box. But someone would need to take them out if they are to be used as security. Would that be a problem?"

Patrick saw his first chance to cross check some details. "It will add some time, but I can enquire. How much did Lars say was needed?"

"A hundred thousand pounds."

Patrick made a note. The figure was the same one Lars had pulled out of the air during his Saturday presentation. "Ok. I'll ask and get back to you." At this stage he was just going to tackle IBP about the principle of advancing funds in London against the security of land abroad, the deeds for which were already in their Head Office. He thought it best to leave any mention of SKRs out of the conversations.

"Great. I'll call the Captain right after our meeting and let him know. Now, I may have a buyer lined up, but it's early days. He's Middle Eastern. You worked there for a bit, didn't you? After Vanuatu, I mean."

Patrick nodded. "I'm up for a more senior job to do that again, but based in London." He'd spent six mostly happy years in Bahrain, travelling around the Arabian Gulf. He had tried, with limited success, to lend money to already wealthy Arabs. He sought to avoid deals with those who merely gave the appearance of wealth. In the years that followed, any marketing failures to lend to the latter category the bank took as triumphs of the Credit Assessment process. Unfortunately, not all marketing efforts to the 'Appearance' lot had failed. Patrick had some credit recovery projects ('Work Outs') to his name. Some had been partially successful. Most had not. And the biggest of all turned out to be fraudulent and had led to the closure of Royal Counties Bank's Bahrain office when the bank wrote off the loan altogether.

"His name's Hamad Al Suleiman. Ever heard of him?"

Patrick chuckled and shook his head. "It's an enormous clan, the Suleimans. To give you some idea, someone with that family name was mentioned by the famous Arabian poet and traveller, Ibn Battuta, and he was travelling around the world in the 1300s. So there might be thousands. I think it's a mainly Saudi name now, but there are likely branches of the family all over the region."

Patrick knew he'd need any other names the fellow had and hopefully his father's name to stand any chance of identifying him with any certainty. "Even then, it is not unknown for Arab men to assume different names, when they travel or do business with foreigners."

Roger's brow furrowed and he bent over the files on the table again. He ran his fingers down a column of names and shuffled some of the papers. "That's the only name I have. I do have his email and cell number, though – any use?"

Patrick wrote them down, thinking to run them past a friend in Royal Counties Bank's Private Banking Division who covered the Middle East, especially Kuwait.

The email address didn't help locate the man's home base – it was a Hotmail account, accessible from anywhere. The cell phone number, though, was Saudi Arabian. It started 00 966 5… These folks usually had several phones since travel throughout the Gulf Cooperation Council territories was freely available. Most preferred to be able to use local numbers as they went.

"I'd be grateful if you could do a little checking on him. I'm told he may be the middleman for a big Arabian investment company. He might be open to doing this on his own recognisance, of course. You know the size of fees these people pay."

The role of the middleman in buying and selling was well-established in Arab circles and was entirely respectable. It avoided embarrassment to either side if there was disagreement. The middleman could approach a seller and ask if his client were to offer a particular price, might that be acceptable? If the seller felt insulted by such a lowball offer, he could reject it without either of the principal parties suffering public humiliation.

More often, there would be several rounds of back and forth bidding and offering until they agreed a particular price level. The real potential buyer could then deal in person with the seller, offer the acceptable figure and both would be satisfied. For this valuable service, the middleman would receive a fee, a percentage of the deal, known colloquially as *'Wahda'*. The Compliance and Governance departments of most big banks, especially the American ones, refused to go along with these payments. They called it bribery. It was a trickiness of doing deals in the region. Patrick had managed to circumvent it in the past, but it was always awkward when it arose.

Many intermediaries were small time players. But some, because of the circles in which they mixed and the products which they trafficked became very rich indeed. Yes, Mr Suleiman might be very interesting for LaDaJ.

They parted. Patrick said he would try to meet Hamad Al-Suleiman when next he went travelling and would have a chat with IBP in London.

As he joined the Villiers Street mass-exodus from London, he placed a call to Jennifer Fisher, formerly his graduate trainee at Royal Counties Bank and now working in securities in IBP. He liked to keep in touch with such folks from time to time. Who knows? He might need to come to them one day for a job.

"Securities".

"Jennifer! You never call - you never write..! It's Patrick. Do you have a few minutes?"

"Patrick!" He could tell she was smiling. "How are you? Of course I do. What brings you to IBP?"

"I wanted to have a chat about something your office might help with for a friend of mine in Manilla. Fancy a game of squash tomorrow?"

"Sure …but can you get a court?"

"If you are free from about 4:30, I'll book as soon after that as I can. The courts at the Barbican are always stuffed but there might be one free in the basement of Head Office."

"I had no idea there are squash courts down there! That would be cool. Ok – let me know when and where to meet. Don't forget your kit! Oh – are there showers?"

"Yup. Even for ladies, although I expect I'll need a shower more than you." She laughed. Actually, Jennifer was quite a decent player, and was fifteen years younger than Patrick. He expected her to stand on the 'T', sending him from side to side and from front to back on most points, until taking mercy and administering the coup de grâce with a vicious sideways slash of her racquet. "Drinks after?" he finished.

"Only if I work up a thirst." She knew how to make a chap feel bad.

"I'll call you tomorrow morning – bye."

-----//-----

In the morning, Patrick telephoned his friend, Tony Valent, from the Private Banking division. Tony's main area of interest was Kuwait, but over the years he had inherited some clients from elsewhere in the Gulf and so usually tagged on a side trip to Abu Dhabi or Saudi Arabia every time he travelled to his own patch.

"Hi, Tony, it's Patrick."

"Hey, long time, no see. What's up?"

"I've been given a temporary release from my New York duties. I'm going to put together a Gulf trip shortly which might include Kuwait. I wondered if you were going to be there. We could have dinner, perhaps."

"That would be great. Actually, I'm going there next week. That is, if Carole will let me."

"Carole?"

"Yeah. We… that is, *she* had another baby last month."

"What? Congratulations! Another boy or another girl?"

"A girl. That makes three."

"Three? Tony, you've been working too hard, my friend. You had four children when last we spoke. Have you lost count?"

"I meant three girls. And yeah, there are two boys as well."

Patrick shook his head in wonder. Tony spent most of his life in Kuwait, attending to the financial whims of some very, very wealthy people. He could only conclude that he and Carole spent a high proportion of his short time in England between trips making babies.

"Isn't it time you got 'The Snip'? I mean, you have an heir and a 'spare' and enough progeny to look after you in your dotage."

Tony's sigh was audible. "I suppose so. I never seem to find the time. Anyway, tell me your travel schedule. Carole's sister is staying with us for a bit and I'm thinking of having a second au pair."

Patrick explained he hadn't firmed anything up yet, but could do with a bit of a chat. Tony always knew the latest inside gossip about the wealthy – and those who merely pretended to be wealthy or claimed wealth connections which turned out to be tenuous indeed. Patrick knew he could pick Tony's brain for information about Hamad Al Suleiman, or whatever he called himself when in Kuwait.

"I'll let you know as soon as I've got some flights booked. Hopefully there will be room at the Sheraton too. I like that hotel."

"Alright. We need a catch up. Bye now."

-----//-----

Patrick's secretary told him that she could reserve a squash court for him at five o'clock, but they'd have to be out sharp at six. Someone else wanted the court then. He relayed the news to Jennifer.

"Don't have too much to eat at lunch, mister," she warned. "I wouldn't want you throwing up on my new shoes."

Patrick laughed. But he also knew he was in for a thorough drubbing. Jennifer was not only very fit, but had a ruthless streak which was serving her well in her career.

"Nothing but salad, I promise. Anyway, I'm not sure I can last a whole hour being run ragged by you."

"You are so defeatist, sometimes, Patrick. See you tonight. I'm looking forward to this. Drinks after?"

"Yup. If I can still raise my arm. 'Course, I may need an intravenous drip…"

She chuckled and broke the connection.

He spent the rest of the day planning his trip to the Gulf. He'd hand the detail organisation over to his new London secretary, Sarah, but he knew some meetings would be hard to pin down.

"Could you make sure there are plenty of blank spaces? There are a number of people I will contact when I get there and I'll need flexibility to fit in with them."

His staff were used to his free-wheeling habits. They told themselves it was just the 'Arab way' even though it seemed risky to spend all that money on flights and hotel accommodation with no certainty of meeting your target clients. Supposing they were out of town? His bosses didn't seem to mind, so long as he got results.

-----//-----

He found Jennifer at the Head Office reception desk, chatting away to the ladies there. They all remembered her, of course, and she wanted to catch up on all their gossip. Patrick sauntered up beside her.

"May I join in with all this 'Girl Talk?"

"Absolutely not," Jennifer affirmed. "The clue to the participants is in the name."

The others smiled. "You tell him, Sister!" one said.

He turned to his visitor. "Have you signed in?"

"I have. And now," she announced, "I'm going to run Patrick around the squash court until he can't even walk."

The ladies loved that. One applauded. Patrick tried hard to look offended, but didn't manage it.

"Come on. Time's a wasting…"

They took the lift down to the sub-basement. Here were the heating and ventilation systems for the whole building, various specialised workshops and hidey-holes for the maintenance workers, a couple of car-parking spaces for the most senior members of the bank's board of directors …and two squash courts.

"I had no idea these were here, Patrick."

"They're a closely-guarded secret. The Messenger staff use them mostly. At least they have time to spare. Um, the changing facilities are …basic. You go first."

He ushered her forwards through a self-closing door marked 'Private'.

"Is there a 'Ladies'?"

He looked about them. "Doesn't look like it. I'll keep cavey for you."

Clearly the building designer in the previous century had not thought that the bank might one day employ female staff.

Jennifer tossed her hair and vanished into the tiny cubicle.

"No peeking," she called. He concluded the door did not have a lock.

Quickly, she reappeared, hair now in a ponytail, all dressed in white with green shoes.

"I'll go and warm up. I brought a white spot ball. Ok with you?

"Fine. I'm not sure that nicety is important to me. I'll be as quick as I can."

He looked in vain for somewhere to hang his jacket. Various items of Jennifer's clothing took up all the hooks. Averting his eyes, he removed his own kit, set his bag on the floor and piled his clothes on top. Shoes and socks and underpants went into the bag and out of sight. It would be alright, he thought, to have his shirt and trousers on show. As he sat to pull on his trainers, something tickled the back of his neck. Without thinking, he reached for it and found himself holding a particularly frilly bra. He dropped it as though it was burning hot. Panicking, he put it back on the hook. He imagined Jennifer might open the door at that very moment, having forgotten something. That would be just his luck.

The regular 'Bang, pop, pop, pop – Bang, pop, pop, pop' coming from the court was evidence of Jennifer's warm up routine. She was pounding the ball along the side walls repeatedly, 'getting her eye in'. There was a pause while she crossed from the forehand side to the backhand side and the noise began again.

Patrick tapped on the glass door as Squash Court etiquette demanded. Her answer was to smash the ball so it rebounded at him.

"Was that Gamesmanship?" he asked, dodging.

"I was passing it to you to warm up." She grinned. She put Patrick in mind of the expression worn by some reef sharks which had cruised by him during a snorkelling expedition in Vanuatu.

And so they began. After the first game, which she won 9-3, Jennifer left the court to put on a knitted sweater.

"I'm not warm enough," she protested. Patrick raised a smile. He was breathing hard. Also, his past injuries sustained at the hands of an *Al Sharika* agent in New York were making their presence felt.

"Having won 3 points, I feel almost victorious."

"Yeah. I was careless. You won't win any points in the next game."

"Ooh. Sounds like a challenge. My serve, I think."

Her forecast of the scoreline proved to be correct. Although they still had some court time remaining, Patrick called a halt.

"Sorry, Jennifer. I'm bushed. Do you mind if we call it a day? Beers are on me." 'And Paracetamol', he thought.

"No, that's fine. There was a danger that I might break a sweat anyway."

They laughed and she headed for the glass door.

"You should keep hitting the ball while I shower. You need the practice."

Patrick knew that Jennifer had always spent hours practising. She wanted to perfect her strokes, her floating serves, the full-length drives which seemed to glue themselves to the back wall and that maddening, sideways slash of her racquet to win a point. Maybe he'd improve a bit if he practised now.

"I know. Honestly, squash is like chess at a hundred miles per hour."

He set to work, walloping the squash ball as hard as he could, trying to vary the length and precise direction of the rebound so it would be most difficult for an imaginary opponent to return. 'Bang, pop, pop, pop – Bang, pop, pop, pop'.

Out of the whole of the five minutes, he reckoned he'd made a single really good shot plus a couple of adequate ones. Maybe he should consider lessons some time? A tap on the glass wall brought relief that he could stop. He stretched his right arm to try to ease his aching shoulder.

Jennifer now looked more flushed after the hot shower than she had during the whole of the game.

"Your turn," she said. "Watch out, though. The water's very hot."

Afterwards, they strode past the reception desk on the Ground floor level.

"How did you get on?" asked one of the receptionists of Patrick.

"As a gentleman, I let her win."

Jennifer giggled. "By a *very* wide margin," she said. "He's much more of a gentleman than even I had thought."

There were smiles all around. Patrick joined in, but felt it was rather at his expense. He led the way towards the Jamaica Wine House around the corner in St Michael's Alley.

"Did you know this was the site of London's first ever coffee house?" he asked.

"I didn't. I always thought the 'Jampot' just sold beers and wines. Anyway – you promised beer. Not that I'm all that thirsty, yet."

"So sharp you'll cut yourself," he bantered. "Come on."

They headed downstairs to the wine bar area. A sprinkling of patrons stood by the bar itself, waving glasses and braying at each other to emphasise their Alpha ambitions. Ties had been loosened; most had rolled up the sleeves of their shirts and their speech patterns had reduced from sentences to clipped phrases. They'd been here a while, then. Patrick shouldered his way through. His brandished ten pound note caught the barman's eye.

"What can I get you, Sir?"

"Two pints of Master Brew, please."

Jennifer found a tiny table for two, squashed into a quiet corner. Patrick carried the beers over with a packet of crisps.

"That's to soak up the alcohol."

"I doubt it. Now, what did you want to talk about?"

Jennifer had always been direct, he remembered. And determined to 'get on' in the world. She'd grown impatient with her promotion prospects at Royal Counties Bank, so had found a position with more seniority and responsibility at International Bank of the Phillipines.

"I ran into a PwC accountant recently I knew from Vanuatu," he began. "We were chatting and he told me about one of his wealthy clients from the Phillipines who owns a large forest in Malaysia."

"Oh yes?"

"Of course, he has some income from that. But it isn't regular and I don't know if he has any other income. He needs a small advance in short order here and none of his assets are exactly liquid."

"And you thought IBP might accommodate him?"

"Something like that. I'm told the deeds for the forest are currently deposited in your head office in Manila. Is that something you could look at?"

"I guess so. Write down his name and I'll try."

Patrick obliged. Jennifer looked at the name when he pushed it across the table.

"Doesn't mean anything to me. Are you sure he's from the Phillipines?"

"That's what the PwC partner said. I have no real idea. It's not an area of the world I know at all. Have you visited your head office yet?"

They chatted for another half an hour and drank more beer. This time, Jennifer called a halt.

"Phew. I'm feeling woozy. I guess that's my fault for combining exercise with alcohol."

"But I thought you said you'd not even worked up a sweat?"

"Ah, but I'm fit – unlike you! I have little tolerance for alcohol. I'd be a cheap date." She looked meaningfully at Patrick's left hand. "You're engaged?"

"I am. We're planning to marry later this year. I met her in Vanuatu and we started to write to each other when I left. Then got together when we were both in England on leave. She's a wonderful person."

"So – no chance of a bunk up, then?"

"Er – no." He blushed. "Um… it isn't that I wouldn't – you know. Or that you aren't…"

Jennifer giggled. She shook her hair and leaned back. "I was half joking. But it's not fair. I keep meeting decent men who are all taken. What does a girl have to do?"

Patrick was trying to recover from this unexpected turn of events. "Jennifer, you deserve a decent man. Don't you dare put up with one who isn't. Maybe stop looking at the squash club?"

"Why?"

"Because anybody who plays squash against you will be embarrassed to beat you and embarrassed if they lose."

"You aren't – are you?"

Patrick shook his head. "It's different. I like playing squash and I don't mind if I lose. I'm not at risk of dropping down the testosterone ladder in the eyes of male club members. Besides, I knew I'd have absolutely no hope of beating you."

"That's how you get to Carnegie Hall." Jennifer told him.

"Sorry?"

She smiled. He'd fallen for her very old and tired joke. "You gotta practice!"

Realisation dawned. "Ah. I see. Your head works faster than mine – as was evident on the court an hour ago."

"I'd better go – really." She shimmied out from the tiny table and hoisted her sports bag.

"Give me a call if you reckon IBP can help with this fellow. It's about a hundred thousand pounds he needs."

"Ok. And you give me a call if you come across any eligible bachelors."

Patrick got up too. Jennifer moved in for a hug. Suddenly, Patrick was over-conscious of her physique and unsure where to put his hands. Her freshly-applied perfume filled his nostrils. He hoped that patting her shoulder blades wouldn't get him into trouble.

"Thanks for the game."

He smiled and watched her sashay towards the stairs. The motley crowd at the bar fell silent as she passed. Patrick was certain that Jennifer would be the hot topic when conversation resumed. He didn't want to hear any of it. He managed to make his pint last another five minutes before he too departed.

Chapter 6
The Pirate

At exactly nine o'clock the next morning, Patrick's secretary, Sarah put a call through to his desk telephone.

"Mr Field? Good morning. This is Agila Mendoza from International Bank of the Phillipines. Mr Ramil Galang asked me to arrange a meeting with you as soon as possible. When will you be available?"

"Hello, Agila. I'm pretty tied up today." He thumbed through his desk diary. "Would Mr Galang be free after work?"

Without pausing, she said, "Yes. That will be fine. At six o'clock in Gordon's Bar, Villiers Street. Do you know it?"

Surprised and intrigued that his casual enquiry to Jennifer Fisher should have gone so high so fast, Patrick agreed to go. Galang was the Chief Manager of IBP's London Branch.

The highlight of his day was Elias Al Masri calling to say Patrick's New York boss had agreed to release him, temporarily, to explore the viability of appointing an Arabian 'Rain-Maker'. If the higher-ups approved budget, the person would bring in investment banking deals from the region using minimal credit exposure.

This excitement made the remainder of Patrick's day drag, but he managed to get rid of most of the mountain of paperwork clogging his In-Tray. And he started roughing out the bones of a trip to his old stamping ground. Five o'clock arrived, and there was still some remaining. Sarah looked up, surprised, when he tidied his desk and made to leave. He was usually the last to go home.

"You're off now?"

"Yup. My brain cell is fried." He shrugged on his coat. "I'll be better in the morning after a good night's sleep. Cheerio."

The London Underground Tube train was heaving with commuters also heading west for Embankment station on their way to Charing Cross. It was a very uncomfortable journey, strap-hanging in the middle of a swaying carriage. He was very happy to emerge into the early evening sun at the bottom of Villiers Street. Patrick stood beside a flower seller at the station entrance to let the wave of humanity wash past. He didn't know what Ramil Galang looked like, but thought it would not be hard to spot a senior man standing by himself in the bar.

There were still five minutes to go before the appointed time. As always, Patrick loved people watching. He amused himself by imagining what individuals might do as a job. At this early hour for home-bound bank workers, most were clerical, he reckoned and unremarkable. But then, standing head and shoulders above everyone around him, the bearded pirate fellow he'd seen before strode by. His clothes were similar in style, but different colours this time, complete with the boots. Amazing!

He may as well head up the street to Gordon's Bar. He fell into step behind the pirate. Walking in the man's wake, he was assailed by a strong body odour. No wonder others gave the fellow a wide berth.

Unsurprisingly, the pirate turned into Gordon's as he had when Patrick first spotted him. The entranceway was cramped and lacked any breeze to waft away the man's smell. Patrick trailed behind trying not to breathe as they descended into the dim half-light of the bar.

The bar itself was half a storey below street level – perhaps testament to the age of the building. Patrick knew that London streets were often ten feet or more higher now than when first constructed hundreds of years before. A previous owner must have added the rickety wooden stairs to adjust for this. The walls of the staircase and the bar itself were covered in peeling, ancient wallpaper, held up, he fancied by large numbers of framed pictures, faded photographs, newspaper cuttings and cartoons from Punch magazine. This was the real thing, he judged. Not what fashion magazines dub 'shabby chic'.

Beyond the bar, arched brickwork storage tunnels had been repurposed as seating areas for patrons. There was minimal standing room at their centre. Woe betides anyone sitting near the wall who tried to rise from their bench to their full height immediately. These tunnels ran beneath Villiers Street. Years of water seeping through had leached salts onto the brick surface lending it a dusty appearance.

He looked about, searching for someone who might be Ramil Galang. The pirate had approached the most likely contender, of vaguely Asian appearance and they greeted each other as old friends. Not him, then.

Patrick tried another of the tunnels. Nobody else stood out. He went up to the bar itself and asked the barman if he happened to know a Mr Galang. The barman did know Galang as a regular client and pointed Patrick back to the first tunnel.

He went back to the man he'd first thought might be the head of IBP in London, now deep in conversation with the pirate.

"Excuse me. Is one of you Ramil Galang, by chance?"

The fellow glanced up. "That's me. You are Patrick Field?"

Patrick nodded. "I'm sorry to interrupt you, but your secretary asked me to come here at six to meet you. I'll wait over there until you are ready."

"No, no," Galang protested. "Pull up a chair. Meet Captain John Santos."

The bearded pirate swivelled around and extended a pudgy paw. Now Patrick was close - far too close in view of the smell - he could distinguish the man's Far Eastern facial features. They had been camouflaged by the excessive growth of beard.

"How do you do, Captain. In view of you being here, I'm not sure whether my meeting with Mr Galang is even needed."

The beard parted to reveal a gap-toothed grin. Patrick added halitosis to his list of the man's afflictions. "Oh, we can make a lot of progress. I'll tell them to bring a third glass." He got up and stomped off to attend to that.

"Is this alright with you, Mr Galang?"

"Yes, Patrick. Call me Ramil. We are going to be great friends."

Patrick smiled, although inside he felt anything but encouraged.

"Very well – Ramil. Jennifer may have briefed you that I had a meeting with one of the partners at PwC, the accountants, recently and…"

"Yes, yes. You met with Roger Hammerson – I know him well. So does John."

Events were running way ahead of Patrick. He struggled to catch up. Why did Hammerson ask him to approach IBP to seek funds for Captain John Santos if the captain was on good terms already with Galang? Was Roger Hammerson guessing that Patrick would know someone in IBP's London branch? Or did he know?

Further internal questions were halted by the captain's return, squeezing himself past Patrick to occupy a space on the bench beside him. One of the servers was right on his heels, bringing wine and three glasses. She splashed a token amount into them all and hurried back to the bar. Another thirsty crowd had arrived, chattering and waving money.

"Good health," Patrick toasted, as the others drained their glasses and Galang topped them all up.

"Now." Galang began. "I'm sure we can accommodate John's need for some short term funds without any trouble. But he has some other questions for you, Patrick."

"Ok…"

"I understand Royal Counties Bank has a branch in the Netherlands Antilles. Is that right?"

"Er, yes. We do. I don't know if it's a full branch, but, yes, we do have an operation there."

"The captain would like an introduction to the Chief Manager there. It will be helpful with the funds raising for LaDaJ."

"I see. I expect I can do that. It may take a little while as I'm departing on a trip abroad shortly. It may have to wait until I return. Would that be alright?"

Captain John's glass was empty again. Galang refilled it, emptied the remnants of wine into Patrick's glass and waved the empty bottle at the server to indicate another was required.

"No problem," Santos said, reaching for his wine. "Where are you going?"

Thinking fast, Patrick remembered what he'd scribbled in his work book before leaving the bank that afternoon.

"I cover the Middle East – banks and other financial institutions. I'm going to Kuwait on Sunday and then Riyadh and Jeddah, returning on Thursday afternoon."

"Ah, good, good. How often do you visit the region?"

"Usually about twice per month. It does vary, I admit. I have to try to do some work in London now and again!"

Nobody smiled at Patrick's little joke. It had landed on stony ground. Just lately, he had been meeting a lot of very serious people.

Galang said, "This is very interesting." And conversation turned to other things – non-financial matters, as far as Patrick could determine. He didn't think he could contribute anything to their discussion – in fact, he could not identify any real help he'd given thus far. The men knew each other already and Galang reckoned finding the hundred thousand pounds for Captain John was easy.

After a while, Patrick interjected, "Gents, I hope you will excuse me. I have another appointment. I enjoyed meeting you both."

He rose. "Thank you for the wine."

They all shook hands and Patrick made his escape from the captain's smell into fresh air. 'It's not only the captain who doesn't smell right', he thought to himself. This had been the meeting equivalent of a money laundering transaction. When monies travel between two or more parties for no particular reason, bankers know to suspect fraud. What had been the reason for this meeting?

Was it to introduce him to Captain John? Patrick reckoned that was about the only benefit anyone might have counted on. The 'pirate', as Patrick would now think of him, was going to finance LaDaJ. The man might have wanted to learn why Lars Heglund had suggested Patrick for the banking role. He walked at a slower pace than usual up the short distance to Charing Cross station. Breathing deeply helped clear Captain John's smell from his nostrils. But it brought no clarity to the hazy situation he was in, no matter how often he turned it over in his head.

-----//-----

By Sunday morning, the episode had slipped from the forefront of his mind. His head was full of the travel arrangements for his Middle Eastern trip – check-in time for the flight at Heathrow; which hotel he'd use in Kuwait City, which suits to take and how to pack some casual clothes into the already full suit-carrier. For years, Patrick had used the same local car service in Britain. The man was reliable, knew all the back doubles to dodge traffic hold ups and could tell when Patrick wanted to chat and when to stay quiet. He hoped the fellow was still working.

He was dead on time for the pick-up – as usual. Today, Patrick wanted to go over his notes and think about what to say to his contacts at Bank of Kuwait and the Middle East. As they sped around the M-25 motorway, some fifteen miles shy of the airport, Patrick's mobile telephone rang, interrupting his preparation.

He didn't recognise the number that was calling.

"Good morning. Patrick Field."

"Ah, Patrick. It's John. Are you heading for the airport?"

John? John Who..? Then the penny dropped.

"Captain John! I didn't recognise your voice. Yes, I'm almost at Heathrow as it happens. What can I do for you?"

"You said you'd go on to Jeddah, I recall. Is that right?"

"That's correct. I'll arrive there on the 30th."

"I'd like you to meet up with my friend and colleague, Hamad Al-Suleiman. Do you have some time available?"

"I do, Captain. There are several people I need to see, but I haven't agreed meeting times yet, so I'm sure I could get together with Mr Al-Suleiman too. How can I contact him?"

Captain John gave him Al-Suleiman's telephone number. Patrick wasn't surprised at all by this. Such an arrangement was very common in the Middle East – it is how business introductions are often made in the region. And this must be the man mentioned by Roger Hammerson.

But when the Captain had rung off, Patrick studied the contact details more closely. The slight oddity was that the cell phone number was a Kuwait mobile starting 00 965. The number given to him by the PwC man was from Saudi Arabia. He shrugged, mentally. Having two mobile numbers was not strange in itself. He concluded the man kept one for work and another for personal calls. But mobiles domiciled in two separate countries? Hmmn.

The car was now very close to Heathrow. But there was still enough time to catch up with his friend Tony Valent from Royal Counties Bank's Private Banking division. He dialled the number. There was no answer so he left a message. He hoped they could get together for dinner that night, provided Patrick's flight arrived on time.

When he disembarked at Kuwait International Airport and turned on his mobile phone again, it bleeped several times. Texts and voicemails sent while he was airborne were downloading. One was from his newly-appointed boss, Alan Pearson. Brief and to the point: 'Call me'. Patrick pursed his lips and frowned. He could only guess at the level of unpleasantness he'd have to deal with when he returned that call.

Much more welcome was a text from Mary-Rose Mattiesson - the lovely young woman he had known since they met in Jeddah. They escaped together from an entrapment scenario – they married in the British Consulate so she could have a UK passport to escape. Her captor, a Saudi merchant, had retained her Norwegian original. They divorced later on, as soon as she was safely out of the Kingdom. Mary-Rose continued to travel elsewhere in the region though, selling her employer's dealing system to bank trading rooms. Her text read, 'Sarah says you are in Kuwait tomorrow – fancy some shawarma'? That cheered him a great deal. But he'd better get the work obligations out of the way first.

The return call to his boss, Alan, went through after what must have been an expansive Sunday luncheon in the Pearson household. The man's plummy tones hinted that more than a bottle of Bordeaux and several cognacs had passed his lips very recently.

"Why are you wasting time with IBP? They aren't your patch".

"Quite so. But through Jennifer – remember her? – IBP have introduced me to a Saudi contact whom I can fit in for 30 minutes between my other appointments.

"What has this got to do with the Caribbean"?

A fast assessment helped Patrick figure that Alan must have met the IBP London

Head at a cocktail party. The request for an introduction to Royal Counties Bank's Netherlands Antilles operation came up when senior men searched for something they might have in common. "That part of it is nothing to do with us", agreed Patrick. "But the Saudi end might prove interesting. I'll check that out before I drop a note to CARLA" – (the Caribbean and Latin America division).

"Bloody waste of time, if you ask me". And with an audible belch, Alan Pearson was gone.

'Well, that could have gone worse', Patrick thought. He was looking forward to seeing Tony for dinner. When he checked in at the hotel, he asked to leave a message with Reception for Mr Valent. As so often happened in the Middle East, the Reception staff were indiscreet. They told him Tony's room number right away and that he had 'gone for a walk to clear his head'.

Patrick smiled to himself. The emphasis on the final phrase suggested Tony seen a client already, for lunch, and consumed a fair amount of alcohol. As the time wound around to seven o'clock, Patrick dialled his friend's room.

"Hello?"

"How was the recovery stroll?"

"Patrick! It was …not far enough. Are you calling for dinner?"

"I am. How's your appetite this evening?"

"For food – not booze. I've had plenty of that today. Do you fancy the Teppanyaki Restaurant downstairs?"

"Sure. It's the only reason I come to the Sheraton. Seven thirty?"

This was why Patrick had toted some casual clothes. A quiet dinner with Tony would be that little space of relaxation that he craved during these trips to foreign lands.

They shook hands outside the restaurant entrance.

"Hey, Tony – good to see you."

"Likewise, my man. It's all been a bit hectic lately."

"Come on – let's find some seats."

The Teppanyaki restaurant had been set up so that several chefs could each stand in the middle of a square island. Hungry patrons would perch on stools spaced around it. Each side of the square had a flat stainless steel cooking surface. The chefs brought out pre-portioned helpings of steak or fish. Each wore smart, white-belted costumes with razor-sharp knives tucked into the belts. They'd wield these with great dexterity and showmanship, together with trowels, to slice and scrape and manipulate the food on the hot plates. It was always quite a performance which the two men enjoyed.

"You said everything had been hectic lately - what did you mean?"

"Everyone is trying to position themselves to succeed Andrew as Head of the Private Bank. You know - sending out spurious emails and notifications designed to bring them to the attention of the higher-ups rather than inform the rest of us. The trouble is, we spin our wheels chasing around to follow these evolving instructions. Honestly, the only peace I get is on trips like this."

"I sympathise. I suppose it's inevitable, working in a big organisation. Some of us do the work. Some design the work and others spend their time politicking."

They had both ordered beef. But on the spur of the moment, they agreed to share a portion of lobster as well. The chef complied with alacrity. He busied himself scooping and scraping a heap of flavoured cabbage shavings, adding splashes of soy sauce from a great height. Pushing the vegetable to one side, he halved the crustacean with precision, chopped it into bite-sized pieces and let it sizzle for a few moments. Patrick caught himself dribbling.

"Actually, Tony, there's a name I wanted to run past you."

"Who is that?"

"Have you heard of Hamad Al-Suleiman?"

Tony thought for a second. I don't think so. How did his name come up?"

Patrick briefed his friend about his current exploration into the world of construction - it would be a radical change. Tony was amused, but gave it six months.

"They're sharks, Patrick and not very clever ones either. Just mean. As I think about it, the name does ring a bell. I met him outside a cocktail party once. The reason I remember him is because the host had just ejected him - thrown him out. Al-Suleiman was fuming on the steps of the hotel, shouting into his mobile. It was the doorman who told me who he was."

"Why would he do that?"

Tony Valent smiled back. "You know my methods, Dr Watson," he quipped. "Actually, I've found that putting a few dinars into the pockets of doormen around the region gives me a great deal of information about who is visiting whom."

They postponed further conversation in favour of attending to the steaming piles of food heaped onto plates in front of them. A waitress brought refills of non-alcoholic beer and they fell to eating.

Patrick slept well that night, even though it wasn't his own bed and the room was unfamiliar.

Chapter 7
Mary-Rose

He breakfasted early, reread his briefing notes and, using his room telephone, began putting together a rough schedule for the day.

It started well. The traders at Bank of Kuwait and the Middle East expressed great delight to see him. Talking to traders was always a short cut to the truth. They didn't have time to waste. Not for them the roundabout conversational jousting of some of the relationship managers. No, they spoke the facts as they saw them, demanded straight answers and reacted openly to Patrick's responses. He booked in a general chat with the Chief Dealer and some of his colleagues at eleven o'clock.

His enquiry of National Bank of Kuwait elicited an invitation to lunch. He didn't have anything particular to talk about but was seeing them out of courtesy as the premier institution in the country. Sometimes such chats were worthwhile.

While he waited outside the bank afterwards for his car to arrive, he called Mary-Rose.

"Hi, there. I've emerged from lunch with NBK. I've got a couple more meetings this afternoon, but are you still free for dinner tonight?"

"Oh, yes. I'm looking forward to that. Today has been rice pudding."

This was her code for uninteresting. Time was dragging for her and she needed something to look forward to.

"I'm sorry to hear that. Any idea what time yet?"

"No clue. I'll text you. Gotta go."

Not only was she as smart as a tack, she had a hard streak. Under the skin, Patrick knew a very lovely person existed. She was much given to wearing high heels and tight dresses, but always on the side of tasteful. Mary-Rose used her considerable charm and good looks to advantage when selling in this very structured and socially restricted society. Patrick suspected that many Arab dealers would tell their directors her company's dealing system was best for the sole reason that they'd receive quarterly 'customer care' visits from Mary-Rose. Medium height, but with honey skin and dark, dark hair down to her waist – after work, anyway – her eyes were bright and lively. She missed nothing when negotiating a price. Patrick liked to meet up with her from time to time to exchange gossip. Her access to dealing rooms and knowledge of at least four languages meant she picked up all sorts of information. Some of it came in handy when doing credit assessment on a bank. Most, though, was about individuals. Personal and commercial chatter, which could be traded for information Patrick could use himself. Over the years, Patrick had amassed a populous Rolodex of contacts in banking and investment management. He was happy to point Mary-Rose in the right direction when she needed.

Their brief arranged marriage to get her a UK passport in Jeddah to escape from forced imprisonment in a merchant's house gave them a deep appreciation for each other. Both knew the marriage was a sham -

a clerical necessity for survival. They divorced shortly afterwards.

Patrick's secretary, Sarah, thought he and Mary-Rose had a loose 'friends with benefits' arrangement going, but they really didn't. Both would acknowledge that there was an undeniable spark of attraction between them. But giving in to it would ruin the low-level but genuine feelings which provided a break from the pressures and undoubted stress of their jobs. It was a general rule that when travelling 'On Business', Patrick knew well that one can never relax. There was always the possibility that a thoughtless remark would be overheard and reported to the authorities. It might be followed by a chance to relax in a prison cell until he had missed a connecting flight – or worse. The old Second World War admonishment that 'Walls have Ears' remained as true in the souks of Kuwait or Riyadh as in a London public house. And for Mary-Rose, being able to say she had a dinner engagement already was a useful first line of defence to ward off unwanted suitors. As they were comfortable in each other's company, and confident that anything said would go no further if it were likely to cause damage, both found an hour or so chatting together released a little of the undeniable pressures of their trips.

Patrick always took the opportunity to take off his tie and loosen his collar – he didn't need to look like a senior banker with her. And Mary-Rose usually donned stretch denim trousers which were a size too small. To be frank, they merely emphasised her exceptional figure, which had got her into trouble in Jeddah in the first place.

His afternoon client bank meetings were straightforward. Some of the more senior members of management worried about computer glitches when the clock ticked over from 31st December, 1999 to 1st January, 2000. He found that the more sophisticated the institution, the greater the level of their concern. He had expected more shoulder shrugging in this Islamic country. Indeed, one man told him, "*Allah karim.*" (Allah will provide). But that was not the wider view. Perhaps they reasoned that Allah would help by giving them the wisdom to write computer programmes to guard against malfunctions.

He noted all these details down. All part of the credit assessment of the banks he visited. His own institution viewed the Kuwaiti banks with a positive outlook. Patrick found their management style to be more conservative than he'd like. Not for them some of the structured products he delighted in suggesting to their Saudi counterparts.

By the end of the day, he had garnered nothing but plain vanilla opportunities. They'd pay for his trip, but little more. He texted Mary-Rose. 'Hope you are still free for Shawarma tonight, Mrs Field?"

She always found this allusion to their previous married status amusing. She texted back a smiley face and suggested seven o'clock. Patrick had never managed to master the language of emojis – communicating with symbols. He regarded them as the modern-day equivalent of Egyptian hieroglyphs. He typed, 'OK. C U at the Sheraton'. There was a brilliant shawarma shop nearby. The hotel reception didn't mind him bringing back food bought elsewhere if he also ordered hotel drinks while they ate.

Suddenly, his day had improved.

"Could you drop me here, please? I'll walk the rest of the way to the hotel."

The driver half turned in his seat, amazed that anyone would want to walk in Kuwait City when they could ride in an air-conditioned limousine. But he agreed. His passenger was the boss. "*Aiwa, Sidi.*"

He pulled the car into the kerb.

"*Shukhran. Eshoufek bahdein, insha'allah.*"

After Patrick had shut the door and thanked him, the driver accelerated hard into a traffic gap which widened just enough to let him in. 'You'll need all the help you can get from Allah if I'm to see you tomorrow, driving like that,' Patrick thought. He stepped sideways into the shade of a shop and looked around.

The roads and sidewalks were always dusty and blistering hot. This was why those who had a car or could afford a taxi would always use them. His smart London suit stood out among the few pedestrians. Everyone else wore loose, voluminous clothing. Light colours or white *thobes* for the men and black *abeyas* for most of the women.

He removed his tie, tucked it into his pocket and took off his jacket. Keeping his pace low, he strolled from shade to shade, pausing on occasion to look into a shop window. To observe the windows of the gold shops was always a marvel. The shopkeepers ensured the shelves would drip with high quality gold – bracelets, chains, earrings, watches – everything you could imagine.

An idea popped into his head. He could buy a block of gold here and have it fashioned into two wedding rings to his own design. There were craftsmen in the Middle East very used to making ornaments and jewellery to a customer's order. It meant he and Jess would have rings which were unique. But he'd have to get hold of her ring size somehow. How could he do that? Even if Mrs Smithson's advice on dress designs was not welcome, she might be able to find out Jess' finger size. He'd score some brownie points with her for asking, at least.

But how much gold to buy? He'd need the design first. This needed some careful thought and planning. What a good job he'd thought of it well before the wedding.

The Sheraton Hotel came into view. He checked his watch. There was plenty of time to have a shower before meeting Mary-Rose.

-----//-----

On the dot of seven o'clock, a taxi delivered Mary-Rose Mattiesson to the hotel. Patrick saw her arrive and met her at the revolving door. They both knew to keep their greeting modest to avoid offending others. But Patrick saw straight away there was tension in her eyes. Her smile was perfunctory.

"I am very happy to see you, Mary-Rose. Are you alright?"

"My last exchange house customer wanted to stir the rice pudding himself – using his hands – if you follow me. I couldn't get out of there fast enough."

"That's tough. You fight 'em off all the time, though, don't you?"

"It wears a girl down, you know. He smelled bad, too." She shook her head. "Come on. I have been looking forward to that Shawarma since I don't know when."

She wore a black shawl in the manner of an ex-pat woman. Not the head to toe covering of an *abeya* like the locals. Instead, she wore normal western clothes underneath but covered more or less with some black cloth. It was clever, Patrick thought. It put people off assuming that her honey-coloured features were Middle Eastern. It meant she and Patrick could stroll together along the streets like a visiting ex-pat couple and not attract undue attention. It was a subtle reminder of how well she knew her market.

There was not far to go to the shop and soon they had a small carrier bag with the wrapped, hot sliced meat and salads. As soon as they returned to the Sheraton, Patrick ordered soft drinks from the waitress in Reception. They found a sofa far away from the comings and goings of the busy main entrance.

Mary-Rose closed her eyes in bliss as she bit into the sandwich.

"Goodness me. Is it that good?"

She nodded, chewing with her mouth full. "It really is. I don't suppose the bar would have any hot sauce?"

Patrick grinned. "You should remember – I always carry some in my pocket." He pulled out a little bottle of Tabasco.

"You, husband, are a star!"

Patrick opened his drink and hers. "Cheers. Here's to unstirred rice pudding."

Mary-Rose managed a weak smile and raised her drink in response. Once again, his attempt at levity wasn't funny.

He said, "I've been doing a lot of thinking recently."

"You want to marry me again?"

"No! I mean… Oh, Mary-Rose, that's not fair." She laughed, this time with genuine pleasure.

Although the joke was on him, Patrick was relieved that she was relaxing enough to tease him.

"I'm sort of falling out of love with banking."

She looked at him with immediate sympathy. "That's unfortunate, given what you do for a living. What are you going to do instead?"

He nodded. "I happened to sit beside a head-hunter on a flight back to the UK. He said he is always moving people from banking into construction."

She blinked. "Construction? Gee. That's a facer. I could see accounting or teaching mathematics or something. But construction? Like in building houses and things?"

"That's right. He says lots of people get into banking because they don't know what to do when they leave school. Finally, they get bored and need a bigger challenge."

She chewed, reflectively. "Don't you have to know about bricks and concrete and all the regulations and stuff?"

"I expect so. But I'm a quick learner, wouldn't you say?"

"You do think on your feet, I admit. And you were very brave, marrying and helping me escape from that horrible man."

"I don't expect to make a habit of doing stuff like that. And, I didn't have to be brave to marry you." She waggled her head as much to say, 'Yeah, yeah, yeah'. "But, to be honest, many of the things I've done, I'd never have had the courage to try them if I understood how dangerous they were."

"Is this what you wanted to talk to me about?"

"Yes. I've been introduced to a group of people with a new building technology. It sounds revolutionary. They need start-up capital, which I reckon they've sourced. But I've been given someone's name as a major seed investor. Have you heard of Hamad Al-Suleiman?"

"Hmmn. Maybe. If it's the person I'm thinking of, several people have encouraged me to call him. They say stuff like, 'He has access to the top level'."

"What does that mean?"

"It's usually code for someone who knows a mid-level prince. Trouble is, they imply his link is close when actually he might just have met someone at a party."

"Ah. How do you tell the difference?"

"It's hard. But there's more – they say this man works across a wide area. The Gulf, North Africa and Turkey too. It isn't possible to be well-connected in so many places. Not only that, but someone said he works in tandem with another man – Riad Al-Sheikh. Now that is a made-up name, so it means your Hamad guy is a bit shady. Maybe even dangerous. So, you see – I'm put off pursuing this Al-Suleiman. I expect he's a bit player."

That made Patrick thoughtful. Mary-Rose's instincts were usually accurate. The likelihood of Al-Suleiman being of use to her were minimal. But if he was an effective middle-man and could introduce LaDaJ to a genuine investor with wealth, he would be worth following up.

As he headed to his hotel room after their dinner, having put Mary-Rose into a taxi, he began worrying that greed and ambition were tainting his reasoning. 'Best sleep on it', he thought. That night, he dreamed about Jess and what she would say when presented with her gold wedding ring.

After breakfast the next morning, he made up his mind. He'd call and maybe meet Al Suleiman. It would be wise to check him out at the very least.

Chapter 8
Hamad Al-Suleiman

"Hello? My name is Patrick Field. Captain John Santos gave me your telephone number so I could try to meet you when I am next in the Kingdom."

"Mr Field – I am glad you call. This is good. Very good. I hope we can do much business together."

"Yes, I hope so too. Um, I will be in Riyadh tomorrow afternoon but in Jeddah on the 30th. Is there any possibility to get together then?"

"Of course. Very welcome."

"I usually stay at the Hyatt Regency – could we meet there?"

"Call me when you arrive. I have business now. I say Goodbye."

"Very well. Goodb..."

The line was already dead.

'Well that went rather well,' Patrick thought to himself. 'At least the telephone number works.' He pencilled in a block of time to devote to Hamad Al-Suleiman and returned his thoughts to the calls he'd make before getting to Jeddah.

-----//-----

So much had happened to Patrick on previous visits to Jeddah. This was where naivety had almost got him into trouble years before. He'd over-indulged in a potential client's home-brewed hospitality. An enterprising concierge at the Hyatt Regency Hotel, named Pauli, had spirited him upstairs to his room. The fellow shielded him from the '*Ulema*' or Religious Police while he slept it off. That same young man had come to the rescue again when he assisted Mary-Rose Mattiesson to escape imprisonment in the house of a wealthy merchant.

His love of the ancient buildings in the Old Town area of this traditional sea port drew him back every time. He always set aside a few hours to wander its narrow, dusty streets, admiring the mud and timber structures, baked for decades by the Saudi Arabian sun. Successive town mayors had spent money installing sculptures and art works on the Corniche – the road running right next to the ocean. The cooler temperatures of early evenings would bring out families and young people to sit by the sea, talking, chatting, gossiping. Some played music. Some would gaze at the sea, dreaming their dreams, lulled by its rolling, inexorable movements, their own pulses slowed by the gentle sounds of wavelets breaking on the shore and the smell of the salty air.

But he needed to be on his guard. Arab memories are long and his appearance made him stand out as a visitor. If one of the servants of the merchant who had captured Mary-Rose spotted him, they might try to kidnap him. This time, Muhammed Al Masri would not let him go.

There were several banks in Jeddah with whom he enjoyed a warm relationship. Patrick delighted in inventing financial structures to benefit some aspect of their balance sheets. The dealers, especially, loved him for this, because his structures would always give them opportunities to trade more. Their personal salaries would thus rise.

The senior people at the banks, especially National Commercial Bank, saw that Patrick took an interest in Saudi Arabian culture. This recognition manifested itself in little ways. His seating position at formal dinners would be near to or even beside the most senior Saudi. The choice of food they'd serve – always local specialities and finally, the after-dinner entertainment. And they insisted that he visit every time he came to Jeddah, even if there was no banking reason to do so.

He knew he would miss many aspects of his travelling banker job if he managed to transition into Construction. This human friendship across such disparate cultures would be one of the hardest elements to let go.

Flying into the King Abdulaziz International Airport, it was always possible to spot the spectacular white tented roof of the Hajj Terminal beside the airport. This vast area was the largest tented space in the world. The authorities built it to shelter Moslem pilgrims arriving from overseas to perform their holy visit to Mecca. Every year, the Government reported greater numbers visiting and the logistical challenge of looking after them grew.

It was late in the evening when Patrick landed. His flight had come from Riyadh, so there were no passport or immigration checks to delay him. Sarah had booked a car to take him immediately to his favourite hotel, the Hyatt Regency and he took the stairs up to the Reception on the Mezzanine two at a time.

Pauli was not on duty tonight, he learned. Never mind. He could say hello to the man tomorrow. He laid out his clothes for the next day. Then, choosing from the room service menu, he jumped under the shower while the food was being prepared.

A final burst of cold water rid him of the mental numbness brought on by travel in the Kingdom. He had found it helpful over the years to assume a particular mental approach. It enabled him to stay calm when the airline cancelled his flight or overbooked it. His car or taxi might not turn up. An Immigration official might threaten to turn him away. It was always better to absorb the news and look for alternative ways to go about his business. But that deliberate retreat inwards to dull the senses wouldn't do when sparring with a potential funder for LaDaJ.

A knock on the door signalled the arrival of his food.

"Room Service, Mr Patrick."

The voice sounded familiar. He opened the door.

"Pauli! How very kind of you to bring my food upstairs. How are you?"

"I am very well indeed, Mr Patrick. I am very happy to receive you back at the Hyatt Regency again. May I ask, how is Mrs Field?"

"Ah, yes. You heard about that? I suppose that should not surprise me." As he spoke, Patrick wondered how on earth a concierge in an hotel heard about the ruse employed by the British Embassy to allow Mary-Rose to escape from the Kingdom. As her Norwegian passport had been retained by her captor, Muhammed Al Masri, she would have been trapped in Saudi Arabia had not Patrick agreed to marry her. That way she could have a temporary United Kingdom passport issued in her married name, so did not need an exit visa.

"We are no longer married, Pauli."

The young man's face fell. "I am very sorry to hear that, Mr Patrick. I hoped you would be very happy together."

It crossed Patrick's mind to explain that this had been a marriage of convenience to save Mary-Rose from a lengthy period of belly-dancing servitude followed by …well, better not to dwell on her likely fate when she was no longer able to gyrate for her captor.

But he contented himself with saying, "It is for the best, Pauli."

He ate his dinner watching some TV news on the main Saudi news channel. He understood only some of it. But found amusing the marching music which always accompanied visits by senior members of the royal family anywhere. It drowned out any hope of hearing snatches of conversation between dignitaries and lesser mortals.

When he had cleared his plate, Patrick called Hamad Al-Suleiman.

"Welcome to Jeddah, Mr Patrick. Are you free to meet tomorrow?"

"That would suit me very well, Mr Al-Suleiman. Let us say eleven o'clock in my hotel? They have very good pastries…"

He heard the man chuckle. Was Al-Suleiman surprised that this British visitor should immediately feel so relaxed in the Kingdom that he invites the Arab to eat and drink coffee with him? But he accepted anyway.

Patrick eschewed his normal number of visits to the Hyatt breakfast buffet. Having never met Al-Suleiman, he had no idea whether the fellow liked to gorge himself on pastries. If this was the case, he'd encourage Patrick to do the same. Or whether he was the type to push a single pastry around his plate and leave half behind.

Patrick chose his seat in the area across from Reception with care. The Hyatt had positioned against one side a couple of two-person sofas at right angles to one another. A low coffee table in front threatened the shins of the careless. The assembly needed a slight rearrangement so he had a direct view of anyone ascending the staircase from street level. He prewarned the waiter that he would desire a plate of assorted pastries, but only to bring them out when his friend arrived.

Hamad Al-Suleiman turned out to be a modestly-dressed, middle-aged Arabian man. He might have been Syrian, or Bahraini or Jordanian – Patrick couldn't tell. He was one of those forgettable people who could fit in anywhere.

Al-Suleiman spotted Patrick immediately. He strode with confidence straight across Reception, extending his hand in greeting.

"Mr Patrick, I am pleased to make your acquaintance. We have many business to discuss." He larded this opening with a broad grin.

"I am very pleased to meet you as well. There are many things for us to discuss. Captain John Santos asked me to introduce you to Royal Counties Bank's branch in the Netherlands Antilles. Someone else recommended I seek your help to fund a project. Do sit down. Would you have some coffee?"

"Yes. I will."

Patrick turned to attract the attention of the waiter, but the man was already there, bearing a fresh coffee pot and a towering plate of pastries.

"Thank you very much," Patrick said. "Could we also have some water?"

The man made a tiny bow and left them to it.

"Here is my card. Although I should like to talk about business which is not for Royal Counties Bank."

"Ah yes. Thank you." Al-Suleiman made no move to reciprocate with his own business card.

"You will see I have written the contact details for the Chief Manager of Netherlands Antilles on the back of my card."

Al-Suleiman held the card closer to his eyes so he could read it. Then tucked it away in his jacket pocket.

"This means I have the last link in a big transaction I have been working on. Thank you very much, Mr Patrick." He selected a Danish Pastry and took a large bite of it, washing it down with the scalding black coffee.

It was always said that you should never talk about detailed business during a first meeting in the Arab World. Standard diplomacy is to allow the person to get to know you and to learn your body language. But if his guest was as sharp an operator as others had suggested, Al-Suleiman will have seen Patrick's face light up at the mention of a 'big transaction'. His natural enthusiasm for a potential New Deal will have caused him to smile, lean towards the other person and adopt an open stance. These are all classic body language giveaways.

Patrick knew this and had made no effort to hide his reactions. So he decided to explore what Al-Suleiman might have in mind.

"Would you be able to share some of the details with me in case I can make some further contribution towards your success? I often construct derivative financial structures for financial institutions to protect or make their returns bigger."

After the briefest of pauses, Al-Suleiman said, "If we are business partners then we share in future successes."

Was this a simple statement of fact or some sort of invitation? Patrick was out of practice in such verbal jousting. To give himself time to work that out, he thought he'd quote an old adage from the world of business in Arabia.

"Good business is good for both parties."

Hamad Al-Suleiman smiled. And took another bite of his pastry. He chewed slowly, watching Patrick.

"I know individuals who are powerful and very wealthy. But their assets are often not well used." Patrick nodded to show he was following.

"There are some banks and other financial houses which advance monies against such assets."

"I have heard of these techniques," Patrick interjected. "Are you meaning Safe Keeping Receipts?"

Now Al-Suleiman leaned forward.

"You know of such things?"

"A senior accountant I used to know in a posting in the South West Pacific has briefed me. I have not come across them in my work at Royal Counties Bank."

Al-Suleiman seemed satisfied with this.

"One of my principals – the most senior and powerful – has much funds to invest. His manager buys large assets to use them up. But sometimes there are smaller investments…" He circled one hand in the air. "Say, five or ten million dollars which he has available to invest. But he does not like such modest amounts. They are not interesting for him."

"What does he do?" Patrick asked, suspecting he knew the answer already.

"He has a network of people like me who can operate with freedom to look after those sums for him."

"I see."

"Sometimes the authorities are not helpful, even when we try our best to make good business."

Was this a reference to tax avoidance? Was this why the man wanted Patrick to introduce him to a bank in a tax haven?

"Is this why our branch in the Netherlands Antilles can be of assistance to you?"

The man nodded and popped the remaining morsel of pastry into his mouth.

When he had swallowed and consumed more coffee, he continued. He proposed to open accounts in the Caribbean in the names of certain companies. They were to take part in his Safe Keeping Receipt scheme, acting as collecting points and investment managers for some of the smaller sums he had mentioned earlier.

"It is important that your branch in the Netherlands Antilles is confidential. They will transfer these sums into London, Paris, New York – many places – to make the investments."

"Will you be able to travel there to open the accounts yourself or do you have a local agent?"

Al-Suleiman looked hard at him. Patrick held his gaze, returning the examination as coolly and openly as he was able. At last, the man said, "We will see."

Patrick changed the subject. "I am considering joining a start-up company in Britain to manufacture a building system. I hope to be able to do this full time when I leave Royal Counties Bank. I was introduced to Captain John as a potential source of funding for the new venture and he has pointed me to you. Perhaps we might benefit from investment of one of your smaller sums?"

"It is possible. Tell me about the opportunity."

So he gave Al-Suleiman the elevator pitch. To his surprise, the man didn't ask about the technicalities, although Patrick was itching to talk about them. Instead, he asked about where Patrick grew up; did he have family, how did he spend his time when not at work? He also threw in questions about what Patrick did for Royal Counties Bank.

In a western context, this approach would have been puzzling. But perhaps his description of the opportunity had been enough to pique Al-Suleiman's interest. Now he wanted to know if Patrick was the kind of person he could work with.

It was nearly lunchtime when they parted. The two men stood, shook hands and Patrick walked with him down to the street level. The Concierge hailed a cab and Hamad Al-Suleiman vanished into the Jeddah traffic.

Walking back to the elevator, Patrick realised their conversation had been very general, in keeping with Middle Eastern etiquette. But in fact Al Suleiman extracted quite a lot of information about Patrick. Not just the geographic area he covered, but his personal background, hobbies and some of the transaction techniques he used – securitisation, foreign exchange, interest rate and other financial agreements like swaps and options.

For his own part, Patrick concluded the other man would be a genial dinner companion, having a fund of stories from his travels, but Patrick had gleaned nothing at all about his background. Even his birth city remained unknown, although Patrick was pretty sure he was dealing with a Lebanese. The family name was common across the entire region, so that was no good for pinning him down. He claimed to be a freelance investment manager for various family offices including some very powerful individuals. Patrick might try to effect a personal introduction for Tony Valent if the man proved trustworthy. The scene he'd made outside the Kuwait Sheraton when removed from a smart cocktail party had made a poor impression on Tony back in Kuwait. Maybe it was unwarranted.

Patrick jotted down some notes for his call report which he'd write up later on. The only mention of Hamad Al-Suleiman would be his referral to the CARLA control office in London. There was a remote possibility of referral fees if they carried out a transaction for Capt. John or Hamad Al Suleiman. He'd have to ensure his own name did not feature in any deal they did, though.

He must also remember to tell Penny Baxter about Al-Suleiman. She could add him into her extensive dossier of Middle Eastern fixers.

Chapter 9
Cem Kaplan

When Patrick disembarked at Heathrow airport and turned on his mobile, there was the usual crop of missed calls and voicemails. Among them was Lars booming at him, "Hey there. Your secretary said you are wasting your time in Saudi. There's a fantastic opportunity in Turkey. It's great news. Call me."

By now, Patrick was familiar with these bursts of 'shiny new toy' fervour from Lars. He knew that after a few set-backs or when the road to progress seemed a little less direct than first billed, Lars would lose interest and move on to the next thing. Wondering if the man had any idea how much progress Patrick had made already towards raising the investment they'd need, he returned the call.

"Hi, Lars, it's Patrick. I've landed back at Heathrow. What's up?"

"Just landed? Well get right back on that 'plane and get your hiene over to Turkey. My contact can arrange for the financing of a new factory near Izmir."

Patrick shook his head, bewildered.

"Shouldn't we get a factory in the UK first? Refine the processes, iron out all the wrinkles in the system and get some certifications?"

"Don' need 'em. I told you, I know how everything will work. My contact has all the biggest contractors in Turkey eating out of his hand. I'm telling you, this is a 'gimme'."

Patrick sighed. Talking with Lars was always tiring and he was worn-out after the flight. He needed a shower and had a dozen other tasks to catch up first.

"I am due to visit Turkey shortly, it's true. Let's discuss it tomorrow. I need to get some sleep."

"Cem Kaplan is his name. He's visiting London right now. We're going to get together tomorrow afternoon. Where's that pub you Brits like to go to? That one in the market with all the shops?"

"You mean The Lamb? That's in Leadenhall Market."

"Yeah, that one. I've told him we are meeting at six o'clock. See you there."

And Patrick found himself talking to fresh air, as Lars had rung off. This was so typical of Lars. He just assumed everyone else would fall in line whenever he wanted.

When Patrick got to his office in the morning, he asked Sarah to begin to outline a plan to visit Turkey and Lebanon. He might go on to Jordan and Bahrain afterwards.

"When do you want to do this, Patrick? Excuse me, but you are looking like you need some rest." She'd spotted the drawn appearance to his face. She'd learned that this meant he was worrying about something or had been burning the candle at both ends.

He didn't argue with her.

"You're right, as usual. I could do with a few days off – a bit of 'R and R'. Maybe I can after this trip – and if I go to Beirut, I'll go to see Monty Hughes. He will relax me."

That made Sarah smile. A confirmed Arabist since leaving SOAS (School of Oriental and African Studies in London) thirty years before, Monty Hughes was well thought of by all the locals. That included all from whichever sect or political grouping happened to be in power that year. They trusted him not to blab. Instead he would indicate in his very old-fashioned British manner (speaking in classical Arabic, diplomatic French or English) whether a particular course of action by the other might be preferable, given what he believed to be the case. Patrick sometimes wondered what bloodshed had been thus averted by Monty over the years. Head Office had tried several times to close the Beirut representative's office. They cited dual grounds for this action - safety of the tiny number of staff, given the constantly warring factions and, essential for a bank, lack of attributable money making. Patrick had spoken up on both counts. He pointed out that Monty was well suited for the role and could not only navigate the local opposing factions, but could unearth and relay valuable intelligence about the entire region. In short, he was an astute listening post. There were always mutterings by the Men in Grey Suits about costs of repatriation and 'Excessive Global Emoluments'. But the Beirut office remained alive, year after year.

"Ok," Sarah said. "I'll make sure there is plenty of space for him in the itinerary."

Patrick's day was a whirlwind of returning calls, pacifying his boss, Alan Pearson and passing along the leads and information he'd garnered while in Saudi Arabia. At last, he saw that it was nearing the proposed meeting time with Lars and this new Turkish contact, Cem Kaplan. He ought to hurry along. What fanciful lines of hope was Lars spinning?

"I'd better call it a day, Sarah."

"That's good. See you in the morning."

He gathered his things and set off towards The Lamb.

Lars and Cem were already two pints along and acting like old friends when Patrick arrived. They had spread out a map on their table. A neat circle on it linked Albania, Greece and Bulgaria. Patrick's enquiry of the significance of the circle revealed that it was only the stain left by Lars' beer glass. Much hearty laughter ensued... Stabbing the paper with his fingers, Lars outlined his plan to begin with a factory in Izmir. Then they would open more factories in Mersin, Adana, Bursa, Ereğli, Karabük, Iskenderun, Eskişehir, Ankara and Gaziantep. Each new factory could be financed by the profits from the previous one. He cited Patrick's cautious spreadsheet projections which demonstrated profits Lars described as 'telephone numbers to Mars'.

"Cem, tell me a bit about your background. How did you come to meet this fellow?" Patrick asked, nodding at Lars.

"I've always worked in financial services, ever since leaving Istanbul University. It's very old, you know. It was founded in 1453."

"Really? That is old. What sort of 'financial services'?"

"Oh, you know. Many types. I ended up at Bina Kredi Bank before going out on my own as an independent financial adviser."

Bina Kredi Bank was one of Patrick's clients. He'd be visiting them on the trip that Sarah was putting together. There might be an opportunity to find out what they thought of Kaplan.

Patrick asked, "Which departments did you work in at Bina Kredi? I guess you got to know some of the important merchant families through them?"

"I was a dealer," Cem replied. "I left because I found I could earn more money being a financial adviser."

"Just financial products?"

Cem shook his head. He admitted to doing 'a little' trade in antiquities. Patrick concluded that many of the crowd with whom he mingled would have had plenty of investible money. This was Cem's opening to declare himself LaDaJ's best route to finding finance. He seized it, describing himself as the ideal person to source funding (whether equity or debt) for the first of these factories. He could also structure a facility to ensure its provision of adequate cash. He knew 'all the major house builders' and selling such a fantastic product to them would be easy, he claimed. At this point, he leaned forward. He could only do this if he understood as much as possible about the way the building system worked and the best ways to manufacture it. He was sure there existed plenty of trainable factory workers and technical expertise to produce reliable panels at a good rate.

Patrick clocked Cem's deliberate use of body language to emphasise his memorable point. Having by now a little experience with Turkish nationals, he considered all these assurances as soft and fluffy. They didn't add anything supportive to his proposition. They were designed more to position Cem as the project's Best Way In than any sort of accurate description of the man's competences.

He listened politely and sipped his beer (a rather lovely pint of Youngs Ordinary, as it happened). The level in Lars' glass dropped at an alarming rate, his gulps of ale spaced apart by vigorous head nodding and loud chuckles of agreement. While he fetched another round, it dawned on Patrick that Lars was being rather more open with the technology secrets than was usually the case.

Many times in the past, such details as the precise density of the insulating core had been muttered to Patrick, *sotto voce*, with a muffling hand directing most of the words through Lars' moustache. Now you could have stood over by the bar itself and learned the secret magic figure and ways to achieve it. Patrick was also less than chuffed to discover as he went to pay for the round that

Lars had told the barman Patrick would be footing the entire drinks bill. He had hosted a Farewell party there some months back and paid with his Royal Counties Bank debit card. He was well known by the staff anyway, so this presumptuous claim was accepted by them without question.

Patrick returned to their table clutching the foaming pints, relieved to realise that the noise level in the whole pub had turned up several notches. It was less likely anyone nearby could make sense of what was being discussed. Still – to be on the safe side, he suggested that such details be left for a proper sit-down discussion another time. Lars gave him a funny look but said nothing. Cem, though, glared at him with palpable hostility, his switch from keen friendliness to glowering resentment being as swift as it was surprising. In fact, it rather startled Patrick. He must have trodden on some nerve or other. But he reassured himself that technology and industrial methods are better explained in a quiet and private room, without the lubrication of several beers. This would be his firm line with Lars afterwards.

He changed the subject and talked about Turkish politics: Turkey's 14th General election had been held on Sunday, April 18th, 1999. The Democratic Left Party under Bülent Ecevit had gained great popularity recently and swept the board in the west of the country. It gained most seats but failed to achieve an outright majority because it did not do well in most of the eastern areas. Ecevit therefore formed a coalition with the second-placed MHP and the fourth-placed Motherland party as junior partner. It proved to be one of the most stable governments in recent years. Patrick wondered what Cem thought about all that.

It was a technique he'd used throughout his region: almost everyone felt obliged to explain to the interested foreigner the finer distinctions between opposing factions. In so doing, Patrick was able to listen to the tone of their story and watch their facial expressions. He knew that any declaration of support for a particular individual or party was unlikely to be genuinely held, because people were always careful to avoid criticising those in positions of power, lest their unguarded remarks be relayed to the police or secret services. But he could learn much about the character of the individual. On this occasion, he felt it telling that Cem Kaplan was uncomfortable at such a discussion. The man returned within seconds to questioning Lars about building houses.

Lars had started revealing test results and boasting about how strong the panels were. This wouldn't do, thought Patrick.

"Lars? Can I talk to you outside for one second?" he asked.

Lars blinked at him, without understanding, the excellent beers having further dulled his already low sensitivity to audience feedback.

"Er, sure." Stepping towards the door, he turned back to Cem.

"Another?"

With a meaningful glance at Patrick, Kaplan said, "Not for me, thank you. I'd better head back to my hotel." He seemed to realise that he'd winkle out no more information that night.

Patrick upbraided Lars for trumpeting much of the content of what he'd gathered was valuable Intellectual Property. Lars promised they would patent it in all countries of the world as soon as they'd raised seed funding.

"Cem is a friend," protested Lars, swaying slightly and with his face a little too close to Patrick's. "Anyway, he can't do anything with it: I kept back The Key," he finished triumphantly.

Patrick couldn't imagine what that was and figured that he himself was in no state for verbal jousting with Lars right then.

"That's good," he finished. "Best get some sleep. Are you going to Waterloo?"

"Aye. Let's get a cab," said Lars. It always amazed Patrick how free Lars was with other peoples' money. The man never had cash on him for more than half a day – just until the pubs opened, anyway. And he'd ask Patrick to pay for the ride, asserting the cab could be claimed on expenses – which actually he couldn't, since no actual bank client was involved.

"Let's not," said Patrick. "A stiff walk will do us both good," and he set off in the direction of London Bridge, with Lars trailing in his wake after a short pause.

"How did you meet Cem?" asked Patrick as they passed the entrance to Monument Tube Station at the start of London Bridge.

"I think it was Captain John who introduced us. He thought Cem and his friends might like to provide some equity - we need seed funding, right?"

Patrick nodded and wondered how those two had crossed paths.

"We do," acknowledged Patrick. "But we have never talked about the proportions of debt and equity which would suit us best, nor the type of equity investor we want to have."

Despite his inebriation, Lars was always able to summon up some comment when it came to matters of money, about which he knew far, far less than he imagined.

"It doesn't matter. We'll be making so much money when this gets going, we won't care what dividends or profit share we give 'em."

That was most unlikely to be the case, Patrick thought, and some of the probable complexities whizzed through his mind. He didn't voice them. As before, their early evening brisk walk towards London Bridge station *en route* to Waterloo would be an attempt to dispel the otherwise pleasant alcoholic fogginess of that wonderful Young's Beer. The activity did not lend itself to a complete and balanced review of the funds raising alternatives.

Chapter 10
The Incident in Villiers Street

It caught Patrick by surprise next day when Sarah put through a telephone call from Cem Kaplan. He sounded quite excited.

"My friend has told me about a 17th Century painting which I could get hold of for only five thousand dollars but it's actually worth between thirty and forty thousand at auction!" He paused for effect. "The only catch," Cem continued, "Is that we have to get him the money by Friday."

Patrick shook his head to try to see how on earth this offered transaction could be anything other than the most unsubtle con. "Cem, I'm way out of my depth here. I know nothing about art and I have to say, when I have heard about deals which sounded so fantastical but had to be done in a short period of time, they all turned out to be fraudulent. Who owns this painting now?"

"Ah," said Cem. "You're talking about *provenance*. It's been valued by Christie's who have seen the line of ownership, and the reason it's likely to fetch so much is that it's a previously unknown painting by a 17th Century Dutch Master named Pieter Claesz. It's *Still Life with Wine, Cheese and a Tobacco box* which Christies think he painted right at the end of his life. You can even see where he signed it."

"And why would the current owner not enter the painting into a Christie's Auction?" Patrick asked the obvious question. "He or she would make six or eight times as much as he's asking you."

"He doesn't know," crowed Cem. "You see, my associate was looking after the painting for him, and thought it a good idea to have it valued – just in case – and what they said blew us away."

Patrick tried to interrupt to find out about this associate and why he might be 'looking after' such a valuable piece of art, but the other man was in full flow: "...And Christie's are holding an auction of 17th Century Masters next month, so we will have a small amount of time to enter it. You can look it up yourself: there are many such painters and their work attracts most wealthy investors from around the world."

He jumped in when Cem Kaplan paused for breath. "Look, sorry to interrupt, Cem, but I've got quite a bit 'on' at the moment; I'll give you a call after work – about seven? Would that be convenient?"

Cem subsided and agreed that he could wait until that evening. Patrick asked him to fax over the Christie's valuation. There was a pause, as though Cem needed to think it through. But he agreed to that too and Patrick told him the fax number to use.

"Sarah?" Patrick called. She popped her head around the door. "Sorry to bother you - someone is faxing a Christie's painting valuation to me in the next few minutes. Could you grab it before Alan catches sight of it?"

Sarah smiled. She was well aware of her boss' eclectic interests: wine, motor cars, fine food – so far, so 'bon viveur'. But he also liked sea fishing off boats, beaches or piers in pretty much any weather. She shuddered at the memory of a Team Building Exercise he'd organised one wet and blowy October day. She'd spent the whole time shivering, wishing she hadn't bothered to wash her hair the night before and trying not to throw up as the boat pitched and yawed in the waves. Patrick had called it a 'moderate swell'. It wasn't so bad when they were motoring out to the designated fishing spot over a wreck, other than the occasional wave which burst over the side and contrived to penetrate her supposedly 'storm-proof' jacket. No, the real problem was when the boat rolled around at the mercy of whichever wave happened along. That and the wafts of stale diesel oil seeping up through the companionway. She had been almost grateful when the sea breeze blew most of it away, except that it sometimes carried icy spray off a wave top which stung like needles when it hit her face. Very 'John Masefield'. How could all the others get so giddily happy when one of them hauled a flapping fish over the side? Patrick was the worst of them - he wanted immediately to gut the fish and use the entrails for bait! Usually the crewmen did this for business parties, especially groups of Hooray Henry bankers. But her boss seemed not to have a squeamish bone in his body.

Was it too much to hope that he was now getting interested in paintings? Art paintings, that is. Not paint-balling, which was another low point from a while ago. She returned to her Trip Outline, keeping a wary eye on the printer a few yards away. This interest could result in a pleasant evening of private viewings at some riverside gallery, she thought. Her mind wandered. There would be champagne cocktails and canapes. She would volunteer to organise that in a heartbeat! She had her eye on a particular dress which was more than she'd usually spend – a lot more, actually, but it would be worth it for such an evening. And who knew what eligible bachelor might attend..?

-----//-----

Trading fine art at the behest of a stranger he had only met once in a pub sounded to Patrick like the beginning of a 'Have you heard the one about…' joke. But if this was something other people did, why should he scoff at it? But rather than call Lars with this update, Patrick felt it wise to run it past Jerry Green for a sustaining shot of reality.

Jerry answered first ring. "Hey, Patrick. I was thinking about you only five minutes ago. Are you calling for advice on how to spend the millions we will be earning next year?"

Patrick couldn't restrain a chortle. "Not exactly, Jerry. I was thinking we haven't chatted for a while and a few things have happened recently, so I thought another cup of caffeinous beverage might be in order. Are you in London today?" It happened that Jerry was attending some military briefing session over lunch in the West End. Although retired from active service, he had a kind of retained hobby advisory role to the Army. He expected to be away from that around four o'clock, so a pastry and whatever coffee concoction Patrick thought he should have at five would be most reviving.

Patrick arrived at the same Starbucks where they had first got to know each other on Villiers Street beside Charing Cross Station. As it was not quite five o'clock, there were lots of seats free and he settled down in a quiet corner. His mobile rang. Hoping it wasn't the office, he pulled it from his trouser pocket. It was Jerry.

"Didn't you like the table I chose?"

Patrick looked around him, blankly. There was Jerry, two tables away, grinning away like the proverbial Cheshire Cat.

"How do you do that?" Patrick asked, with mild exasperation that the other man should be able to hide in plain sight. Jerry shrugged.

"You need to keep your eyes open, mate." They shook hands with genuine good feeling.

"Right. First things first: do you know what you want, or shall I choose?"

"You drive." Jerry made a sweeping gesture with his hand as though passing responsibility to Patrick. "I'm in your hands, but I would like a cinnamon roll."

"Coming right up," said Patrick, laying his coat on top of his briefcase on the seat. Five minutes later he returned with a couple of cups of steaming coffee, a blueberry muffin for himself and a cinnamon roll. They were all balanced on a tiny tray such as a butler might have used in the last century to bring an urgent, hand-delivered letter to his employer.

"Why are these trays so small?" he grumbled. "It wouldn't take much more plastic to make them actually fit what people buy."

"Overheads, dear boy – overheads," quoth Jerry with no further explanation. Patrick took an appreciative sip of his Americano brew and extracted his briefcase from beneath the coat.

"That's better. Now, I told you about my trip with Justin to see that modular building company in the midlands. It would be a complete money pit for us, at least until our own building system is up and running. They have no orders, few staff and costly premises which have reduced their bank balance to nothing much. I said to leave it well alone."

Jerry nodded. The cinnamon roll was very good, especially after the plain and stale Army biscuits which had constituted 'lunch' for him.

"Moving on, Lars is working on exactly how we can construct the panel samples which BRE are to test. There is a series of laid down tests which all such systems have to meet to get certification, he says. We'll need to test seven panels, at least five corners and at least three joining wedges. We'll have a chat next week about how to schedule production, order the cores and have them laminated up."

"Right. Makes sense," Jerry agreed.

"Ok. That's the second thing. Next - you'll remember I met with PwC again up the road the last time we met. The partner introduced me to a Philippino captain – he dresses like a pirate, but he's retired navy, I think. The partner, Roger Hammerson, had posited this chap as controlling a large area of Malaysian rain forest. It produces an income for him, but he wanted either to bring forward some of that income or to make the asset work a bit harder. He could do that by borrowing against it. Roger is thinking of using Safe-Keeping Receipts rather like the repo market, as I explained in our Team Meeting. To start with, he pointed me towards International Bank of the Philippines in Manilla who might put up some seed money for us as they are holding the title deeds. I know the London office of that bank and hoped to speed things up. They introduced me and I had a longish chat to this Captain John fellow. What's interesting about him, or maybe just odd, is that he seems to know quite a lot of senior financial people around the City."

Jerry raised a questioning eyebrow. "What do you mean?"

"I'm getting the idea that there is a network of people in London and elsewhere who all know each other but it isn't clear which one is Boss."

"Does there have to be a 'boss'?" asked Jerry. "The brokers I come across on business linking networks all seem to be one-man bands. They hope that by introducing me to one of their mates, they will come in for a share of whatever commission or fee the business generates in the end. They are all very good at reminding me of introductions they have made on my behalf, asking for updates on progress. They want to know if they are close to receiving money from me. But none of them seem to be in charge, as it were."

"That sounds annoying," sympathised Patrick. "But I don't feel this is a pool of brokers, like you describe. It's more…" He paused, searching for some descriptive word. "…organised, I suppose; like everyone has a role to play in an organisation."

He set out the sequence of events, from finding his low-level enquiry of IBP kicked upstairs fast to Ramil Galang, the London General Manager and then talking to Captain John. Also, following his casual mention of an upcoming trip to the Middle East, the Captain pointed him at Hamad Al-Suleiman for a meeting in Jeddah. He was the man mentioned by the PwC partner, Roger Hammerson – but with a Kuwaiti mobile number.

Jerry smiled: "And you think there is a Mr Big somewhere?"

He had to admit this wasn't much to go on. Maybe he was a little tired. "But when I did meet Al-Suleiman, he wanted my introduction to our branch in Netherlands Antilles, as did Captain John. Why couldn't he call them himself?" Patrick finished, a little lamely, knowing full well the power of such an introduction from a senior member of bank staff.

"I wouldn't worry about it," pronounced Jerry, glancing at the remaining sandwiches over at the counter.

"There's something else; well, someone else. I had another beery evening with Lars so he could introduce me to a Turkish fellow named Cem Kaplan."

"I'm listening," Jerry said, his attention now focussed back on Patrick. "Who is he?"

"He seems to have bounced from bank to bank in Turkey, winding up at one of the quite decent, medium sized ones, Bina Kredi Bank. He also does what he describes as antiquities trading, on the side. Lars sees him as being able to pull in some funding for us. Seed funding, at least, as he says he knows lots of wealthy people who might want to be early investors in our building system."

"And what does he want for doing this? He sounds like a broker to me."

"We haven't got to that stage, yet, Jerry. This morning, Kaplan called saying he can buy a 17th Century Dutch Old Master painting for one sixth of its true worth – he has all the provenance and a Christie's valuation to prove it. Look – here is a copy he faxed over to me."

Jerry actually laughed. "And he wants us to put up the purchase money so that it can go to auction and he shares in the profit? Yes?"

"Something like that." Patrick felt his face colouring up. He realised as he told the story, the prospective deal sounded more and more like one of the oldest scams in the world. Why had it seemed so attractive when Cem described it? So …real?

"Forget him," Jerry dismissed Cem Kaplan with a slight wave of his hand. "That PwC partner's Safe-Keeping Receipts thing sounds dodgy enough, but arbitraging 17th Century Masters paintings? That's more flakey than a '99' ice cream!" He looked around at the counter again. "I might investigate those sandwiches before they disappear," scraped back his chair and headed to the front.

Patrick checked his watch. It was nearly 6pm. He ought to tell Cem that he wasn't interested any more in fine art opportunities, so as not to waste his time or Cem's time. But as he scrolled through for the number, the phone rang. It was Lars.

"Great news!" (Lars' usual opening line). "Cem has found some seed capital for us. We're meeting in an hour to discuss terms."

Patrick looked up to see if Jerry was coming back. He was at the stage of paying for his sandwiches. "I'm in a meeting right now and I was going to call Cem at 7 – can the meeting be rescheduled"?

"I know," said Lars. "But don't worry – we'll come to you." And the line went dead, leaving Patrick open-mouthed.

"I got one for you as well," Jerry settled himself into his seat, laying out a couple of sandwich packets and plates. "Tuna or Ham and Cheese?"

"Um …I don't mind," Patrick replied, waving his phone. "That was Lars – he says Cem has found our seed capital and they are both coming here to discuss terms."

"Here?" Now it was Jerry's turn to look startled. "Did you tell him we were here?"

Patrick shook his head. "He knew." Jerry stopped chewing for a moment.

"That puts a different complexion on things. Maybe your secretary told him?"

Patrick doubted it and shook his head. He had told Sarah he was meeting someone in the West End but not who or why …or where. She might have guessed it would have been somewhere to drink decent coffee or beer or wine.

"I wasn't followed," Jerry said. "I was careful. Were you?"

"I have no idea." This was alarming Patrick now. His eyes widened. He could see that Jerry's military training seemed to have kicked in. "Why would I notice anybody following me?"

Jerry nodded. Without turning his head to look at the glass front of the cafe, he asked, "Is there a man, mid-30s, short black hair, brown jacket, jeans and sunglasses reading a magazine across the Road?"

Feeling self-conscious, Patrick turned his head as though to rub a sore neck. It was difficult to spot anyone in particular, as Villiers Street thronged with home-bound commuters heading up to the Charing Cross side entrance or down to Embankment Tube station. But, yes. There *was* such a chap, currently gazing down the road and looking down again to study his Evening Standard newspaper.

Patrick nodded. "Yes – there is. How did you know?"

"He took up position right after you came in. He's mates with a thick-set man - Asian, who keeps station for him while he nips down the road, probably to pee. I wonder why he isn't going to the station toilet?"

"But this is absurd! It all sounds like a Graham Greene novel with spies watching each other." Patrick sat back in his chair. Jerry continued to look serious, though. At least he was still eating his sandwich.

"These are not bad – you haven't started yours: do you want it?"

Patrick went through the motions of wrestling with the polythene wrapper and wiggled one half of a ham sandwich out of its waxed paper carton. "I do." He took an exploratory bite. "It's ok. Thanks."

"I'm going to visit the Gents' at the back," and Jerry got up again, leaving Patrick to wonder about his sandwich of Farm cut Ham, Cheddar Cheese and Roasted Tomato on Granary bread. What distinguishes 'Farm Cut' ham from regular ham?

Chapter 11
The Puzzled Curator

Jerry was spending quite a long time in the toilet. Patrick knew he had some sort of sensitive gut which misbehaved on occasion. He remembered his own father had returned from the Second World War with Amoebic Dysentery and a profound sensitivity for certain foods. They caused his bathroom breaks to be frequent and prolonged. He assumed something of the sort was the case with Jerry too, as he also had served abroad in lots of countries where he did not have the choice to stay in four-star hotels. He was not especially surprised when some ten minutes elapsed before his companion returned.

As Jerry sat down again, there was a kerfuffle outside and an emergency vehicle siren sounded, its driver trying to get through the human river blocking the narrow street. An ambulance pulled up right outside the cafe, lights flashing. A small crowd kept trying to gather to watch proceedings, but, like flotsam caught on an overhanging branch, was washed away by those desperate to catch the 6:32pm train to suburbia. The sea of humanity and the ambulance itself hid the causal event. Patrick said, "Well at least that has blocked the man's view if he is spying on us." Another siren lit up close by as he spoke.

"You might want to let Lars know that we cannot meet here tonight," said Jerry, his face neutral. "I'm expecting them to block the road for a while."

Now it was Patrick's turn to raise his eyebrows. "How so?"

"The Police always do that if there is a fatality. It's so they can collate evidence and work out what happened. Come on. Time to go."

And with that, Jerry stood up, gathered his things and waited for Patrick to drain the final drops of cold coffee from his cup. As Patrick picked up his coat and stuffed the Christie's valuation back into his briefcase, Jerry turned towards the rear of the café. Seeing his companion's puzzled face, Jerry offered, "This way's quicker." He steered them between the gawping customers, all of whom were staring at the action out of the front window, of course.

Beyond the toilet was the emergency Fire door which was not quite closed. "Mind where you step," cautioned Jerry, weaving between cases of coffee, themselves piled with boxes of other comestibles. The smell of roasted coffee beans was distracting for Patrick, but he did what he was told. They twisted and turned down various alleyways. Once they went through a building, down some steps, only to emerge up a loading ramp on to Craven Street. Patrick glanced up to get his bearings. A blue plaque high on the wall was dedicated to Herman Melville, the 19th Century American novelist, writer of Moby Dick and various romanticised accounts of his adventures in Polynesia. He was familiar with these, because of his own time in the SW Pacific. He thought them wistful, rather than factual. Even so, they were a nice way of adjusting memories of some of the harsher realities of what he had found all those years ago.

"Now, where shall we go?" Jerry was striding away. "Have you called Lars yet?"

Everything was happening a little too fast. "I'll call him now." Patrick paused. "I need to think through first what I'm going to say."

"What's the problem?" Jerry queried. "It's quite straightforward. We are not going to get involved in buying dodgy artworks and we don't know anything about this man Kaplan. We ought to do some checking on him first, before even thinking of sitting down to discuss funding via him and his friends."

"True. I can call some contacts at Bina Kredi Bank to see if they know him and Ak Bank as well. He worked there for a spell."

"But how well do you know those contacts?"

Patrick admitted he knew them only in a functional sense. On reflection, he couldn't trust any character reference from them. He always met the staff on bank premises - they'd discuss trading lines, the economy, interest rate scenarios and the like. Rarely they might have lunch together or a dinner. Even though there was usually some light 'cocktail party chatter' about holidays or family matters, both sides were conscious that the sole purpose of meeting, even in such convivial surroundings, was business between their two bank institutions. That was why Patrick's boss was prepared to sign off on his expense claims for flights, hotels, taxis and food.

"Ok. I'll do the checking. First, though, tell Lars any meeting is out of the question until we have checked this guy out in depth. Tell him we don't want to get into bed with anyone who will steal our technology – you know how protective he is of 'our' Intellectual Property."

"Should I tell him you are checking Cem out?"

Jerry nodded.

Patrick dialled Lars' mobile. It went to voicemail. He looked up and said as much to Jerry. "I guess he's on the Tube - shall I leave a message?"

"Yup."

"Lars, this is Patrick. I was having a catch up with Jerry and there has been some sort of incident outside the café, so the Police have closed Villiers Street. It means we can't meet there. Anyway we both feel that this talk of funding via Cem is all a bit too rushed. Jerry is going to check him out as fast as he can. After all, you wouldn't want to let someone steal our technology, would you? Sorry I couldn't call you back earlier but everything happened in a bit of a rush here."

He cut the line. He and Jerry went their separate ways.

As Patrick boarded the train to head home, his phone rang. There was a tension evident in Lars' voice. He was getting to recognise when the man was controlling his emotions. It was usually anger that something hadn't gone the way he wanted.

"Tell Jerry I'll take care of it. In fact, I have already. I have contacts in the Federal Reserve who are checking him out right now. That's how I checked you guys out too, you know."

This sounded as unlikely to Patrick as the prospect of trading profitably in Old Masters had sounded to Jerry. He couldn't resist asking, "Oh yes? Who is that, then?"

"Someone very, very high up - in a secret part of the Fed that nobody knows about. In fact, I could tell you but I'd have to shoot you," Lars finished, in a lame attempt to lighten the conversation. "I told Cem that something had come up – one of your big deals – and you had been called away. But he is very keen that we meet ASAP, otherwise the opportunity will slip away."

Patrick sighed. "Is this anything to do with oil paintings, by chance?"

Now it was Lars' turn to sound surprised. "He did say something about that, but it's all above board and he has a Christie's valuation and everything. But there is more. That's just for starters - you know me. I like to cut deals with people. He has the biggest Turkish investors in the country who have so much money it embarrasses the Government. They have to get rid of all their money – art, motor cars and what-have-you. I told him, they could invest in the best building technology in the world. With us! And then they have steel plants which are idle, so they can buy them and put people back to work…"

"Hang on, hang on," interrupted Patrick.

"…by converting all this waste material…"

"Lars – wait a second. Let's do one thing at a time." Patrick had raised his voice to make himself heard. He was conscious that people in the carriage were staring at him. Lars did stop, though, mid-sentence, taken by surprise that anyone else would speak while he was in full flow.

"I'm scared that this technology is so good and so useful that many people will want to take it away from us – cut us out completely. That is why, rightly, you are talking about patenting all around the world. We both know that patents are often circumvented by people abroad, even in quite civilised countries. The resultant law suits would tie us up for years."

"But Cem is a friend – I can control him," protested Lars.

"Ok. If you say so. But many of those he represents may not be friendly. And they will smile and take us to dinner and cheat us out of all our hard work – *your* hard work."

"What they see, what Cem tells them, won't mean anything. They won't understand it. I won't give them *The Key*."

Patrick could see where this was going. Lars always thought he was more clever, more experienced, had better lawyers - he could best anyone. "I'm sure that's right, Lars, but they will attempt to reverse engineer the system. They may fail and they will put out some pale imitation which won't perform as well. Heck, it might even fall down and kill people, and some of that mud will stick to us! No matter how much we protest that it wasn't a licensed operation, didn't use our original technology and was nothing to do with us, nevertheless, mud will stick. People here will think our system failed."

There was a short pause while Lars thought about this drawback.

"I see what you mean," he relented. "But we can be more clever. We'll tell them we are not going to explain it all unless we are allowed to run the factories. They'll pay the license fee upfront so we won't care and only have to visit twice a year to collect the royalties. I'll call Cem now and rearrange the meeting. They'll have to wait until next week."

And with that, he was gone. Patrick tapped out a text to Jerry to brief him that the latest imminent Lars-inspired crisis seemed to have been averted. But they should expect some sort of resumption after the weekend.

That night, watching the Ten o'Clock News on television, Patrick's jaw dropped when they showed shots of Villiers Street. Police were taping off a crime scene. A young man had been knifed without passers-by noticing anything wrong. There was talk of gang-related violence. As always, reporters were thrusting microphones into onlookers' faces asking what they saw. Again, as always, the more truthful talked for thirty valuable seconds before admitting they'd seen nothing amiss. Others asserted that they had seen the fellow collapse, but assumed he was drunk and stepped over him. 'So why were they still hanging around at the scene' mused Patrick. Nobody from the authorities was available for comment. The reporter claimed a duty Constable had given him the boiler-plate reply that enquiries were ongoing. "Back to the Studio," he finished, grimly. Patrick noticed his tie was askew.

-----//-----

It seemed that mysterious telephone calls were becoming part of Patrick's daily routine now. This time it was Captain John.

"Patrick. What's going on? I need that introduction to Netherlands Antilles."

"Captain John. Good morning. I met with Hamad Al-Suleiman in Jeddah. I passed him the contact details and I'm now preparing a report to go to our controlling office for the Caribbean."

"How long is this going to take? We need to get going."

"I would estimate a few more days – a week at the outside. What's the sudden hurry?"

"It's getting urgent. Call me this week."

He rang off. Not ten minutes later, Sarah put through a call from Lars.

"We gotta talk. Can you meet tonight?"

Patrick thumbed his diary. It was getting crowded with all these impromptu meetings. But he agreed. Over the inevitable pints of beer, which Lars bought, for a change, he leaned towards Patrick over the table.

"What do you think of Jerry?"

"I like him," Patrick replied. "He's a pretty straight shooter, it seems to me. Feet on the ground and all that. What's in your mind?"

Lars stroked his moustache. "But can he be trusted? Capt. John and other people have heard bad things about him."

"I try to take people as I find them. I think he is trust-worthy. What are these 'bad things' you have heard?"

"Jerry had to leave the Army, you know – they kicked him out."

"I'm sure he feels like he was kicked out, but he was injured in a parachute jump. That's why he limps and that's no good for a serving officer."

"Is that what he told you...?" Lars left the question open.

"So what do you think happened?" Patrick pressed for details.

Lars shook his head. He was sowing seeds of doubt and Patrick found it unsettling. The man refused to be drawn on what he meant. Patrick decided to keep this enquiry to himself, but to be more observant when dealing with Jerry.

-----//-----

"Patrick?" He looked up from his desk. Sarah was standing there. "I'm getting on with your trip but I can't seem to get hold of the people you wanted in Bina Kredi's dealing room. They're always on a call or 'off the desk'."

Patrick frowned. Sarah was usually good at this aspect of preparation. Maybe there was a problem of some sort.

"Leave it with me, Sarah. I'll try the Chief Dealer towards the end of the day when things calm down a bit."

"They told me Mr Mungan has been on vacation and nobody wants to commit him to any meeting."

"Ok. Thanks." He knew these things were always subject to the day's trading conditions. It was best to remain flexible. Mert Mungan wouldn't hesitate to keep Patrick waiting if the US dollar started moving or one of their positions was looking iffy. Not that he cared, but he knew Patrick wouldn't mind in the least.

"Mert – it's Patrick Field from Royal Counties Bank. I'm heading to Istanbul and wondered if you might be game for some cold beers after work?"

Mert chuckled. "Is your Pope a Catholic?" They juggled dates and times and he accepted. Patrick hoped to pump him for information on Cem Kaplan, whom he ought to know, if what Cem claimed was true.

-----//-----

Patrick had an hour or so to kill before visiting Bina Kredi Bank, so, attracted by a poster advertising a current display of 17th Century Dutch Masters, popped into the Sakip Sabanci Museum for a wander through. 'Obviously the fashionable art period *du jour*', he thought. His eye was caught by a Rembrandt: '*The Music Lesson*' painted in 1626, when the artist was only 20 years old. The Dutch had been adventurous travellers and traders for centuries by this time. Patrick knew this from the number of times he'd visited local Middle Eastern sites which had some sort of link with Holland. Some had been created or changed by a visiting Dutchman hundreds of years before. The little history card beside the painting explained in Turkish and English that Rembrandt was not known to have visited the Middle East. But Ottoman trinkets, clothing and spices would have found their way to Holland for at least a hundred years before young Rembrandt picked up his paint brushes. They often featured in Dutch culture, sometimes in subtle ways, such as dressing subjects in Ottoman-style clothing, as in this picture.

The paintings were arranged in date order. He moved on. There, right in front of him was a 1627 painting by Pieter Claesz – whose *Still Life with Wine, Cheese and a Tobacco box* was the subject of Cem Kaplan's great excitement. This one was called *Still Life with a Turkey Pie*. Patrick immediately checked the notes beside the picture. It was on loan from the Rijksmuseum in Amsterdam. They had acquired it a few years before from a private collector for eight hundred thousand Euros!

Patrick whistled.

He read the notes again. Claesz died at the end of 1660 (and was buried on New Year's Day, 1661) so this was a relatively early painting. He stood back and surveyed the 75cm x 132cm canvas from a distance. He wished he knew more about painting techniques and art generally. It looked much the same as the photograph which had accompanied the Christie's valuation document Cem had sent him. The initials were in the same area of the picture and looked to Patrick's eye much the same. Perhaps he should reassess the opportunity Cem had offered. Even if the later work somehow didn't fetch quite eight hundred thousand Euros, it might sell for a great deal more than the five thousand dollars Cem said they'd need to buy it.

His focus on the picture had been intense. He became aware that a smaller, older man had stood quite close to him. "Excuse me," the man asked. "Do you particularly like Pieter Claesz pictures? We have two others in the next room from his later period."

"Thank you," smiled Patrick. "I don't really know anything about this artist in particular. It's just that a friend of mine has a chance to buy one from nearer the end of Claesz's life and has asked for my help to do so."

"Allow me to introduce myself - I'm Bülent Aksoy, curator of this exhibition."

"I'm very pleased to meet you – Patrick Field," said Patrick. "I'm afraid I don't know either what a curator does - other than get hold of items which have something in common. Then arrange the display so that visitors can learn more about the topic."

Aksoy smiled and said that pretty much covered his job. He motioned Patrick towards the door to the next room.

"Claesz was famous for still life representations like that one. He concentrated on what we term 'breakfast' pieces, using monochrome colours. His special talent was achieving a rich effect of light playing on different angles and textures of the items in the painting. Now, this one…" he went on, nodding at a canvas roughly half a metre square, entitled *Still Life with Drinking Vessels*, "…This one, he painted in 1649. Look at how much better he has caught the folded cloth and the reflections in the glasses."

Patrick peered at the picture, blinking.

"Try standing back a little."

Patrick obliged and realised that the fussy detail of the brushwork had confused his eye. Viewed from an extra yard away, the picture took on a photographic quality. He realised that his perception of shades and textures had been influenced by that diligent brushwork.

"This painting looks darker than the one my friend is interested in," offered Patrick, hoping to sound at least slightly erudite. He wanted not to make a fool of himself.

"Oh, that's not surprising," said Aksoy. "Lighting his work from this earlier period is a challenge because Pieter Claesz is noted for subtle variations of closely related monochrome colours. In his later, more Baroque work, they became stronger. Claesz's work after 1640 was more and more decorative and included quite lavish still-life displays. The earlier works all position the viewer at a higher level, too, than paintings he did towards the end of his life."

Patrick was trying to take all this in.

"So it isn't just a matter of whether the painting needs a clean, then?"

Aksoy politely indicated that that would be too simplistic.

"Which of Claesz's paintings is your friend interested in?" he asked.

"*Still Life with Wine, Cheese and a Tobacco box*," answered Patrick. "I understand the artist painted it towards the end of his life."

The other man's forehead furrowed.

"Claesz painted around forty pictures in his last ten years – or thereabouts. We are lucky to have these three on loan, but they are earlier, as you see. Would you excuse me for a moment? I can look it up for you so you have a bit more information about it."

"Oh, that would be very kind," Patrick smiled. "If it isn't too much trouble, I'd be very interested." He glanced at his watch. There was still plenty of time before his meeting. He could mooch around the rest of the exhibition while he waited.

"Give me ten minutes. I'll meet you back here at …shall we say, at 4pm?"

"Thank you." Aksoy disappeared through a door marked 'Private'.

He circled around some of the other pictures, not recognising any of the artists' names. Soon his watch told him it was nearly 4 o'clock. Bülent Aksoy was there already.

"Hello again," Patrick opened. "What did you discover?"

"Are you sure about the name, Mr Field?" asked Aksoy. "I cannot find any reference to a painting with that name."

"I think so," Patrick frowned, fumbling with his briefcase. He thought he might still have the faxed Christie's valuation tucked at the side. He found the paper and handed it over. "Here is a valuation Christies provided, with a small photograph at the bottom."

Aksoy examined the paper, holding it up to the light to see it better.

"Well, well. This is quite exciting for me. I haven't seen this picture before and I thought I knew Claesz's body of work quite well. May I ask where is it now?"

Patrick confessed he didn't know, except that it was being looked after by a third party.

"If your friend does proceed with the purchase, do let him know that we would be greatly honoured to include it in this exhibition as an example of the later work. Here is my card. The exhibition will run for another four months, so there might well be time – it will show how Claesz's style changed during his life." He handed back the valuation with his business card.

Patrick reciprocated with his own card and murmured something to the effect that he'd be sure to pass along the request. They shook hands, warmly and Aksoy returned through the staff door.

Patrick reckoned that a gentle stroll towards his 5 o'clock appointment would be a wise course of action. He crossed to the shady side of the street and proceeded, deep in thought, towards the Bina Kredi Bank offices.

-----//-----

Patrick called at the Bina Kredi Bank a few minutes after 5 o'clock and asked for Mert Mungan at the reception desk.

The man was emerging from the lift at that moment. Mert greeted him like an old friend, grabbing him by both shoulders and kissing his cheeks. The thought flashed through Patrick's mind that it would be preferable to be scraped with sand paper than Mert's five o'clock shadow. But he put up with it and manfully slapped the other on the back.

"You look as though you could use a beer," he offered.

"Damn right," agreed Mert. "Let's get out of here."

He wiggled his fingers at one of the receptionists as they left and Patrick saw that the woman smiled shyly and cast her eyes downwards at her keyboard. He knew Mert was married with a couple of children.

"You dog!" he murmured, and held the door open. A faintly raised eyebrow from his companion acknowledged the comment. Mert led the way towards a nearby bar and restaurant, which served quite delicious fish, fresh from the dock.

The Bosphorus Grill at the Ciragan Palace Hotel boasted a wonderful view over the Bosphorus River. Most importantly, though, they offered a fantastic selection of foods, straight from the market or dockside. Prawns, calamari, sea bass, dorado and grouper all featured on the grill menu. It was that part of the menu which always drew Patrick to them. More predictable offerings of lamb, chicken and beef were there too, for the less adventurous. Plus they served the local Efes beer in large glasses which were constantly but discretely refilled by the waiting staff. A bonus was their 'smart / casual' dress code, which Patrick figured Mert would appreciate, as bank cocktail parties called for a smart suit. He'd seen the man showing his resentment at having to wear a tie in formal settings by knotting it at half-mast.

They were led to a table closest to the water. Pretty soon the waiter reappeared with foaming glasses of Efes and small plates of grilled calamari and tangy shrimps. Mert made half of his first beer disappear in one draught. He sat back, wiping his lips. "I needed that," he explained. Something else Patrick knew Mert hated about official functions was that you were supposed to sip your glass of wine in a delicate manner. Downing half a glass of beer at once was not permitted. The unspoken rules for the trays of food were similar. You ought to nibble little more than would be consumed by an off-colour sparrow. "I'm glad you called," Mert said. "Corporate are working on a big deal to finance a construction project. We haven't won it and we might lose the mandate to one of the other banks, but it would be the biggest we've ever done. Can you help?"

"Go on," said Patrick. Already it looked like he'd not only get the chance to ask about Cem Kaplan but also, possibly, have a sniff at a real bit of Royal Counties Bank business.

"We'd handle all the local distribution and run the books, but would Royal Counties Bank arrange and co-front it with us?"

Patrick knew well that Bina Kredi Bank had absolutely no chance of selling a deal of $100 million or more by themselves to the international market. They would need the *imprimateur* of a global name like Royal Counties Bank with its 'AA' credit rating, sophisticated syndication team and the prestige which went with it. So Royal Counties could pretty much name the size and percentage of fees they could demand out of the deal. There would be much angst in his credit department because the amount of country risk Royal Counties Bank had left for Turkey was modest. A fully-underwritten transaction would be out of the question. But, fronting a syndicated loan for a short time which would then be sold down in the market could represent a very valuable earning opportunity for a short-term use of those country limits. Patrick foresaw lively internal discussions in his future back at base.

He'd also have to weigh up whether he would do better to partner with one of the larger Turkish banks from which Royal Counties Bank garnered more significant earnings every year than Bina Kredi Bank. It didn't do to annoy such powerful institutions. Still, Patrick told himself, as an investment banker, he ought to have a transactional view of the world. This went against the grain with him to an extent. But if it all succeeded, he told himself he'd reject any accusations by the larger banks by saying 'Bina Kredi asked me first'.

"How much are we talking about?"

"Two fifty million dollars over five years," replied Mert and drained his glass. The man's voice gave away that he was asking more in hope than certainty. Patrick whistled. Given the state of Turkey's economy right now, that might be quite a stretch.

"I'm not saying 'No', but such a size and time span, especially in the construction sector, requires considerable thought – and beer!" he finished, as a waiter materialised with two more Efes bottles. Mert wanted to keep the name of the borrower private for the moment. He said that he'd relay Patrick's interest in principle to his own management and Corporate Team.

"I came across an interesting chap the other day," started Patrick, "And he mentioned he'd worked with you a while back. Do you remember Cem Kaplan?"

Mert replaced his glass on the table with studied care. "Sure. Can we order first and is Royal Counties Bank paying for this?"

Patrick nodded. "Yes to both. Here's a menu."

Judging by what Mert ordered, his appetite for food matched that for beer. Patrick reckoned to be a hearty eater, his hunger sharpened by the salty sea air, but he had to give best to the Turk. It took the entirety of their meal for Patrick to learn that Cem had been a junior trader for some months. Both were distracted by chili and lime marinated İskenderun prawns, followed by grouper fillet marinated with aromatic herbs and lemon; yoghurt, turmeric and garlic-marinated chicken döner kebab and Tahini halva with several very strong Turkish coffees to finish. Eventually, Mert said that Cem hadn't demonstrated the staying power his early performances promised. He was not actively disliked by the back-room staff, but they also had no particular regard for him. And there were rumours. Rumours of what, Patrick asked. Mert would not be drawn. He'd already been more open than Patrick expected when he introduced the topic by saying that a friend in London was looking to find a job for Cem and had asked his opinion.

"I asked him to move along," Mert confided. "He resigned. Bina Kredi doesn't write references other than to confirm the dates between which they worked here. Cem never asked even for that."

Chapter 12
Monty's Wise Words

Patrick moved on to Lebanon. Royal Counties Bank had a Representative office there reporting to Dubai, now that the Bahrain office had closed. It had sourced locally several of the finer traders who now worked in the Dubai trading room. Patrick found it interesting that all were women. They seemed to have an ability to think with clarity and logic when there were big currency moves happening in periods of volatility. Some of the younger men didn't. The women also didn't have quite so many trading car crashes as their male counterparts – not always trying to outdo others, Patrick concluded. He liked to drop in to chat to the permanent representative in Beirut when he had a day free in the region.

Sarah had asked Monty Hughes if he could spare Patrick a little time during the late afternoon of his day in Beirut. The man was effusive in his insistence that Patrick should stay for dinner. "And I have a special surprise for him," he enthused. "I can think of nobody I would rather share this with."

Sarah didn't dare ask the great man what manner of surprise this might be, but had an inkling it might have something to do with her boss' passions for food or wine.

"I'm sure he would be delighted, Mr Hughes – you are very kind. When should he come to your office?"

"Nonsense, my dear. It's no trouble. And tell him to come straight to my house. Shall we say at six o'clock?"

So it was that Patrick found himself staring at the clothes he had brought on his trip, laid out on his bed in the hotel, wondering what would be appropriate for the occasion. His wardrobe was, of necessity, limited. He preferred to travel as light as he dared, knowing that flights sometimes changed terminal at short notice and he would need to jog to another carrying all his possessions. Airline ground staff in Arabia had little sympathy for perspiring foreigners at the wrong terminal!

At last, he selected some oatmeal slacks and a short-sleeved shirt. A quick search of the room's wardrobe revealed an electric iron, so he could try to press out the worst of the creases in the trousers. His favoured method for achieving the same result with shirts was to hang them in the bathroom before he showered. The steam and the shirt's own weight would manage what several minutes of ham-fisted wielding of an abused hotel iron might not. Experience suggested that hotel irons came in two varieties - too hot and not hot enough. The trousers could put up with this, but likely not the shirt. Now - shoes? Monty came from a generation and class in which you would never ...*never* wear brown shoes in the evening. Yet this was a visit to the man's home rather than a formal occasion. Would brown brogues be acceptable?

Thus attired, Patrick closed the door to his room with an audible click, pocketed the key card and pressed the button for the lift. Tinkling piano music drifting up from the hotel lobby. Two others joined him to wait for the lift door to open. One he guessed was a Lebanese businessman, judging from his puffed jowls, jet black hair and dark shirt bulging over his trouser belt. Even his feet seemed chubby, as the shoe uppers swelled beyond the sole edges. The other was probably Saudi, Patrick estimated, as his pure white thobe and red and white *ghutrah* topped with the black rope *agal* were all pristine. The central crease in the *ghutrah* was positioned right in the centre of the man's forehead. These garments had been ironed by more skilful hands than Patrick's.

"*Salaam aleikum*," they murmured as they joined him.

"*Aleikum as'salaam*," responded Patrick and then, partly out of habit, he took half a step backwards and motioned with his hand for the others to enter the lift first – "*T'fuddr – baedec.*"

Patrick was always fascinated that the elaborate rules of politeness in Arabia persisted, irrespective of the meanness of the surroundings or circumstances. Greetings and language might be gruffer at the back of the souk or on a building site, but the structure of approaching others and being invited to join them were a constant.

In some circumstances, there might now begin a sort of 'After you, Claude' dance. Patrick had invited the others to go first. They now might step back and counter-invite him, ensuring they made sweeping movements with their right hands, lest he take offence at the use of a left hand. Clearly this could become silly, and it was often the lift door starting to close again which caused someone's nerve to break and they would enter, bowing slightly, right hand on their heart. But the Saudi didn't have time for such pantomimes and stepped forward at Patrick's first invitation. He did at least mutter thanks, "*Shukhran*" as he did so. Manners are not entirely dead, thought Patrick. He returned the Lebanese man's smile and inclined his head towards the lift, so securing the ritual victory of being third through the door and, by default, the most humble.

The same ritual took place when they reached the lobby, but this time, Patrick felt comfortable in stepping out on to the marbled floor first, the Saudi close on his heels, striding towards the entrance. He swept past them both leaving a faint cloud of perfume hanging in his wake. Patrick turned to alert the front desk that he'd likely be returning late and would not be requiring dinner.

The doorman waved in a taxi for Patrick and opened the rear door. "Where to, Sir?"

Patrick answered, "Aaramoun, east of Ghazir – I know the house when we get there". The doorman ducked his head down to the driver and explained the destination. There are two towns named Aaramoun in Lebanon, one to the south of Beirut. Monty's house was in the one to the north, however, up the Beirut Highway and then turning right at the Casino du Liban through Ghazir - about twenty five kilometers from Central Beirut. Patrick settled back to watch the scenery, the traffic and the sea to his left.

His driver was silent for the most part. After a couple of basic questions to make his passenger feel comfortable, the driver agreed a fixed price for the return journey, gave Patrick his telephone number and turned off the meter. The sun was still hot as they sped north, windows open. Pretty soon they neared the famous Casino where the rich gambled and sunbathed even with the sound of gunfire outside. The driver turned off at the Ghazir exit and Patrick started navigating him up into the hills.

Ethelbert Montague Peregrine Hughes occupied a sprawling older-style villa high up in the village of Aaramoun with glorious views west to the Mediterranean and south, down the coast. He had converted the foundations of the house into an air-conditioned cellar. There, he had amassed an amazing collection of wines from Europe, the Americas, South Africa and most especially from the local region, for Lebanon has been a wine-growing area for thousands of years.

Patrick's knock at the door was answered by Monty's houseboy, Ahmed. Salaams exchanged, Ahmed explained that Mr Monty was in the garden and showed Patrick into the main sitting room. Liberally hung with carpets and paintings, there was a small area of wall devoted to photographs of Monty with senior politicians, visiting dignitaries and recognisable celebrities, the dates trackable by the amount of first grey then white in his always neatly-trimmed goatee beard. A much-faded degree certificate from SOAS took pride of place in the middle of the display.

"Patrick, my dear boy," boomed Monty as he erupted into the room, arms wide in greeting. "It is so good to see you." It was impossible not to like the old man: he was unfailingly optimistic and warm and generous and had the knack of making everyone feel that they were his most special guest, even in a crowded cocktail party.

"I told your young lady …ah, Sarah, isn't it, that I have a special surprise for you. Well, for us both!"

Monty always referred to Patrick's secretary as 'his young lady' – Sarah knew well that Patrick shared Monty's epicurean delight in wines, and rumours abounded in the London Head Office about what was actually contained in Monty's house. It was the Bank which owned the building, of course. It was acquired for the use of whichever senior members of staff should happen to be stationed in Beirut. At different times in its history, it had contained riches – gold, silver, bundles of cash and share certificates transferred for safety from various branch premises during the tidal flows of hostilities. There were still some valuable artworks, shielded by the Bank on behalf of the most powerful politicians from time to time. Now they may have been forgotten by their owners, whose fates could include departure from the country or death.

In fact, the foundations had been opened out over the years in quite dramatic excavations by local workers. They were paid by Monty out of his own pocket and under strict vows of silence, to construct a wine-lover's dream cellar. Here Monty kept his life's collection of fine vintages. Once before, Patrick had ventured down to the cellar, to wander its narrow corridors between walls of wine bottles, all racked in order of producer and year of bottling. There were all the classical French vineyards represented as one would expect; but many Italian wines too. Monty was especially keen on wines from Puglia and from the tiny Barolo region, which unusually has different soil types in all four quadrants of the producing bowl. There were some wines from the New World, but his most prized collection was the locally-produced wines.

Patrick had previously been treated to a sumptuous bottle of the local Chateau Musar, 1991. He remembered that the growing weather that year had not been optimal and the crop quantity was below average - due to frost and the cold weather in the Spring. All of Musar's wines were blended. This one contained Cabernet Sauvignon, Cinsault and Carignan grapes. As usual, they aged the wine for 12 months in French oak; blended, then bottled in 1994. All this background information came from his research back in the UK. He recalled its dark ruby colour - bright and beautiful with a nose of chocolate, animal, tobacco and leather. Very complex and rich, red fruits, spices and olives. Swirling this precious wine in a large and delicate glass and sipping sparingly produced a feeling that all was right with the world. He was very keen to repeat the experience.

Monty called out to Ahmed, who had returned to the kitchen: "Ahmed, I'm going to visit my other office. We'll be only five minutes," and winked at Patrick. He led the way to the corridor and the small door leading downstairs.

"My friend, Serge, allowed me to buy a couple of cases of his Special *Cuvee* for the Millenium." Monty was referring to Serge

Musar, of course, current head of the famous Chateau Musar.

He continued, "Serge's winery was hit on several occasions during 1989 as there were hostilities raging all around back then. He tells me they used the cellars as air-raid shelters, but never stopped making wine! There had been a dry winter and a mild summer and so an excellent vintage was produced. But there was a particular vineyard in the Bekaa Valley which produced what he considered a quite exceptional vat of Carignan grapes."

The old man led the way between the shelving, checking labels as he went. "Although, as you know, all Musar's wines are blended, it prompted Serge to try to prove that a humble varietal could be made into a really special wine. It spent its twelve months in French oak barrels and then was bottled in 1992 to celebrate Serge's fiftieth birthday. Two thousand bottles only were labelled 'for the Millenium 2000'."

With a showman's timing, he stopped and turned to Patrick. His eyes were wide and bright. "I have a couple of dozen of them!" Monty announced, triumphantly, drawing one out of the rack and on to one palm. He cradled it lovingly, like a new-born baby.

Patrick protested weakly that it was still 1999 and not yet the Millenium, but needed little persuading to follow the great man back up the stairs and out to the terrace.

Little plates of foods were laid out on the table as *mezze*: Pickles, Hommous, *Baba ghanoush*, fresh pittas and olives. The pitta breads were still too hot to hold, as Ahmed had extracted them from the clay oven moments before. Patrick's face lit up. "Monty, this is wonderful. You are so kind."

"A meal shared is a pleasure doubled," averred his host. "*Beiti beitak*". (My house is your house).

Monty found a foil cutter and corkscrew in his pocket and gently extracted the cork, peering at it for a second using light from the sitting room. He also noted with satisfaction that the wine did not appear to have thrown any sediments. Even so, he decanted it against the light into a plain decanter. They manoeuvred around the wooden benches under Monty's favourite olive tree and sat on the cushions provided. A comfortable silence descended upon them as they fell on the food, appetites sharpened by the evening air and the sea breeze.

Ahmed busied himself at the barbeque on the other side of the terrace, brushing kebabs of lamb with sprigs of rosemary.

Knowing the amount of food which was likely to be coming to the table, Patrick restricted himself to a couple of scoops each of the appetizers. They began to chat about Beirut and Monty shared a political joke he had been told at a recent cocktail party. Finally, he asked, "Do you think we are ready?"

"For what? Oh …I see", Patrick grinned. "Let's find out what the Millenium has in store for us."

Monty reached around for the decanter and poured a little into two glasses. They swirled and peered. "I smell coffee …and tobacco", volunteered Patrick. Light from the flickering barbeque glinted on his glass, emphasising the deep ruby contents. He couldn't suppress a smile forming as the sweet, full, rich and uplifting flavours of fruits and chocolate filled his head and monopolised his senses when he sipped the wonderful liquid. He tilted the glass towards his companion and met the old man's eye. "To the future," he said.

They sat in companionable silence for a bit. Monty refilled their glasses. Ahmed pushed the meze starters to the edge of the table and brought an oval plate of bulghur wheat topped with lamb kebabs. There were dots of pomegranate peeping out from the bulghur. Monty sat forward and served them both with heaping plates of the wonderful food. They tucked in with gusto.

Afterwards, Patrick asked, "Do you eat like this every night, Monty?"

"Not *every* night." Monty paused for reflection. "Now take last month, for example…"

Patrick laughed. He thought his friend was about to identify a single day when his consumption was more modest.

"I'm sure I must have eaten less on at least *one* day."

They smiled together. Of course it wasn't true and Patrick knew that. Monty would be the size of a house if he did eat like this all the time. In fact, despite his age, the man was trim and looked to be in good health.

Suddenly an unpleasant thought occurred to him. It filled his head. He struggled to make his brain move on – or return to the blurry pleasure of their sumptuous meal. He found himself sitting with the most knowledgeable Arabist and historian who could answer most of his questions. Yet he was reluctant to spoil the mood by enquiring about *Al Sharika*. But the organisation had reared up in his consciousness and refused to go away.

"Monty? I need to seek your advice on a …wider matter."

The man waved his hand. "Anything, dear boy. Anything." But then he looked at Patrick. "Is this something serious?"

Patrick nodded.

"I feel very bad for even raising it. I was enjoying this wonderful food and wine but I am living with a significant worry and it intrudes every so often."

"My God – are you badly ill?"

"No, no – nothing like that. I didn't mean to alarm you. It's …something else."

Monty reached over to top up Patrick's glass. "Very well. Here's to Salvation and the Banishment of whatever ails us."

That made him smile. Maybe *Al Sharika* was beatable after all.

"Gosh. Where to start? For the whole time I have worked abroad for Royal Counties Bank, I have been picked on by a terrorist organisation as having potential to help fund them. I'm told that their usual methods are to find out some unsavoury secret about a person. Or they trap people to force them into compliance."

Monty was paying close attention and stayed silent, his hands interlaced on his stomach.

"With me, they began in the New Hebrides – trying to get me into trouble with the Chief Manager and the local Police. Actually, a colleague and I found out later they'd already co-opted the Chief Manager." He paused. "Look – this is all a bit confidential as the man is still in post. Inspection and ...'others' wanted to keep quiet about the role they know he is playing."

At last Monty asked a question.

"Who are these 'others'?"

"MI-6."

"I see." Monty blinked. So – this was not some internal malfeasance restricted to Royal Counties Bank. It was bigger. "Go on," he said.

"Next, I went to Bahrain, of course. I ought to say that I pretty much fell in love with Arabia. I don't know why. I found myself wanting to learn more conversational Arabic, but was never in one place at one time enough to learn the phonetic sounds and how to write it."

"That is the usual way," agreed Monty.

"One of my potential customers in Jeddah tried to film me having sex with a belly dancer."

"Well that's one way to secure a customer mandate! I'm sorry to interrupt, but I was always told the best way to learn a foreign language is to find a girlfriend who speaks it. But I guess that wasn't the intention, eh?"

"I was drugged. I was also very fortunate that the dancer had other ideas. She used me to escape – she'd been imprisoned by this man, you see. We both got away, so that attempt failed. What was more serious for me was what happened to a syndicated loan led by Royal Counties Bank to Abdulla Al Hassan. It was a hundred million dollars in all. He hopped on his camel and disappeared into the desert with it. I petitioned the Sharia Court to get the money back - and won!"

"I heard about that. Remarkable."

"It turned out he paid all the money to a terrorist organisation and they didn't bail him out by giving it back. He was executed by order of the Court."

Monty slapped his knee. "That's why I heard about him. It was a big scandal at the time. I didn't know you were involved."

"I almost wish I wasn't. I tried to fly out of the Kingdom after the hearing, but was kidnapped and driven far into the Rhub Al Khali and left to die."

"My! The Empty Quarter. How did you escape? Who kidnapped you?"

"I was very lucky. I don't know who ordered it, but I came across some *bedu* who looked after me and took me to a truck stop on the road to Dammam. I boarded a dhow across to Bahrain."

The host shook his head in wonder. Did the young man understand his enormous good fortune? Monty was in awe of the Arabian desert. It was wonderful. Magnificent. Unforgiving. Bedouin tribes had taken centuries to master the ability to survive in the desert. They alone appreciated and knew how to overcome its dangers.

"This organisation found me later in Bahrain too. They sent an assassin to carry out my execution by sword. You remember the Bahrain Manager, Mike?"

"Of course."

"He rounded up some ex-army colleagues and rescued me."

"You keep saying 'this organisation'. Do you know who they are? Do they have a name?"

"They do. The young woman assigned to me in MI-6 told me their name is *Al Sharika*."

Monty jerked his head up. He asked Patrick to repeat the name to be sure he had heard correctly. He steepled his fingers and tapped his lips in thought.

"I am aware of them. There were texts I found in the library at SOAS. Ancient texts, telling of the uprising against the Crusaders."

Monty creased his face trying to remember more details.

"It was a Sultan who founded them... Oh, what was his name?"

"Qualawun."

"Yes! Sultan Qualawun. That was him. It grew up around Tarabulus, I remember now."

"Your memory is extraordinary, Monty. I'm amazed at your powers of recall."

"There was mention of their role in the Spanish war as well, I believe. But only vague references to them mounting opposition to the Christian west after that. But I do remember that name – *Al Sharika*."

"They are alive and well, I'm afraid, according to MI-6. They believe Ghaddafi is their current figurehead – you said 'Tarabulus'? That's the original name for Tripoli, in Libya isn't it? They are active everywhere I've worked, including New York. I have seen evidence of all kinds of money laundering, market manipulation and outright theft. They are gathering funds for some sort of major assault on the West."

"What are the authorities doing about it?"

"Trying to identify the higher-ups, I think. At least, that's what an F.B.I. chap told me." Monty's eyes widened, noticeably. "He used me as bait to catch a New York Imam named Fawaz Damra."

The old man gazed into the far distance where waves lapped silently against the shoreline as the evening light faded. He examined the effect the changing light conditions had on his glass of wine. And took another sip.

"There is much evil in the world." He looked back at Patrick. "You said you needed my guidance."

"I do. In two respects."

"Two? Gracious… Go on then."

"I am exploring some …other avenues for life after Royal Counties Bank."

Monty nodded sagely. "Wise, dear boy. Wise. Having more than one string to the bow is a good thing, these days."

"One of those head-hunter fellows is introducing me into some company which is manufacturing a revolutionary construction product. They need seed funding, of course, since there's to be a raft of tests carried out on the prototype product in order that it can gain certification for use in the UK – maybe elsewhere."

"And they've asked you to fund them?"

"No. Although I expect they thought about it. No – actually they want me to represent them in the search for funding. And doing the figures for them after that."

"As a Royal Counties Bank employee, you will lend credence and gravitas – not to be under-estimated."

"I suppose so. The trouble is, the methods they keep talking about using to get the money are a bit flaky."

"Like what, pray?"

"Well, SKRs, to start with – Safe C[K]ustody Receipts."

"Ah," said Monty. He raised one eyebrow.

"And one of them can get hold of a 17th century Old Master painting for a few thousand pounds. He says we could enter it into the next Christies' Auction for such items. The estimate is that it might fetch more than half a million Euros – that would be plenty to get the company started."

Monty's second eyebrow joined its brother and they vied for the lead towards his receding hairline.

Patrick smiled. He knew how naïve this sounded. "Yes, I thought so too."

He decided not to share with Monty that he'd been taken in completely to begin with. It was only when Jerry Green had accused him of being gullible that he'd reconsidered.

"Thing is, Monty, the chap has a valuation from Christies complete with its *provenance* and it would seem to be on the level."

He thought he caught a weary shake of the head. But he waited for the older man to turn it over in his head.

"When you are going to lend money to a company or a bank, you examine their recent accounts, no? And you check that the firm of auditors are of good quality, don't you? I mean, Messrs Check, Bodgeit and Scarper, Accountants to the Gentry, would not weigh much on the positive side of the credit scales, would they?"

Patrick's smile was fading a little. Monty went on.

"If I may suggest, it might be worth visiting Christies yourself one evening and meeting with the person who signed the valuation. Just in case, hmmn? Signatures can be forged, as you know well."

"Oh yes," Patrick put in. "I planned on doing that." Was his face flushing from the wine or from embarrassment that he hadn't thought of it?

"And as for the painting itself – there have been some wonderful forgeries circulating in the international art world. Some good enough to fool any but the most specialised expert." Monty reached for the wine again. "Actually, it's a subject which interests me."

"What? Forgeries?"

"Indeed. The sad thing is that the best forgers are often excellent painters in their own right. Their bad luck is that their paintings haven't broken into the wider market yet. So they succumb to the lure of big bucks, painting to order. One of the paintings I stored here turned out to be such a forgery. The Minister was mortified when it was revealed."

Patrick couldn't speak. He had always rated Monty as a human onion skin – he had so many layers – and the man was warming to his new theme. He cleared his throat.

"If the forger uses ordinary house emulsion, he can stir in KY jelly to get the right consistency to the paint. It mimics oil paint, you see. The frame and canvas are tricky, but he can create new stretchers, with appropriate age wood. Then he has to find some old canvas, cutting it to size and he remounts it. He secures the canvas with tacks, washing with salt water to corrode them. Or he might even find a period-correct painting which is near worthless and remove the original paint. That is to say, strip off the paint, but not completely, to keep the lower layer, the 'surface signature'. Then he does a sketch first with pale chalk – that doesn't show up in X-Rays. To make it look antiquated, he has to put dirt on the back of the canvas. One technique I've heard of is to empty the vacuum cleaner on to it. A good shake around gets dust and particles in behind the canvas."

Now it was Patrick's turn to shake his head, but this was in wonder at the extent of Monty's knowledge.

"I do a bit of painting myself, as it happens. That's how I know about such things. Some forgers try to recreate known pieces, but this is too easily caught. The best idea is to create a similar style painting."

At this point, Patrick felt he should relate his recent experience in the Sakip Sabanci Museum. "They say the painting they are talking about is by Pieter Claesz. The museum in Istanbul happened to be having an exhibition of 17th century works including a few by him when I popped in there. The curator of the exhibition was walking around when I visited. He kindly looked up the name of the work - *Still Life with Wine, Cheese and a Tobacco box* – and was very excited because he thought he knew the entire body of works by Claesz – but hadn't seen this one."

"Oh dear," said Monty. "Still, all is not lost, my boy. Forgers know that ordinary oil paints take half a century to dry properly. They have to use siccatives to make the paint dry faster. They leave the forgery under ultra violet light for a month to oxidise and maybe another month in a warm room to dry out completely. This is why dealers examine paintings with UV lamps looking for fluorescence in the glaze."

Monty saw his guest was slumping in his chair.

"Don't despair, laddy. My guidance, as I said, is to visit Christies yourself. If the valuer remembers seeing it and confirms it is genuine then you have nothing to worry about. Now, drink up. I'm already a glass ahead of you. There was something else?"

"Of course, yes. I am to marry soon."

"Oh, congratulations - that's wonderful. Is it that lovely young lady, Sarah, who telephones me?"

Patrick grinned. "No, no. Not Sarah. She is my secretary - she is lovely, but a lot of years ago, I met a junior doctor in the New Hebrides. Her name is Jess Smithson. There's something special about her…"

"You are a fortunate man, Patrick, to have found someone like her."

"I know. In fact, she pointed that out to me before I left for this trip."

Monty's laugh coincided with him swallowing more wine. The resultant coughing and spluttering made him red in the face. But he managed to gather himself and say, in a weak voice, "Do go on. I'm fine – really."

"What concerns me, Monty, is that when we marry, I will be bringing her into the firing line of *Al Sharika*. In fact, that Fawaz Damra fellow had a go at her in New York. It was only her first day there, too."

"Tell me what is special about her. You said she is a doctor?"

Patrick nodded. "She isn't afraid to try techniques you won't find in a medical textbook, if it means saving a patient. She was the doctor in the New Hebrides – the only doctor for the islands. What a baptism of fire it must have been for her - only the year after she qualified, too. I'm sure she faced all the usual range of illnesses, but some odd ones too. People with coral growing from their ears... Others who were convinced they'd die because the medicine man had put a spell on them. It was a tropical zone, after all. You can't look that up in a medical textbook. The hospital wasn't well-equipped, either. She didn't have big supplies of blood for operations – on one occasion she hooked me up to a woman who had been stabbed and was losing blood. She needed time to perform the surgery necessary to save her."

Patrick looked at Monty. The man was smiling.

"Why are you smiling?"

"Patrick, you have nothing to worry about with this Jess. She obviously has all the internal determination to resist whatever threats *Al Sharika* visit upon you both. I believe you will be very happy …in the end."

"That sounded ominous."

"The 'in the end' bit? Yes. Well… there will be testing times, I'm sure. But I do believe you couldn't hope for a more worthy companion. You are lucky, you know."

This time, Patrick helped himself to more of the wine.

Chapter 13
Penny is in Trouble

When he landed at Heathrow airport from Beirut, Patrick had a spring in his step. What had caused his cheerful demeanour today? He sat in the back of the car taking him into London and mused on the possibilities.

He was going to marry Doctor Jess – that was enough, more than enough to account for any excess of gladness. But there was more: he was taking his first steps into the unknown world of construction. Well, manufacturing a construction material, anyway, but construction for all that. And it felt good that he might contribute in a way to making other people happy and warm and comfortable in their homes. He was also attempting something way out of his comfort zone – and felt good about it. Energised. Nothing he had done in his ordered past prepared him for this.

As so often was the case, his mobile telephone buzzed repeatedly with new messages when he turned it on having left the aeroplane. One of the messages was from Lars. He was arranging for some trial panels to be made and had pestered the Building Research Establishment in Watford to test them. Dave and Justin had agreed to put up a couple of thousand pounds between them towards the cost – could Patrick contribute as well?

He turned the request over in his mind. He could afford one thousand pounds, but what was the likelihood of success? And anyway, weren't they supposed to be receiving seed funding from Captain John? He'd give Lars a call later.

First, there were some Royal Counties Bank matters to deal with. He called Sarah at his office to get some files ready.

Later on, after the immediate bank tasks had been taken care of, he called Lars.

"Give me Good News."

"Hi, Lars. I suppose it is, in a way. How are you?"

"Just dandy, Patrick. Just dandy. Listen…" Patrick heard rustling on the line and he was sure Lars was covering the mouthpiece with his hand. "We need to pay the proformas from the moulding and laminating company. Do you want to join the deal of a lifetime? Are you in?"

Lars didn't expect a laugh in answer, but that's what Patrick did. He was beginning to pick up Lars' conversational patterns and was delighted that he had predicted this one.

"Very probably, Lars. Tell me – am I buying shares in LaDaJ Ltd or in something else?"

"Sure. We can do it that way. It doesn't matter now. We need to pay these invoices."

"Has LaDaJ Ltd been registered?" Patrick knew it hadn't been. He had checked on the government website called 'Companies House' and there was no listing – yet.

"It's being done. Our accountants are doing it."

Patrick asked some more qualifying questions. He established that the accountants for the head-hunting firm had bought a company off the shelf. They would soon open an account at a bank for it, when they had changed its name to LaDaJ Ltd.

And Captain John said he would be 'wiring funds in the next day or two'.

"Ok. I'll send my money to the accountants to be held in escrow pending establishment of LaDaJ Ltd. You might want to tell Dave and Justin to do the same."

Lars could see this would prolong the procedure and delay sending money to the factories which were to make the test panels. He protested, but gave way when he found Patrick wasn't budging. He rang off with ill grace.

Next, a call to Christie's was needed. He peered at the signature on the bottom of the valuation report. It wasn't that clear, as he was looking at a photocopy. The first name could be Henry or Harry and the surname was Pelham-Browne. The surname, at least, was clear.

"Sarah? Could you get me Christie's on the phone? I need to speak with a Mr Pelham-Browne."

After a few minutes, his desk phone rang as she put them through.

"Mr Field? This is Holly Pelham-Browne. How can I help you?"

To his surprise, Patrick found himself speaking to a youngish woman. "Ah. Um, good afternoon. I, er, wanted to ask some questions about a recent valuation you have given for a painting by Pieter Claesz."

"I beg your pardon?"

"A valuation? I understand you have kindly examined a painting by Pieter Claesz and issued a valuation dated… hang on. Ah, here it is. It was on the 3rd of March this year. I believe Christies are holding an auction of such works shortly."

"Is this a joke, Mr Field?"

"What? Gosh, absolutely not. Are you saying you have not issued such a valuation?"

"For a painting? I think I'd remember if I had."

"Crikey. Look, I'm not sure what to do, now. Could I show you the valuation and have your opinion as to how it has been given?"

"It's possible I miss-heard you — by all means, do come to our offices this evening. Do you know where we are? I work at the Central Way, Park Royal, office."

"I'm sure I can find it. I'll try to be there by five thirty, if that's ok."

-----//-----

Patrick was five minutes late, but that didn't faze Miss Pelham-Browne in the least. She welcomed him with a firm hand shake into what appeared to be a staff rest-room. The chairs and sofas were threadbare and worn. Teabags and a jar of instant coffee were prominent on the only work surface beside a tiny sink in the corner. A varied selection of used mugs and cups and spoons jostled on the drainer while they waited to be cleaned. A half-empty bag of sugar hung its head beside the kettle.

He started to extract the photocopied valuation from his briefcase.

"Would you like a drink, Mr Field?"

"Oh, no – thanks very much." He had seen how his drink would be prepared and preferred to wait. He handed over the three-page facsimile.

Holly Pelham-Browne was in her late twenties. Everything about her was very brown. Her sweater, her dress, even her shoes and stockings were all shades of brown. As she read, her brow creased up and she held the papers a little closer as though to make sure she was seeing the words correctly.

"Do you have the original paper, Mr Field?"

He admitted he did not, but thought he could probably get hold of it if that would help.

She looked up. "How did you come by this valuation?"

He gave her a brief explanation. He saw that she was nodding towards the end of his tale.

"This is my signature." She tapped at the bottom of the third page. "But I study Chinese Export porcelain produced between the 16th and 20th Centuries. Most came to Europe and only later to America. The earliest items were destined for the Middle East. It is those which I find most interesting."

She folded the papers up again and read from the front page.

"This document refers to an oil painting of which I have no knowledge at all." She looked at him as though reaching a decision. "It is quite possible that the document has been pieced together from others to represent a false assertion."

"Are you saying it might have been forged?"

She nodded. "I'm afraid so. That is why I asked for the original document. The signs of forgery would be more obvious on that. Perhaps that is why you were given this photocopy."

"I'm rather embarrassed, Miss Pelham-Browne. I'm afraid you may be confirming what I feared all along may have been the case."

To his surprise, she was smiling. It was genuine warmth, though. Not a forced rictus at the conclusion of a commercial interaction.

"There is still the painting itself, though. Even if the valuation isn't genuine, is it safe to assume the painting is too?"

He didn't know what to say. If Patrick had been a betting man, he would have said that the odds-on favourite likelihood was that the painting was a forgery too. Who knew if it was even a decent forgery which one could stick above the mantlepiece to impress visitors?

"I admit I haven't seen the painting itself. I'm told it's being 'looked after' by a contact."

"Well, why don't I introduce you to a colleague who can say for sure?"

"Oh, I don't want to waste anyone's time."

"She won't mind – honestly. Look, I'll see if she's around. You can make an appointment to see her. She's busy preparing for the auction of 17th Century works, so will be clued up on this Claesz fellow."

Patrick accepted. It was a very, very long shot. But he ought to run it to ground. If, by chance, the painting was genuine, it would be a most exciting find, and could be worth even more than the one he'd seen in Istanbul.

Despite the hour, Lucy Worthington was still in her tiny office. It was a working space, big enough for her alone. The lack of a second chair confirmed it was not for receiving visitors. Patrick felt awkward for her. But she brushed a stray hair out of her eyes, stood and welcomed them both. Holly explained why Patrick was there and showed her the forged valuation.

"So you see, although it is likely the painting is a forgery too, I thought you might want to check."

"Yes, yes. Very exciting. We have a Claesz in the sale already. It's one of his 'skull' series – very depressing, in my opinion. I'd love to see *Still Life with Wine, Cheese and a Tobacco box*. I haven't heard of it before. Even if we cannot attribute it to him, it is possible somebody painted it 'in the style of'. It may yet be interesting."

That cheered Patrick a little. He took the woman's number and promised to return with the actual painting as soon as he could. He thanked Holly Pelham-Browne for her patience and headed out into the early evening bustle.

-----//-----

As he walked, he dialled Lars' number. It rang several times – that was unlike Lars not to answer immediately. Perhaps he was with another client.

"Give me the Good News!"

"Oh, there you are. I was afraid… Am I interrupting you?"

"No problem for the banking expert in our team. What can I do you for?"

Patrick thought the snuffling noise he could hear was Lars being amused at his own little joke.

"This painting Cem says his friend is looking after – can he have it brought to Christies? They'd like to see it before considering putting it into their auction."

"But they've already authenticated it."

"Nevertheless. Can he bring it over to them?"

"I don't see why they have to have it again. They've made all their checks, they issued their valuation, there was that list - *provenance* you called it - and all that crapola. How do you know they want to see it?"

Lars was putting up quite stout resistance. Patrick sensed this was not just a battle of wits – alpha males tangling over some point of order. This sounded very much like Lars trying to avoid him discovering that the painting was fake.

"Well, if we are to buy it and enter it into the sale," he answered, "We are going to have to give it to them sooner or later. It may

265

as well be sooner. I have a friend who works there. She said they are pretty strict about this sort of thing. They have to protect their reputation, you see."

He waited. Would Lars accept this rather loose explanation? He had somewhat bent the truth about the status of his association with the Christie's member of staff. He'd not, of course, revealed that he'd deliberately opened the enquiry with them.

"Sure, sure. I'll ask him. Anything else? Oh – I almost forgot. Have you paid your money to the accountants yet? BRE are chasing me for a date for testing and the panels aren't made yet."

"No, not yet, Lars. I'll give them a call tomorrow and arrange it then."

"Great. Gotta go. I got people to see. You know how it is."

"I do. That's all for the moment, Lars, thanks. Bye now."

Patrick carried on walking. He could smell petrichor and felt the first few drops of rain. He glanced up at the lowering sky. Was this emblematic of some parts of his life right now? Caught in a possible rain shower without a raincoat?

-----//-----

Lars must have got through to Cem Kaplan very fast. He must have prompted whatever further communications were needed with Cem's associate, because Cem was on the telephone to Patrick by mid-morning. In contrast to the obstacles Lars had raised, Cem seemed keen to fix delivery instructions to the Christie's address. Patrick knew they accepted deliveries between half past eight in the morning and half past four in the afternoon. He relayed that information.

"Will it go in a taxi, Cem, or will you use a delivery company? The company might be better as they will have all the insurances needed."

"It's too important to let someone else bring it. My associate will transport the painting himself."

Patrick wondered why Cem kept referring to his 'associate'. Who was this mysterious person? Was this some feeble attempt at restricting knowledge spread?

"What is the name of the person - your associate? In view of the importance of the painting to LaDaJ Ltd, we ought to know."

"LaDaJ doesn't own it yet. I'll tell you what Christie's say."

Now that was distinct resistance. But Patrick thought he'd make his own enquiries of Lucy Worthington later on.

"Fine. I look forward to hearing from you." Patrick rang off. Time for some Royal Counties Bank work.

-----//-----

"This is Penny. Can we meet?"

It was unusual for Patrick's mobile telephone to ring while he was in the office. Using a mobile on Bank premises was generally frowned upon. Royal Counties Bank believed there could only be two reasons somebody would call in that way while in the Investment Banking area. Either you were taking a personal call and therefore not working or – and this was the greater sin – you were relaying or receiving confidential information. That was strictly forbidden. Either of these offences, if proven, were grounds for firing the member of staff concerned.

Patrick was therefore hesitant even to take the call, but he answered it more out of surprise than anything.

"Hello, Penny. Um… Of course. When would suit you?"

"Today. Tonight. It's important."

"This sounds alarming, but… alright. There's a Starbucks coffee shop in King William Street at the Bank of England end. It's got a few perches by the window. I can reserve one. Would five thirty be ok?"

"See you then."

She rang off abruptly.

This wasn't like Penny at all. She always seemed so 'in control', her life paced according to her wishes. Yet he also remembered when he and Jess had been driven off the road by some *Al Sharika* operatives, how she had become clipped, brusque and efficient. She'd ordered up a service helicopter to whisk them out of danger. Then arranged collection of their wrecked car and instructed the local Police to track down the vehicle used by the attackers. Truly, a woman of action. This brief exchange had been with *that* Penny.

The hair on Patrick's scalp prickled. It made him shiver. His mind leaped into action, imagining all sorts of terrible scenarios. It was evident that whatever Penny had to say cannot be good.

He dragged his concentration back to the realities of working in a pressured environment. Here, you were paid according to your results. You risked being let go if you failed to make some pre-set minimum return.

At last his watch neared five o'clock. Nobody would leave their desk this early unless they had an official function to attend. He muttered something to Sarah about needing to meet a contact at five thirty and picked up a random bunch of papers so he could appear to be taking work home.

"'Alfway for ladies..?" Alan Pearson queried, as Patrick hurried by his office door.

"Something like that," Patrick replied, not wanting to stop in case he was quizzed further. He'd have to establish an alibi by tomorrow morning. Pearson was a micro-manager who claimed to trust his staff, especially senior staff like Patrick, but he'd also check up on them from time to time. So annoying...

To his relief, the lift doors opened as soon as he pressed the button. He glanced at the papers he'd scooped up from his desk.

They concerned National Commercial Bank in Jeddah – his favourite institution in Saudi Arabia. Lady Luck was smiling on him and had steered his hands to the best pile of paper, because that bank had a London representative office in Cornhill run by the estimable Jinx Grafftey-Smith. Jinx's family had a long association with the Kingdom, stretching back to the 1920s and his knowledge thereof was encyclopaedic. He also knew a thing or two about wine and it took little persuasion to open a bottle with him for sampling purposes. 'Yes,' Jinx answered Patrick's mobile call with glee. 'Of course I'd like to'. He was free around half past six. Patrick was to ring the doorbell at number 78, Cornhill and they'd venture out to a nearby wine bar to establish a firm and unbreakable alibi.

Thus protected from the wrath of his boss, Patrick headed for his assignation with Penny Baxter.

-----//-----

Patrick couldn't remember how Penny liked her coffee, so just settled down on a stool in the window of the Starbucks with his own black Americano. He passed the time going over his NCB paperwork. Several pertinent questions arose that he could put to Jinx later on. Pertinent enough that he wasn't being entirely untruthful with Alan Pearson. A little disingenuous, but there was no harm in that.

He had been keeping an eye on people passing by in case he needed to wave to Penny to confirm that this was the correct location. But she was suddenly right beside his elbow. He shuffled across to the seat in the very corner, making a place for her to sit.

"Hello, Penny. You surprised me – again! Can I get you a coffee? Maybe a muffin or pastry?"

She shook her head. "I can't stay long. We have been infiltrated. There is someone in my section of MI-6 who belongs to or has a link to *Al Sharika*."

"Blimey. That's serious. Why do you think that?"

"There have been several incidents – things which only I know but which have circulated around the department. Jesus, even Christopher found out."

"Do you suspect any one person in particular?"

She shook her head, but said, "I have three possible people lined up. I'm thinking of setting a trap to try to narrow it down, but haven't figured out yet how to do that. As you are the most prominent of their targets, it would make sense to involve you in whatever I can devise. Would you be okay with that?"

So… That was why she needed to see him. But why was it so urgent?

"Of course, Penny. Whatever I can do to help. But I rather gathered when you called that it was extremely urgent that we meet. If you haven't figured out what to do yet, why the hurry?"

"Someone is following me. Jonathan says I shouldn't walk anywhere by myself for a bit. He insists on driving me everywhere. I think some of my emails have been intercepted too."

"This sounds bad. But do you have any concrete proof of any of this?"

"No." She gazed out of the window, watching. "But you develop a 'nose' for this kind of thing." She turned back to him. "I think I'm in trouble and the thing about this place is that I can't just go to my boss and complain and ask for protection."

"I was going to suggest exactly that."

"It could be him."

Patrick snorted with derision. "That's daft, Penny. Sir Christopher Sherrif? Head of MI-6? No…" He shook his head. "That isn't possible."

Now she looked cross and worried at the same time. "I thought you of all people would take me seriously, Patrick. I see that I was wrong."

She turned and started out of the café. He caught her arm.

"Penny. Don't go. Of course I believe you – you have been the calm voice of sanity when I've got myself into all sorts of scrapes before. Perhaps I need to reflect on this a bit longer. You have to admit it's unlikely to be him, at least. Are there not more obvious candidates?"

She allowed herself to be led back to the stool by the window. She wriggled onto it. "Maybe I'll have a coffee after all. Black, please. Two sugars."

Patrick ordered. Then he waited for her to open up a bit more.

"The job I do has different challenges every day. There are situations where of course I tell Christopher what is going on – he's my boss. But more often than you might expect, I have to keep information under my hat. I have to sort stuff out by myself. It can be …lonely."

Patrick nodded in sympathy. Sometimes he felt a bit like that, but it wasn't usually a matter of life and death as he imagined it could be with Penny's job. Or Jess' job, for that matter. At least, when he was in New York, he could sit with Jess and go over the events of the day. It was always helpful. But Penny dealt with State secrets and other information he could only dream about. The Official Secrets Act prohibited her from sharing with a spouse. Not that she had one, as far as he knew. The burdens were hers alone to bear.

Her drink was ready. He collected it and added a couple of sugars, passing the wooden stirrer to her.

"Um, Penny, I know you can't tell me what is going on, but I promise to listen to whatever you can tell me. And I will definitely take part in whatever scheme you dream up to find out who it is."

The corner of her eye was moist. He thought he saw her hand shake as she gulped at her scalding coffee. He found himself looking at Vulnerable Penny. He hadn't seen her before.

"I'd better go," she said, putting the top back onto her drink. "Wave to Jonathan."

Patrick looked out of the window, searching for Penny's long-term driver. There he was, slouching against the wall over the road, watching what was going on in the Starbucks. Patrick had not realised he'd been under observation all this time. He put on a smile and waved. Jonathan acknowledged with a dip of his head.

"You trust him?"

She nodded vigorously. "That's why I've kept him all these years. We are loyal to each other. Thank you for listening, Patrick. And, if I think I'm in danger, then you are too, don't forget. They think you owe them – a lot."

She got down from the stool and gave him a peck on the cheek. "Take care. I'll be in touch."

Unaccountably, Patrick's throat wasn't functioning again. He wanted to say goodbye. He said it, in his head and his lips moved, but no words emerged. Dammit. This was why his father could never manage emotional situations – perhaps he too was struck dumb when he very much wanted to say the right thing.

Chapter 14
The Overweight Panel

"Great news!"

"Hello, Lars. How are you?"

"Just dandy, as you Brits say. Just dandy. Listen – those panels have been made and are being transported down to BRE this morning. A testing slot opened up tomorrow morning and we can go watch. Wanna come?"

"Er… Of course I'd like to. Let me see…" Patrick flipped over his diary pages. There were a couple of items he simply must take care of, but maybe if he stayed late tonight?

"Yes, I can. What's the address?"

Lars told him where to go. He was to report to Building twelve on the BRE site in Watford, where they carried out all the heavy-duty testing. He needed to get there by nine o'clock for the Safety Briefing and then the actual tests started at ten.

-----//-----

His name was on the list, so the BRE gateman let him pass.

"Down there, mate and turn right at the bottom. You can't miss Building twelve – it's the biggest there."

"Thanks."

The BRE campus consisted of several characterless buildings, scattered about, with driveways and walkways between them. The remainder of the land was grassed over with a few trees here and there. It looked like an old industrial complex, built when land was not in such short supply.

There was no obvious place to park. So he tucked his car up against the side of the building, out of the way of anyone going past. He knocked on the big, steel doors. There was no answer. Was it locked?

He pulled at the handle and the door swung open. It took a moment for his eyes to adjust to the relative darkness inside. Confronting him were three enormous machines which he couldn't identify. Yellow-painted walkways demarcated safe routes for pedestrians between them. Nobody was around. Maybe he should wait outside? But as he turned back to the door, someone called from deep in the building.

"Hey, is that you Lars?"

"No," Patrick called back. "I was expecting to meet him here. I'm Patrick Field, his ...er, colleague."

The young man jogged over to shake Patrick's hand.

"Hi, I'm Rob. I'll be running the tests for you. Come on. The panels are over here." And he pointed to one side and began heading away beside a tall press.

"Shouldn't we wait for Lars?"

"Oh, no. He'll show up. We keep telling him he isn't allowed in certain areas because it's dangerous. Or we might be testing materials belonging to other people, so they are commercially confidential. But he takes no notice. I expect he's fiddling around with the panels already. Oh – have you had the Safety Brief?"

"Uh, no. They told me it would be here at nine am."

Rob scratched his chin.

"Well, look, it's pretty straightforward. I'll cover the main points now. Keep within the yellow lines; don't touch stuff and wear one of these when we are lifting things." He handed Patrick one of the white hard-hats hanging inside the doorway.

The hat was a hard outer shell with an inner, soft plastic strap which he needed to adjust to sit around the crown of his head. He tried it for size. The previous user must have resembled a silver-back gorilla. He wrenched at the strap to make it smaller. The hat was giving off a faint, unpleasant odour. Maybe it really had been worn by a gorilla.

Rob was staring at Patrick's loafers.

"Those aren't steel-capped boots, are they?"

"No. I didn't know I had to wear them."

"Hmmn. There's a spare pair in my office. Is size ten ok?"

"Gosh – spot on. You must have known I was coming."

"Right. Follow me."

Rob threaded his way towards a tiny cubicle wedged into the corner of the test hall. He rummaged in a drawer beneath his desk and extracted a pair of slip-on boots.

"Leave your shoes here. We can collect them later."

Patrick obliged and trailed after the man again to the rear doors of the building. Immediately inside, lined up by the yellow markings, was a pile of composite panels. Patrick hadn't seen them before, in the flesh, as it were. He ran his hand over them. The surface texture reminded him of dried out snake skin, sloughed off before the animal's next growing spurt. The boards, which were the outer skins of the panels, appeared to be made from pressed fibres. The core resembled coloured polystyrene. How could these be such a wonder product? Patrick thought them flimsy.

He heard voices nearby. Lars' American boom was unmistakable. He guessed Rob was the other.

Both men came around the side of the panel stack.

"Ok, we're ready for the first test. Could you two stand back, please, and Bill and I will crane the panel over to the rig."

Patrick obliged and took two paces backwards. But Lars, of course, ignored the request and fussed around the panels. He was giving unnecessary instructions to the laboratory assistant, Bill, how to insert slings under the edges of the panel without breaking it. It would never occur to Lars that a person in Bill's job might possibly have used slings a few times before.

Rob himself operated the lift with buttons on a remote controller. Bill guided the panel into the holders on the rig and secured it in position.

"You watch this," Lars told Patrick. "It's gonna blow 'em away."

Patrick could only stand there, open mouthed, while Lars strutted up and down, looking at all the fasteners.

A steel beam lowered onto the top of the panel and Bill zeroed the instrumentation.

"All ready?" Rob asked.

"Go for it," said Lars, eager for the result.

They watched. The low humming of the rig, which he hadn't noticed before, increased in intensity. Patrick could sense that the beam was pressing down on the panel. Now and again a tiny piece of dust would ping out of the side. He was trying to watch the instrument panel.

"What are the different readings, Rob?"

The engineer pointed to the first dial.

"This one is the U.D.L. – uniform distributed load. We run it up to a preset level and leave it for five minutes. Then we check for deflection on this other dial. We do that in two steps upwards if it doesn't break beforehand. After that we just run the machine up until failure. The machine will record the graph of increasing pressure and deflection until it breaks."

Patrick nodded. This sounded like a severe test.

"Why run it until failure?"

"We don't only want to know that it can meet building regs. We want to know how strong it is and we repeat the test to check consistency of failure point and mode."

"Ah." There was little else Patrick could say.

The rig gave a little creak. But no deflection registered. Rob checked his watch.

"Ok. That's five minutes. Increasing pressure."

The humming noise rose in volume and pitch. Another fleck of board flew off and landed at Patrick's feet. He watched the panel, fascinated and in awe at how much the beam must be pressing downwards now. Rob levelled off the pressure and they waited another five minutes. He tapped the dial which was to record deflection. The needle hadn't moved.

"Was this tested?" he asked Bill.

"Uh, huh. Last week."

There was another creak. But still nothing dramatic could be seen.

"Alright," said Rob. "Let's go all the way."

He wound the control knob fully to the right and the pressure needle crept immediately and inexorably up the gradations.

"Engineered timber would have failed back here," Rob said to Patrick, pointing at a reading behind the advancing needle. "This is pretty good."

"Told you!" crowed Lars. "It's going all the way to the stop."

"Unlikely," opined Rob. "This press will squash steel blocks, so I think failure might be close."

But it wasn't.

Rob was starting to think the machine was malfunctioning as he tapped the deflection dial again. And again.

At last, the dial showed a millimetre of deflection.

"It's going," he warned.

The deflection figure increased gradually and then with a rush as the top metre or so of panel compressed into a concertina.

"Yes!" shouted Lars, punching the air. "Told you."

"My. That was …quite good," came the tentative engineering opinion.

"What were the readings?" Patrick asked.

"I'll get the print out," Bill said.

"We need seven of these. Then we'll do the bending and floor attachment tests."

Patrick looked at the stack of panels.

"Are there going to be enough to do all that?"

"Oh, yes." Rob nodded. "You see, for the bending tests we cut out lengths three hundred millimetres wide from one panel. We suspend the lengths with a U.D.L. in a controlled environment and wait for a month to see how much deflection we get."

He scratched his head.

"Having seen this, I'm not expecting there will be much, you know."

"Of course not," boasted Lars. "I keep telling people – this is the strongest, stiffest system BRE has ever seen."

"Yes, well. Perhaps we'd better wait until the full battery of tests has been done, eh?" Patrick always hated triumphalism. The panels sounded promising, but it would be foolish to declare victory after just one test.

"Let's go and celebrate."

"What, now?"

"Sure? Why not? The others are going to be the same or better. Tell you what – let's have an early lunch. Rob? You wanna join us?"

"Er, thank you, but I'd better get on with the tests. I usually don't eat lunch anyway. Just an apple, maybe."

So Lars led the way back through the building to where Patrick had parked. He was bubbling with gratified excitement.

"See? This system is going to take over the world. Brick and block? Pah! When we show these test results to investors, they'll be queuing up to finance a factory. Many factories. Why not? Let's start with half a dozen in Britain then we can go to France and Germany …and Turkey. With Cem's contacts, we'll sweep the market."

"It's very exciting and a great prospect. I'm glad I came today to see that. We'll have to be very careful, though, about keeping the intellectual property safe."

"Why bother? We'll be first to market. With our low price, why would anyone even try to copy it? Buying a license from us will be their cheapest way in."

Patrick knew that when Lars was in this kind of mood, he'd not be talked out of his own, unique view of the future.

"Talking of Cem, do you think he has taken the painting to Christie's yet?"

"Let's ask."

Lars pulled out his own mobile phone and dialled. Patrick heard it ringing.

"Hey. What's going on? Great news! We passed the testing at BRE. They think our panel is great…. Anyway, Patrick here was wondering if you have dropped off the painting to Christie's. Give me a call. Ciao, Baby."

Lars was obviously talking to Cem's voicemail.

"I'll try him again later. Right. Come on. When do they start serving beer around here?"

-----//-----

They drove away from the B.R.E. campus together in Patrick's car. He didn't ask how the man had got there in the first place. Lars had been told about a pub west of the North Orbital Road named the Swan. He repeated the directions he'd been given.

When they went in, the manager said they weren't yet serving lunch but he'd be happy to give them the brunch menu. Lars shrugged. He just wanted to eat something to soak up the beer.

When they'd chosen and the pints arrived, Lars tried Cem's phone again.

"Hey, Cem. More great news. I'm sitting here in the Swan pub with Patrick celebrating passing these tests. Shame you can't join us! Anyway ...give me a call."

He frowned as he put his phone away. They clinked glasses.

"Here's to commercial success." Patrick said.

"Aye. And taking over the world."

Then Lars' phone rang.

"Talk of the devil!" he said, pulling it from his pocket. But didn't recognise the number when he looked at the display.

"Hello? Oh, hi, Rob. Yeah, we're in the Swan celebrating." His wide grin narrowed. "What? Now?"

There was a pause.

"Give us an hour and we'll be back. Use the others 'til we get there."

The call ended.

"What happened? Was that Rob from B.R.E.?"

Patrick waited while Lars drained his beer completely. He belched.

"That's what drinking before lunch does for you." He wiped his moustache.

"Does Rob want us to go back?"

Lars nodded.

"He said they've been weighing the panels before the tests and they're all about ninety Kilos. Except one. That is a hundred and seventy."

"What? That's… almost twice what it should be."

"He wants to cut it open to see how it was made but won't do it until we get there."

At that point, the server arrived with two large and heaping plates of fried English Breakfast.

"Let's eat first. Oh …Miss? Can I get another of these?"

Patrick had barely sipped his beer. He hadn't really wanted one this early in the day and anyway, he was driving. He waved his hand at his glass to indicate 'no more'.

They fell on the food, using the last scraps of toast to wipe their plates clean of baked bean sauce. Patrick had asked for a coffee. He wasn't sure how agile his brain would be after such a generous helping of greasy food. Lars pushed back his chair while Patrick was still finishing his coffee.

"Come on - the stagecoach is leaving now."

"As I'm driving the stagecoach, it'll leave when I've finished. And we need to pay, don't forget."

"I'm buying," Lars called as he pushed open the pub door towards the car park.

'In my dreams…' Patrick thought, extracting his credit card and waving to the server.

It never failed to amaze him how Lars managed to get others to pay his way. He could always find money for his cigarettes and beers but rarely bought a round for others.

Arriving at his car, he unlocked the doors. Lars started to get in. He was starting to light a cigarette.

"Hey. No smoking in my car. We've talked about this."

With ill grace, Lars gave a final lung-straining drag on the cigarette and dropped the stub on the ground. To Patrick's horror, he was still expelling the lung full of smoke when he closed the passenger door.

"Lars!"

"Well start the engine already – I'll open the window. I'm gonna call Cem again. He should know better than to ignore all my calls."

Patrick didn't answer. Lars stabbed at his mobile and held it to his ear.

"Bloody voicemail. What is wrong with that boy?"

No further words were uttered during the journey back to B.R.E.

-----//-----

"Do I recognise you, mate?"

"Yup. We're back again. Rob in Building twelve asked us to come back to look at something."

The gateman dialled somebody from his little shelter and soon waved them through. They parked and went straight inside the building. Rob and Bill were bending over some paperwork beside one of the huge lumps of machinery.

"Ah. There you are. We're all set up to look inside the panel. Was it made in a different way?"

"Nope." Lars was very sure.

"So can you account for this weight difference?"

"Uh, uh."

"Alright. This way, then. Hard hats…"

Patrick took his, but Lars was already half a dozen steps away and refused to wear them, 'on principle', he had said. Rob handed over the work boots again.

"I guessed you'd need these."

Patrick's hat fell off as he bent over to change his footwear. "Thanks, Rob – whoops - I'm not used to this stuff!"

They arrived at what they said was the offending panel. It laid flat on a work table. They walked around it, looking for any obvious differences.

"I can't see anything weird," Patrick said, "Although someone managed to leave a hand print on the polystyrene core. I bet that was hot when he did that."

He sniffed. "It smells a bit funky. Can't see anything wrong, though."

"Ok, let's open this sucker up," commanded Lars.

Bill had plugged in a circular saw before they arrived. He now donned safety goggles, ear defenders and gloves and started cutting across the top board. As the cut began, Rob took photographs to record what they were doing.

The cut was shallow, intended to be the depth of the ten millimetre board. He got part way across and stopped, putting the saw down carefully and blowing away the dust. They watched as Bill peered at the cut he'd made. He rubbed at it and they saw his fingers came away red. There was a red smear on the outside of the board.

"Rob? I'm not liking what I think I'm seeing."

"What's the problem?" Rob restrained Lars by putting a hand on his shoulder and climbed onto the panel.

There was viscous, red liquid oozing gently from the cut. It contrasted with the whiteness of Rob's face. His eyes were very wide.

"Patrick? What did you say about a hand print?"

"It was over here… yes. Just here."

Rob hopped off the panel and came around to look. He turned briefly to a work bench behind them, selected a chisel and began digging out polystyrene around the hand print.

"What are you doing to our panel, Rob?" Lars asked.

He didn't reply at first. But then said, quietly, "I think we need to call the Police."

They all clustered round. He had begun excavating around the hand print, but the polystyrene had fallen away.

It was not a hand print. It was a hand.

-----//-----

The only one who was unfazed by the experience was Lars. He couldn't wait to tell someone what he had found.

He began prodding buttons on his phone, then put it to his ear.

Patrick heard it first.

"Who are you calling, Lars?"

"Bloody Cem – again. I'm going to tear him a new one when I see him."

"That may not be necessary," Patrick said. Lars looked at him oddly. "Somebody may have done it for you."

Lars' face fell. He didn't understand.

But Bill and Rob did. They too had heard the faint ringing of a mobile telephone - from inside the panel.

Rob took charge.

"Gents, we need to walk back to my office and wait there. Bill? Would you tape off this whole area and alert Health & Safety? Tell them I'm calling the Police."

"Right. I'll come and see you when I've done that."

Lars looked at them all in anger.

"Hey, where are you all going? We need to finish investigating the panel – and there are the others to test as well. I'm paying for this, don't forget."

"Lars – this is not the time or place. We'll talk about it in Rob's office."

Patrick ignored Lars' spurious claim that he was paying for it. Actually, the cost was supposed to come from LaDaJ and who knows if Lars had contributed anything to that.

Chapter 15
The Factory Plan

Patrick wanted to drive away from B.R.E. with Lars as soon as he could, to get away from the awful, mind-numbing horror they'd just seen. At least, Patrick wanted to. He wasn't sure about Lars. The man didn't seem to have processed what had happened. If he had, it wasn't affecting him. But the Police told them to stay. They were to give statements. A more senior officer wanted to interview them; more senior than those in the patrol car which had answered the call.

Almost certainly, the body in the panel *was* that of Cem Kaplan, if the presence of Cem's mobile phone was any guide. He was not a large person. The factory might have blown the normal amount of polystyrene bead into the mould before laminating the boards on to the core. The difference, Patrick estimated, between the expected weight and the measured total would be about Cem's weight plus clothes.

Questions flickered through his head – first, what a horrible way to die, assuming Cem wasn't already dead when put into the mould. But how did anyone get access to the factory? Once inside, how did they operate the machinery? Two or three strangers would soon be spotted creeping around the moulding machines. The operator would know if somebody paused his machine, opened up the mould, inserted a body and closed it up again. Could it have been done in the dead of night? The machine needed power and a supply of steam at the right temperature and pressure. The night watchman and security staff would see or hear. Those elements needed other machines to be turned on, run up to temperature and… It all beggared belief.

Unless the machine operator was in on the plot.

Also, why would somebody go to all this trouble? If Cem had done some bad deal or failed to pay money he owed, it would be easy enough to kill him in some regular way with a knife or a gun. Why all the showmanship? Was this to get at Lars for some reason?

Patrick remembered Mert Mungan, the Chief dealer of Bina Kredi Bank in Turkey, wasn't impressed with Cem. He'd remembered rumours of the young man dealing in antiquities 'on the side'. Patrick expected the characters who operated in that market were unsavoury. But they'd not know how to carry out this ...horrific deed. And why bother?

What had happened to the Pieter Claesz painting? Did it reach Christie's? At least he could telephone one of his new contacts there to ask. Of course, if they hadn't taken delivery, there was now no way of finding it.

"Mr Field? The detective is ready for you now."

"Thank you."

Patrick uncoiled himself from his hunched position, enforced by the confines of Rob's office in Building twelve. He followed the uniformed officer across the grassy space to another building.

There was blue and yellow striped tape everywhere. 'Police' and 'Do not Enter' were printed on both sides as the tapes fluttered in the slight breeze. He was shown into another tiny cubicle in the new building. It boasted a plywood desk with a jumble of papers stacked in a heap at one side, as though someone had swept their arm across it to clear the space.

The balding, middle-aged man behind the desk half rose and waved Patrick to the chair in front.

"I'm Detective John Henderson. Please sit down."

He did so.

"I understand you and Mr …Heglund were here to attend the testing of some prototype building panels. Is that right?" Patrick nodded.

"And that you witnessed the first panel being tested before leaving?"

"That's right. I would have stayed longer, but Lars - Mr Heglund - is an impulsive sort of chap who wanted immediately to celebrate the excellent result."

"So you departed?"

"Yes. We drove to The Swan a few miles away and ordered Full English breakfasts with beer – they were very good actually."

"Mr Field."

"Yes. Um... we had not been eating long before Rob, the structural engineer running the tests, telephoned Lars and asked us to return."

Detective Henderson made a note in his book.

"And what time was this?"

Patrick puffed out his cheeks. He hadn't kept track of time. He thought for a bit and said, "Between ten thirty and eleven, I suppose."

"What exactly did Rob say?"

"He spoke with Lars so I don't know for sure. Lars told me Rob claimed the panel was almost twice as heavy as it should be. So they wanted to cut it open to see why it was different."

Henderson grunted and made another short note. He then pressed Patrick to recall exactly where he stood when Bill started to cut the panel, who said what and how the sequence of events unfolded.

Patrick remembered inspecting the panel visually before Bill went to work on it.

The only things he noticed were its smell and the hand print. Well …the hand, as it turned out.

"And you suspected the individual inside this panel is Mr Kaplan?"

"Yes. Because Lars was trying to get in touch with him. He'd dialled Cem's mobile phone and I thought I heard muffled ringing. Then we listened carefully and we all heard it. I suppose someone else might have his phone, but that would be odd."

"I think it's pretty odd to have a body squashed inside a laminated panel, don't you?"

"Er, yes. Of course."

"What is Mr Kaplan's relationship to you?"

"None! Nothing! I mean, he was one of Lars' contacts. I'd never met him before. Well, actually, that's not true. Lars introduced him to me when we met in a pub in London."

"Are you sure? Mr Heglund said Kaplan was one of your banking contacts."

"That's not… Um. Mr Kaplan told us he used to work for Bina Kredi Bank in Turkey – they *are* one of my customers – I work for

Royal Counties Bank, you see, as a calling officer."

"Go on."

"I asked the Chief Dealer about Mr Kaplan. There was nothing in writing, but I gathered he wasn't much good at dealing and they asked him to resign. And there were rumours about some unofficial trading in illegal antiques and things. All reputational risks for the bank which the Chief dealer didn't want to take."

"Are you saying he was mixed up with a bad crowd?"

"That was my impression, yes."

"Hmmn." Another note.

Patrick waited while the detective continued to write.

"And what was your impression of Mr Kaplan?"

Patrick was starting to wish he was somewhere else. His words mattered, of course, but he ought to preface them with some explanation of his experience in this arena.

"The straight up answer is I thought him untrustworthy. I should explain and I hope this …er, doesn't have to be relayed to my current employers?"

Henderson remained silent and impassive.

"Well, I have always worked in a regulated financial institution. I suppose one meets a certain type of person in banks and things. I've recently decided to …look around for a different career path. A head-hunter introduced me to Construction and to Lars - Mr Heglund, that is. To raise capital for our start-up company, I have been meeting some …well, unusual characters, let's say. Different types of people, you could call them. And I'm not experienced at judging them yet - you know - can they actually be trusted and all that."

"But Kaplan struck you as untrustworthy? What made you think that?"

"Gosh – it's hard to say, really. I suppose it was his manner. His persistence at trying to get information out of Lars – confidential, commercially-sensitive information. And I was beginning to feel uncomfortable that Lars has no honesty filter. He just blurts stuff out while insisting nothing he tells people could actually be useful. I'm not so sure."

"Could Kaplan have been relaying this information to others?"

"Yes. Or, I don't know, maybe trying to position himself as some sort of big deal-maker who had to be paid for information." Patrick puffed out his cheeks. This was pure speculation. Detective Henderson may have thought so too. He hadn't written it down.

"Is there anything else you can tell me?"

The painting. Should Patrick tell him about the painting?

Henderson was sitting there watching Patrick's face. He raised one eyebrow.

"Well?"

"I'm not sure it is relevant."

"Tell me anyway."

"There's this painting. Hang on. One step backwards – Lars and a couple of colleagues have formed a company to own and exploit this building panel. They've asked me to work in the company. We need to raise some capital. Cem Kaplan said he can buy a 17th century oil painting for a small sum. If it goes to auction at Christies soon, it might fetch a great deal – maybe several hundred thousand pounds. That money could pay our start-up expenses."

"And you suspect Kaplan came by this painting illegally?"

Patrick remembered an old Chinese saying. He had no idea if it really was Chinese, but the loose translation was something like, 'When in hole, stop digging'.

"I don't know. As I sit here today, telling you all this, it sounds more and more flaky. As told to me, the painting might be an unknown work by Pieter Claesz. His genuine paintings sell for many hundreds of thousands of dollars or Euros or whatever. Kaplan showed me a Christie's valuation which I now know was fake. I went there and checked with them. But Christies themselves still want to see the painting as it might be by a pupil of Claesz or even a genuine, but previously unknown work. Kaplan had agreed to have an associate deliver it to them. That's all I know."

He sat back in his chair. His clothes stuck to him. They were uncomfortable and no longer fit as well. This was becoming a grubby business and he felt dirty – soiled. It was so unfair – he was trying to be ambitious in his career choices and wanted very much to succeed. But everywhere he looked there were greedy takers. He was now being interviewed by the Police as a witness. Maybe more. His career ambitions had made him jump the gap between his protected life in Royal Counties Bank and this corruption. That gap was narrow. The swirling eddies of mucky commercialism were proving alarmingly distasteful.

Henderson asked some more questions about his contacts in Christies and Lars' colleagues. But then snapped his notebook shut.

"Right. That's all, Mr Field. Thank you for your time. You may go. Do not discuss this with anyone else – even Mr Heglund."

Patrick gave a bitter laugh.

"That might be tough. I have to drive him home and you know how he chatters."

"Do your best. Give your contact details to the officer outside. We'll prepare a formal statement and you may be required to attend the Coroner's hearing."

"Oh. Ok. Um, thanks. Cheerio."

-----//-----

Patrick went and found Lars. He was pressing Rob to carry on with the tests. Rob protested that B.R.E. themselves had embargoed Building twelve and no staff were allowed in or out of it, maintenance staff included. No work would be undertaken today and maybe not tomorrow – not until forensics had extracted the body and taken away the remains of the panel for close examination.

"They can't do that! That's my panel." Lars was almost shouting now and waving his arms.

"Out of my hands, Guv'nor. Take it up with my boss." Rob rolled his eyes.

Patrick thought he should rescue the poor chap. It wasn't fair to berate him.

"Lars! It's not Rob's fault. It's best if we just go home and work out what to do next."

Grumbling, Lars subsided. He stomped off in the direction of Patrick's car.

"I'm very sorry about all this, Rob. Like Lars, I'm upset as well, but he shouldn't have erupted like that. It's not your fault."

"I know. Thanks. If he does anything like that again, we might have to ban him from coming here. It's very disruptive."

"I see that. Sorry again. Could you let me know when the Police say you can continue the testing?"

Rob agreed and pocketed Patrick's business card.

They shook hands.

At the door, he stood for a second and took a couple of deep breaths. Enormous reserves of patience and guile would be needed during the trip home. Patrick couldn't just sit there, mute. Who could guess where Lars' mind was off to?

In the event, his passenger was as quiet as a lamb the whole way back around the M-25. He didn't even ask to stop for a smoking break. They pulled up outside Lars' house. He got out with a muttered, "Thanks." And went straight inside without looking back.

Now that Lars had gone, the atmosphere in the car didn't have that charge of tension any more. Patrick could feel his pulse slowing. He had been keyed up, anxious that Lars might have pressed him to talk about Cem, about what the Police had said and what he had told them.

Apparently, Lars was caught up in his own thoughts, which was fine by him.

For the rest of the drive home, he set his unconscious mind going to figure what they should do next. And concentrated hard on driving safely. He used the same technique sometimes before going to sleep. Magically, upon waking, he'd often have an answer or at least another angle on a knotty problem.

Switching off the engine at home, he decided to do two things. First, he'd call the women at Christie's – maybe the painting had been delivered before Cem was killed. And he'd also contact the factory where the panels were made. That was an obvious call for the Police to make, but it wouldn't hurt for him to make enquiries as well.

Still quite full from the enormous meal they had at The Swan, Patrick made himself a small sandwich and a pot of coffee. Then dialled Christie's.

"Good afternoon. May I speak to Lucy Worthington?"

He waited while the telephone exchange made some hissing noises.

"Hello? This is Lucy."

"Ah, Miss Worthington. It's Patrick Field. You may remember I was enquiring about a possible…"

"Of course, I remember. It's very exciting, Mr Field. I've been examining it for much of the morning."

So – the painting had been delivered.

"Oh, good. Well, I'm not chasing you. I just wanted to check it had got there safely. One point, if I may?"

"Yes?"

"Do you know who delivered it?"

"No. But I can ask the receiving staff in Deliveries. They are very attentive, as you might imagine."

"That would be most kind. As for the painting itself, have you noticed anything …ah, untoward about it?"

"Oh no. It's a lovely example, and in such excellent condition for its age. It's quite exciting, actually. We'll have to establish the provenance before the sale, of course, so perhaps you could forward that to me?"

"But you…" Then Patrick remembered the provenance, the chain of ownership which had been passed to him by Cem

Kaplan was probably as fictional as the supposed valuation document.

"Oh, yes. Right. Um, will it be possible to prove its authenticity beyond doubt by then?"

There was a slight pause. Lucy Worthington was choosing her words carefully.

"Time is tight, Mr Field. I cannot be certain about that."

"I see. Well, then. I'll leave you to it. Thanks for confirming it arrived safely."

He poured some more strong coffee into his mug. The true ownership of the work might now be hard to establish. With Cem out of the picture – he wiped the guilty smile off his face at that unintended witticism – Christie's might assume he, Patrick was the owner. But the picture would have little or no value on the open market unless it was both genuine and true ownership could be proven.

He looked through his papers and found the name of the factory which had made all the panels. He didn't know any of the staff. They were Lars' contacts. But he couldn't ask the man to make the call. The trouble with that was that he couldn't trust him to ask the right questions and to relay wholly and truthfully the answers they gave. Time for an update to Jerry Green. He'd know what to do.

"Hi, Jerry, it's Patrick. Do you have five minutes?"

"I do. It won't be five minutes, though, will it?"

Patrick gave a nervous laugh.

"Probably not. We've had …some developments. Thought you'd like an update and I'd value your input."

"Sure. Ok. Clock's running…"

"Ha bloody ha. Ok. Here we go. The painting valuation by Christies is fake."

"Uh huh. Go on: surprise me."

"But the painting itself might possibly be genuine."

"Really? Ok. I admit, I'm surprised."

"I don't mean to sound like Lars, but the woman who is conducting the upcoming auction of 17th century oils thinks it looks real. She cautioned it might have been painted 'in the style of…' but if it's anything less than a brilliant fake, she'd probably see that. There is the provenance document

Cem sent us which might not be genuine. You probably know that even a genuine painting needs provenance to achieve its full sales potential."

"Can all this be verified before the auction?"

"I asked that. I don't think it can, but the woman at Christies was reticent to say anything."

"Hmmn. Anything else?"

"Oh yes. A lot more. I went with Lars to B.R.E. to watch the first tests of the panels. The first one did far better than they expected. Lars insisted on going out to celebrate – you know how he is – but then the engineer called us back. They'd found a panel which was much heavier than the others and wanted to open it up with us watching."

"Why was it heavier?"

Patrick paused.

"This is pretty hard to believe. They started to cut it open and found ...a body inside."

"What?"

"A body. We think it's Cem Kaplan. Lars called his mobile and we could hear it ringing inside the panel."

"Jesus."

"We've all been interviewed by the Police. And testing is abandoned for a while, of course."

"It sounds like his past caught up with him, eh? If it is him."

"Indeed. I've been wracking my brains to figure out how he could have got in there. If bad hats got to him, why not just kill him with a knife or a gun or something?"

"It's a message."

"I agree. I'm thinking of calling the factory to have them explain how it could have been done. I don't know anyone there, though."

"They are all Lars' friends, aren't they?"

"Yup. I'd ask him to do it, but I doubt we'd get an accurate picture."

"I know," Jerry said. "How about we get him to book a factory visit? Then we all go."

"I'd be up for that. I'll try to get more time off. I can feel the headache coming on as we speak…"

"I'll call Lars and tell him to fix it. You're too involved. I'll say you briefed me and this is the right course of action."

"Hmmn. You might want to think of some way to let him think it was his idea. Then he'll be all for it. You could try, 'Patrick said you mentioned we ought to visit the factory to find out what's happening' and I support your idea."

"Good plan. I'll do that. Ring you back…"

Chapter 16
C.C.T.V.

"Hey, Patrick. Have I got some great news for you." Lars was speaking even before Patrick had the telephone against his ear.

"Good morning, Lars. Do tell. I need some cheering up today." In truth, he really did. Alan Pearson had shouted at him earlier for some infraction. Patrick was not guilty, but it was now his responsibility to sort it out. A little voice in his head shouted, 'It isn't fair', but another voice squashed that. 'Since when did everything have to be fair?' He was a bit bruised, emotionally after the encounter. Coffee might help, but he was short of time. He could do without having to deal with Lars' next Shiny New Thing.

"I've told Jerry that we need to visit the factory and I want you to come too. Cem didn't get inside that panel by himself."

A tiny smile began to form at the corners of Patrick's mouth.

"That's a great idea, Lars. When can they receive us?"

"I told them we are coming on Friday and they'd better be ready."

"Ok. Do you want me to pick you up? How's Jerry getting there?"

"Meet me at eight. We'll be there by eleven. You can buy me breakfast."

Patrick started to say that he would eat his breakfast before he left home. That would be at six if he was to collect Lars first, but realised he was talking to fresh air. The man had rung off. Still, Lars appeared to have got the idea that he had dreamed up this visit all by himself, so that was good. The man had ignored his question about Jerry's travel arrangements, though. He dialled Jerry's mobile but had to leave a voicemail.

In the event, Jerry left home very early to drive to Patrick's house. They continued north, stopping only to collect Lars, who wasn't ready by eight as he'd promised. It took fifteen minutes of faffing around for him to get dressed, smoke his first cigarette and join them in the car. The man was so tiresome!

Traffic was kind to them and they arrived at the factory a little early. It was a sprawling, single storey building with a double height covered area at one end for storage. Several rows of cars lined up in front of the building, evidencing the number of people working inside. Patrick pulled up at the end of one of the rows.

Jerry and Patrick had pumped Lars for a briefing on the people who worked there. Other than a couple of names and their inflated titles, Lars had little information to offer. Each, he claimed, was the most prominent and experienced in his field. Because Lars knew such a lot about the technology, he had singled out this factory as being the pre-eminent manufacturer in Britain - he said…

"I only work with the Best People," he finished, with a verbal flourish.

Neither of the others said anything. Such bluster no longer moved their Interest dials.

Lars led the way up to the door labelled 'Reception'.

There was no Reception desk. It was an entrance hall with several doors leading from it. The machinery noise from the door immediately ahead of them suggested it might lead directly on to the factory floor. Lars made for it.

"Hold on there, Lars. We'd better announce ourselves – they will want us to put on Hi-Vis tabards and things. You know – health and safety rules?"

The big man stopped.

"You're kidding me, right? This is the factory which put a human being into one of our panels and you think they worry about health and safety? Gimme a break!"

But at least he didn't plunge onwards and stayed in the hallway.

Patrick knocked on the door on the left. There was no immediate answer, so he pushed it open and went in. This was the administrative office with lots of men and women working at computers.

"Hello – we're from LaDaJ, here to see …Brian Kemp."

A bespectacled young man with the beginnings of a goatee beard rose from his chair. He'd been peering at a large computer screen with a technical drawing on it.

"Good morning. Mr Kemp will be in the Board Room upstairs. I'll go and tell him you are here."

"Thanks. My name is Patrick Field. Mr Kemp knows my colleague, Lars Hegburg."

The fellow excused his way past Lars and Jerry and disappeared up the stairs to a mezzanine level. Patrick had half-wondered how the single storey building could have an 'upstairs', but perhaps he would soon find out.

"I'll be right back," said Lars. He took out a battered packet from his shirt and tapped the filter end of one cigarette hard against the wrapper to firm up the tobacco.

Jerry watched him leave through the front door again with ill-concealed disgust.

"That man is addicted," he said. "He can't seem to leave 'em alone."

Of course, Brian Kemp came downstairs to welcome the guests long before Lars returned.

"I'm sorry — Lars had to ventilate his lungs again after spending so long in the fresh air of my car. He'll be in very soon, I'm sure. I'm Patrick Field."

They all shook hands.

"And this is Jerry Green."

"Brian Kemp. I haven't met you gents before. Just …Lars. I guess you are here to talk about the panels we made for you?"

"That's right," Jerry began. "Early indications of the testing are very positive, so we'd like to say 'thank you'."

Kemp beamed. Perhaps he had been concerned that they were going to complain about something.

"It's good of you to come all the way here to say that. Not all our customers are so appreciative. Let's go upstairs. Then we could have a tour of the factory. Would you like to do that?"

He stepped forward a couple of paces and opened one of the other doors.

"Diana? Could you rustle up some drinks for our guests?"

A matronly woman emerged, smoothing her dress and took their orders for tea and coffee. Jerry nodded over his shoulder towards the car park.

"Our colleague, Lars will join us shortly. I have no idea whether he'd like some tea."

The woman's face broke into a wide smile.

"Lars? Lars Hegburg? Oh, I know exactly what Mr Hegburg will want. Leave it to me."

Patrick and Jerry exchanged glances. Trust Lars to butter up the secretarial staff. Maybe that was a head-hunting technique.

"Follow me," commanded Brian Kemp. And up they went.

The Board Room had restricted height, but was more than adequate for such meetings. A long, polished, wooden table dominated the room and the walls were hung with various industrial awards.

"Take a seat, take a seat," encouraged their host. "Diana will be up in a ticcy."

"I suppose we'd better wait for Lars to join us, if you don't mind. In the meantime, can you tell us about these awards? There are so many."

Brian Kemp didn't mind boasting about the awards at all. He was just getting going when the door banged open.

"Hey, Brian. Great to see you again. Whatever these guys have been saying about me, they don't know the half of it."

"Hello Lars. Haven't seen you for a while. How've you been?"

They all shuffled sideways to make room so Diana could put down her tray. She had followed Lars up the stairs. She handed a weak tea to him.

"I hope I got that right, Lars. Not too much milk, right?"

The others had to help themselves.

When everybody had taken their first sips at the scalding liquids, Jerry got in first. He knew that leaving the conversation starter to Lars would prolong the day more than somewhat.

"Brian, the main reason we wanted to visit was because one of the panels sent down to B.R.E. was much heavier than all the others. I won't bore you with the whole story, but it turned out that it contained a human body – that was why it was so much heavier."

Kemp had been about to take another sip of his coffee. He paused the cup halfway to his mouth.

"I beg your pardon?"

Jerry repeated what he'd said.

"Lars – is this right?"

"Sure is. I got me a theory, but we'd like to get your take on it."

Patrick put in, "We don't yet have a positive identification, but we think it is a man named Cem Kaplan. It was his mobile phone which rang inside the panel when we dialled him. Forensics are taking the panel apart to investigate. In fact, I'm surprised they haven't come up here to talk to you yet."

At last, Brian Kemp was able to have his desired sip of coffee. He replaced it on the saucer, spilling some of the liquid.

"My God. How is that possible? Did you say, 'Cem Kaplan'?"

They all nodded.

"Mr Kaplan came up here with some colleagues a few weeks back when we were making the panels. You'll remember, Lars – he said you'd told him to bring some potential investors to watch."

"Me? Nope. I didn't tell 'im nuth'n."

"But he said you'd encouraged… never mind. Oh, God – this is awful."

Kemp sat with his head in his hands. He knew this would bring a visit from the Police, from the Health and Safety Executive – all sorts of inspectors and his factory would be shut down. He'd be laying off staff… This was a disaster.

"Tell us what happened, Brian," Patrick said. "Who were these other people?"

"I didn't really talk to them very much. I think they came from Turkey. Cem did all the talking. Our Production Manager, Andy, walked them around. We had moved on to laminating so at the end of the tour they said they wanted to go back to see the core moulding stage."

He was shaking his head. His whole world had fallen apart.

"I thought Andy was with them. Maybe he wasn't. Perhaps he was called away for a few minutes – I don't know."

For a few seconds he sat, speechless.

But then he looked up.

"I know - there's the visitors' book – and we have CCTV in the factory. I'll see if we still have the film from back then."

He scraped back his chair.

"I'll go and see Diana."

When he had gone, Patrick looked at Lars.

"I thought you said, 'Cem is a friend'. You can control him, you said."

"He is. Was. They still don't know squat."

Jerry said nothing. He'd recognised long ago this would be a risk with Lars. The man couldn't keep his mouth shut. Silence reigned until Diana reappeared.

"Mr Kemp says can you join him in our office downstairs? He's going through the CCTV film from when your friends visited."

They all trooped after her.

The CCTV machine had its own little screen with enough resolution to confirm that something had recorded. But it wasn't good enough to recognise details.

"When you find them, Brian, can you show that film on a bigger screen?"

"Maybe. Yes, I think so."

Kemp looked up.

"Diana? Can this be transferred to a computer screen? I can't see much of anything on here."

"Yes, Mr Kemp. I'll bring a screen over."

He kept looking.

"Are you sure it was the eleventh? Ah. Here they are. He straightened up. I can see them arriving at the front door."

"Right," Jerry stepped in. "Let's get the screen hooked up first and we'll run it from there. Where are your cameras positioned?"

Kemp and Diana explained between them. The screen burst into life. Now, although grainy, much more detail could be seen.

"Could we back up say, two minutes, so we see their car arriving? We might get a registration number."

They had no such luck. When the men first appeared there had been no vehicular movement apart from a curtain-sided truck moving away, slowly, in the background. Maybe they parked some distance away.

"There's Cem," Patrick said, pointing at the screen. There were four others. Three had overcoats, the fourth had a leather biker jacket. They all watched as the men disappeared from view into the Reception area. Another camera picked up the tops of their heads. They saw Brian Kemp emerge to shake everyone's hand and lead them straight through to the factory floor. Kemp handed them over to another man who must be the Production Manager, Andy. More handshakes.

They all tracked the visitors from screen to screen around the factory. This was all new to Patrick and Jerry, of course, as they hadn't had the tour yet.

"There!"

Patrick had spotted one of the guests whip out a measuring tape when Andy wasn't looking. They were all standing beside one of the lamination tables and Andy was checking the lay-up of some cores on the first board. The man in the biker jacket checked how high the top plate of the lamination machine went. He then put the tape back in his pocket.

They saw Andy check his watch and they gathered round him, discussing something. There were heads nodding, Andy pointed to the side and shook their hands. He then departed from the picture and all five guests headed the other way.

"Where did they go?" asked Jerry.

Everyone looked from picture to picture.

"They went in the direction of the moulding machines," Kemp told him. "We might pick them up on this camera."

He was right. Someone's head passed across one of the other screens and vanished. But soon, all five strode into view on the expected screen, heading for machine number two. Cem led the way. Two of the raincoats hung back and ducked around the other side of the machine. It was about four metres high and perhaps eight or nine metres long.

An operator was visible at the control panel beside it. Cem approached him and they talked for a moment. The operator pressed a large button on the panel and then held down a second while he peered under a side supporting rail. It looked as if the inside part of the machine was separating. At length, he undid a guard gate and stepped into the machine itself.

They could see him gesturing at both sides of the machine and making squashing motions with his hands. Everyone nodded and they all stepped clear. The gate closed again. The operator held down a third button until the machine closed up. He then stood, checked his watch and walked away.

"He must be on a break," Kemp told them. The visitors all stayed where they were. Biker jacket looked around and nodded to one of the overcoats. He stepped up close to Cem and appeared to punch his chest multiple times.

As Cem collapsed, one of the men pressed the button to separate the machine and opened the guard gate.

"Christ – look at that," Lars almost shouted. "That's how they did it…"

Two of the men dragged Cem Kaplan through the gate and hauled him up into one half of the machine. They backed out, closed the safety gate and the button was pressed to bring the machine back together.

But they didn't disperse. They stayed there, chatting as though this was nothing out of the ordinary.

"Why haven't they gone?" asked Patrick.

"They're making sure the job is finished," Jerry replied, tight lipped.

And sure enough, the operator came back, resumed his seat and began pressing the buttons to continue to make cores. They stayed to watch two more cycles before shaking his hand and leaving.

Then strolled away, cool as you like.

"Where are they? Where have they gone?" Brian Kemp asked. He couldn't stand still.

"Out through the bloody front door," Lars pointed to the camera covering the Reception area.

The visitors were in no hurry. They saw someone emerge from the secretary's office and walk past them, half raising a hand to wave goodbye. The final screen showed four heads ambling along, smiling and joking as they headed into the carpark and off the premises.

"And then there were four…" Patrick breathed. "Agatha Christie would have been proud."

"You need to back up those films, Brian," Jerry said. "It's important that they are not lost. You may want to make contact with the Police yourself. Better not wait for them to get in touch. Also, is there any chance we could have a copy? It's about our panels after all."

"Sure, sure. Um… Sure. I don't know… Erm, Diana?" She came scurrying back. "We must make sure these tapes are not wiped. They must not be cycled back into rotation.

Got that? And make two copies, please. One back-up for us and one for these gentlemen."

"Yes, Mr Kemp. Right away." She half-curtseyed. "Anything for Mr Hegburg."

"Actually, I'll hang on to that, if you don't mind," As he was ex-Military, Jerry felt that security matters were his domain. "Patrick? Could you give Brian the contact number for the Police detective who is running the inquiry? He has interviewed Lars and Patrick here and will undoubtedly follow up with you in due course. Scene of the crime and all that."

"I know we have to get back home, but I wouldn't mind seeing that tape again before we go," Patrick asked. "Could we do that?"

Diana said she'd make the copies first and then take him back to watch the original through on the bigger screen.

"While Diana does that, could we have a look at the visitors' book and maybe tour the factory?" Jerry asked.

"Of course. I'll get Andy. You could ask him about the visitors."

Brian went through to the factory floor. He was back almost immediately with another man. He made introductions and then retired upstairs. Patrick wondered if he had a bottle of comfort secreted in his desk for stressful occasions like this. Diana returned with the visitors' book. She turned the pages backwards.

"Here we are – the eleventh – here's Mr Kaplan. Oh. It says, "Cem Kaplan plus four colleagues." She looked up. "They didn't say who they were."

Andy handed out ear plugs. Lars flicked his onto the floor. Everyone else dutifully rolled them and inserted them into each ear.

"Do you have time to show us the process from the beginning?" Jerry yelled as they went through the door. Andy nodded.

They made for the hoppers where they kept the raw polystyrene bead before blowing measured quantities into the moulding machines. Although they'd seen these machines on film, Patrick gasped at the sheer size of them. They must weigh many, many tonnes, he thought. The operator showed them how opening the safety gate stopped the machine immediately. But this was necessary to put various inserts inside to create shapes in the finished article. They all stood in awe as the steel goliath hissed and clanged and belched steam before ejecting a dripping wet block of polystyrene onto a pile.

Patrick looked carefully at the latest block on the stack. All the surfaces were concave.

"It's not very flat, is it? Is it supposed to be flat?"

Andy smiled. "That's where post-expansion comes in, mate."

Patrick thought he understood. He guessed that the beads expand initially in the mould when steam is pumped in but then, even when they are cooling after ejection, they keep expanding a bit. It would be tricky to gauge, he realised. There was more to this moulding process than Lars had let on. Had the visitors figured this out? Were they even interested?

"Andy? Remember when those guys came around with you a few weeks back?"

"Yeah. Foreigners. Didn't speak much English, 'cept one of 'em."

"Did they ask lots of questions?"

"Hard to say. They kept talking to each other in some foreign language. Then the one asked me stuff in pretty good English. I wouldn't say they really understood the process, though."

"How so?"

"'None of the questions followed on from each other. They were, like, random. Know what I mean?"

Patrick nodded. He was mildly relieved to hear this. It implied that the group didn't really know how to make their panels, but it would be foolish to count on that. He kept his thoughts to himself while they moved on to the lamination area. He didn't understand how the men could assemble boards and a core together without noticing that the core was much heavier than usual.

They all gathered around one of the lamination tables. It was quieter here and Patrick and Jerry removed their ear plugs in order to hear Andy more clearly.

"Andy, we've seen CCTV of their visit and watched as one of them was killed and shoved inside the moulding machine."

"You what?"

Patrick realised that nobody had explained to Andy what had happened.

"I'm sure Brian was going to tell you all about it, but it turns out that the one who spoke some English was killed beside Number Two machine. The operator must have gone to the toilet or something. While he was away, they opened the mould and shoved the man in there, closing the machine before the operator came back."

Andy opened his mouth to say something, but didn't.

Patrick went on. "It's really hard to credit, I know. But they managed it – it's all on film. The operator started up the machine again and kept making cores as normal."

Then the next thought occurred to him. "Surely the guys over here by the lamination table would have noticed?"

Andy thought for a second. He stuck out his bottom lip. "Probably not. They push the trolley with all the cores over here and this loader machine pushes one of them out when the men have sprayed glue onto the first board. See? They press this bar, here, with their feet and out it comes. So, unless some part of him was poking out, they wouldn't see."

There was a distinct smell of the volatile gasses from the adhesive in this area of the factory, and already it was beginning to make Patrick light-headed. The workers who did this for hours on end must be as high as kites by the end of their shift, he reckoned. They'd not notice anything. It struck him that Cem could have waved his hand at them and they'd just keep going.

Chapter 17
The Turkish Connection

"Who was the operator on machine number two back on the eleventh?"

Andy looked at Jerry and shrugged his shoulders. "I dunno. I can look at the roster."

"Thanks. Ok if we wait here?"

"Sure."

Lars walked away with him. "I need a cigarette," he said over his shoulder.

Jerry watched him go. "And *we* need another idea," he said to Patrick. "No matter how great this building system thing might be, Lars shouldn't be anywhere near the process of getting it going and certainly not near the ongoing operations."

Patrick nodded in agreement. He thought the same. But he still liked the idea of this simple building panel which seemed to be so strong. How could they stop the outflow of information from Lars?

Andy was coming back.

"It was a man named Aydin Agha. Bright guy. We took him on about a week before. He's already away on compassionate leave, though. His aunt was sick or died or summat, so he had to go back to Turkey."

Jerry and Patrick looked at each other.

"Ok. Thanks, Andy. Erm… He probably won't be back, you know. You may want to hire a replacement now."

"Aw, give the guy a chance," Andy said. "'Least 'til the end of the month."

"Thanks very much for showing us around," Patrick said. "It's clear that making good panels isn't quite as easy as we thought to begin with."

"Any time. I'll be here."

Patrick and Jerry headed for the door out of the manufacturing area. They reached it as Lars was coming back.

"Let's say 'goodbye' to Brian," Jerry said. "There's nothing more we can learn here. We've got a great deal of thinking to do."

"You go up there, then," Lars said. "I'll go see Diana."

"See?" Jerry hissed at Patrick as they mounted the stairs. "He has no idea how to behave."

-----//-----

Brian didn't bother to hide the tumbler of pale liquid in front of him on the table. He stayed slumped in his chair when he waved them in.

"We'll be off now," Jerry told him. "Thanks for all your help."

"Welcome. So problem. Any sime." The half empty bottle on the table explained why he was slurring his speech.

"Andy told us the machine operator was a chap named Aydin Agha. He'd joined you quite recently, I believe. Is there any chance you could let us have an address for him?"

They waited while Brian considered. His eyes hadn't focussed on them and his brain struggled with the request.

"Thass confidensh... Iss pirate."

"Oh yes. I realise. Thing is, Andy was told Agha's aunt died and he's gone back to Turkey. We don't believe he'll be back."

"Worrever..." Kemp waved his arm.

"Right. Thanks again. Um, see you soon. Bye, now."

They left Brian Kemp surveying the ruins of his business from inside his bottle of whisky.

Back on the ground floor, there was no sign of Lars. Patrick tapped on the door to the secretarial office and went in. He thought they too should thank Diana for her help before leaving. They found Lars looming over her typewriter, stroking his moustache. Diana gazed up at him, hanging on every word.

Jerry came to her rescue. "Diana? There was one more thing before we all head off – Brian said we should ask you for the contact details of Aydin Agha."

"Oh? Aydin? What a nice boy. He's gone to Turkey, I'm afraid. It's so sad – his aunt is very sick. He needed to leave in a hurry." She sniffed. "He hasn't been with us long, either."

She rose and side-stepped around Lars. She unlocked a tall filing cabinet and peeled through the folders. Then, with a frown, started again from the beginning.

"Sorry about this. I can't lay my hands on his records right now. I wonder where they are..." She closed the drawer and looked around the office.

"What's the matter, Diana?" asked one of the others.

"I can't see Aydin Agha's personnel file. Do you have it?"

"No. But I remember he asked to photocopy something in it last week. P'raps he put it back in the wrong place?"

"I've looked. Hang on."

Diana went through all the folders again, one by one.

She turned to Jerry and Patrick. "It isn't here."

"Don't you have to send quarterly returns to the employment office, or something?" Patrick asked. The hair on the back of his neck prickled. This was beginning to look like what Mike, his manager back in Bahrain, would have called 'naughtiness'.

"Oh, yes, of course. Silly me!"

Diana went to her computer. Half a minute later she pressed the 'Return' key triumphantly and went to the printer. It stuttered into action. She handed the emerging piece of paper to Jerry.

"Here you are. I would like to know where that folder went, though."

"Better start searching for it, Diana. I expect the Police will want to see whatever records you have on this guy."

Her eyes grew wide.

"The Police? But …he wasn't anywhere near the machine when that man was killed."

"Exactly. He left the way open for them. Now, we'd better be on our way. Oh, and Mr Kemp will be wanting a pot of coffee, some Paracetamol and a taxi home in a short while."

Her face crumpled. "Was he..?"

Jerry nodded.

"I need a pee break," Patrick said. "I'll be right with you."

"And I need another cigarette."

Eventually, they gathered by Patrick's car.

"It's probably far too late, but let's go around to this address. It's not far from here."

Jerry navigated. They were looking for a flat at number eighty five, Church Street. The numbers ran out at seventy five. Beyond that was a cross roads and the road names changed.

"Could eighty five be around the back, somewhere?" Patrick hazarded.

"No. This was a false address Agha gave them. We may as well keep going home."

The mood in the car as they drove south was grim. It looked very much as though Lars' bright idea had been stolen from under their noses.

Nobody felt like saying anything until Jerry said he needed the bathroom. Patrick pulled in at the next services area.

"We need more fuel, anyway, and I fancy a sandwich. Anything for you chaps?" he asked.

"Sure. Why not? I wanna burger and fries – a cheese burger. And a large shake."

"Jerry?"

"Well, ok. A small sandwich for me, thanks. And a tea. Or a coffee – not one of your fancy coffees, though."

"Is that what you Army types call a 'Wet and a Wad', Jerry?"

The other man laughed.

"There's a burger place over there, Lars. I'll meet you back here when I've got the sandwiches and coffees."

"Aren't you getting a burger too?"

Patrick shook his head. "It would give me indigestion."

Lars chewed his moustache for a moment. "Oh, alright. I'll have a sandwich, then. I'll come with you so I can choose."

Despite his Christian upbringing, it occurred to Patrick that Lars' choice of food was influenced less by taste than who would pay for it. Lars expected Patrick would pay for everyone's sandwiches along with his fuel top up. 'What an unworthy conclusion – even if it's accurate,' he told himself off.

Lars found a triple-decker bacon, lettuce and tomato with mayonnaise. He also snagged a packet of crisps, a bar of chocolate and a pre-made cold coffee. Patrick and Jerry selected more modest fare.

"Just write it off to expenses," Lars told him. "This is company business so it's legit."

"But the company doesn't have any money yet," Patrick protested. "It has to have funds to be able to pay expenses."

"Formation expenses," said his greedy passenger, as though this was the answer to everything.

Knowing argument was pointless, Patrick paid. He saved the receipt in case, some time in future, the cost could indeed be refunded by LaDaJ as a formation expense. He and Jerry watched Lars light up again and dial someone on his mobile phone – perilously close to the fuel pumps. These actions drew the ire of the cashier at the till.

"Pump six – no smoking at the fuel station and turn off your mobile phone immediately, please."

Lars ignored the loudspeaker.

"Oi, mate. Get rid of the fag and the 'phone," shouted a builder in a grubby vest. He was filling a Transit van with diesel from the next pump in line and would like to have lit up too. But rules are rules and he didn't want to burn to a crisp.

That got through to Lars.

To an extent, anyway. He dropped his lit cigarette on the ground. It flared, for a second, because of the spilt fuel there and he stamped on it.

"The phone!" came over the loudspeaker again. The cashier hurried out, hastily-donned Hi-Viz jacket flapping and carrying a bucket of sand.

She shouted at Lars, "Are you stupid or something? You could ignite this whole fuel station."

Using an unnecessary amount of vigour, she emptied the bucket all over the spot where he had ground out his lit cigarette.

Lars ignored the display. He turned his back and stomped towards their car.

"What's their problem?" he asked, rhetorically.

"I think they want to avoid a conflagration," Jerry replied with mild sarcasm, to Lars' evident puzzlement.

"Confla… what?"

"They don't want a big fire, Lars. Come on. Back in the car and don't drop crumbs all over the inside."

Their conversation for a few miles was restricted to comments about the quality of the food they'd eaten. But then Patrick broached the topic they'd all been thinking about.

"How are we going to track these guys down? We have no clue who the visitors were. Talk about slack procedures! Nothing in the visitors' book, no real contact address for the Aydin Agha chap – not a sausage. Any ideas, guys?"

After a moment, Jerry said, "Everything points towards this being an organised group, yeah?"

"Right…"

"And there might be a bit of a Turkish theme going on. Cem Kaplan was Turkish. This Agha man is Turkish. It's likely all the other four who came to the factory with Cem are Turkish – remember Andy said they spoke a foreign language?"

"It makes sense – because Cem was boasting of all his Turkish contacts to you, Lars, wasn't he?"

"Aye. He knows …knew all the biggest contracting companies in the country and we were going to open factories all over."

"So – isn't it likely that Cem's 'associate' who was going to deliver the painting to Christies might be Turkish as well?"

Patrick snapped his fingers. "Good thinking, Jerry. I can call that painting expert woman there – she said her colleagues in Deliveries were always extremely thorough. She might be able to tell me who it was."

He pressed the accelerator a little harder. The speedometer flirted with an indicated seventy five miles per hour. Soon, another service area came into view.

-----//-----

"Lucy? It's Patrick Field here. We spoke about... Yes, that's right. You have a good memory."

"Hardly, Mr Field. It's only been a day or two. You speak as though everyone talks to me about a previously-unknown Pieter Claesz painting."

"Ha, ha. Yes, of course. When we spoke last, you indicated you might be able to ask Deliveries the name of the person who brought the painting to you."

"Oh yes. I have that here, somewhere. Just a moment."

He could hear shuffling noises.

"Here we are. It was two men - Deniz and Mehmet Arif. They both signed the release documentation."

"That's great, Lucy. Do you have contact details for them?"

"Of course. This is Christies."

Patrick turned on the speaker function on his mobile phone. Jerry wrote down the details as she dictated.

"Thanks ever so much, Lucy. I never doubted you! Oh – right at the beginning of the conversation, I gathered from the way you spoke, that the painting is genuine. Did I hear correctly?"

"Perhaps." She breathed out. "I suppose I shouldn't have said anything, but it does look very much as though you have an exceptional and exciting 'find'. From the style, I can gauge roughly at what stage during his life it was painted, but I'd love to do some more research. We have links with specialist investigators who can research the *provenance*, the materials – what we call *examen minutieux*. All such matters including prosecution, where necessary. Would you like me to instruct them? I can send you their scale of fees."

Sudden movement made Patrick look up. Jerry was making frantic cutting motions with his hand across his throat, indicating he should end the call.

"Um, gosh – Lucy, that's …reassuring to know. Er, could I come back to you on all that? I can see we will need to gather all the information we can about the painting before spending any money on such a process."

"Well, if you are sure. It's just that everything will be needed if the painting is to reach its best value in the auction. 'In the style of' isn't as valuable as 'attributed to' and certainly not as valuable as the Holy Grail of 'By'. You understand, of course."

"Of course. Thanks for the information. I'll be in touch. Good bye."

Patrick hadn't realised he was sitting forward in his seat, tense with excitement at what Lucy Worthington was saying. Now he sat back and tried to relax. Could they really have within their grasp a genuine work by a seventeenth century Dutch master?

"I told you we should go for it," Lars opined.

"Shut up, Lars. That isn't helping. This is a very mucky business. We are getting involved with some potentially dangerous people and could easily find ourselves in trouble with the British Police."

"We haven't done anything wrong," Lars protested.

"How about 'handling stolen goods' for starters," Jerry shot back. "Patrick – you are squarely in the firing line here. Are you alright with this?"

"I suppose so. But we have to pursue it, don't we?" He thought for a second. "I might have a way of checking on those blokes who delivered the painting."

"So do I," Jerry affirmed. "Mine's Military. Yours?"

"I'm not sure what you'd call them – governmental, I suppose."

"Well, I'll check 'em out with the Federal Reserve and the CIA and the FBI," claimed Lars, not wanting to be outdone in the checking stakes.

Jerry shared a cheeky half smile with Patrick.

"You do that, Lars. We can compare notes afterwards."

-----//-----

Patrick had no intention of letting either of the other two know that he was in touch with Penny Baxter at MI-6. So he waited until he got home before calling her. He insisted Jerry at least drink half a glass of fruit juice to boost him for his further drive onwards. The man had had a very long day – and then dialled her number when he'd gone.

"Baxter."

"Penny, it's Patrick. Are you ok to talk?"

"Yes. What do you need?"

"There's a bit of a long story involved here, which I can tell you if you want. I need to check out two men - brothers or cousins, maybe. They're Turkish, I think."

"Give me the names."

"Deniz and Mehmet Arif."

"Spelling, please."

Patrick obliged.

"How have you come into contact with them, Patrick? Can you not live a normal life for once?"

"Sorry? Have you heard of them before?"

There was a little laugh on the phone. More ironic than girlish, Patrick would have said.

"It's fair to say I have heard of them. That's why I'm concerned how you have come into contact with the Arif family."

So Patrick told her the story from the beginning. Only once did she ask a question. That was to find out how Lars had met Cem Kaplan. He didn't know that. When he finished, there was a little pause. He heard her blowing out a long-held breath.

"Patrick Field. You must have been born with some sort of criminal magnetism. Let's skip to the chase here. Have you heard of the Kray brothers?"

"Of course. Ronnie and Reggie."

"The Arifs are a Turkish-Cypriot family, based in South London. When the Krays were banged up, there was a turf war for control of the London underworld. The Arifs were considered the leading crime family throughout the late 1980s. Most of them were arrested for armed robbery and drug-related stuff in the early 1990s.

The two characters you just told me about, Deniz and Mehmet lead the gang together with their brother, Doğan. I remember Mehmet was shot by police in Surrey or Sussex during a robbery which went wrong. They smuggle drugs – all sorts – why not artwork?"

"Oh, Penny. I don't know what to say. It isn't fair. Everything I try…"

"If your friend Cem Kaplan got on their wrong side, they'd have no hesitation in rubbing him out – as the Americans say."

"Given what you just told me, is it odd that they waltzed up to Christies, handed over a potentially valuable painting and then signed with their own names?"

"It is. Could be someone impersonating them, but that, as you will now understand, is extremely dangerous. I wonder if Christies checked I.D.?"

"I can ask. The valuer woman, Lucy Worthington, was insistent that the Christies receiving staff are very careful indeed. Perhaps they took an address or driving license or something."

"Even if they did, I don't suggest you knock on their door, Patrick. Even you wouldn't do that?"

Patrick was silent. How was he going to establish the chain of ownership of the painting? Was there any chance of protecting LaDaJ's intellectual property – the know-how of making and putting together these wonder panels?

At last, he said, "I agree, Penny. They sound like nasty folks. I ought to run in the opposite direction. We have to work out what to do. Anyway – enough about me. How are you? Are you any closer to …you know?"

"Just make sure you do leave the Arifs well alone. I may not be able to rescue you next time. As for me? I'm a bit worried about my father. I fear he has a nasty infection which modern medicines find hard to tackle. We'll see how it goes."

This was the first time she'd ever spoken about her family to Patrick. He'd always assumed she had to fight to keep personal stuff private and not to bring it into the workplace.

"I'm sorry to hear that, Penny. I hope it isn't catching, whatever it is."

"I don't think he's infectious, but one never knows."

"Hmmn. Oh well. Look, if you want to talk about it at any stage, my shoulder is always free."

There was a sound on the line which was halfway between a cough and a laugh. "I'll remember that, Patrick. And thank you."

Chapter 18

"Another Port, Please"

Patrick called Jerry and relayed the gist of Penny's news about the probable identity of the two men who delivered the painting to Christies.

"Hmmn. Well, I have good news and bad news, Patrick. Which would you like first?"

"Oh, the good news, every time."

"Which is that these men were certainly not Mehmet and Deniz Arif. They may be other members of the family, but we think they are from some other group. Think about it. How old must the Arif brothers be now if they were ruling the roost back in the late 80s and 90s?"

"Oh, yes. I see that now. If they were someone else, that is a good thing. So what's the bad news?"

"We don't know who they actually are."

"I should have guessed. Darn it. So – how do we track down who was keeping the picture? And we still don't know who were the four men who killed Cem."

"That's all true. I do have some feelers out with the local Police to see what motor cars drove past cameras around those times, but I'm not holding my breath. It's likely that the cars had false number plates anyway."

"Great. So what now?"

"Dunno, mate. Back to the day job, I guess."

"S'pose. I do have a lot on my plate right now. Call me if anything comes back from your Police friends."

This was dispiriting. Everything that Patrick tried these days began with excitement and promise but soon dried up in the dust. He sighed. 'Back to the Day Job', indeed.

He was supposed to be preparing for another trip to the Middle East to include Jordan and he still hadn't finished the follow-up to his brief stop in Turkey. The truth was that this recent experience made anything Turkish unpalatable. 'But the bad stuff is not connected with Royal Counties Bank', he admonished himself. 'Better get on with it.'

The most important Turkish business which he ought to take care of was the request from the Chief dealer at Bina Kredi Bank, Mert Mungan. The man had asked whether Royal Counties Bank could help them launch a two hundred and fifty million dollar deal for a Turkish corporate operating in the construction sector. Royal Counties Bank's Credit Risk Management division laughed when he mentioned the amount of Turkish risk. But they thawed a little when he explored ways to structure the deal to lower and shorten the risk profile. In the end, he got approval to keep talking to Bina Kredi Bank at least.

He dialled Mert's telephone number.

"Hi, Patrick. How's my deal coming along?"

He chuckled. The man was on form today. Sharp as always. "Not bad, Mert, not bad. Can you send me some details of the corporate customer and their last couple of annual accounts? Also any notes your colleagues have written about them. You know – local press cuttings, reputation, management changes – that sort of thing."

"Sure, sure. When are you hoping to launch, then?"

"Woah, there. We haven't even said we'd do it, yet. We want to know where our money is going before we ask other people to contribute their share."

They chatted back and forth a little more. Mert passed along a joke, which he considered hilarious, but which obviously lost something in translation and then rang off. Five minutes later, Patrick's computer dinged. It heralded the arrival of Mert's email.

He opened and scanned the message. In short, the customer was quite a new company, but was run by experienced management culled from rival contactors. They reckoned to have a laundry list of projects to build, some for the government, some for private buyers. So far, so speculative.

But then Patrick's eyes widened. He couldn't believe what he was reading. He shook his head and read the page again. The company proposed to use a revolutionary building system, using panels. There was an addendum which described how the panels were made. He opened the attachment.

There, laid out as clear as day, was the manufacturing method for the panels Lars and he and Jerry were testing at B.R.E. For a moment, the computer screen blurred. It was as though Patrick's brain shut down his eyesight, overwhelmed with the enormity of what he had seen. Blinking rapidly helped. He rubbed his eyes and refocussed.

The description lacked a lot of the minute detail which would be essential knowledge for anyone hoping to make good quality panels. It was arguable whether they needed that level of detail for a credit proposal. But did they know those details? Had Lars spilled them through his moustache at high volume to Cem during some beery session? As that thought framed itself in his head, Patrick knew it would be useless confronting Lars with this evidence. He was finding out that the part of Lars Hegburg which kept him going was the part which reinvented history to suit his present dilemma. Patrick was convinced the man had some sort of mental condition enabling him to tell untruths in a convincing manner.

At the time of telling, Lars genuinely believed in what he was saying. Presenting irrefutable evidence to the contrary wouldn't budge him.

He read on through the rest of the paper. Some of the money to be raised would fund a factory near Istanbul. The balance would buy land and build out the planned houses and apartments. Selling them would repay the loan.

It was a simple proposition.

Patrick shook his head. This was because of Lars' big mouth. He kept replaying some of Lars' claims in his head. 'Cem is a friend'. 'I can control him'. And then the man's propensity for shouting confidential details about the system and the manufacturing process in public.

Patrick slumped back in his chair. Stupid, stupid, stupid. Lars had something which could have made them all very wealthy and make thousands of wonderful homes for people. His big-headed arrogance had thrown it away to greedy and lazy people who wouldn't even do it right. They'd likely cut corners in the quality of making the panels. One day a big building would collapse. There would be a national scandal and everyone would be very sorry, pointing fingers at everyone else.

But then he sat bolt upright. Hang on! In these papers might be information about the men who had stolen the technology. Perhaps also the individuals who had done away with Cem Kaplan too, when he outlived his usefulness.

Yes. Another thought occurred to him. Oh, and this was devious cleverness beyond compare. They got rid of Cem in a way which also stymied the people who were trying to get the original product to market in the UK. That would give the thieves a head start in a world market. These men must have reasoned that a Police investigation plus a delay in the testing regime at B.R.E. would set LaDaJ back months. That was why they went to the trouble of this murderous charade – pushing Cem into a mould at the factory.

Patrick's hand was shaking as he pressed the numbers on his phone to call Jerry.

"Yes, Patrick? …Hello? Are you there?"

"Er, I am. This time, I have Good News and Bad News for you."

"You don't sound very sure. Are you ok?"

"I'll get back to you on that. I've had a bit of a shock."

"Well, come on. Don't keep me in suspenders…"

"So – um, good news first. I might know who are the people who killed Cem – or at least, had him killed."

"Who is it? How did you find out?"

"Well, that's sort of the bad news as well."

Patrick explained how he found himself looking at this syndicated loan opportunity.

"As portrayed to me by the Chief Dealer, he felt they were in competition with other Turkish banks. I now think that because Cem worked at Bina Kredi, he will have a friend in their corporate department. No other bank in Turkey would touch the proposition, but maybe his friend pushed it forward. Who knows what that individual's motivation was? Maybe it doesn't matter."

"I think I follow. It's a bit circumstantial, though, isn't it?"

"Don't you see? The dots all add up. It's like following a trail of crumbs from the biscuit barrel with the loose top all the way back to the hole in the skirting board."

"Ok, I'll give you that. So who are these mice?"

Patrick clicked through the corporate information.

"Kemal Aksoy is the founder and CEO of this company. Baris Ozturk is the Financial Director. Those are the only names listed. They are thirty eight and forty one years old respectively."

"Right. Let's go check 'em out. Can you sit on the proposal for a few days?"

"I suppose so – at least, if I'm right about them not approaching other Turkish banks. I can always say I wanted to make preliminary enquiries to avoid Royal Counties Bank looking foolish."

"Crack on."

As he replaced the telephone receiver, Sarah knocked on his office door. He looked up and smiled.

"Sarah. I owe you a bit of an apology. I know I've been a bit self-absorbed the past few weeks and I'm sure I've been grumpy. So – sorry. Have you come to chase me up about going to Jordan?"

She returned the smile and placed his passport on his desk.

"Apology not necessary, but received and I forgive you for whatever you think you might have done. Your Jordanian visa came through. I've got the visit all teed up for next week, so shall I book the flights?"

"Yes, please. That would be good. I …er, need to go for a short walk. I reckon a breath of fresh air might clear my head. I have to think carefully about an opportunity which I came across in Turkey. I was going to fetch a coffee. Do you fancy one?"

"Yes, I do. Thank you, Patrick. A cappuccino, please, with chocolate sprinkles."

He couldn't imagine ever doing that to a cup of decent coffee, but forced himself to smile in a welcoming fashion.

"A cappuccino, it is. I'll be around forty five minutes, I expect."

She headed back to her desk. Patrick checked his mobile telephone still had some charge left.

"Hey!" called Alan Pearson as Patrick strode past his office.

"Coffee run," Patrick explained, over his shoulder. And then he was outside. He really didn't want to be buying his boss coffee to justify absence from his desk.

Once around the corner from his office building, he pulled out the mobile.

"Baxter." She answered on the first ring.

He didn't bother with preliminaries either.

"I have a couple more names for you. There may be a connection to the forced demise of my associate."

"Shoot."

"Kemal Aksoy and Baris Ozturk. Aksoy heads CAV Construction. Ozturk is the Financial Director. The company has just sought a big loan from the Turkish bank where Cem Kaplan worked for a bit. The bank has asked us – me, to help them launch it."

"Do you believe in coincidences, Patrick?"

He chuckled. "I hadn't thought about that, but it would be odd. I mean – what are the chances? But I don't think it's all that coincidental, though. The reason I've connected these dots is that it says in the application they're planning to use a panel system exactly like the one I am pursuing. Royal Counties Bank is a sort of UK partner to Bina Kredi Bank, so it would be natural to come to us."

"I see. You think they've nicked the technology? I'll call you back."

She cut the line. He was going to ask about her father's health, but she was too quick to end the call. He must make sure to get that question in when she came back with whatever information she could dig up."

He strolled off to join the queue at the Starbucks down the street.

One of the machines in the Starbucks had broken down. The poor baristas looked harried. They were having a terrible time keeping up with customer demand. But he bought the coffees and was almost back at his office when his phone vibrated.

"Hello? Patrick Field."

"Patrick, these guys belong to the 'Grey Wolves' – they're Turkish Mafia. You do not want to mess with them either. Moreover, they belong to the Islamic branch of the Grey

Wolves. They're radicals. You have to stay away from them."

"Oh, just great. Why couldn't they be low-level criminals for once?"

"Well not only should Royal Counties Bank keep well clear of them, but you might want a friendly word with your Turkish bank friends to watch their step also. It's up to them, of course, but Aksoy and Ozturk are very bad news. There's an international arrest warrant out for them. It's that bad."

"Before I forget, Penny, I wanted to ask after your father? You were a bit concerned about him when we spoke before? Remember? About the Arifs..?"

"Penny?"

"I was closing my door. I'll give you an update when we get together next. Perhaps you could treat me to another of those steak sandwiches?"

"Oh – sure. That would be super. I don't have my diary right now but how about we say tomorrow evening? Around six, maybe? If that's ok, let's pencil it in and I'll call if I'm booked elsewhere."

"Done."

"I do hope he's on the mend ...Penny?" But she'd rung off.

That girl was living such a stressful life, he thought. Her clipped delivery was even more abrupt than usual. She must be really worried about the man. He tucked the phone back into his pocket. It always spoiled the hang of his jacket. He ought to buy one of those holders which clipped onto his trouser belt, like his Lebanese friend Camille had. He always looked sharp and smart, even when not wearing his suit jacket. Patrick's suits generally had braces rather than belts to hold up the trousers. 'Suspenders', as his American colleagues had it. Maybe there was a model of holder which fastened to the braces buttons. For the moment, he'd have to put up with the pocket sagging.

"Thank you, Patrick. Ooh – just what I need – and extra sprinkles if I'm not mistaken?" Sarah grinned up at him.

"That's right. The barista had a twitch."

She giggled. Patrick went to see what was to be done about a trip to Jordan. Could he come back via Turkey..? As Istanbul boasted it was the 'Gateway to Europe', it ought to be possible. He thought for a few minutes. Was this as stupid as it sounded? Would Royal Counties Bank think it odd if he, a relationship manager for banks, went to visit a corporate in Turkey? Well, they would, but he could always claim he was visiting other Turkish banks to assess how much of the underlying risk they'd buy if Royal Counties Bank underwrote the whole deal for Bina Kredi. It would need careful handling with Alan Pearson, who always seemed suspicious of Patrick's motives.

'He's just jealous', Patrick told himself.

-----//-----

"I'm going to miss The Lamb," he sighed, entering Leadenhall Market from Gracechurch Street the next evening. He strode past the New Moon pub which was right on the corner. For some reason he'd never bothered to work out, he had no desire to try it. The pub looked fine from the outside. Probably they sold decent beer. Their failure to attract him inside was caused by the lure of The Lamb, a few steps further in, at the cross roads.

Patrick was contemplating how his life might be if ...*when* the building panel business took off. Maybe he'd have to move house to be nearer the factory. Not too near, obviously. But it was unlikely he'd be travelling up to London every day, especially to the City. This was like the Finance Souk of London. There was also the West End, which was where most of the cultural or artistic stuff went on. Likely some financial businesses too, but he believed real money travelled through the City of London. The City handled the business of money.

Time to begin to play the game he and Penny always played when they were meeting up. He scanned all the pedestrians, men and women. Her range of disguises could achieve either with the flick of a scarf. He'd never yet spotted the woman before she wanted to be seen. But, like playing squash against his best friend, Barney, being eight nil down didn't stop him trying to win just once.

Alas, he went all the way up the stairs to the non-Smoking bar before he spotted her. And it was clear she had seen him first. She was looking right at him. At least she'd bagged his favourite table near the window.

She scanned the room as he approached. Then, as he got almost close enough - just before opening his mouth to greet her, she gave an almost imperceptible shake of her head.

He stopped in his tracks. She was still looking directly at him but the corners of her mouth were turned down. There was no welcoming smile of recognition.

To defuse the obvious awkwardness of his actions, he crouched to retie his shoe lace. He could see her left hand below the table. It was waving in a dismissive manner. She wanted him to go away. She was cancelling the meet!

This was scaring him. What should he do? He straightened up. How could he confirm this?

"Excuse me? Is that seat taken?" he asked her.

"I'm afraid I'm reserving it for someone. Sorry," she said. It was clear she didn't want anyone to think she knew him.

Jesus. What should he do? They'd have to rearrange the meeting. Why was she behaving like this? She must be in danger of some sort.

"Um, could I buy you a drink while you wait?"

Alarm flashed across her face. But then she understood the opportunity he was giving her. Her face cleared. "You are very kind. I'd like another port, please."

"I'll be right back."

Penny didn't drink port. What was she trying to tell him? Did it have a meaning or was it just a throwaway drink she made up on the spot? They'd never discussed what he knew was called 'Tradecraft'. Techniques and methods used by spies to communicate with each other in a surreptitious manner. Might 'another port' mean 'another meeting place'?

He reversed and went to the bar.

"Yes, Sir. Nice to see you again. A pint of Ordinary?"

"That would be grand. Thank you. And may I have a small port as well, please?"

"Ooh? Who is the lucky lady?" the bar girl teased.

He grinned back at her, hoping his nervousness would come across as embarrassment that he'd just met a girl he fancied.

"I don't know her name yet, but she's over by the window – blond hair?"

The mischievous look on the bar girl's face vanished.

"Are you Patrick?"

He nodded. How did she know his name?

"She said you need to go to the New Moon. I think there is someone here who is making her feel uncomfortable and she wanted to meet you there instead."

His head raced. Penny was in some sort of danger. Should he just walk out? He'd just ordered drinks. It would look weird if he left his pint on the bar.

When the girl finished pouring his drink and pushed the glass of port across the counter, he held out a ten pound note.

"She's already paid," the girl said. "I'll take her the port."

"Er, right. Please say, 'Thanks'."

Time for a 'Down-Down', as his mates from the Hash-House Harriers might have said. Fifteen seconds later, his glass was empty. It was a bit of a shame to treat such excellent beer like that, but the occasion demanded swift action.

He didn't turn around again to look at Penny. He headed for the stairs down to the market and out to the New Moon. How funny that he had mused about that very pub on his way to The Lamb. Some sort of pre-cognition, perhaps?

Chapter 19
Penny is Followed

Ok. Here was the door into the New Moon. A long bar made of polished dark wood stretched all the way to the rear. There were several groups of beer taps, all with the same selection of lagers and ciders. No regular ales – no wonder he hadn't been in here before.

There was a healthy sprinkling of young bankers and insurance clerks to provide cover for him. They probably preferred lager, anyway. He could see some stairs leading downwards at the far end. That was likely a dining area. But he'd better stay up here to catch Penny's eye when she came in. He found a spot inside the door.

"D'ya have Fosters?"

"'Course, mate. Pint?"

"Sure."

He didn't have long to wait. To his astonishment, he actually spotted Penny before she spotted him. This was the first time he could recall doing that. She walked straight past him, eyes searching the bar, and he startled her when he said, "Penny."

But she recovered fast. "Follow me."

She strode the length of the bar and took the stairs he'd spied earlier.

The stairs did lead to a brasserie and at the back there were two doors either side of the little bar. One looked like a store cupboard. The other was a fire escape. She marched over to it and stood, looking back over the heads of the diners.

"What's going on, Penny?"

She looked up at him with wider eyes than he'd seen before.

"I thought I was being watched but now I *know* I'm being followed. I keep seeing a couple of people in places I wouldn't expect. It's the same man and a woman."

"Could they be MI-6 staff practicing?" Patrick hazarded. He had the idea that being a spy was not something you attended a three month course to learn and that was it for the rest of your career. Probably, they'd encourage staff to take refresher courses.

That earned a withering look. "I told you I have narrowed down the *Al Sharika* infiltration to a couple of possible people. But I can't seem to pinpoint the guilty party. Remember, I said I might need your help to do that."

He nodded. That memory was crystal clear. "Of course. Anything I can do to help."

"If you are sure, Patrick. You aren't paid to take these risks – I am."

He couldn't suppress an ironic laugh.

"Alright," she agreed, "I do see. Trouble seems to follow you. It's just that…"

"What?"

"One day you might not be so lucky as you have been so far."

He knew she was right. But it was only fair to point out that she had rescued him from several serious scrapes and he assumed *Al Sharika* was still after him. So they needed to try to help each other.

When he explained that, she said, "Ok. I may have an idea. There's a British Trade Mission to Libya in about a month. If you are ok with it, I can ask Christopher to send you an invitation."

"To Libya?"

She nodded. "I figured it's the home of *Al Sharika* – the Mission will start from Tripoli itself where the movement started all those hundreds of years ago. I don't know what to tell you to do. I guess try to meet with Colonel Ghaddafi and keep your eyes and ears open. It would be like visiting the lion's den. But it might bring things to a head."

He rubbed his chin. She had resumed gazing around the room, her eyes always returning to the stairs coming down at the other end. He reckoned he could swing a trip to Libya – he could fit it into a visit to Turkey, Jordan or Egypt. Then come back via Tunisia and Libya. He'd tell Alan Pearson that he could represent the British Export Credit Guarantee Department and do his best to land a deal to sell equipment to the country.

"How come Sir Christopher can issue the invitation?"

"Unusually, he is leading it. He's not from the Department of Trade and Industry, of course, but they have briefed him and the PM agreed he should go in view of the security situation."

Patrick sipped at his lager. Fosters lager always made him think of his years in the New Hebrides, which was a pleasant memory. But it was also the first place *Al Sharika* had found him and tried to co-opt him into their service. The slightly sweet taste didn't sit well with the Youngs beer he'd downed a few minutes before. He put the glass on the bar top, thinking it wouldn't be so bad if he had to leave it there. Also, having a belly full of gassy beer wasn't great preparation for running or having a street fight.

"Is Jonathan driving you today?"

She nodded.

"Does he know you shifted to the New Moon?"

"No. At least, I don't know if he does. He parked over the road and may have seen me come in here. He's pretty good at this stuff."

That was not hard for Patrick to imagine.

"If these people you think are following you come down here, are you going out through the Fire Exit? I could wait here and delay them if you do."

She thought about that, but said, "I'd rather have you with me. They wouldn't both come down here. One would stay at street level – probably the man – and you can help me more with him. Don't forget, Jonathan will also see them enter this pub if they tracked us. He would recognise them."

"Ok. That's good. Now, the main reason I wanted to get to talk to you without either of us being overheard is that you said your father might have some incurable illness. Do you want to talk to me about that?"

She looked him full in the face and shook her head slightly.

"Sometimes, Patrick Field, for a bright man doing clever investment banking things, you are really, really slow on the uptake." She pursed her lips.

What had he said that was wrong now?

"When I said I was worried my 'father' had a nasty infection, what I meant was that one of the very few people I suspect of being the *Al Sharika* plant in MI-6 is Sir Christopher."

"What?"

"It's ridiculous, I know. Like you said in the coffee shop. But I haven't been able to eliminate him. There are a couple of others too, but it ought to be so easy to cross him off the list. I can't do that. That's why, if you travel around with him, you'll pick up signs or hints if he isn't who he pretends to be." She looked past Patrick at the other end of the bar. Seeing nobody untoward, her gaze returned to him. She spread her hands apart in a gesture of uselessness and shrugged. "It's an awful lot to ask, I know. But I can't think of any other way of clearing him. Sorry, Patrick."

To give himself a moment to think, he gulped more Fosters. And immediately regretted it, remembering his earlier conclusion that lager and running were not comfortable bedfellows.

"I'll do it," someone said. He looked round. There was nobody close by. And when he turned back to Penny it was just in time to receive the closest, warmest hug he'd experienced since saying 'Goodbye' to Jess back in New York.

"Thank you, Patrick. You are mad but I love you for saying that. I'd better get back to Jonathan. Come on."

She dragged him by the hand through the Fire Escape door. His protest that it might be alarmed didn't slow her down one bit. In the event, it wasn't. They rattled up the iron staircase outside and emerged halfway to The Lamb, beside a shop which sold Caviar by the ounce. After a quick scan of the passers-by, Penny led the way towards the sunshine of Gracechurch Street and the shiny government car parked there. Jonathan picked them out immediately and pointed at the New Moon entrance. He was signalling that Penny's pursuers had gone in there.

Patrick shepherded her across the road and into the back of Jonathan's car. It took off, at a brisk pace, running a red light at the junction with Cornhill. He waved, but couldn't see through the tinted windows if she waved back.

-----//-----

Patrick stood on the narrow pavement watching the car disappear into the distance. Somebody bumped his shoulder and brought him back to earth.

"Sorry," he said, automatically. He had been careless to block the whole pavement. He found himself in front of a taller man, red in the face, scowling at him.

"You stupid idiot," the man spat at him. "You got in my way."

"Well, I'm sorry for occupying part of the earth you consider to belong exclusively to you," Patrick replied, his anger rising faster than normal following his recent exposure to spies and spying.

"Piss off," the man bellowed. "You just cost me…"

He stopped, part way through his accusation, realising he might be saying more than he should.

Sensing this, Patrick stepped forward. "Cost you, what?"

"Nothing." Like a punctured balloon, the ruddy-faced lout subsided and turned away.

"No, I mean it. What did I cost you?"

"Get away from me." And the fellow broke into a run.

Was this one of the people who had been following Penny? Patrick knew he'd recognise him again. He had quite a distinctive face, complete with five o'clock shadow, ill-kempt brown hair and bland jacket and trousers. Not a City Gent at all. There was an intensity in his eyes which

Patrick found unsettling. Yes, he'd remember this man alright.

Chapter 20
The Grey Wolves

"Alan? Have you got a minute?"

Patrick's boss looked at him with suspicion. He was used to Field avoiding him unless there were expenses to claim or it was time to negotiate his annual bonus.

"What do you want?"

"I've been offered a chance to join a UK Trade Mission to Libya. They know I speak enough Arabic to get by and I can pair it with a visit to Tunisia. As you know, that's the only way to get into Libya, but nobody has visited the Tunis banks for months and it would be great experience for Daniella."

"You reckon she'd be alright going to Libya?"

"Oh, no. No, that wouldn't be necessary and anyway, there's only one invitation to join the Mission. It was issued personally to me."

Pearson made a sort of harrumphing noise. He was always displeased when one of his staff was lauded and he couldn't bask in reflected glory.

"You'd better make it worthwhile. Go there via, I dunno …Turkey or Egypt or somewhere. Shouldn't you be chasing up that syndicated loan opportunity in Turkey?"

Patrick couldn't believe his ears. "Oh, right. Yes, of course, Alan. Good thinking."

Pearson stared at Patrick's back, trotting away towards his own office. He had an uncomfortable feeling in his water that Field had got one over on him, but he couldn't think what.

-----//-----

"Sarah? Could you join me in my office?"

She noted the wide grin splitting her boss' face.

"You seem especially happy. What's brought this on?"

"I'm going to Turkey. Well, and other places too. But just now I very much wanted to go to Turkey and couldn't think of an excuse to go again so soon. Alan just gave me one. Isn't it great?"

"Er, I suppose so. Is it that good?"

Patrick paused. He could trust Sarah with all sorts of information. He was certain it would go no further. But there was nothing to be gained by taking her into his confidence now. He'd bring her up to speed one day about the Turkish men who'd killed Cem and tried to steal the panel technology – but not today.

"I guess I always enjoy Turkish food. Listen – I've been invited to go on a Government Trade Mission to Tripoli, and I want to call on Turkey and Jordan on the way. And then Tunisia, of course. So I'll need flights and accommodation in the first three. Could you arrange for Daniella to meet me in Tunis? It'll be good experience for her and help me with the rapid-fire French they speak there."

"What dates are you going?"

"It'll all pivot around the Libyan visit. I'll give you the invitation when it arrives. It'll be next month some time."

"Ok. So – nothing to do yet?"

"Nope." He rubbed his hands together. "I'm looking forward to this."

-----//-----

There were several Turkish banks for Patrick to visit, but he started with Bina Kredi Bank. This time, his meeting with Mert Mungan, their Chief Dealer, would be short. More of a courtesy, really. Spending more time with some of their corporate officers would be valuable background, especially the one responsible for the new construction company wanting to use LaDaJ's panel technology.

"I'm here to see Kaan Yildiz, please."

"And your name, Sir?"

He gave it.

"Please wait here for a moment. Mr Yildiz is expecting you."

Two minutes later, a tall and wide, older man appeared, smoothing his hair and tugging at his jacket sleeves. They introduced themselves and he ushered Patrick into a small meeting room. Patrick couldn't help but notice the way the man moved – his thighs were especially thick and caused him to waddle as each moved past the other. His jacket was not small, yet his arms and chest filled out the garment – there was no hope of fastening it at the front. Yildiz looked like a body-builder gone to seed.

The receptionist reappeared shortly afterwards to offer drinks. Patrick asked for Turkish coffee with a little sugar. Stuck in London for a while, he'd been missing this little luxury.

"Mr Mungan approached me recently with a general request for my bank to join with you in launching a syndicated loan for CAV Construction. I am pleased to say we view this opportunity positively. That is why I have come to build up our knowledge of your customer and learn how they intend to use the money."

"Ah, yes. Good, good. They are very good customer. We know them for many years."

"Many years? I thought they were a new company. Were they not formed especially to bring this new building technology to Turkey?"

"Yes, yes. That is right."

"But even though they are new, you have known them for years?"

"Yes."

"I do not understand. When did you first get to know the company?"

"We know Kemal Aksoy and Baris Ozturk for long time. CAV is Kemal's latest company."

"Alright. I see. Has Mr Aksoy had banking business with Bina Kredi before?"

"I do not know. Perhaps."

This was not proceeding as Patrick had hoped. The man was supposed to be the new company's corporate officer at the bank. It was odd indeed if he wasn't able to share information about the most important man in the customer company.

"Mr Yildiz, I'm sure any participants in the syndicated loan will expect Bina Kredi and Royal Counties Bank to have performed at least minimal due diligence on the beneficiary of the loan proceeds. At least we will need to tell them if the man has repaid loans before."

"Mr Aksoy is very wealthy."

"Excellent. I'm pleased to hear that. Has he put capital into CAV Construction? The syndicate will expect him to share the risk with them."

"Yes. Many capital. All is shown in their accounts."

This was better. Patrick or a corporate colleague would be able to look through the accounts to assist their credit assessment.

"Ah, good. May I have a copy, please?"

"I do not have it."

Patrick could almost feel Alan Pearson sitting on his shoulder and telling him to walk away. It all sounded bad. Was Bina Kredi seriously asking Royal Counties Bank to underwrite and sell on a loan to a company which they themselves didn't know? Not only was this making the syndicated loan impossible to do, it was a black mark against Bina Kredi Bank. Until now, he'd considered them a little racy, but basically sound. This was turning into a visit to the local betting shop, but with millions of dollars at stake.

"Does anyone here know the company well enough to talk me through their figures, their management competence, their potential customer sales leads and …er, their building methods?"

"I am their account officer. I am responsible for everything. I know everything about CAV Construction."

"But you don't have their accounts?"

The man shook his head. What to do?

"Could you introduce me to Mr Aksoy and …" Patrick checked his notes, "Mr Ozturk?"

"Of course. Are you sure you want to meet them?"

"Yes, of course." Why would a lending banker not want to meet his client? This was becoming stranger by the minute. "How long have you worked at Bina Kredi?"

"I am new since three month."

"I see. And where did you work before?"

"Many place. I do many things."

"Right. Thank you very much. How might I meet Mr Aksoy and Mr Ozturk? Do they live in Istanbul?"

"I show you." By creasing his mouth into a smile, Kaan Yildiz showed he was pleased. Here was something he could do. Patrick was beginning to suspect it would be something which would please the seniors at CAV Construction more than his bank.

"I would welcome that. Thank you very much, Mr Yildiz."

"You call me Kaan."

"Ok. Kaan it is. Thank you. And you should call me Patrick."

The big man banged the flat of his hand down on the table and gave a short, barking laugh. Patrick's empty coffee cup spun in a small circle and settled again, the right way up.

"We drink Raki together. Then friend for life."

The violence accompanying this offer of friendship suggested it might be conditional in some way, but Patrick produced the expected grin and held out his hand to show acceptance.

The physical interaction which then proceeded was less a hand shake and more a hand mashing. Yildiz had the grip of a steam hammer.

Afterwards, Patrick flopped back in his meeting room chair, massaging his bruised knuckles under the table. Meanwhile, Yildiz contrived to dial a number on a tiny mobile phone. He used his pinky finger to press the buttons. All the other fingers were the size of bananas and quite useless for such precision work.

His call went through. There followed a lengthy exchange in Turkish conducted at such volume it crossed Patrick's mind that the parties would hear each other just by listening at the window. The help of the telephone was really not necessary. At last the call ended.

"We go," thundered Yildiz.

"What, now?"

Patrick's host was already stomping towards the door. "Come."

He collected his things, bundled them into his briefcase and trotted after the man. When in Rome…

As they emerged from the front doors of the institution, a taxi appeared and Yildiz waved at it. Patrick climbed into the back seat, viewing the plasticised upholstery with distaste. What messes had been wiped from it over the years? The assorted smells produced by its springs taking his weight suggested a range of organic origins imperfectly masked by Essence of …Something Else.

Patrick could not see much out of the front, partly because he had sunk a long way into the seat. The shoulders and neck of his host blocked the view. The man occupied fully half of the taxi's front seat and spilled over towards the driver. His terse instruction was to take them to one of the entrances to the *Kapalıçarşı* or Grand Bazaar. This extraordinary building, started in 1456 by order of Sultan Mehmet II, has survived many fires and earthquakes. Patrick had wandered through it and made a few purchases during previous visits to Istanbul. It is vast. But its sixty passageways split into areas for different products, bringing order to the bewildering array of produce.

Instead of entering the market itself, he was disappointed to find Yildiz headed for a small restaurant close to the entrance. The man squeezed through the doorway. The restaurant owner welcomed his outsized guest with genuine joy. 'Perhaps,' thought Patrick, 'he expected to serve a significant amount of food and drink. Such a large frame requires many thousands of calories of fuel.'

A table in the middle had been set already with little bowls of melon and cheese. Two men were there already and sat on one side of the table. They stood to welcome Yildiz. Patrick watched as their greeting ritual suggested subservience on the part of the banker. Were these two the principals of CAV Construction?

They shifted their gaze to him. Kaan Yildiz introduced Patrick with a fair attempt at pronouncing his name correctly.

The first man had a darker complexion and curly, black hair going white at the edges. He offered his hand.

"I am Kemal Aksoy. This is Baris Ozturk. He is my money man. Have you brought money for me?"

'Woah, Neddy,' Patrick thought. But he fixed a professional smile to his face and said, "Not yet, Mr Aksoy. Our friends at Bina Kredi Bank asked me to help them raise a syndicated loan for CAV Construction. To do that, we at Royal Counties Bank must work with them to appraise the company, its management and the projects you will undertake to give other bankers a fair view of the credit risk of joining in."

"So you do not have the money?"

"Not yet. But if we work together on this, I believe we will."

"How much do you want?"

"Oh, it's too early to assess the pricing level, Mr Aksoy. We have to perform due diligence first."

"Half a million dollar?"

Patrick shook his head. He wished he spoke some Turkish to be able to describe the information gathering process he was trying to do. The loan would be priced at percentage points over LIBOR – not as an outright dollar sum. Aksoy took his confusion as refusal of his offer.

"Ok. One million dollar. We agree now. You tell Baris account number and we pay today."

It began to dawn on Patrick that Aksoy was offering him a personal bribe to raise the entire sum of two hundred and fifty million dollars. Was this how business was usually conducted in Turkey? Penny needed to hear about this – when he got home.

"Mr Aksoy. You are very generous but I promise you I do not need ...um, financial inducement to structure a loan which will get your business off to the best start. I do this for you free of charge."

Yildiz had looked from one to the other, like a spectator at a tennis match. Now he sensed Aksoy needed time to reappraise the situation. He turned slightly in his chair to attract attention from the restaurant owner. The chair legs gave an ominous squeak. He snapped his fingers.

"Bring Raki."

The owner bowed and scribbled on his note pad. He called to someone at the back with more complex instructions.

A waiter appeared bearing a small tray stacked with an open flask and four narrow tumblers. There was also a tiny jug of water. He placed glasses between the four diners and filled them with the colourless, viscous liquid.

They all reached for a glass, Patrick a second behind the others. He wanted to see what they did. Nobody added water. Had they done so, the liquid would have turned cloudy, earning its nickname of 'Lions milk'. The group proceeded to clink the bottoms of the glasses – not the rims.

"*Shereffay*", they said. ('Cheers'). "*Saligina*" ('To the health') came the response.

And then sipped sparingly at the drinks.

Yildiz smacked his glass down on the table with unnecessary force. But the glass was stout, and the narrow diameter prevented any Raki spilling out.

Patrick guessed that Raki tradition has rules, much like the Arabic coffee ceremony, to promote politeness and to avoid giving offence. He watched his hosts to be able to mimic the movements of the others. He learned later that clinking the bottoms of the glasses indicates you consider the other to be your equal – neither superior nor inferior. And knocking the glass down on the table toasts the honour of a lost or loved one as well. That might explain Kaan Yildiz's treatment of his glass. Not only did they sip, rather than knock back their drinks in one, like you might a shot, he saw that everyone sipped together. They all waited until Aksoy picked up his glass before sipping at their own, confirming him as the leader, the senior one at the table.

The strong taste of aniseed was very much to Patrick's liking. It made him think of Arak from Arabia which he would certainly have mixed with water as it is so strong. Ozturk picked at the melon pieces and indicated Patrick should try some. It was not very sweet but had reached the perfect level of ripeness. He took some cheese too. The man had a pinched face and narrow eyes, making him appear Asiatic. Looking at spread sheets on a computer for too many hours would have the same effect, Patrick reflected.

"Are you married, Patrick?" Ozturk asked. "In Turkey, we say no man is complete without a woman."

The man's fluency in English took Patrick by surprise almost as much as the change of subject.

"What a wise saying. In that case, I am happy to say, I am complete. Although she is English, we met some years ago in the South West Pacific. She is a doctor."

"So," Aksoy continued, "She look after you when sick."

This was an unsubtle attempt to make Patrick feel at home, he thought. But he supposed some headline details of his personal life were fair game for discussion. He needed to inquire quite closely into Aksoy's background and how his earlier business ventures had done. So he nodded and gave a gentle smirk to play along.

"She looks after me in many ways," he responded. "Especially when I am not sick." A raised eyebrow would be enough, he felt, to convey a slight lascivious tone to his words.

He was right. Aksoy and Ozturk broke into wide smiles and Yildiz pounded his back to signify 'We're all lads together, eh?' Patrick made a mental note to keep at arm's length from the man. Prolonged proximity carried a risk of severe bruising. Maybe a cracked rib. Another round of sipping emptied everyone's glasses. The waiter appeared to refill them all. Yildiz jabbered away and he wrote furiously on his pad, then scuttled away towards the kitchen at the back.

"Tell me about your business history, Mr Aksoy. What did you do before founding CAV Construction?"

"Kemal, please, Patrick. Now we drink Raki, we friends." He raised his recharged glass.

"Very well - Kemal. As I understand CAV is a new company, our syndicate will be very interested in how well you have done in previous businesses."

"I have many activities. Some I tell about. Some are …private. I own fuel stations in Istanbul and Marmaris. I do import / export business. And transport."

"Ah, that is interesting, Kemal. What goods do you trade in?"

The man gave a sly smile. "Anything, Patrick. Whatever people want to sell or buy. What do you want to buy?"

"Um, nothing right now, thanks. May I ask how many fuel stations you have?"

"Baris?" Clearly Aksoy didn't know, or maybe wanted to give that impression.

"Thirty seven."

"Have you worked in construction before?"

"Of course. All apartments in one area of Istanbul – all me."

"Is that where your office is?"

"One of them."

"Tell me about the apartment blocks – how did you build them?"

"What do you mean?"

"Most apartments I have seen in Turkey are concrete – reinforced with steel bars. It looks slow. You have to wait for the concrete to dry before adding another storey. And it's heavy and there are lots of earthquakes around here, so I expect you have to dig deep foundations. Doesn't it take a long time to build things?"

"I have new way. I use strong panels."

'Bingo,' thought Patrick. It is them.

"Are the panels made from concrete?"

Aksoy shook his head. "They are new. Light. But very strong. Stronger than concrete."

"The syndicate will be very excited about this," Patrick told him. "Will the panels speed up the process?"

"Very fast. My men say I can do four buildings in the time I used to take for one."

"My goodness. That is impressive. Do you have plans for the factory?"

"Not yet. Do you have my money?"

Patrick smiled. "Not yet. Alright. How are you going to make these panels? Do you have a sample to show me?"

Aksoy scratched the side of his face. There was an old scar there Patrick hadn't noticed before. "I think you good man. I show you."

Aksoy leaned across the table and clinked his glass against Patrick's. The others all responded.

"Now, we eat."

A tray of little dishes of food and a pile of breads appeared. Most of these foods Patrick knew – *hommous, babaghanoush*, slivers of toasted bread with anchovy. All presented with careless insouciance and real artistry.

He could see that Kaan Yildiz was relaxing as time went on. He'd had a suspicion from the start that Yildiz actually worked for Aksoy – that was why he seemed so …unbankerly. Had Aksoy planted him in the bank to progress the loan raising. Did he know Cem Kaplan? Patrick would save that enquiry for later.

More Raki came to the table. Patrick wondered if it would be impolite to ask to mix some water into his drink. These were obviously hardened drinkers, used to putting away quantities of neat alcohol. He wouldn't be able to keep up at this rate.

"Excuse me, Kemal. I am needing the bathroom."

Aksoy gestured with his head towards the rear of the restaurant. It was Patrick's plan to ask for a drink of water as he passed the kitchen. Then he could continue to drink the neat Raki – for a while, at least.

He walked past the tiled walls with their swirling blue patterns and went up to the server.

"Where is Bathroom?"

The man removed his white paper hat, wiped his brow and pointed at the nearest door.

"Could I have a drink of water, please?"

The server's face clouded in doubt.

"Water?"

"Ah."

The man turned and found a jug beneath the working counter. He filled it from the tap. Patrick realised he must think the request was for water to wash himself. Mentally, he shrugged. It was probably not potable water, but would have to do. A few more glasses of neat Raki would kill off any bugs.

He returned the empty jug on his way back to the table. He found a large white plate in his place. It had already been piled with several kinds of fish and rice and beans. There was another round of sipping. It would be fair to describe the style of eating of these three men as 'enthusiastic', with Yildiz leading the way.

His face was flushed and shiny as he shovelled food into his mouth. Yes, the combination of Raki and what he felt to be imminent success of his money-raising task was putting Yildiz into a very good mood.

Patrick was sure that his own cheeks would be flushed, betraying the quantity of Raki he'd consumed. Was it three glasses now, or four? But the food would help him remain sober enough to keep out of trouble. He hoped…

Aksoy called for, "Sweets." The plates and their food remains were swept away. The waiter replaced them with more little dishes, this time of sweetmeats. Sticky Turkish Delight of several flavours and halva with pistachio nuts.

Patrick was almost in his element - wonderful food, delicious alcohol, served in a restaurant frequented by locals. Almost. Except that he was unable to relax mentally. It was easy to appear comfortable with his hosts, to pay attention when they spoke, to laugh in the right places, to nod and clap his hands in delight when appropriate. But in his head, he was on edge. These were dangerous people. Penny had warned him they belonged to the Grey Wolves. It was an ultra-right wing organisation established in the late 1960s, dedicated to bringing back what they considered to be the True Turkey. Anything or anyone viewed as leftist or liberal had to be removed, with violence if that was easiest. Were Aksoy and Ozturk likely to resort to violence if he crossed them? He didn't want to find out. But he did want to discover how advanced was their knowledge of LaDaj's panel building system. And how likely was it that they could bring it to fruition? He had to play along.

There was a final round of sipping Raki before the server was told to bring Turkish coffee for everyone.

Patrick didn't see anyone pay for their meal. Perhaps Aksoy owned this restaurant too.

They headed outside and boarded a dusty Mercedes saloon car. Fortunately, Yildiz went to the front seat and Patrick found himself astride the transmission tunnel at the rear. Baris Ozturk had something hard under his jacket. It was digging into Patrick's kidneys. He hoped the site he was to see was close, so it wouldn't be for long.

The driver seemed to know exactly where to go without further instruction. He accelerated into the flow of traffic, merging between two trucks. Patrick admitted to himself that his seating position was uncomfortable, but at least he was far from the doors of the car. Just as in Cairo, traffic was heavy, yet moved along at a passable rate. All the vehicles maintained a gap of no more than a foot or two. But he thought them uncomfortably close, all the same.

Turkish drivers would laugh at the British Highway Code. It compels drivers to leave plenty of braking distance between themselves and the vehicle in front. Cars were close together at the sides, too. Nobody could have opened a door enough to get out. Yet he saw few vehicles which had dents. Most looked to be in decent condition.

To his amazement, they were often overtaken by small-capacity off-road motor bikes. The riders seemed to have a death wish as they passed within inches of the door handles. Unafraid of the narrow spaces between cars and trucks, they would buzz along, weaving through the traffic, always keeping on the move.

It took Patrick around ten minutes for his brain to acclimatise to this blizzard of sensory input. And then, it became normal. All the windows of the car were wound down. This exposed the occupants to widely varying clouds of smell – thick diesel fumes from ancient trucks, wafted perfume from a female motorcyclist or Oleander trees hanging over the roadside; leather from a shop selling waistcoats and over-coats.

Nobody spoke during the drive. After a bit, this struck him as odd. Why wouldn't a Turk comment on or point out features of his home town as they passed by? And there were several notable monuments and features – Patrick spotted the Ozturk Carpet store just a couple of minutes into their journey. Was this one of Baris' personal investments? There were several mosques which looked very old. The men would know Patrick wasn't Moslem, but still – these were important buildings of which any native of Istanbul would be proud.

Patrick decided to break the conversational silence by asking some questions. He was about to open his mouth to ask Baris if the carpet shop owner was any relation. But there was too much noise. Two motorbikes drew level with the rear doors of their car as they wriggled through the traffic. They swayed more than usual, having pillion passengers, making them top-heavy.

All the other bikes had sped onwards without delay. Although Patrick could see gaps ahead, the riders weren't taking advantage of them. The bike engines were far too loud, revving repeatedly. Nobody would hear a word he said.

The pillion rider on the left looked directly at him. He could appreciate someone who enjoyed the thrill of riding in such a dangerous environment. He rather thought it was a woman, riding side-saddle. But he couldn't tell for sure. She was wearing a bulky biker jacket and helmet. He smiled back.

In slow motion, she drew a pistol from inside her jacket. She steadied her aim and fired two shots through the open window at Baris Ozturk. Patrick felt Ozturk jerk violently and there was a blow on his own forearm. The pillion nodded to him and tapped her rider on the shoulder. At that signal, he revved up and raced off.

The riders on the right did exactly the same. Their simultaneous shots were for Kemal Aksoy. He slumped forwards and then backwards again as the car driver stabbed the accelerator pedal. The car leaped forwards, but only a few yards because the traffic was too solid.

Both bikes buzzed away into the distance. Now, the driver braked hard and slewed sideways. Kaan Yildiz was doing his best to turn around to assess what had happened, but his bulk would not permit that. They lurched to a halt in the middle of the five-lane street. Car horns blared. A truck ground by them in low gear, filling the interior of their Mercedes with foul exhaust fumes. Someone was yelling.

Patrick realised that he was doing the yelling and closed his mouth. His face was wet. He looked down and saw his coat and trousers were covered with blood and specks of white matter. His left arm ached.

The driver turned off the engine, opened his door and sprinted away through the traffic.

For some incongruous reason, some famous words uttered by Oliver Hardy to Stan Laurel floated up into Patrick's brain. "Well, here's another nice mess you've gotten me into."

He didn't say them out loud, though. He thought it unlikely that the only other living occupant of the car would recognise them, far less see the humour in it.

"Kaan? I think we might have need of the Police. Do you know how we can contact them?"

There was a sort of 'Harrumph' noise from the front seat.

"Kaan – the Police?"

This produced no movement or action. Patrick was trapped between two very dead people but reached across Ozturk to push his door open. He shoved at the inert body. It flopped out of the seat and onto the road like an unwanted teddy bear. There was screaming from a woman inside a passing car which had nearly taken off his door as it drove by. Patrick got out into the traffic, seized Ozturk and bundled him back inside without ceremony. His plan was to try to restart the car and at least drive it to the side of the road and out of the way. He realised he'd be disturbing the crime scene, but he had a feeling that wouldn't matter very much to the Turkish Police.

He slid into the driver's position. The keys were still in the ignition! Praise be... The starter motor churned and the engine burst into life. Yildiz watched, aghast, as Patrick did this, but said nothing. Did sudden shock always strike people dumb?

Selecting Drive made the car creep forward. He put down the indicator stalk to try to move to the left side of the road. Unlike in the UK, nobody understood what he wanted. Nobody gave way to let him through. He stuck his blood-spattered arm out of the window, wondering why it hurt so much. A car pulled up right beside him, very close. The front seat passenger looked with horror at Patrick's hand. Blood was flowing from it in a steady stream. A little splashed on to the other car as he continued to signal left.

The passenger shouted at his driver. They jerked backwards, making room for Patrick to cross in front.

The big wheels of the Mercedes mounted the rough stone kerb without difficulty. He parked up and killed the engine. Yildiz hadn't moved and showed no sign of doing so. Patrick hurried into the nearest shop intending to ask someone to call the Police. Various brass ornaments and kelim carpets hung from the ceiling and the walls. The counter at the far end sheltered two older folks, sitting on stools and drinking coffee. They looked up as a sprung bell over the door announced Patrick's arrival. But their welcoming smiles turned to revulsion as their gore-streaked customer approached. The man had got up, clasping his painful back. He intended to lead Patrick towards the most expensive of their wares. But without meaning to, he stepped backwards, away from the walking horror show. He raised one hand as though warding it off.

"Could you call the Police, please?" Patrick began. "There has been an attack on the car I was in."

Frozen indecision turned to frantic action on the part of the old woman behind the counter. She grabbed her telephone, dialled and began yelling at someone. From outside, a siren started up.

"Ah, that may be them now," Patrick told her. He turned and headed back outside. Rounding a bend in the distance, flashing blue lights shone from the top of a white van. It twisted and turned through the river of traffic, the whooping siren growing louder by the second. Shortly, the blue stripe around it was visible with the word 'Polis' in the centre.

"This is the police – thank you anyway," Patrick said and raised one hand in a part wave. He found himself unable to walk in a straight line back to the Mercedes and leaned on its boot to stay upright. Suddenly, he was light-headed and feeling faint.

And that was the last he remembered for a while.

Patrick came to with a Turkish policeman kneeling beside him slapping his face and shouting. He raised a protective hand to try to stop the onslaught. This evidence of consciousness satisfied the policeman. He rose and went back to the Mercedes mortuary.

Rolling sideways and manoeuvring himself into a kneeling position was Patrick's way of getting up slowly. The world began to rotate again, so he lowered his head to the ground and breathed deeply. He was kneeling in a pool of blood. The thought crossed his mind that his dry-cleaner was going to be very cross, but then he saw he'd torn his trousers as well. Probably they wouldn't be worth cleaning, even if mended.

There was another siren going. Patrick only noticed it when it cut off abruptly. It was an ambulance. The medics onboard tumbled out in a hurry and checked the occupants of the car. Then moved on to helping Kaan Yildiz to walk over to the back of their vehicle. One sat him down and gave him tea. The other came to Patrick and checked his vital signs. They removed his jacket revealing a bullet wound in the fleshy part of his forearm. It was obvious that his blood pressure was low, probably due to loss of blood. The man yelled an instruction. His colleague produced a stretcher and together they positioned Patrick on it. A tourniquet was applied and they strapped his arm down to his side.

Just before he was pushed into the ambulance one of the policemen asked in broken English for his contact details. Patrick requested that they telephone his secretary in London so she could cancel the remainder of his trip. But then he felt woozy again. His last conscious memory was relief that he'd not crossed swords with *Al Sharika* for a change – just ordinary, common-or-garden gangsters. Somehow that was comforting. He hoped Jess and Penny would agree.

He woke up in the Kolan International Hospital. Their Accident and Emergency Department was heaving with broken people. Some were in wheelchairs, some hobbling or using crutches.

Patrick stubbornly refused a wheelchair when it was offered. He did accept their drinks of water, though. And stayed seated until he was called to see a junior doctor. Lacking any English, she communicated what she wanted him to do using pantomime. It was successful, and he ended up laying on a trolley with his injured arm on a stand beside. She pulled a powerful light over to shine on his wound.

He began to feel a little like a patient visiting the dentist. The white-coated dentist looms over you, asking questions about your health, your holiday plans and so on. But you cannot answer – there are too many sharp objects inside your mouth. Here, he had the freedom to speak, but had no idea what he was being asked.

She removed the temporary bandage put on by the ambulance crew and sprayed his arm from elbow to hand with antiseptic – at least, that was what he assumed. It stung like fury to begin with. But then, he realised his forearm had become numb. He could wiggle his fingers by thinking about it, but couldn't confirm this by feel.

He saw her pick up a probe and begin to dig around in the wound. The spray must have been some sort of local anaesthetic to take away the feeling. Otherwise, he was sure he'd have hit the ceiling, shrieking in pain.

After a few moments, she paused the excavation. He sensed she was tapping the probe on something – a dull knocking sensation communicated itself to his brain. Was this one of the bones in there? The doctor bobbed her head down for a better view, adjusted the light and reached for a pair of over-sized tweezers.

The knocking feeling came again and then she withdrew her tool with a small cry of success. She held a misshapen lump of metal up for their mutual inspection.

"Ha!" she said. It clanged into a metal tray at her side.

"That wasn't supposed to be there, was it?" Patrick inquired. He ought to contribute something to the process.

She smiled in triumph. "This – gun. For you - after."

She thought this was a bullet? It didn't much resemble a bullet.

"You think that is a bullet?"

She nodded and tapped the hand of his injured arm. "You lucky."

Patrick said, "Thank you." But he thought, 'Better lucky than rich.'

To his horror, she began to use a nail brush on the open wound, scrubbing at it to remove every trace of dirt. Of course, despite the tourniquet, the wound was bleeding all the time, so the brush had to be alternated with dabs from a wadded-up dressing.

At last she seemed satisfied and anointed the gash with some kind of beige paste. A needle and thread closed the sides of the wound and then several plasticised stitches finished the job. A nurse took over to fix a dressing on top with several turns of surgical tape.

The older woman fixed him with a stare. "No water," she said, a stern expression on her face, wagging her finger for emphasis and tapping his wrist. "No water."

He mimed drinking.

She shook her head. Then waved her hands in the air to imitate showering.

"Ah! I understand. No showering. I must not get the dressing wet," he confirmed.

The doctor produced a small plastic bag containing the remains of the bullet. She put it into his good hand and squeezed it shut.

"Now you go. Bye, bye."

"Thank you so much," Patrick said, swinging his legs over the side. He tucked the plastic bag into his pocket. Would the Police want the bullet as evidence? They hadn't been keen to take his statement or even talk to him. Perhaps they hoped he would disappear from the scene. As a visiting foreigner, he would complicate any paperwork they had to do.

His mangled and bloody jacket was given back to him in a plastic laundry bag. It still had his wallet and enough local currency to pay a taxi back to his hotel. He would call Sarah from there and rest up before his onward flight. He wondered if he could he claim for a new suit on expenses.

Chapter 21
Amman, Jordan

"Sarah? It's Patrick. You'll never guess what has happened to me."

"Do I get a prize if I'm right?"

"I guess not. It's all a bit complicated, but due to being shot at, I'm not going to be able to finish my visits in Turkey."

"Oh, you should have let me guess. Though I wouldn't have guessed that. Are you alright?"

"My arm has been better, but I'll be ok if I don't lift heavy weights for a while."

"I'll start cancelling your meetings. Shall I rebook your flight home?"

"No. That's alright. I reckon I can carry on with the trip, just not the Turkey bit. To be truthful, it's probably better if I leave Istanbul. I'll go to Jordan and then home."

"That doesn't sound like a wise idea, Patrick."

There was a pause. He heard her say, "It's Patrick. He has to cut short his trip in Istanbul."

There was a loud clunk on the line as the handset was picked up.

"This is Alan. Are you ill? Why are you cutting short your trip?"

"It's a bit of a long story, Alan, but I was in a shooting incident – well, I was a rather close witness. And the Police might want to interview me. A hospital patched up my arm so I'll be fine to go to Jordan. Oh – that syndicated loan you reminded me about? The principals of the borrowing company are dead. It won't be proceeding."

"Hmm. Well, go and find another."

He rang off.

There was another call he needed to make. Well, two more. One was to Jess in New York. He ought to tell her that he was fine. But then he'd have to explain what had made him possibly *not* fine and finding the words to say he'd been shot, but it was ok – this would not be straightforward.

The other, rather easier call was to Lars.

"Hi, Lars – great news!" Patrick couldn't resist aping the other man's usual telephone greeting. Anyway, it really was great news.

"Gimme the Gospel."

"I found and tracked down the Turkish gangsters who killed Cem and stole our technology."

"Great! How'd you do that?"

"I have my methods, Lars." Patrick was enjoying this. He risked stretching the truth a little. "I had them shot. They won't bother us again. The way is clear to develop our building system."

"Say, wha'?"

"I said the way is clear."

"Yuh, I caught that. It was the other bit – about having them shot."

"Oh, don't worry about that, Lars. They were very Bad Hats. Ever heard of the Grey Wolves?"

"Sure." Patrick knew this was untrue, but pressed on anyway.

"Well, one was the leader and the other was the money man. I got away and am heading for Jordan. See you when I get back. Take care."

As Patrick replaced the handset, he heard the beginnings of Lars' badgering for details. He smiled at the telephone, sitting there - mute - on the room's desk. Later on, he'd need to deflect and dodge all sorts of subtle and not so subtle digging by Lars into what, exactly, had happened. He'd tell Jerry chapter and verse – it would go no further and he was sure Jerry had been in many more dangerous firefights. But then his smile faded. He still had to bring Jess up to speed.

In the event, and somewhat to his relief, Jess didn't answer when he called. He left a message on her voicemail. He didn't mention anything about getting shot. Better to wait until they were together before explaining one of the bullets which hit Baris Ozturk had gone straight through him and grazed his forearm. Jess could check him out, examine the stitching and give a professional opinion of the medical competence of the Turkish doctor.

Patrick thought he'd reward himself with a decent dinner and a couple of Efes beers. The nurse hadn't said anything about not drinking alcohol.

-----//-----

The next morning, he caught a flight south to the Hashemite Kingdom of Jordan. He felt honoured to have Bank Arabia as a client. It had been founded before World War 2 in Jerusalem, but was now head quartered in Amman.

In fact, Patrick had inherited the institution from a colleague. In truth, the relationship came about between the two banks because of historical closeness rather than the personality and skill of the current Royal Counties Bank account manager.

When the British Mandate Authority withdrew from Palestine in 1948, Bank Arabia lost its branches in Jafa and Haifa. Customers forced to leave the country asked for their deposits, Bank Arabia paid out in full, initiating a reputation for customer loyalty which continues to this day. Later civil disturbances caused the Nablus, Palestine branch of Bank Arabia great difficulty. On a previous visit, the current bank chairman explained this to Patrick in some detail. For the old man, these events were as clear and real as though they happened yesterday.

One Henry Smythe, a contemporary member of staff at the Royal Counties Bank branch in Nablus, permitted Bank Arabia customers to do their banking operations out of the Royal Counties Bank branch there until all his cash ran out. Memory of this great service and evidence of loyalty between institutions lived on to the present day.

Such 'on-the-spot' credit decisions would never happen now, but gave a clue to how the two banks regarded each other. It put Patrick in the lead to transact several meaningful deals for Bank Arabia over the years which might otherwise have gone to a competitor.

As always, Patrick was invited to lunch with some of the board members. They wanted to sound him out about raising money for an acquisition in Egypt - target undisclosed, but it would be a retail bank with many branches. Patrick thought he knew which one it might be, but there'd be plenty of time to discuss that later. The first order of priority was to talk about how to raise the cash. Issue a bond? Run a syndicated loan? That would be ok for short-term borrowing and be repaid by selling unwanted assets from the target bank, or sell more equity? These were all viable alternatives, with different advantages and disadvantages. The choice might be clear a matter of weeks before going public with the proposed transaction. Patrick and his head office colleagues would need to consider the health of the local stock market (or another if a dual listing might be possible). Also, the types of current holders of stock (individuals or institutional), their appetite for more stock and the bank's desire to broaden the stock-holding base and appetites within the syndicated institutional market and the bond and debt markets generally. Internal discussions back in London would determine what would be most helpful for Bank Arabia. He'd need to establish for how long they needed the money – how sure were they of being able to repay it? What might be their view of the interest rate environment?

It remains a truism that the greatest thing about debt is that one can repay it – and the worst thing is that you *must* repay it. The degree of any doubt about repayment would guide the choice of funding instrument.

On this occasion, a most splendid luncheon was hosted by the Chief Financial Officer but with the Treasurer in attendance. So Patrick did more thinking, listening and talking than eating. He cast rueful glances at his barely-touched plates of delicious food as they were whisked away by smartly-uniformed servers. The time reached half past two. The CFO rose and left Patrick to the Treasurer and several rounds of strong coffee. Which was fortunate, as he was then subjected to heavy-duty quizzing about economics, interest rates, global volatility and the likely reactions of ratings agencies to such a raising.

Head spinning, Patrick retired to his hotel to gather his thoughts and write up some notes. He took the opportunity to swallow several Paracetamol tablets. His arm ached as well. At least it hadn't started bleeding again through his shirt.

Once the notes were done, he changed into casual clothes and went for a walk. A lover of Arabic culture, he always tried to stroll through the old parts of cities he visited. Here, he could feel a little part of history and sense all those whose lives were lived there. Now in Amman, he wandered towards the Roman Theatre, Taha Al-Hashemi Street in the Hashemi Plaza, which once held up to six thousand people. It had been built during the reign of Antonius Pius (138 - 161 CE). Behind the theatre could be found remains of the Temple of Hercules. His brain was exhausted from the meeting. The hike up there would do as adequate aerobic exercise for his body. Besides, the view of the city towards sunset was well worth it.

After eating relatively little at the Bank Arabia lunch, Patrick was hungry for dinner. He ducked into a workers' café when he reached the foot of the slope. He asked for whatever they had in abundance. They brought an over-full plate of freshly-shaved shawarma lamb with pickles, lettuce, breads and yoghourt. He was the only man in western clothes – everyone else wore the workers' *shalwar khameez* or a simple *thobe*. The meal proved filling, and he sat back, permitting himself a modest belch – as was polite in Arabia then. The proprietor asked if he'd like anything more and he realised that hot tea would help him digest all

437

that rich meat. A small boy was sent running down the road to a tea shop, returning with a large glass of steaming, sweet mint tea, leaves bursting from the top. Glorious. Patrick relaxed against the back of the wooden bench. His head was no longer bothered with interest rates and equity percentages – at least for a while.

He would sleep well tonight. Provided another dose of Paracetamol kicked in quickly.

Chapter 22
Where's Penny?

Back in London, he texted Penny to set up a meeting to bring her up to date. She always seemed to enjoy having a beer and maybe a steak sandwich at The Lamb, so that was where he suggested. He leaned up against the walls of the pub and watched people go by. There was lots to report to her. He ran through a little mental checklist to be sure he wouldn't forget anything. He checked his watch for the third time. It wasn't like Penny to be late. He looked carefully around, trying to spot her, knowing she liked exercising her skill at being able to approach him undetected. Her disguises were usually subtle, but effective. Rarely could he see her before she wanted to be seen. And that was despite him knowing that her timing was almost always spot on, so he'd be on heightened alert at the appointed hour. It had become a source of merriment between them.

The slightly bent older woman over the road proceeded on her way without pausing. She had been his prime suspect. But she didn't straighten up and cast a beaming smile his way. He kept an eye on her pained departure in case. But every step into the distance notched down the likelihood that it was Penny.

He cast his gaze elsewhere and lit upon a thin young man, a clerical type, dragging on a cigarette and lounging against the pillar box. Gee. That would be a great disguise if it was her. But he kicked the pillar box, and examined the effect it had on his shoes. He didn't look like Penny, either. Besides, she wasn't a smoker. The young man had glanced up as the older woman plodded by, but didn't find her interesting and resumed contemplation of his shoes.

Where was Penny? Perhaps he'd got the time wrong. He opened his Filofax. Nope. Five o'clock was right. It was now almost a quarter past. She hadn't acknowledged his text from that morning either. The signal in Leadenhall Market was rubbish so perhaps the reply hadn't arrived yet. But she'd never been this late. He turned and went back into the pub.

"Excuse me? Could I use your telephone?"

The bar staff knew him well by now. "Sure. Here you are."

He pulled out Penny's card to double-check her office number and started to dial.

It rang several times. That was unusual, too. He had grown accustomed to her business-like barking of 'Baxter' into the phone when it had barely begun to ring.

Patrick was about to ring off when a soft female voice answered, "Miss Baxter's phone. May I help you?"

"Hello? My name is Patrick Field. I was supposed to meet Penny this afternoon – at five o'clock, actually. And she's normally on time. Do you know if she is still at work? Maybe she has been delayed?"

There was a pause. And then an odd noise on the line. He pressed the receiver closer to his ear. "Hello? Are you still there?"

That odd noise came again. And a distinct sniff, followed by someone blowing their nose.

"I am. I'm sorry. It's just that…"

"What's the matter?" Patrick asked. "Is she alright?"

The woman began to cry. "Noooo," she wailed. "She's ...been taken to hospital."

"What? Which hospital?"

"I can't say. I'm sorry. I've got to go. Sorry..."

"Wait!" Patrick cast around for a way to find out what had happened. "Could you put me through to her driver – er..." He snapped his fingers in frustration. "Yes. Jonathan? I'm – a friend of his."

"Oh. Er. Ok. Just a minute. I don't know... ah. Here it is."

He heard rustling and imagined pages of some internal directory were being turned. He hadn't thought about Penny's driver for ages. How he managed to dredge up the man's name from his memory he couldn't fathom. 'Necessity is the mother of invention', he thought. 'Or something'.

"I'll put you through, although I don't know if he'll be there."

"That's fine. I'd be most grateful. Thanks..."

A melange of electronic noises suggested the transfer was being effected via several goldfish bowls and a drainage pipe.

"This is Jonathan. Who is this?"

"Er, hello. Are you the driver who works with Penny Baxter?"

"Who is this? How did you get my number?"

"It's Patrick Field. You've driven her to various meetings with me but you and I haven't actually met for ages – you dealt with an aggressive bloke outside a pub Penny and I were visiting in Kent several years ago. And then kindly drove me back to Petts Wood."

"Oh yes. I do remember that. How did you get my number?"

"I called Penny's office – we were supposed to meet at the Lamb in Leadenhall Market, as usual. But she hasn't shown up and I'm concerned. The woman who answered the phone said she has been taken to hospital. I couldn't think of any way of finding out where she is other than asking for you. Is she going to be ok?"

"I couldn't say, Sir."

Patrick gripped the phone harder and gazed at the ceiling for inspiration. "Look, I'm really worried about her. Can you at least tell me where she is? Which hospital?"

There was a pause. "I'll meet you, Sir. Can you come to St Thomas Street, by London Bridge Station?"

"Yes. Of course. Give me ..half an hour." Patrick knew that Guys Hospital was right beside London Bridge Station. Was this Jonathan's way of telling him but not telling him her location?

He handed back the telephone to the bar staff and joined the train-bound throng of commuters as they crossed London Bridge. He had always been a fast walker, but now found himself cruising past groups of people, their homeward pace blunted by the day's toil.

How would he find Jonathan, though? He cursed himself for not agreeing exactly where they'd meet. Would Jonathan remember what he looked like? He decided to make for Guys Hospital. He slowed when he passed the Shangri La restaurant on the right and the back of the hospital on the left. He'd have to leave St Thomas Street and turn into a side alleyway to reach the main entrance of Guys.

A tap on his shoulder made him jump. He recognised Jonathan right away.

There was no smile of recognition on the driver's face, though. Just a horny hand extended for a formal handshake.

"Is she in there?" Patrick asked, nodding his head towards the featureless brick building on the left.

"Follow me, Sir." Jonathan turned and strode away along the alleyway. It rejoiced in the name 'Great Maze Pond'. They crossed the main thoroughfare in front of the hospital entrance and went into a news agents. Jonathan led the way through the shop to the very rear and stopped beside the end of a magazine rack. He faced Patrick.

"I have heard Penny talk about you and she trusts you more than most people. I hope she won't object to what I'm about to say."

Patrick opened his mouth, but Jonathan held up his hand and continued.

"She was attacked as she left for work this morning. She reckons a terrorist organisation is after her and, worse, she thinks they have an operative in our agency."

"Jesus."

"It was two weeks ago she said that. I've been driving her everywhere ever since. Today was the first time she was not escorted."

Patrick's mind raced. "Who knew you wouldn't be with her?"

Jonathan smiled, for the first time. But his face had a grim set. "That's just it, Sir. Very few people and I've narrowed down the list of real suspects to …well, three or four. The trouble is, most are not people you'd suspect."

"Go on. Who?"

Jonathan sucked his upper lip. "You understand that this knowledge might endanger you further, Sir?"

"Ok, ok. I understand. Penny had told me that if she was in danger, so was I." He was impatient for the information.

"Alright. Her secretary, who is a fifty eight year old spinster and a couple of the clerical staff in her department. That's all."

"Tell me about them."

"There's not much to tell, really. It's true that one is a Middle East expert, but he has been with us for many years. He's British. Went to SOAS. The other is a management trainee – an Oxbridge graduate. He only joined last year. His father is something in the City."

"SOAS? Is that the School of Oriental and African Studies?"

Jonathan nodded. And then added with that grim smile again, "Sometimes known as the 'School for Spies', I believe."

This wasn't much to go on. And Patrick still didn't know where Penny was being treated and how badly she was injured. Jonathan was being very sparing in what he said.

"Can you tell me what happened to her this morning?"

"She was hit by a car. She was crossing the road to the Tube station."

"That's awful. Poor woman. But it sounds pretty innocent to me." Patrick remembered an occasion when Penny had steered him across a busy street through the moving traffic to get to her favourite bar. She had no fear of London traffic and would weave her way between busses, taxis and messenger cyclists with confidence.

"Not so innocent, Sir. The driver reversed back over her. Then sped away."

Chapter 23
St Thomas'

Patrick stood there, open-mouthed with astonishment. He didn't know what to think. That secondary action put a completely different complexion on the incident. It had surely been deliberate. Could it have been a case of mistaken identity?

"Gosh. That's terrible. But could she have been in the wrong place at the wrong time? I mean – could she have been mistaken for someone else? The true target?"

"She'd found out someone in the office was not who they made out to be. I don't think she was absolutely positive, so couldn't raise an official alert. She didn't tell me who it is. But she shared her overall concerns with me. I was to let her know if anybody was especially curious about where she was, who she was seeing and so on."

Jonathan pursed his lips and gave a slight shake of his head. "They all suspect each other of stuff in '6'. I can't keep up with it."

Patrick puffed out his cheeks.

"Well, we have to do something. I trust her, if that counts for anything. And I'm one of her 'contacts' – if that is the right word. So I kind of feel I ought to look after her – if I can."

Jonathan seemed to be wrestling with his conscience. He looked Patrick square in the face.

"Alright. She could do with a friend right now. They took her there, I think." He jerked his head in the general direction of Guys hospital. "But she isn't allowed visitors. I know. I tried. I'm not family. And there's Plod all over the place."

"Thank you," Patrick said. "'Plod', you say? She has Police protection? Well that's something. Maybe I can make up some story and get to talk to her, or at least check her condition. Um, how can I get in touch with you?"

Jonathan pulled a mobile telephone out of his pocket.

"Penny is the only one who knows this number. Work don't know about it and I sometimes take out the SIM card - if you follow me?"

Patrick didn't like using mobile telephones very much. There was a lot written in newspapers about them causing brain cancer due to excess radio waves close to the users' skull. Because he worked for Royal Counties Bank, they had issued one to him. But often it couldn't get a signal and the battery had a short life. He used a land line whenever he could. But he carried the thing out of habit. He pulled it out now and registered surprise that there was enough charge remaining for him to be able to enter Jonathan's number.

"I've had a thought. If Penny felt herself to be in danger, she would have told her boss, Sir Christopher, wouldn't she?"

"Like I said, Sir, they all suspect each other – that works up and down the seniority ladder. Best ask her, if you can, before bringing him into it."

Sir Christopher Sherrif was a pillar of the establishment, a peer of the realm. For some security reason, Penny had said 'the

PM had given permission' for him to head a UK Trade Mission to Libya next week. As she had suggested also, Patrick received an invitation to join it as well on behalf of Royal Counties Bank. If he needed to approach Sir Christopher, he could do it then.

It was not commonly known that Sherrif ran the UK's Secret Intelligence Service, MI-6, responsible for collection, analysis and dissemination of all foreign intelligence. It was unusual for the UK's top spy to go on a Trade Mission. Perhaps he was going on the Mission to do some information gathering of his own? Patrick didn't know and hadn't given any thought to it since Penny told him. It was unthinkable for the British Government to have appointed a foreign operative in such a sensitive position.

"It would be ridiculous to suspect him," he managed. "The vetting such a person would undergo, the interviews with colleagues, the family history… It's impossible."

Jonathan smirked. "But is it? Think back to some of the most infamous spies in our recent history. Take the Cambridge Five for instance – Burgess, Philby, Maclean,

Blunt, Cairncross – establishment figures, the lot of them. Penny thinks whoever it is, has been hiding in plain sight."

"Ok. I'll tell you how I get on at the hospital."

They shook hands and went their separate ways. Patrick approached the main reception desk.

"Can I help you?"

"Yes, please. I have just found out that my friend, Penelope, was in a road accident and was brought here. I don't know which ward she is on. Can you tell me?"

"Your name, Sir?"

He gave it. And for reasons he didn't understand, pretended Penny's surname 'Baxter' was her married name.

She tapped at her computer.

"She isn't here, Sir. Our A & E Department is at our twin hospital St Thomas' in Westminster Bridge Road. She was admitted there at …nine o'clock this morning. Do you know where that is?"

Patrick scribbled the street directions on the sheet of paper she passed to him. It would take about thirty minutes to walk and maybe half that if he was lucky with a taxi.

He thanked her and jogged out in search of a black cab.

Fortune was with him. He hailed it. Usually, black cabs which are available for hire vanish when it rains. Threatening clouds were now beginning a gentle drizzle – the kind which soaks to the skin any who think 'it's only a short distance – I'll walk'. Without a word, the cabbie clicked off his sign and started the meter. Less than fifteen minutes later, Patrick was put down right where ambulances off-load their patients at St Thomas'. His gaze was drawn to the curious sculpture of two figures reaching towards each other on the building's flyover above. Rain water dripped off their hands. He hurried through the entrance.

A nurse appeared from one side.

"Excuse me? I was sent here by the receptionist at Guys - I understand my, er, sister was admitted this morning after a road accident. Can you tell me how she is?"

"What is the patient's name?"

He told her.

"Wait here, please."

The nurse checked with someone at a desk beside the entrance way. She made a short telephone call. Returning to Patrick, she said, "We are not able to give out information about Mrs Baxter. I cannot confirm or deny that she is here. If you would like to wait for a short while, a Policeman will take your details. Perhaps we will be able to give more information then, Sir."

Patrick persisted. "I would really like to speak with someone who has treated her. I am anxious for news."

"Of course you are, Sir. There is a waiting room through there." She indicated another doorway to the side.

Patrick murmured his thanks. This was very bad. It looked as if he wouldn't be able to talk with her either. He went to the waiting room to think. Then he remembered he had promised to update Jonathan.

There were a couple of other people waiting and he didn't feel comfortable talking to Jonathan out loud. He tapped out a text on his phone. As he was about to send it, someone cleared their throat in a pointed manner and gestured at a sign on the wall above his head. He craned his neck around. It read, 'Mobile Telephones are prohibited'.

He smiled back at the glowering woman. "I'm not calling – just sending a text."

She bristled and for a moment he thought she'd explode. But she subsided, muttering to herself.

-----//-----

Patrick found the artificial lighting inside the hospital somehow draining and claustrophobic. He'd always preferred being outside, even if it was dark. But his chosen career had compelled desk work in an office. Perhaps that was why he was always happy to go travelling in search of customers. His watch told him he'd been in the waiting room for a little over half an hour. His lower back was complaining that thirty minutes was a gross underestimate. The plastic chairs had been shaped to fit some other human being. He wriggled to ease the creeping ache in his core muscles. They protested as though he'd adopted this unnatural position at least two hours before.

The door opened and all eyes swivelled to inspect the new arrival. It was a young man, barely Patrick's age, but sporting blue scrubs, slip-on shoes and a stethoscope.

"Annabelle Cartwright?"

A man in the corner raised his hand and rose.

"Come with me, please."

Patrick subsided back into his chair. Could he continue to pretend to be Penny's brother or cousin or something? He straight away felt a wash of guilt for this imagined deception. More her 'Brother-in-Arms', he told himself to assuage his conscience. This fellow looked like a doctor, not a Policeman.

He found himself rising to follow the two men out into the main reception area again. There was another room next to A & E. The door was labelled 'Relatives'. If he was going to be her brother, he'd better go in there. But it was devoid of people, and the atmosphere was stuffy. It smelt of worry, grief and sadness. Although the chairs and table dated from the 1960s, they appeared to have more cushioning than the plastic bucket he'd been perching on.

Another man opened the door and shuffled in. He too wore scrubs, but lacked the obvious identifying feature of a doctor – a stethoscope. The fellow plopped down into a chair with an audible sigh. He stretched his head one way and then the other, making his neck crack loudly. A plastic pencil case was pulled out of his trousers pocket and a packet of cigarette papers from the other. With practiced ease, the man began rolling a cigarette using tobacco from the zippered case. He repeated this twice more.

"You don't mind, do yer?"

Patrick shook his head. "No. I don't mind."

They stood, facing each other.

"Someone you know in here?"

"Er. Yes. My …sister. Penny Baxter. She was run over by a car."

The man's face creased up sympathetically. "Nasty."

"Apparently there's a Policeman on guard so I can't see her. But I'm really worried that she is badly injured."

The man looked behind him to check they were alone. "I think I know the young woman. I'm a porter here. She came in this morning and I took 'er through. Look – do you smoke?"

Patrick shook his head.

"Never mind. I'm going outside to have one of these. If you want, I might know a bit about her."

Figuring any news about Penny would be better than none, Patrick trailed behind the porter, trying hard not to look as if they were together. They just happened to walk out of A & E at the same time.

"My name's Patrick. What's yours?"

"Don."

They had hesitated at the entrance while Don figured out the wind direction. He strolled a few steps downwind so his smoke wouldn't pollute Reception. He leaned back against the building to shelter from the drizzle, one foot resting on the brickwork. He thumbed his lighter. Patrick guessed this was a favourite spot for Don and other smokers, as there were dozens of squashed cigarette butts on the ground.

"You were there when Penny arrived?" Patrick prompted.

"Uh, huh. She was in a bad way. I took the stretcher off the paramedics and pushed her through to Dr Harrison to be admitted. She was unresponsive at that time and he got me to take her up to the ICU."

"ICU?"

"Yeah. 'Intensive Care Unit'. I went on a break later on and the consultant looking after her said…"

He paused and scratched his head to help him remember the words.

"He said, 'she has a laundry list of contusions and fractures to both femurs and her hip'. That was why she lost so much blood, you see."

"Poor woman. Did the consultant say anything else?"

"Are you sure you don't want one of these?"

Patrick shook his head. Starting to smoke was the very last thing on his mind right now.

"He was explaining to one of the junior doctors that she's got bleeding on the brain. They've stuck 'er on a ventilator trying to stabilise her. She was out of it for some time before the ambulance got her here."

"Christ. Bleeding inside her skull? How can they stop that?" Patrick knew the porter wouldn't have any idea and didn't expect an answer. Don shook his head to convey the gravity of the information he was about to impart.

The fellow took a deep last drag on his rollup and ground it into the dust beneath his heel. He puffed out a final cloud of smoke.

"'E's doing a 'Frankenstein'. 'E's putting a bolt into 'er 'ed to relieve the pressure. That's all I know. I gotta go now."

"Thank you, Don. Um…" The porter was half way to the door.

"Yup?"

"What is a 'bolt'? How long will she be like this? I mean, is there a chance I could speak with her tonight?"

"No idea, Mate. Best you go home, I reckon. She's in good hands. I gotta go," he repeated.

Patrick stood for a moment looking at the sky. Then he walked slowly back inside and into the 'Relatives' room. He flopped onto the nearest Ercol 'Windsor' style chair, not caring about the puff of dust which escaped its sides. For a moment, his mind was blank. He didn't know the extent of Penny's responsibilities. How many other 'Patricks' was she running? Did she have a portfolio of terrorist 'customers', much like he had a list of regional banks in the Middle East and America before that? When it came down to it, he didn't know that much about Penny at all. Did she have a flat in London? Were her parents alive? Where did they live? Gosh – someone ought to tell them their daughter was lying in St Thomas' Hospital in a coma. And why hadn't a Policeman come to question him? Maybe the officer had been told to stick close to the patient.

He clutched his head to stop it bursting with this maelstrom of consequential thoughts. He couldn't ask the hospital if they had contacted her parents – as her 'brother', he would know whether they were alive and he couldn't risk being questioned for their contact details. He'd call Penny's office number again. Or ask Jonathan – yes – that was safer.

In a daze, he left the A&E department and stood outside, close to the unofficial smoking area, sheltering from the insistent drizzle. He dialled Jonathan's private mobile number. It rang twice and then stopped.

Was it an open line? There had not been an answer. Patrick said, "Hello?"

"Yes."

Ah. So Jonathan *had* answered.

"Someone listed off loads of injuries and they are trying to stabilise her. But he thought there would be no change overnight and told me to go home. Does Penny have any family? I mean, are her parents alive? Does she have brothers or sisters? They ought to know where she is."

"I'll pass along the information."

"Are her parents alive?"

"If there's nothing else..?"

"No – wait. I'm sure she wants to keep her life away from work private. She probably has to do that. But …if I'm going to do a passable impression of being her brother, I'll need to know some basic facts."

There was silence for a bit. At last, Jonathan seemed to relent.

"She's an only child. Her parents live in Chalfont St Giles. They run a shoe shop."

When he clammed up, Patrick said, "Thank you, Jonathan. Could you give me their telephone number?"

Realising that he had now opened the metaphorical bag holding the cat of knowledge for Patrick, Jonathan sighed. "Ok. I'll text it to you. Do you want to call them or shall I? You've actually got inside the hospital and spoken to them, even if they didn't tell you much. They know *of* me but I don't have the level of information you do."

"Don't worry. I'll call. I mean, I owe it to Penny to let her parents know what's happening and it'll boost my credentials with the hospital. Thanks, Jonathan."

Patrick's phone went dead. He headed home.

Chapter 24
Mr and Mrs Baxter

His first attempt at calling Penny's parents came to nothing. The telephone number Jonathan had texted him was for the shoe shop. He listened to the answerphone but rang off without leaving any message. The delay was frustrating, but he had to wait until the next morning. He had more success then.

"Baxter's Shoes. May I help you?"

"Yes, Good morning. May I speak to Mr or Mrs Baxter, please?"

"This is Mrs Baxter. How can I help you?"

"My name is Patrick Field. I'm a ...*an associate* of Penny's. I was supposed to meet her for a drink in London last night but she didn't show up. When I telephoned her office I found out she had been in an accident. A car hit her."

There was a gasp.

"Oh, God. I knew she'd get into trouble with all this secret Government stuff she was doing. Is she alright? Where is she?"

"I am told she was admitted to St Thomas' Accident and Emergency at nine o'clock yesterday morning. I think they are doing some sort of operation on her, but I don't know the details, I'm afraid."

He could hear the woman calling for her husband to come to the phone. "Andrew? Andrew – where are you? Penny has had an accident." She came back on the line. "How is she? Is she going to be alright?"

"I'm afraid I don't know any of that, Mrs Baxter. I did go to the hospital last night but nobody would give me any details. I'm not a relative."

"No, no, of course not. Andrew? Leave that. And shut the shop. Yes, shut it. Penny has been hurt."

"Mrs Baxter? I spoke with Penny's driver, Jonathan and learned of her whereabouts from him. He is very protective of your daughter, you know. I'm sure he would welcome any news you are able to find out about her. As would I, of course."

"Do you work with Penny?"

"I suppose so. In a manner of speaking."

Andrew Baxter had arrived at the telephone, so Patrick listened to an abbreviated version of their conversation. The phone was handed over.

"Hello? This is Andrew Baxter. What is your name?"

"I'm Patrick Field. I'm an associate of Penny's. I found out about her car accident quite by chance."

"Yes, yes. We'll get ourselves down there. Did you say St Thomas'?"

Patrick gave them the street address and the hospital's general telephone number. It occurred to him to wonder why Penny's employer hadn't contacted her parents. The hit on Penny, for he was convinced that's what it was, had been carried out twenty four hours ago. Yet nobody from MI-6 had called them. Not her secretary - not her boss, Sir Christopher – nobody from whatever they called 'Personnel'. Was MI-6 so hidebound with security measures that such a simple act of humanity was forbidden?

This impersonal corporate attitude made Patrick cross, he realised.

"Mr Baxter? Would you like me to meet you when you get to London? Perhaps we could have a cup of tea after you've been in to see Penny."

"Yes. Alright. What's your telephone number?"

-----//-----

Patrick waited in the Illy Café, a tiny coffee house on the ground story of an enormous glass-walled building across a busy road from St. Thomas'. Andrew Baxter had promised to call his mobile when they came out of the hospital. He hoped they would have news of Penny's condition. He was dawdling with his second cup when an older couple came to stand outside the shop, looking from side to side as if to make sure this was the only Illy Café.

He rose and went to the doorway.

"Mr and Mrs Baxter?"

The wife spotted him right away.

"You must be Patrick Field."

They all shook hands.

"What news of Penny? The nurse on Reception told me there was a Policeman guarding her and they wouldn't say anything about her condition."

He saw that Mrs Baxter was flushed. As he watched, she extracted a well-used cotton handkerchief from her sleeve and blew her nose. Dabbing at her eyes, she said, "Penny is not at all well. They've kept her in intensive care."

Mr Baxter thought he should take charge. "She is no longer critical, the doctor said, but they have to keep her hooked up to some machines monitoring her condition. She has to have this thing inserted into her skull to check the pressure there."

"Were you able to see her? Could you talk to her?"

They shook their heads. "Dr Harrison came out to talk with us. The poor man looked exhausted. He was very kind, though. They might remove the 'bolt thing' tomorrow, he said."

"Did he say anything else?"

"Not really. Although she kept going on about a 'sofa', he said. Wouldn't shut up about it. Oh yes – it must have been you she meant," Mrs Baxter's eyes gleamed. "The doctor reported she was saying, 'Tell Patrick it's sofas'."

"Sofas? As in chairs with several seating positions?"

They nodded.

This made no sense. But then, she'd had a major knock to her head which will have jumbled all her thoughts. A secret part of him was pleased that the thought which made it into the open from her poor, battered brain was his name. But he didn't say that to her parents. It would have been wrong on several counts.

He asked Mr and Mrs Baxter to let him know if there was any change in her condition.

Dialling Jonathan's secret mobile phone, he relayed as much of this information as he could and promised updates whenever they came. Although the man's response was gruff and abrupt when they said goodbye, Patrick sensed he cared very much for Penny. He must have felt awful that he'd let her out of his sight.

-----//-----

The rest of his week was uneventful. He selected and packed what he thought he'd need for his visit to Libya. The journey would be by aeroplane to Tunis where he could visit some of the Tunisian banks. He'd then join others on the Trade Mission nearer to the Libyan border. After passing through Immigration, the plan was rather looser. In theory, he'd fly to the Tunisian island of Djerba and take a car to their first destination of Tripoli, the capital city.

What seemed like an age ago, Sir Christopher and Penny had briefed Patrick that they believed the current figurehead of *Al Sharika* was Moammar Ghaddafi, President of Libya. In view of the number of times the organisation had tried to kill Patrick, he realised it seemed like the height of madness to go anywhere near Ghaddafi. But maybe going as part of such a prominent group would offer him some protection. He peered at his carefully-folded clothes before clicking the hasps into place. A gun or a big knife would have been handy for protection, but the airlines would discover them and he didn't know how to use them, anyway.

A young, female colleague named Daniella would go with him for the visits in Tunis. Her linguistic skills in Arabic, French and Italian ought to keep Patrick out of trouble. They stemmed from her multi-cultural family background. Born in Cairo to Egyptian and Italian parents, she now lived in London with her boyfriend and two small dogs.

When they met up in the airport Departures lounge, she handed him a sheaf of briefing papers, all updated the night before. He intended to skim read them during the flight and then read each in detail shortly before each visit. Patrick's grasp of French was rusty, at best. His 'O' level school qualification had been adequate for his time in the New Hebrides. The colloquial French he'd picked up there made him sound like a native speaker - which confounded fluent speakers when they lost him before the end of their first rapid-fire return volley. He couldn't yet distinguish formal speech from language of the streets.

Chapter 25
Rebellious Goats

They were received at their first meeting at the Banque de Tunisie by the Head of International, a willowy man in a sharp and shiny suit, with straight, brown hair slicked down to his head. His shoes gleamed, his manners were impeccable, greeting them in the banking hall and ushering them before him into the lift. Exactly two minutes of polite enquiry about their travel experience and chosen hotel segued into the intended meeting purpose. They chatted about foreign exchange trading, deposits and letters of credit. It was a good and fruitful meeting. Then Patrick noted, with mild alarm, that they were almost late for their next appointment. As soon as he could, he interjected, "*On perd du temps ici.*"

The genial smile on the face of the Banque de Tunisie man froze. Daniella went as white as a sheet. Of course, he was trying to say that time had slipped away without their noticing. But by mistake had told their host that he felt they were wasting their time. The mood changed right away. Patrick sensed that something was wrong. Daniella gabbled away to excuse his verbal slip. But the damage was irretrievable. Patrick's excellent accent gave the lie to her claim of his lack of fluency.

A stern secretary shooed them into the lift and glared as they crossed the banking hall to the doors.

Once out in the street, Patrick asked, "What? What did I say?"

Daniella could not restrain her giggles. It was only when they were ensconced on the back seat of their car and on the way to their next destination that she was able to explain.

"Well …I didn't like him anyway. He obviously doesn't have a sense of humour."

That set her off again.

"I'll look forward to seeing your call report of that one." Patrick shuffled his briefing notes to find the next bank. This time, he would try harder to avoid ruining another Royal Counties Bank relationship.

There were four more meetings to get through. He restricted himself to comments in English which Daniella translated, so they passed peaceably enough. When the last one was over, he perked up very much at the thought of dinner. Food in Tunis was always excellent and Daniella was an amusing and interesting companion. Plus, she could enquire delicately of the waiter which items of seafood were actually fresh thus helping Patrick avoid digestive troubles during the night. Tomorrow she would fly back to London and he would take a small aircraft to the island of Djerba, off the Tunisian coast. From there he'd be ferried by car the short distance to the border with Libya. It was not possible to fly direct to Tripoli as the country was under severe trade and travel embargoes. Some of the other participants on the UK Trade Mission were driving the whole way from Tunis. This would take between six and seven hours. He expected to feel a great deal fresher than them on arrival at the overnight accommodation at the Ras Ajdir border crossing.

-----//-----

The border guards had been pre-warned of his arrival and showed him into a typically gaudy, marble-clad room in a building next to the crossing. This, they said with pride, was where Colonel Ghaddafi usually rested until his chauffeur turned up. Through-wall air conditioners laboured to bring the temperature down. They made quiet conversation impossible. Several rounds of tea, coffee and iced water later, his bladder announced that he ought to be using the Colonel's rest room facilities.

"*Wayn al marhad, min fadlak?*" One of the flunkeys showed him the way.

Perhaps because of the importance and personal preference of the regular user of this building, the toilet was western style - not for the Colonel a traditional hole in the concrete floor. There was a shower too, equipped with towels, soap and so on.

When Patrick emerged, there was Sir Christopher Sherrif being treated to his first tray of assorted refreshment.

"Sir Christopher! You have made good time. I didn't expect you for some hours."

The man looked up. "One of the benefits of seniority, Patrick. Was your flight comfortable?"

"Very, thank you."

Hang on. How did the man know Patrick's travel plan? Perhaps he guessed. The arrangement was that participants would make their own way and gather in Al Naher Hotel off Tariq Street near Martyrs' Square and the Old Town in Tripoli. Everyone else was driving the whole way. He hadn't told Penny his flight plan to Djerba – or had he? Maybe she had asked his secretary? This was quite ridiculous. He had to be so careful what he said near Sir Christopher. Maybe he was just over-thinking everything now. Should he even mention that he'd heard about Penny being run over?

"The Colonel is sending his chauffeur to collect us. I expect he will be here soon."

"His own driver? Gosh."

And at that very moment, a squat, moustachioed man in drab, military fatigues came into the room, saluted and addressed Sir Christopher.

"*Salaam aleikum. Minfadlak, sayara kharij, Sidi.*" (I come in peace. If you please, the car is outside, Sir).

"Ah, Abdul-Daim, *aleikum assalaam. Kheiful haal?*" (And peace be to you too, Abdul-Daim. How do you do)?

"*Kheiful haal, inter, Sidi. Ya'allah.*" (How do you do, Sir. Let's go).

Patrick listened in some astonishment. He knew from previous meetings that Sir Christopher had, in his own words, 'knocked around the Arab world a bit'. He might be expected to speak some Arabic. But this exchange was conducted with utter fluency and, Patrick noted, a recognition and recollection of the name of the Colonel's driver.

"Coming?"

"Oh, yes. I'll just pick up my bag."

A dark coloured, dusty Mercedes 450 idled smoothly outside, its air-conditioner humming. Abdul-Daim opened the boot for their luggage and the left side rear door for Sir Christopher. Patrick was left to his own devices. He hefted both their bags into the boot and closed the lid firmly. And then opened his own door. He swung his legs in rapidly because the heavy door was beginning to close under its own weight as the driver planted his foot on the accelerator pedal. They were off.

-----//-----

Despite its age and bulk, the 6.9 litre V-8 Mercedes displayed an astonishing turn of speed. Abdul-Daim liked to steer using one hand; the other held a microphone. Every so often, when an obstacle appeared in front of them, he would yell into it, and loudspeakers transmitted his commands to clear the way. The local citizenry was accustomed to the urgent passage of their Glorious Leader. They would straightaway drive into drainage ditches or scuttle behind date palms so the thundering Mercedes could proceed at greatest speed.

Patrick couldn't help but admire the driver's competence at rounding bends on the dirt roads. He knew the route well and could hold the big car in a controlled power drift, steering with the throttle and using the entire width of the road. All went well until they came around a blind bend and encountered an unusual obstacle. A bent old man with a stick was shepherding his goats across the road. The man was probably deaf. And the goats didn't understand Abdul-Daim's commands to move out of the way 'in the Name of the Glorious Leader'. If they *did* understand, then this was their moment of stubborn rebellion.

We will never know if the goats had become politically active. Abdul-Daim allowed the car to skid further off the track, avoiding the herd of dissident ruminants. Dust clouds billowed around them as he kept his foot in, sawing at the steering wheel with his hand but not dropping the microphone. Patrick opened his mouth to congratulate the man for these lightening reactions and admirable car control. But then he saw they were heading for a berm, a mounded-up hillock, at undiminished velocity. His '*Mahbruk alleic*' was strangled at birth by a plug of viscous fear in his throat. In slow motion, he reached for the grab handle above the passenger door. As his fingers grasped it, the Mercedes reached the berm, diagonally.

The plush, leather seat rose up beneath him; Patrick's head was jolted forwards and down. He wondered why the engine note had risen so much, before the truth dawned - they were flying. Their fate was now in the hands of Allah, as Abdul-Daim's efforts could not control their destiny while airborne.

Happily, there were no further obstacles awaiting the two tonnes of automobile the other side of the berm, not even rebellious ruminants. They returned to earth, still travelling at some sixty miles per hour, with a cushioned bump. Abdul-Daim resumed what passed for control of their direction. With much energetic single-arm action and stabs at the throttle, they slewed back on to the main track to Libya.

Sir Christopher hadn't uttered a sound throughout this off-road adventure. Now he enquired after the driver's health.

"*Eshoanak, inter*?" He might have been asking if the car was alright. Patrick couldn't tell. He was obviously a very cool customer.

"*AlHamdullilah.*"

And with this assurance, Abdul-Daim confirmed that they were unscathed only due to the care of the Almighty.

Patrick tried to calm his breathing and thus his pulse rate. An odd, triumphalist urge rose within him at escaping Death's clutches yet again. But it would be unbecoming to punch the air, as well as awkward, due to the confines of the luxurious passenger compartment.

He decided he would not share this particular detail with Jessica when he got home – if he arrived at all.

Drawing closer to Tripoli, he began to see evidence of agriculture – quite lush agriculture, actually, with neat, well-tended plots on the inland side of the coast road. The trees groaned with fruit – he thought he saw orange and lemon trees – and other fruits too.

"Are those oranges?" he asked Sir Christopher.

"They are. You are in for a treat when we arrive at the hotel."

He did not elaborate. Patrick kept quiet. He liked surprises – pleasant surprises, anyway.

The El Khan Hotel in the Old Town district looked down-at-heel, but its sun-beaten, dusty exterior entrance concealed a most gracious and elegant interior. Cool, tiled floors and soaring columns supported traditional arches. Cushions and sofas lay everywhere for guests to take their ease. It was a very welcome sight for any weary traveller and especially one who had recently come very, very close to meeting his Maker.

Sir Christopher led the way to Reception to check in. Patrick was in no hurry and waited a short distance behind the British Government Grandee. He couldn't help noticing that the entire process was conducted in rapid-fire Arabic. His own knowledge of the language might manage to stumble through provided there were no alternatives offered; no choices to be made. In the event, it turned out that a block booking had been made for members of the Trade Mission. Patrick was given a key at random and pointed towards the stairs. He could manage that just fine.

"Dinner's at seven," Sir Christopher told him. He looked past Patrick's shoulder to one of the arches.

"We'll all gather through there beforehand for drinks." He picked up his bag.

"I need a whisky."

"See you later", Patrick said to his retreating back. Whisky? In Libya? A

Moslem country? Perhaps Sir Christopher had smuggled a bottle in his luggage and would consume it in the privacy of his room.

Chapter 26
The Tour Leader

Patrick was in Room five. The solid wood door squeaked on dry hinges but opened and closed well enough. The room was on an upper level, boasted a small balcony and looked towards Tripoli Port. Someone had propped open the narrow French windows and a gentle sea breeze flapped the thin floor to ceiling curtains. Its salty tang carried a whiff reminding him of the *souk alhoot* (fish market) even though that was some way to the south east. Maybe the day's catch of fish was being unloaded right now. He stood on the tiny concrete balcony with its rusted, ornate wrought iron railing and took several deep, relaxing breaths. Wheeling gulls cried in the distance. Why was this wonderful country so wracked by conflict, internecine wars and political infighting? He knew from conversations with friends in British Gas that Libya's long coast had enormous petrochemical deposits a short distance offshore. There was no reason why the country could not exploit these and be as rich as Saudi Arabia or Kuwait or some of the other Gulf States. If only the population could stop fighting among themselves, they could be wealthy.

But he was part of a Trade Mission hoping to help them achieve some of that. In view of the politics involved, it would be a steep mountain to climb. The itinerary choices for the group included visits to several factories and other sites of interest. One of these would be a steel mill, largely mothballed, north west of Sirte, along the coast. Because of fears that the country would manufacture armaments from steel, countries overseas, including the UK, had embargoed shipments of steel pipes and other materials. Few spares were available in country, therefore, to repair machinery which broke. Perhaps Patrick's group would only achieve an update to UK Government records about the state of economic deprivation of the country.

'But this is defeatist thinking', he scolded himself. He turned around to start to unpack.

On a table at the foot of the bed was a bowl of very large oranges. Zesty scent filled the room as he peeled one. He could tell from the way the peel came off and how the segments separated that the fruit was at its peak of ripeness. It had a glorious taste, juicy and not too sweet. He ate with greed and gave much thought to having a second. Was this the treat Sir Christopher promised them at the hotel? The orange was exceptional. Time would tell.

He checked his watch. If they were all to meet downstairs at seven, he could shower and change and wander down in good time to start to meet the other delegates.

-----//-----

Most of the delegates were from household name British companies. A notable exception was a young man, named Brian, who described himself as an 'Import / Export' specialist. Unlike everyone else, he had paid his own travel fares to get out there. Patrick spotted him loading his pockets with food from the buffet to avoid having to buy dinner later.

Not sure about how to treat this behaviour, Patrick nevertheless engaged him in light discussion.

"Hello. I'm Patrick Field from Royal Counties Bank."

"Brian Wilson. Erm …from Brentwood." He smiled.

"What brings you to Libya, Brian?"

"Dunno yet. But I'll know it when I find it. You?"

"Someone suggested I come along. I s'pose this mission is more for companies wanting to buy and sell stuff. Though I reckon it does no harm for me to understand which companies here can be relied upon, if you get me, and which to run far away from."

"I expected the Government to send some low-level bureaucrat, not Mr Stuffed Shirt Sherrif over there."

Patrick adopted a hurt tone. "I say! You can't mean 'Sir Stuffed Shirt' surely."

"'E's a 'Sir'? Blimey. How do you get that, anyway?

"You should ask him. I'd like to know as well, so let me in on the secret when you find out. Cheers!"

They clinked their glasses of orange juice – freshly-squeezed and chilled orange juice.

"I could do with a beer, meself. But these Moslem lads don't go in for that, do they?"

Patrick shook his head. It crossed his mind to warble on about the well-stocked bars that some wealthy and powerful Arabs enjoyed at home, but that might sound boorish.

"Have you looked through the itinerary? There are some side trips which sound interesting to me, but I'd prefer my boss in London didn't find out about them."

"Like what?"

"Leptis Magna for starters."

"Who's that, when 'e's at home?"

"It's a place. Actually, many of its archaeological remains go back to Phoenician times, but the best-preserved ones are Roman. I am told there are more Roman remains here than in the whole of Italy."

"No!"

"That's what I read."

"Well, well." He took a pull at his drink. "Um, are there – 'artefacts' – lying around, do you know?"

"You mean, pieces of history which you can gather up and sell to collectors?"

"Maybe."

"I doubt it. And I suspect you'd create a diplomatic incident if you were caught trying."

"Bummer."

"Had you thought about selling goods into Libya?"

"Yup. But I like to get paid, so... that's off the table."

"I hear you. It's a shame we can't get their oranges in our supermarkets – did you try one in your room?"

Brian shook his head.

"You should. They're outstanding."

Further conversation was prevented by someone at the front clapping loudly and calling for quiet. Their Libyan governmental 'minder' and someone else 'from Whitehall' introduced Sir Christopher Sherrif.

The Head of MI-6 stepped up onto a raised part of the floor, cleared his throat and let an air of expectancy build for a second or two.

"Welcome to Tripoli, gentlemen. I am glad you have all arrived safely. A selection of visits has been arranged by our hosts to include industrial facilities, some ministers and their government offices and one or two of the larger companies. There will also be opportunities to see some of the cultural riches Libya has to offer, although numbers will be restricted, I'm afraid, due to particular travel restrictions in place for some of them."

He did not explain what these restrictions might be. Nor did he list the cultural centres which featured. Perhaps the organisers were waiting to see what might be the demand before choosing destinations or allocating busses. It was all a bit mysterious, Patrick concluded. But then this was a Trade Mission – not a cultural tour group – and was supposed to focus on business and things economic.

Sir Christopher went on. "There are lists and short descriptions of the various trips on those tables over there." He waved vaguely at the side of the room. "Please put down your name for the visits which interest you and then join us for a buffet dinner at eight in the dining room."

There was a dignified rush towards the visit lists. Patrick hung back, hoping to ask Sir Christopher for advice about the best one to go for, but his quarry made for the dining room. Patrick would have to take whatever was left.

He followed Sir Christopher towards the smell of food and into the dining room. At least he'd have a chance to bag a seat beside the group leader.

"Ah, Patrick. I wanted a quick word with you away from the others."

"Oh? Is there something I can do to help?"

"No. I have arranged a private meeting for you with the Colonel tomorrow. I think it will be more important that you meet him rather than go to any of the ...more public visits."

"Gosh. Well, thank you. That would be quite an honour ...for Royal Counties Bank as well as me, of course. Um..."

"What?"

Patrick lowered his voice. "You and Penny had told me you reckon the Colonel is the current head of *Al Sharika*. Isn't it a bit unwise to go to see him?"

"Oh, no. You'll be with me, remember. You'll be perfectly safe. We'll set off right after breakfast – say, nine o'clock? Meet me in the lobby."

"Righto. Thank you very much. I wanted to ask you about the other visits on offer. Are there any you'd particularly recommend?"

Sir Christopher flashed him a look as though Patrick had asked a loaded question. He had not. He was still trying to comprehend why Sir Christopher had singled him out for the honour of meeting the country's leader. His boss in London would be hugely jealous. Patrick was afraid it would put the man's nose out of joint. His face registered only puzzled innocence and the Head of MI-6 saw that.

"The steel mill at Sirte. Don't bother with the ministers or companies. They'll do what they're told. But the mill is very short of equipment, spares and new machinery. If you can approach Export Credit Guarantee Department to organise a loan facility, I'll pull some strings inside government for the approvals. Do you think you can do that?"

Patrick nodded his head energetically. This would be quite a coup and could earn a lot of money for the bank.

Sir Christopher looked around. Delegates were beginning to file in.

"Not a word to the others, eh?" He tapped the side of his nose.

"Of course. Sure. Not a word."

Chapter 27
The Bab Al Aziziya

Next morning, the driver delivered them to Colonel Ghaddafi's compound, the Bab Al Aziziya, a short distance away from the port. They pulled up in front of a pair of plain iron gates set into the twelve foot high wall.

A smartly-dressed guard stepped up and opened Sir Christopher's door. He stood ramrod straight and saluted as the Mission leader stepped out of the car. Patrick couldn't help noticing he'd gathered his hair in a bun beneath his military cap. But then, looking more closely, as they made their way towards the compound gates, Patrick realised the guard was a woman. Another female guard had remained in the sentry box when her colleague stepped forward to greet them and now stood to attention as well.

This put Patrick off his stride. How was he supposed to behave towards them? Should he say all the traditional Arabic greetings he'd usually employ when entering a room full of men? He realised he hadn't conversed much with Arab women – there hadn't been the need or the occasion. All his carefully memorised greetings and conversational gambits were male gendered. It would need great concentration to get the word pronunciations correct. Perhaps he'd stay quiet and follow Sir Christopher's lead.

The great man strode past the guards as though they didn't exist. One guard fell in three steps behind them and escorted the visitors towards a small buggy resembling a golf cart. The guard waited for them to settle themselves before accelerating towards the main buildings in the distance. They passed between fields and lush lawns edged with white-painted concrete. Patrick pointed out a swimming pool to his companion. He rubbed his eyes. It was about fifty yards away. In the bright sunshine it was hard to be sure, but there appeared to be women in bikini costumes walking beside it.

The buggy swerved left and right between administrative structures and drew up in front of the entrance archway of a two-storey block.

Patrick had half expected the Colonel's residence to be some gaudy palace such as he'd seen in the Arabian Gulf. This building was as plain as the iron gates to the compound. It looked almost military and designed for efficient operation rather than ego boosting.

More female guards stood to attention and led the way inside. It was striking that their behaviour did not include any of the usual modesty required of Arabian women. Even in Bahrain or Cairo, which were more open societies, women would avert their gaze and avoid stepping forward as the centre of attention. But these guards gazed at Patrick openly and without shyness, exactly as any male soldier would have done.

Once again Sir Christopher led the way into the first anteroom. The inevitable round of cardamum coffees got under way almost immediately. They were still settling on the over-stuffed sofas when a teenaged boy in a most colourful costume approached. His orange pantaloons clashed joyfully with his white shirt and scarlet waistcoat. And his toothy smile of welcome was topped by an outsized brown turban. Accepting his second cup of coffee, it hit Patrick that he very much loved this traditional ceremony, performed all over the Arab world. He'd be sad when the time came that he could no longer visit the area.

A sideways glance as the coffee poured from a great height into the tiny cup revealed that his delight was not shared. Sir Christopher had rejected a second cup, and might not even have finished his first thimble-full. This refusal teetered on the edge of impoliteness. Maybe he couldn't abide the stuff.

With a slight bow, the lad gathered his coffee-making impedimenta and retreated backwards, his slippers making little sound.

Patrick sat back to contemplate their surroundings. The plain theme continued. Muted colours and dull, polished concrete with sparse furnishings suggested this was not a building for impressing foreign dignitaries. Was this Colonel Ghaddafi's personal taste?

As they waited, it didn't seem right to start pointless conversation with Sir Christopher. He might take it as betraying nervousness. Anyway, Patrick had nothing to say, even to pass the time.

But there wasn't long to wait. They heard footsteps on the concrete floor coming towards them. A middle-aged man rounded the corner, smiled and gestured with his hand that they should follow him. He wore a western suit, complete with tie. This struck Patrick as odd. Western clothing was ill-suited to the temperature variations and extremes of Arabia. This must be an administrator, for his clothes and bearing were not military at all.

They rose together. But Sir Christopher said, "I'll go first to lay the ground. You stay here. I'll send the man back to fetch you."

Taken aback, Patrick could only murmur, "Ok." He sat back down. The footsteps retreated further into the heart of the building. It was easy to distinguish the footfall of Sir Christopher as he had a set of steel 'Blakey' heel protectors fitted to his shoes. They tapped away on the concrete like a Guardsman on sentry duty at Buckingham Palace.

Patrick rehearsed in his mind what he'd say to the Colonel. He remembered that Sir

Christopher had encouraged him towards trying to finance renovations for the steel plant. Should he plunge right in to that topic? Surely some diplomatic toing and froing should come first? But then, as Ghaddafi was a military man, he might want to dispense with all that polite faffing about. Patrick determined to introduce himself first as Royal Counties Bank's representative on the UK Trade Mission. He was keen to increase Libyan trade, perhaps starting with… Yes, that would do.

Ten minutes went by before he heard any movement. Were there so few people in this building that nobody had occasion to hurry past in pursuit of their duties, whether military or civilian? Sure enough, it was Mr Western Suit who appeared, now wearing a smile to go with his tie. Sir Christopher must have 'laid a lot of groundwork' in that ten minutes, Patrick thought.

Western Suit knocked softly on a door, opened it and stepped inside. Patrick followed. He expected to see Sir Christopher sitting with the Colonel, deep in continued discussion, but instead, the Colonel was alone. He reclined on a chaise longue on a raised platform. Patrick was led towards the inevitable sofa a little way in front.

Ghaddafi wore a white robe and sun glasses. He didn't acknowledge his visitor at all. As Patrick watched, he reached forward to a large bowl on a table and stirred it with his hand. The dry sound was loud in the otherwise silent room.

Should Patrick remain standing? He cleared his throat in case the Colonel was hard of hearing and was unaware of his presence. Patrick eyed the sofa with dislike. He was certain it was one of those where you sank into it and had to peer at others from between your knees. Also, he didn't like to sit before the host invited him to do so.

"Good morning, Colonel Ghaddafi. I am very honoured that you have agreed to see me. I work for Royal Counties Bank in London and am keen to discuss how we can help Libya with some trade finance facilities."

The bowl contained pistachio nuts. Ghaddafi cracked a couple with his teeth and flicked the empty shells over his shoulder. They bounced on the floor and were still. There was no evidence that Ghaddafi even knew that Patrick was there, less than ten feet in front of him. He tried again.

"Sir Christopher tells me you might be especially interested in renovating the steel mill near Sirte. I'd be pleased to see what we can do towards helping with that as a first step."

He waited for some response.

Ghaddafi stopped chewing for a moment. "Royal Counties Bank?"

Patrick nodded.

"Nest of spies and vipers. Which are you?"

This aggressive response was the last thing Patrick expected. Ghaddafi's naturally cruel mouth showed no sign of a smile. Sun glasses shielded the eyes so Patrick could only conclude the man was serious and not trying to be funny. It was easy now to see why Sir Christopher believed him to be head of *Al Sharika*. He wasn't behaving like one assumed the premier of a country would behave. His manner exuded restrained hostility and - Patrick had to admit - evil. If Ghaddafi was a psychopath, Patrick knew he mustn't show weakness.

"I'm neither of those, Colonel. And, as part of this UK Trade Mission, I really am interested in helping Libya. Is the steel mill at the top of your list?"

Ghaddafi swayed to the side and farted, loudly.

A tiny piece of pistachio nut had lodged in the Colonel's moustache. He brushed at it with his left hand. There, on his finger was an elaborate signet ring. As Patrick waited for the reply to his question, he tried to discern the marking on the ring. It was Arabic script but easy to read despite the distance between them. Three numerals – seven, nine and zero.

Adrenaline lent clarity to his brain. He saw right away that the characters would read upside down as a dot, followed by lower case 'B' and lower case 'L'. It resembled the one Sir Christopher wore. Patrick froze. Were they linked somehow? Why would they have the same rings?

What could '790' mean?

"You ask about the steel mill. What did Sheikh Cephas tell you?"

He opened another pistachio nut and consumed it. 'Cephas'? Who is Cephas?

"I apologise, Colonel. Who is Sheikh Cephas?"

Ghaddafi raised his hands in mock despair. "You are playing games, Mr Field. He brings you to me and you ask who he is?"

The penny dropped. 'Cephas' must be Arabic for 'Christopher'.

"Ah! You mean Sir Christopher – well, he suggested that among the most useful assistance we can give Libya, would be help to renovate the steel mill. But we are open to other works if you prefer them."

Ghaddafi chewed with no expression on his face. "Can you do this?"

"I believe so, yes, Colonel."

"Then I let you go."

"I am grateful for this audience, Colonel. I will write to you when I return to London and outline how Royal Counties Bank can assist your country. I will leave my business card with your assistant. Thank you for receiving me."

Patrick bowed his head very slightly and tried to make a respectful and dignified withdrawal. But his brain raced faster than his elevated pulse rate. What an extraordinary encounter. What did Ghaddafi mean, 'I will let you go'? Patrick recalled the man had been educated in England, so his grasp of the language ought to be decent enough. Did he go to the military academy at Sandhurst? Maybe not. Perhaps that was just a rumour. Was there ever a possibility that he'd be stopped from leaving Gaddafi's compound? This could have been 'Let you go' in the American sense, meaning, 'It's time for you to go'.

He opened the door, thankful to escape Ghaddafi's pungent flatus and made his way back along the corridor. He wondered where Sir Christopher had got to. They'd have an interesting discussion in the car on the way back to the hotel. Patrick paused where he'd waited before, expecting his Mission leader to join him there. Maybe Sir Christopher would have a few departing words with the Colonel before leaving.

Chapter 28
Sofas and the Unmasking

There was audible movement deeper in the building. The concrete floors and walls reflected sound almost as well as it travels over flat water at night. Then someone shouted something. The words were in Arabic and remarkably clear. With growing horror, Patrick realised it was Sir Christopher. His voice was harsh.

"Ayha al-balhaa. Turkete jedhab. Mahe mushkeltke"?

This was like the shock of cold water pouring over Patrick. Roughly translated, he knew this meant he was accusing the other person of being an 'imbecile'. Sir Christopher had said, 'You let him go. What is wrong with you'?

The other person was replying, but his words were muffled. It was a man, Patrick could tell that. And the voice was quite deep. But he was gabbling his words, rushing them in desperation to apologise and seek forgiveness for whatever he'd done to incur such displeasure.

It was plain that the other man knew he was in the wrong. He was emphasising utter subservience in the face of the verbal onslaught.

Patrick felt sorry for the man right away. Sir Christopher was evidently unused to being questioned or crossed. This misbegotten creature must have spilled his drink or tripped him up or something.

He wasn't afraid this might develop into a diplomatic incident. Rather, he worried it could risk the UK's chances of landing a mandate to renovate Libya's industrial machine. Patrick hurried along the corridor, intent on pacifying his Mission leader. He headed for the source of all the noise. It was the door behind which he had met Colonel Ghaddafi. By this point, Sir Christopher was suggesting the other man was the unfortunate product of a union between his mother and a passing diseased camel. It would have been amusing if the circumstances were not so serious. Who was this poor fellow and what could he have done to incur such an outpouring of wrath?

For a single heartbeat, Patrick hesitated. Should he go back in?

But then, propelled by a mixture of national pride, desire to win a valuable deal and plain sympathy for the target of Sir Christopher's ire, he pushed open the door.

-----//-----

The scene burned into his memory. Colonel Ghaddafi sprawled on his knees, his hands raised in supplication. A man towered over him, brandishing a curved sword. The man's feet were bare. They poked out from suit trousers held up by bright red braces. His collarless linen khamis (shirt) billowed as he moved. The mop of silvering black hair was covered by a sandy cimama (turban). His signet ring flashed in the light as the being Patrick knew as Sir Christopher turned to confront whoever was interrupting him.

He roared at Patrick, flecks of spittle fanning out from a familiar face now contorted with hatred. Patrick back-peddled as fast as his legs could manage and made it through the door with seconds to spare. He slammed it shut. He tried to stop the handle turning as the madman crashed and pounded against it.

Mad man, indeed. What had happened to Sir Christopher? This wild creature cannot be him. Yet, Patrick noticed the incongruity of pairing Saville Row suit trousers and braces with bare feet and a sort of pirates' linen blouson and turban. What had Ghaddafi called him? Sheikh Cephas?

Somehow, Sir Christopher Sherrif had morphed into a Moslem warrior.

Then realisation dawned like a dousing with freezing cold water all over again. That was it! The design on the signet rings - the numerals 790. That was approximately the year when Penny and Sir Christopher told him the *Al Sharika* movement was born. That was when Sultan Qalawun rallied Moslem fighters to expel the Christian Crusaders from the area now known as Libya.

But …if they said Colonel Ghaddafi is the current Head of *Al Sharika*, why was he grovelling before Sir Christopher …or Sheikh Cephas as Ghaddafi called him?

Unless… Was Ghaddafi only the figurehead? Was it conceivable that the UK Trade Mission leader and current head of the UK's Secret Intelligence Services could be the *actual* leader?

He remembered Penny's driver, Jonathan had told him Penny believed someone in MI-6 was 'not who they appeared to be'. But hadn't had proof. Or maybe she did get proof – perhaps she discovered or at least suspected it was Sir Christopher and that was why she had to be done away with. And when he met Penny's parents outside St Thomas' Hospital, they reported Penny kept insisting someone should 'Tell Patrick it's sofas'. But she wasn't saying, 'sofas', but 'Cephas'.

The pounding on the door redoubled in ferocity. Running footsteps presaged the arrival of help. Four of the women guards approached, guns drawn.

"*Anzel, sidi, anzel,*" ('Get down'), the leading guard commanded.

"*La*" ('No'), Sheikh Cephas *ladih al-aqid al-Gaddafi.*" ('Sheikh Cephas has Colonel Ghaddafi').

The guards conferred rapidly. The most senior sent one to fetch help.

Still struggling to hold the door shut, Patrick called, "*Laqud jen najunu.*" ('He has gone mad'). It occurred to him this extra explanation might be unnecessary. The obvious tempest raging the other side of the door indicated this was the case. He hoped they'd see he was on their side.

Another four female guards came to join in. They must have heard the commotion.

"You talk English?" one asked.

"Yes." Sweat was breaking out on Patrick's forehead. "Your Colonel is in there being attacked by Sir... I mean, 'Sheikh Cephas'. The man has a sword and has gone quite mad."

The shouting and roaring behind the door had changed to more of an agonised howl. All the guards had drawn their weapons. Patrick had no real plan, except he knew he would soon tire and would not be able to keep the door closed.

"I'll open the door and step aside. Then can you get him under control?" He looked around, hoping for understanding.

The guard who spoke some English translated for the others. There was a short exchange with the senior guard during which Patrick caught the words, "*La. Mush mumkin*..." This was bad news. Something in his plan was 'not possible'.

"What?" he asked.

"If it is Sheikh Cephas, then we cannot."

"What? Why? He's waving a sword. You have guns."

Heads shook in denial. To his dismay, they were lowering their weapons. Then, one by one, they all knelt on the ground, bowing their heads.

"No, no. This isn't some Sheikh – this man is Sir Christopher Sherrif - from the British Government. And he has gone mad. You have to help me subdue him."

Their answer was to begin to ululate in unison. Patrick had heard women perform this high-pitched trilling sound at weddings and other happy events. But he also knew that pre-Islamic women encouraged their men in battle this way.

The guards had turned against him. It could only be a matter of time before he was forcibly removed and left to the mercies of Sheikh Cephas or whoever Sir Christopher had become.

At school, Patrick had played rugby as a Centre. Despite his size, he had been able to sidestep reasonably well, even if he didn't have the outright speed of a wing three quarter. He saw a gap between groups of the guards, took a deep breath and let go of the door handle. He feinted left and then dodged right and through the gap.

The nearest guard rose to grab for him but couldn't hold his arm. The others were distracted by the door swinging open. They all looked at the hideous, sweating monster who stood there, fiery eyes searching for his quarry.

"*Wayn al Inglesi*?" ('Where is the Englishman?') Cephas thundered, shoulders heaving.

It took the senior guard a couple of valuable extra seconds to answer, "*Lay aalam*" ('I don't know'). But Cephas spotted several of the guards were looking down the corridor where Patrick had run and he guessed she was not telling the truth.

He snarled, "*Ant taketeb*." ('You lie'). The long sword swirled. Those closest to her were splashed with crimson and the guard was silenced for ever. Everyone's eyes followed the collapsing body as it slumped, her life pulsing like lava from a volcano.

Cephas brandished the stained sword and shouted, "*At ebah – y'allah*" ('Follow him - quickly').

It had only taken Patrick a few seconds to get back to the big front door. He dragged it open, stopped himself closing it, as that would have wasted a precious second or two. He dashed for the compound gates.

Alas, the pursuing guards must have radioed ahead, as his way was barred. The Gate Guards stood in his direct path, legs akimbo, guns drawn in a classic shooting stance. Patrick took all this in as he sprinted towards them.

"There is a mad man with a sword," he yelled. "Er, *fi ragoul majnan bisen!*"

"*Waqf!*" ('Halt'), they yelled back.

He couldn't chance trying to run past. He'd have to try to persuade them without naming the sword-wielding attacker. Patrick pulled up a few feet short of the lead guard. Her kohl-rimmed eyes narrowed against the bright sunlight and gave her an especially fierce expression.

"Sheikh Cephas want you," she said, simply.

His shoulders slumped. It was all over. He should never have listened to Sir Christopher Sherrif's bland assurances that he'd 'be fine' if he stayed with him during the Trade Mission to Libya. His choices were now to be killed or wounded at least by this guard. Or waiting meekly to be put to death by whatever Sir Christopher had now become. Was he the reincarnation of some early Islamic warrior – the real present-day head of *Al Sharika*?

Footsteps pounding behind him announced that the other guards had now caught up. He looked back. More than twenty had appeared. In their midst was the red face of Cephas Sherrif and his sword. A spray of crimson marked his tunic; evidence of the recent punishment meted out to the wavering guard.

Those flanking him stepped a couple of paces to each side and Sherrif advanced more slowly. He was muttering something but appeared to be taking a second or two to recover from his exertions. Many plentiful lunches and cocktail parties and too much coffee and stress had padded his formerly robust frame.

Very conscious of the guns trained on his back, Patrick tried to convince himself that those guards were unlikely to fire in case their shots missed him and hit their leader.

Looking past the man's turban, Patrick saw someone else in a bright, white robe and sun glasses. It was Colonel Ghaddafi. He did not seem to be injured, but was walking slowly with deliberation. Each step was taken with care to make no noise. He pressed his heels then the sides of his feet down into the dirt, much like a cat advances on its prey. Ghaddafi's eyes could not be seen behind the glasses, but Patrick fancied they were focussed directly on Cephas Sherrif.

Sherrif paused some ten feet from Patrick.

"You have caused much trouble for us, Field," he began. The voice was the plummy, well-bred, educated tone of the Head of the UK's Secret Service. And Patrick was fascinated that the lips of the Islamic warrior moved exactly in time to the English words.

"You have resisted our advances. You have avoided joining us and you have frustrated our activities in many places. You have caused the death of my brother, Abdullah Al Hassan, *bismillah al-rahman al-rahim* ('In the Name of the Most Gracious, the Most Merciful)."

Sherrif waited, as though to let the weight of his accusations sink in. And then, in an echo of Al Hassan's own words, hissed at Patrick as he left the Sharia Court in Riyadh, Sherrif pronounced his own sentence.

"For this, you will die."

Patrick knew he ought to say something. To make some objection. Without even considering it, he knew pleading for his life, as Ghaddafi had done, was a waste of time. The eyes glowering at him had no soul, no humanity to which he could appeal. Sherrif would only understand force. And Patrick had none with which he could resist. There was a rushing sound in his ears, like the roaring of millions of gallons of water as he stood behind Niagara Falls. All other sound was blanked out. He couldn't hear anything else Sherrif said, if he did speak again. Instead, he found himself staring at the crimson stain on Cephas

Sherrif's tunic. He had first noticed it when the guards stepped aside to reveal him clearly. But now the stain was growing and spreading.

Instead of a thin line of blood spray, it was expanding quickly across the whole lower part of the tunic. It was not quite the same colour as the braces holding up his suit trousers. A very poor match, Patrick thought.

And then Cephas Sherrif toppled forward onto his face and was still.

Patrick looked down at him, not understanding what he was seeing. He raised his eyes again and looked beyond to see Colonel Ghaddafi in the centre of the crowd of guards. The gun in his hand was still raised in Patrick's general direction

. The light breeze blew acrid fumes from the gun towards him. Ghaddafi lowered his arm and addressed the guards, demanding fealty to him alone.

"I am your leader. Your Glorious Brother Leader. Do I not look after you? Treat you well? Provide food, refreshment – all this?" He swept an arm around in a wide arc to illustrate his beneficence.

One by one, the guards holstered their weapons and knelt as a sign of their loyalty. But Patrick didn't see any of that. He had fainted and collapsed in an undignified heap. Ghaddafi ordered him to be carried back inside and for the guards to dispose of Sherrif's body.

Chapter 29
The Colonel Escapes

He came to lying on a cool, concrete floor. Trying to sit up right away was a bad idea, as a blanket of wooziness threatened to descend again. Someone had given him a small bottle of water. He unsealed it and sipped repeatedly, levering himself bit by bit into a sitting position. His head was still swimmy, but the room as a whole was cool and a pleasant change from the heat outside. Dehydration was a terrible thing, he decided. Pursuit by sword-wielding reincarnations of ancient Islamic warriors was pretty terrible too. Arguably, worse, in fact.

The room came more into focus, its walls remaining still and straight. The floor no longer rippled and shimmied. His finger pressed on the inside of his wrist to reveal that his pulse was thready – he needed more blood volume. The last of the water swirled around his mouth and Patrick took and held a deep breath, bracing himself to rise to a standing position.

He managed, although that awful tide of faintness stirred. He kept it at bay by breathing deeply several times and leaning against the supporting wall. The room was new to him. It wasn't where he'd first met the Colonel. That room at least boasted some minimal furnishings. This one more resembled an office. There were filing cabinets and a couple of desks with computer screens. The computers were not switched on, though. Some inner part of Patrick's brain told him that his thought processes were working slowly. Like a car in 'limp home' mode. He had to concentrate; not let his mind wander.

Closing his eyes helped. He had to get out of the compound and return to the hotel. Maybe there would be a taxi or perhaps he could offer to pay a passing motorist.

He had made up his mind to start to walk towards the door when he became aware of people running in the corridor. There was urgency in the calls and shouts people made. He reached halfway across the room when the door banged open to reveal two more guards.

"*Ta'ale manna*," ('Come with us'), they ordered. "*Ya'allah*."

"*Aiwa*," Patrick acknowledged. They seemed to be helpful, and might have more water. "*Fi mai*?" he asked, hopefully.

"*La. Ya'allah, Sidi*."

Oh well. Maybe he could find some wherever they were going.

His legs weren't working fully, yet, so dragged a bit, but with the help of the two strong women, he made his way deeper into whichever building this was. They rounded a couple of corners and finally paused at a door. One guard put her ear to the door and listened. Satisfied, she took a key from her uniform pocket and unlocked it. Steps led downwards in a gentle curve. The ceiling was low and as they proceeded further, headroom became even more limited.

Low voices could be heard ahead. Another bend revealed a small, open area with seating and cupboards on the wall. There was a group of guards with Colonel Ghaddafi at their centre.

He looked up. Without his sunglasses, Patrick could see the man's eyes for the first time. They were dark. Expressionless.

"*Salaam aleikum*, Colonel. You shot Cephas Sherrif." He didn't mean it to sound like an accusation. Ghaddafi nodded.

"I think he was going to kill me. *Shukhran, yah Sheikh*. Thank you."

There was the slightest tilt of Ghaddafi's head in acknowledgement.

"We go to my son, Mutassim," Ghaddafi said. "We need transport to Sirte. Rebel forces attack us here in Tripoli. Maybe you help Libya in future."

With that, Ghaddafi stood up, and with him, his coterie of close protection guards. Patrick stumbled after them as they made their way swiftly along the remainder of the tunnel. By the time he and his two helpers reached the steps up to the exit door, the Colonel had boarded a Toyota pickup. As he watched, it sped out of the warehouse following another vehicle. Several others fishtailed in pursuit.

Patrick's guards left him there and sprinted for the last pickup. One waved and smiled from the cab as the driver revved its engine.

So, what now? Who were these 'rebel forces'? Ghaddafi had sounded almost welcoming with his parting words. Patrick was aware that Arab lands rarely stayed in the control of one man for long. Ghaddafi had been in charge for more than forty years. Usually a ruler's son would seize the chance to overthrow his father, then at least the same tribe stayed in control. But in Libya, there were several warring tribes which would relish the chance of controlling the country. Then he remembered he was hoping to generate a large restructuring loan facility to restart the country's steel mill and hence revive its industrial economy. If tribal factions began shooting each other once more, he could kiss that opportunity goodbye.

On the bright side, he was still alive. And, maybe even more positive than that, the actual head of *Al Sharika* was dead. But with Sir Christopher Sherrif's passing, would the movement crumble? He doubted it. He now knew it was so old and so widespread that another would rise to take Sherrif's place. Not Moammar Ghaddafi – it was clear he was just a figurehead, as Penny had intimated.

It was depressing to think that someone would succeed Sherrif. But he looked forward to telling Penny what had become of her erstwhile boss. How would the British Government handle the unmasking of their most senior spymaster as head of a powerful terrorist organisation, dedicated to the downfall of the western way of life?

He'd leave that to Penny – if she recovered from her injuries. He couldn't wait to tell her.

And Jess. With a guilty start, he remembered they were getting married later this year and he hadn't thought about her at all.

'I've been a bit busy', he told himself. And her memory wasn't really in context with hot and dusty places where everyone plotted against everyone else.

In the distance, there was shouting.

He'd best get out of the compound. Who knows what manner of armed militia men might burst in and think he was loyal to the Colonel?

Chapter 30
Brian from Brentwood

How was he going to be able to leave Libya?

Ghaddafi had fled east towards his tribal homeland near Sirte. Egypt was in that direction, a country which might be friendly towards Patrick – he had visited frequently and knew influential and powerful people there. But it was several hundreds of kilometres away.

No, Tunisia was much closer. And the route would be easy to follow – pretty much straight along the coast, the way Ghaddafi's driver had brought him.

First, he ought to return to the El Khan Hotel. His luggage was there. Maybe he could arrange some transportation too.

He had come to Bab Al Azizya in a taxi with Sir Christopher. The driver had taken a direct route, twisting and turning through the back streets. Probably this was the shortest way which used less fuel. But Patrick was scared of getting lost. It would be longer but more straightforward to head for the coast, turn north east and walk until he reached the little seaside park he'd spotted from his room.

The two downsides would be the route was longer and those main roads would be the ones rebel forces would use to begin with as they closed in on the heart of Tripoli. On the plus side, he wouldn't get lost so easily.

So he set off at an easy pace. He could skirt the built-up area and cross an open park. In the distance, he could see the Sheraton hotel, which was right on the waterfront, so he aimed to the right of it, staying in the gardens and parks. The on-shore breeze ruffled his hair. It carried the smell of the sea. His steps quickened.

Soon he could see the ocean as well as smell it. He thought briefly of his plaintive pestering of his parents when, as a small boy at the back of their family car, he'd asked repeatedly, 'Are we there yet?'. The answer was always, 'Not yet, dear,' or 'We'll tell you when we are close.' But after what seemed like a whole agonising day spent on the A-303, travelling nose to tail with hundreds of others bound for Devon or Cornwall, he was able to make that triumphant announcement, 'I can see the sea!'

Time always flew after that.

He smiled to himself at the memory.

By now, he could hear the waves breaking on the shore. He turned northeast.

There was little traffic on this coast road. Perhaps the local business people were aware that armed soldiers were headed their way. It would be natural to restrict journeys to the most urgent errands for supplies. They could be in for several days of sheltering in their homes and places of business. It was only a few kilometres to the hotel now.

As he had found in the past when needing to walk for a considerable distance, he took comfort in the metronomic repetitions of striding left, right, left, right. It took his brain to a restful place. His conscious brain, anyway. He reckoned that unconsciously, his mind was puzzling away at what to do next. What were the alternatives? Could the hotel organise transport for the remaining members of the British Trade Mission? Would he be better off finding a taxi and paying over the odds for a speedy ride to the Tunisian border? What would he do if there was no transport?

He recognised a couple of the streets near the hotel, turned a couple of corners and there was the Hotel El Khan.

Patrick was always conscious that reception and concierge staff first judged guests by their appearance and secondly by their behaviour. He felt himself to be well-dressed – he'd prepared that morning to meet the President of the country, after all – but his suit and shoes displayed evidence of his recent adventure. Hotel staff would knock some marks off for that. He hoped they would see his drab exterior as similar to the exterior of their own hotel and perhaps postpone final judgement, recognising that, in the same way, outward appearances might not reflect *his* interior.

As he passed beneath the portals, he consciously straightened his back and marched to the reception desk.

"*Minfadlak, al khamsa.*" (Room five, please). The Reception clerk handed over his key. Patrick was about to enquire after some transportation but spotted 'Brian from Brentwood' loitering in the corner.

"Brian! Good to see you. What's the news? What have you heard?"

"Me? Nuffink, mate. 'Ole place has gone deaf, I reckon." He nodded his head at the Reception desk. "It could be that I don't speak the lingo, but them blokes don't know what time of day it is."

He eyed Patrick up and down.

"Which visit did you go on, then? Were you attacked by wild animals? Was it that …'Leopards Magma' place?"

Patrick couldn't help grinning, despite their predicament.

"Ha, ha. Very funny. No. Not 'Leptis Magna'! I expect my day might have been a little more peaceful if I had gone there. Actually, I had something of an altercation with an ancient Moslem warrior named Cephas Sherrif. He's …not going to be a problem any more, though."

"Sherrif? Like in our 'Sir Stuffed Shirt Sherrif'?"

"The very same, my friend, the very same. I understand there are rebel forces heading our way to depose Ghaddafi. He has escaped towards the east and so I'm planning to head west, towards Tunisia. Have you heard about any of this?"

"You wha'? Rebel forces..? 'Ow did you 'ear this?" Brian's face was registering shock and disbelief at the same time.

"Believe it or not, I heard it from Ghaddafi himself. He and his guards were about to jump into a pickup truck along with a couple of dozen others in a convoy. That's why I asked what have you heard. If there are any others from the Trade Mission, we might try to find a truck or some cars and get them out too."

"Christ. I can't leave yet. I haven't done any deals with anyone."

This was the difference, Patrick realised, between an entrepreneur, living on his wits and counting every penny he spends in pursuit of making money and himself. He had the luxury of not needing to worry about that. Of course, if he failed to bring in profitable business in the medium term, he'd be fired. But Brian's monetary worries were immediate. If he didn't pay for this trip with a deal, he'd be bankrupt. 'Game over', as they say in America. Still, he needed to convince Brian that the Game might be over in a more serious and terminal fashion if they didn't depart very soon. Being fired at had been a sobering experience.

"Look, Brian, I've been visiting the Middle East and North Africa for a number of years. My knowledge of the region suggests that few rulers die peacefully in their beds. Most rulers take power by force and lose it by force. That means gunfire – and the soldiers they use won't have had the disciplined training of the British Army. What I'm saying is that they'll keep firing at anything that moves and happens to be between them and the target their commander gave them."

"You fink this is dangerous?"

"Is the Pope Catholic?"

They were both able to smile at that little rejoinder, at least. Patrick smiled, because it was how he remembered Mert Mungan, the Bina Kredi Bank Chief Dealer, reacted when asked if he'd like to have a few beers after work. Brian from Brentford might not have heard the expression before.

"Guess we'd better scram, then."

Patrick nodded. "Yes, I'm afraid so. Is anyone else here from the Mission?"

"Yeah. A couple of blokes who came wandering into town with me to see a minister. They didn't get anywhere either." He looked around. "They went upstairs. The bar's a bit dead. Where's 'Stuffed Shirt'?"

"Oh, he's not coming back with us. He's …er, well-connected locally."

"Oh. Right. Well, 'e can sod off, then. I'll get me bag."

Patrick turned to the Reception.

"*Mumkin, sayaara 'ujrat 'iilaa Tunis?*" *(*Is it possible to get transport to Tunis?)

"*Kam eadad alrukaab?*" *(How many passengers?)*

This stumped Patrick, briefly.

"*Laheder shwei.*" (Please wait a short time). He'd have to check around to see if any other Mission members could be scooped up to take away to safety.

He trotted through to the other receiving rooms, lounges and the dining room. He didn't recognise anyone. Brian was waiting for him in the reception. His bag must have been packed already.

"I couldn't find anyone else. I don't like to just leave them here. Who knows what'll happen?"

His Brentwood companion was more sanguine about the situation. "They took the same risk we did. It ain't up to you what 'appens to them."

"Hmmn. I suppose not. Still. I don't feel great about abandoning them."

"Everyman for 'imself. That's what I say. Come on. 'Ave they got a car or summink?"

"I'll ask." Patrick attracted the attention of the bored reception clerk. *"Faqat nahn aliathnayn"* (Just the two of us).

"Tammam – laheder, Sidi." (Ok. Wait, Sir).

The clerk picked up his desk telephone and muttered rapidly into it.

"Antazar khams daqayiq, min fadlak." (Please wait five minutes).

Patrick asked for his bill. The receptionist eyed their baggage and asked if Brian from Brentwood was checking out too. The question confronted him with a moral quandary. He was certain Brian couldn't afford to pay, especially as he hadn't managed to conclude a deal during his time in Libya. But could the hotel afford a non-paying guest? He said he didn't know but noted that Brian was nowhere to be seen. While waiting for his credit card transaction to go through, Patrick looked around the hotel's atrium. As he turned back to the reception desk, he thought he noticed one of the ornamental ferns move in an unnatural manner.

Why was his life so full of moral choices, just lately?

He decided to wait outside. This was both to save Brian's blushes if he had difficulty paying and also to collar the taxi driver and stop him driving away. There wasn't long to wait. A dusty Toyota saloon pulled up and the driver jumped out.

"*Sayed Patrick?*"

"*Aiwa. Isme Patrick.*"

The young man stepped forwards to grab Patrick's suit-carrier. This was better service than Ghaddafi's driver had given him. But then, Sir Stuffed Shirt wasn't there to absorb all the limelight. The bag went into the car boot and the man went to close the lid. Patrick stopped him.

"*Sadiqi sawf yati qariban*" (My friend will come soon).

"*Tammam.*"

They both got into the vehicle to wait. A couple of minutes went by. Surely this had been enough for Brian to find his credit card or cash or however he was going to pay? Leaving his car door open, Patrick asked the driver to wait and went back inside the hotel.

Brian's luggage was no longer stacked beside a chair in reception. The potted ferns along the far wall were unoccupied and the Reception staff were bent over some paperwork on their desk. Where had Brian gone?

"*Wayn sidiqi?*" Patrick asked them. (Where is my friend)?

They shrugged.

"*La fikrat ya sayidi.*" (No idea, Sir).

He frowned. This was frustrating. Perhaps the reception staff decided they were unlikely to extract any more money from him, now he had checked out. They had little motivation for helping. He didn't feel like searching through the hotel to find Brian. It was true that the level of danger for them both was rising — the ruler and presumably his forces of law and order were no longer in power. Who knew what manner of rebel soldiers would be streaming through Tripoli in the next few hours?

He made up his mind. Patrick raised one hand to wave goodbye to the men at Reception, turned and headed for the door. Brian would have to look out for himself.

But when he arrived at the waiting taxi, there was Brian, hunkered down in the back seat. The boot lid was now closed.

"There you are. I was looking for you in Reception. I saw your bags had gone and didn't know whether to leave or not."

"Let's get out of here." Brian's eyes were darting all over the place.

"*Yallah.*" Patrick told the driver as he closed the door. (Let's go). He turned to Brian, still hunched down in the seat. "Are you ok?"

The man straightened up to a normal sitting position as they rounded the corner.

"Yup. I'm fine, as long as we keep going." He twisted in his seat to look back and didn't face forwards again until they had made two more turnings.

At first, they were nervous and watchful, looking into all the side roads and scanning the open spaces they passed for signs of advancing soldiers. But nothing untoward was visible. 'Not even a herd of revolutionary goats,' Patrick thought. The driver increased speed as they reached the open coast road. They did not go as fast as Abdul Daim had driven Ghaddafi's Mercedes, but neither man was in a mood to complain. In fact, neither exchanged any conversation at all, as they were lost in their own thoughts.

The slight swaying motion of the car was almost soporific. Patrick began to relax a little as the adrenaline-soaked memories of his recent brush with death softened in his head. Why did that happen, he mused to himself? In the immediate moment of danger, everything was sharp and well-defined. Or it seemed so, at least. Yet, no matter how clear and well-defined were the sights and sounds and smells of danger, the passage of time melted the edges. Made hazy the details.

Was this some evolutionary adaptation? 'If I was being hunted by a sabre-toothed tiger, I'd want to smell or hear it before I was attacked. And if I had a weapon, I'd want to be able to see the animal in exquisite detail to be able to target its vital organs as it moved. But why do these high-definition images soften in the aftermath? Is it all too big for my brain?'

Patrick tried hard to commit to memory as many details of the past days as he could, replaying his meeting with Ghaddafi, witnessing the transformation of Sir Christopher Sherrif into Sheikh Cephas Sherrif. And, of course, the latter's death at Ghaddafi's hands.

As he sat at the back of the car, he found himself fiddling with the *Gris-Gris* around his neck. This was the protective charm he'd been given by a Voodoo priest in New Orleans what seemed like years ago.

Was it the *Gris-Gris* which kept him alive when Fawaz Damra tried to drown him in New York? And again when he was caught up in the assassination of two top members of the Turkish mafia group, the Grey Wolves? And now, in Libya, Ghaddafi's driver had not crashed when avoiding a herd of goats during the journey from Tunisia to

Tripoli. Ghaddafi himself, whom he believed to be the head of *Al Sharika*, had not killed him when he had the chance. And finally, he'd escaped capture and likely death when Cephas Sherrif, the actual head of *Al Sharika,* revealed himself.

If the *Gris-Gris* was responsible, he knew it would become a mental burden. If he believed the thing kept him safe then he had to keep *it* safe – at all costs. And that could become ridiculous. He'd never go swimming again, since it smelled bad as it dried out. And although he took it off to shower, it was always just a few feet away from him. Actually, it was the first item of clothing he put on after towelling himself dry.

What did Jess think about it? He'd seen her nose wrinkle when first she saw it. Did she believe in it? She had witnessed one of Patrick's junior members of staff in the New Hebrides fade away and die because a witch doctor had put a spell on him. Yet, she'd examined the lad carefully and concluded there was nothing wrong with him. It was all in his mind, she said. But that belief was a powerful thing.

It followed that if Patrick allowed himself to believe the *Gris-Gris* kept him safe and he lost it, then would he be *un*safe? Would he have exactly the amount of fortune he'd have experienced had he not visited New Orleans? Or maybe he would experience 'fortune deficit' – 'like going into overdraft', he thought. What would be the consequences of that?

Patrick closed his eyes. This was the danger of thinking too much. He should live in the Here and Now. Wasn't that a Yoga thing? To be more Present. More conscious of how and where you were right now.

What was going through Brian's mind? What was he thinking? Patrick decided to enquire gently. If Brian wanted to be alone with his thoughts, he'd shut up for the rest of the journey.

"Are you ok, Brian? What are you thinking?"

"Me? I'm trying not to think. It does me 'ead in, thinking too much. We're goin' to Tunisia, right? Mebbe I can do a bit of buyin' and sellin' there. I'll think about it when we get closer. You?"

Patrick shook his head. "I'm thinking too much. It's been an exciting couple of days. Unfortunately, I've achieved nothing."

They were silent for a few minutes. Patrick began to realise that in fact he *had* achieved something. He might well have resolved his *Al Sharika* problem, for the time being, anyway. Common sense suggested others would replace Sherrif in time. The network was too old and too established and well-financed to evaporate just because the head was no more.

But he had a promising new career in front of him, a wonderful woman he could now marry and little to stand in his way.

He just had to find his way back to the UK.

Chapter 31
A Military Escort

They stopped only once for fuel. Patrick treated Brian and their driver to some stale pitta breads, hommous and water. He didn't even try to protest when the driver lowered his window and threw the food wrapping onto the road. He was too tired.

There was an enormous queue of cars and trucks at the border. They sat in the broiling sun, crawling forward a car length at a time. At long last, they drew into the shade of the border building and a guard in uniform approached and snapped his fingers for their passports. He took them inside for inspection. Patrick never liked losing control of his passport for more than a minute or two. It was his only documentary protection in places like this.

He was about to get out of the car to follow the guard and find out what he was up to, when the man scurried out of the guard house. He ran to Patrick's door, stood ramrod straight and saluted. He began to gabble apologies in Arabic. Then started shouting at his colleagues to move other cars in front out of the way. He handed the passports over with a stiff bow from the waist and saluted again.

The taxi driver and Brian from Brentford watched all this with growing amazement.

"Oo's yer mate, then?" Brian enquired.

Patrick realised the guard must have recognised his name from when he passed through the border with Sir Christopher and was shown into the Colonel's quarters to rest.

Despite the guard's shouting, they made little forward progress. Over the noise of the cars queuing around them they heard diesel engines revving up. Brian looked behind.

"'Ere. There's army vehicles wanting to come through. They'll be lucky. Mebbe that's why they want us to move."

Patrick thought so too. But he was wrong. They were getting an army escort all the way to Djerba in Tunisia. The guard explained to their driver that he had to follow in line behind the third vehicle.

"I must have friends in high places." Patrick told Brian. He tried to look mysterious. It was said half in jest, but he didn't think he ought to try to dissuade the guard. If his explanation included anything about the fate of Sir Christopher or Colonel Ghaddafi, their futures might be far less certain. Better to go along with the arrangement.

The trucks and armoured cars ground along, much slower than they'd been travelling until now. Such a show of force ought to have brought Patrick a sense of comfort and safety. But the reverse was true. Moving slowly was bad enough, but he reckoned travelling in an armoured column was drawing far too much attention to them – making them an obvious and slow-moving target. Of course, they were now in Tunisia, not Libya. Surely, rebel forces wouldn't seek to attack them in a neighbouring country. Would they?

The only occupant of the car who was in any way comfortable with this was the taxi driver. After a few minutes, he turned on his radio and began to sing along with the song.

It was Rai music. Patrick liked Rai and thought he recognised the singer.

"*Hal hadha Cheb Khaled?*" (Is this Cheb Khaled?)

"*Aiwa. Hu al'afdal"* (It is. He's the best).

Even Brian seemed to like the music.

"What do you call this? It sounds like some of that Hip Hop stuff the lads round me play all the time."

"It's Rai music. It originated here in North Africa. My fiancée Jess bought me a world music album which has a couple of tracks by this artist. I don't understand it and it's too exotic to whistle on my way to the station in the mornings. But it kind of sticks in your head, doesn't it?"

"Yeah." Brian looked out at the passing desert scrub with the sparkling sea in the distance.

"What are you thinking, Brian?"

"Me? Nuffink. Well, not nuffink. I might 'ang around here for a day or two, now we're out of Libya. There's people that lives in Djerba, ain't there? They'll be wanting to buy stuff, yeah? Mebbe I can 'elp 'em wiv that."

Patrick smiled. Brian reminded him of one of those childrens' toys. You knock them over and they'd spring right back up again.

"Yup. Maybe you can. How's your French?"

"French? I dunno. How's their English?"

The man was irrepressible. He'd be fine, Patrick was sure. "They speak Arabic here as well, of course, but if you have a few phrases in French, you'll do alright. I don't know how much English they'll have – it depends upon their education. Anyone who tries to sell to tourists will have a smattering of English, German, Italian – you know – enough to get someone to buy whatever they're selling."

"Sounds pretty kosher to me. Thanks."

"Er, I don't think you should be using Yiddish expressions, Brian."

"Oh. No, I suppose not. They don't really get along, do they?"

"Not always, no. But they do when it comes to matters of business, I have found."

Brian stared at him. "You don't say..? Huh." He looked out of the side window again.

Patrick's thoughts turned to how he'd get home.

-----//-----

With some ceremony, the Libyan soldiers escorted Patrick and Brian into the little airport at Djerba. The local Police and Security were unhappy with armed soldiers marching onto their territory. But someone explained to them that these Englishers were emissaries from Colonel Ghaddafi and were to be treated with utmost care. Some French is spoken in Libya and they are used to speaking it when visiting Tunisia, although it isn't their mother tongue, of course. The result was equivalent to Patrick's schoolboy level of linguistic fluency. He could follow the discussion just fine, his memory and imagination filling in the gaps in vocabulary.

Ceremony done, the soldiers saluted and left them to the tender mercies of Tunis Air.

"You want to stay here, Brian?"

"Might as well. I'll give it a go."

"I need to get back to Britain. Look – here's my card. Give me a call when you can. We can have a beer, perhaps."

Brian grinned at him. "If you're paying."

They shook hands and Brian wandered off to find a taxi. Patrick made his way to the check-in desk to enquire about flights back to Tunis and onward to London.

-----//-----

When the aeroplane touched down at Heathrow, he sat upright in his seat. Somehow a great weight had lifted from his shoulders. He had his passport and would probably find his luggage on the carousel. He was home.

Immigration scrutinised all the stamps in his passport with minute attention. The officer called his supervisor over and whispered in his ear. The senior man told Patrick to go with him into an interview room.

There the man opened with, "You have spent quite a long time in the Middle East, haven't you?"

"Indeed, I have," Patrick conceded.

"Do you have any Arab friends?"

This took Patrick aback. What an odd question. Immediately, he tried to gauge what the fellow was trying to get him to say. If he said 'no', this would lead to examination of his travel itinerary, person by person. 'Are *none* of these people your friends?' Yet if he said 'yes', he might be accused of being an Arab sympathiser, a likely funder of international terrorism and possibly worse. He'd have to try a different tack.

"I have been on a government trade mission lead by Sir Christopher Sherrif. Perhaps you should take these questions up with him."

The name meant nothing to the Immigration official. And why would it? What would he know of the head of …well, the *former* head of MI-6?

The fellow licked his thumb and turned the pages of Patrick's passport, rotating it to see the stamps where they had been placed askew.

"And you visited Turkey," the man observed. This was a statement of fact, so Patrick remained silent.

"And Saudi Arabia and Kuwait. And Bahrain… Are you sure you don't have any Arab friends?"

"I work for Royal Counties Bank and am responsible, with others, for some of the bank's relationships in the Middle East. That's why I travel there frequently."

The man looked hard at him. Then pushed the passport back across the table.

"Alright. Off you go."

It took some effort on Patrick's part not to utter some crisp rejoinder. He was being treated as a criminal who hadn't been caught – yet. Did many foreigners experience entry to the UK in this manner when they arrived? Perhaps Immigration was on the look-out for a particular person resembling him and who was wanted for genuine criminal activities. All the same, he felt aggrieved.

Just as his mood had lifted when the wheels touched the runway, so did his spirits rise again as he strode through the Arrivals gate to the rank of taxis.

For once, the journey by road into the City of London took just an hour and twenty minutes. Having paid off the taxi, Patrick pushed open the heavy swing doors of the Lombard Street Head Office of Royal Counties Bank.

"Oh, Goodness. What happened to you? Is everything alright, Mr Field?" one of the receptionists asked. She eyed his dusty trousers and jacket and unshaven face with alarm.

"I've had a more eventful trip abroad than is normally the case. I just want to dump my bag and have a shower and shave before I go upstairs. Would that be ok?"

"Of course, of course. You know the way."

Ten minutes later, the streaming hot water of the sub-basement shower revivified Patrick. He was now a whole lot more positive. There weren't any fresh clothes in his bag, so he did his best to freshen up what he had been wearing. It was time to return to his normal world.

His attempts to improve his appearance didn't fool any of the women in his project group, though.

"Hey, Patrick. Welcome back. Looks like you've been working hard for your money," Annabelle observed. "Do you want a quick briefing or do you want to go straight home?"

"That bad, eh? Hmmn. Sorry. The Trade Mission was quite …trying."

"What did the other guy look like?" Judy was grinning at him.

"I didn't know you were a fan of blood sports." Patrick shot back.

They all laughed. "I'd like to know where we are up to in the project, but actually, I could do with making a couple of calls first. Do you mind?"

"Just say when you are ready." Diana told him.

Patrick was itching to see how Penny was. And he should tell his Mum and Dad that he was back in the country again and, when enough time went by, he most wanted to hear Jess' voice. She was still in New York, of course. He wanted to catch her before she went on duty at the hospital.

He dialled Penny's desk telephone. Would she have recovered enough to go back to work?

"Baxter."

"Oh, fantastic. Penny, I'm so pleased to talk to you. What a relief. How are you? When did you get out of hospital?"

"Er, this is Patrick, right?"

"Yes, yes. Of course, it's me. Sorry. I should have said."

"Where are you?"

"In London. At the bank."

"Well, that's a good thing. Did you hear about the Trade Mission?"

Patrick chuckled. "Did *you* hear about Sir Christopher? Or should I call him Cephas Sherrif?"

"That's what I kept trying to tell them. They all thought I was raving. I suppose that was natural after my …accident."

"It wasn't accidental, though was it, Penny?"

"Uh, uh. Jonathan worked it out. Christopher was the only person it could have been who was after me."

"Did you confront him?"

"No. I overheard a call he was making on speakerphone. He was careless. The conversation was in Arabic, so he thought nobody would know what they were talking about. But I have heard enough Arabic to recognise when someone is addressed by name. The person on the other end called him 'Sheikh Cephas'. I was walking past his office at the time. I think he saw me go by, so knew that I knew, if you follow."

Patrick shuddered. What a cold-blooded man Sir Christopher had been. "I have my own little story to tell you about him – and Colonel Ghaddafi – when you are free."

"Ghaddafi's been overthrown. We don't know for certain yet, but we think rebels from the National Transitional Council captured him. Maybe his sons too, although the most likely one to succeed him, Saif Al-Islam, has vanished. Mutassim also. There's no word on any of his other offspring."

"So… Libya's a bit of a mess right now?"

"You could say that."

"Tell me about you, Penny. I was trying to see you but couldn't get into the hospital."

There was a pause. He heard a door shutting. Then Penny came back on the line. "Jonathan and my mother and father said you were very kind. I couldn't have talked to you if you had got in, though. I was heavily sedated after being run over by that car. I'm using a wheelchair right now while I recover. It's good exercise for my arms and shoulders."

"Is Jonathan driving you everywhere? Does he cram the wheelchair into the boot of the Jag?"

"He does. It's collapsible, you see."

Patrick thought for a moment. "I guess you're on loads of medications and shouldn't really drink..?"

"I'm sure I could make an exception – just a little one."

"If you're sure – that would be great. Or we could meet for coffee. Maybe a meal?"

"Give me a call when you are free, Patrick. I'm master of my own timetable right now. Christopher isn't breathing down my neck any more."

He thought of saying, 'He isn't even breathing any more,' but contented himself with, "I'll figure something out, Penny. You sound much happier. Far less stressed!"

"You can say that again. 'Course, everyone round here is speculating who will take Christopher's place and all the security people are scouring their records to make sure it wasn't *them* who approved him to the job. It wasn't me, obviously. Quite the reverse."

Patrick chuckled. It was exactly the same in the bank. When something goes wrong, everybody points at the people sitting either side of them. 'It wasn't me' they protest, trying to deflect any blame.

"I'll call you. Give my best to Jonathan."

He rang off and dialled his own telephone number in his apartment in New York. Considering how early it was there, a remarkably lively voice answered, "Doctor Smithson."

"Hi, Jess. It's only me. Thought I'd better let you know I'm back in the UK."

"Oh, it's you. I've missed you. Are you coming home soon?"

"I'll be heading home on Friday. I flew back to London from Tunisia just now. I've missed you too. I've got lots to tell you."

"Hey, I thought you said you were on a Trade Mission to Libya? Did I hear there was a revolution or something? Was that Libya? Are you alright?"

"I'm just fine, Jess. Especially now I've heard your voice. There was ...*is* a revolution which overthrew Ghaddafi. He's part of my story, as a matter of fact. But more importantly, are you ok?"

"Yes. I am. Just tired, I suppose. Hang on…"

There was a bump and a scraping noise.

"Gee. I have to go, Patrick. I am doing Post-Take this morning so there will be a queue of juniors and nurses wanting to hand over their latest patients. Sorry – see you on Saturday morning. Love you!"

"Love you too."

The line went dead. Someone cleared their throat just behind him.

It was Annabelle. "I couldn't help overhearing. You went to Libya?"

Her eyes were wide.

Patrick nodded. "Yup. I was asked to go on a UK Trade Mission there. It's a shame about Ghaddafi being overthrown. We were getting along so well, too. I almost had a mandate to finance a steel plant for him."

To Patrick's dismay, she hooted with laughter. "In your dreams, Patrick Field. In your dreams... Next you'll tell us you got caught up in the fighting."

There was nothing he could say to that.

"Perhaps you could bring me up to speed on the Project?"

-----//-----

In truth, by now, Patrick had contributed most of what he knew about relationship management. It was satisfying to see it all represented on a series of slides prepared by his team colleagues in his absence. He made a couple of minor comments, but they had it all, really. When Annabelle's briefing was over, he said, "You know, I reckon I don't have much more to say on all this. You've got it pretty well summarised."

"We still have to present it to the Board. They may have questions – in fact, some of this runs so much against accepted wisdom, I'm *positive* they'll have questions."

"When are you presenting?"

"Probably tomorrow. I'm planning a bit of a party afterwards. You'll come, I hope?"

"If it's tomorrow …oh. I forgot. There's someone I *must* go to see tomorrow."

Annabelle's face fell. "That's too bad. Although we'll be starting about three in the afternoon – whatever the Board says."

"At three? Great. In that case, I'd love to come for a little while. I've really enjoyed working with you ladies."

"Ever the gentleman. You can buy us all a drink afterwards."

-----//-----

About the Author

Richard Sexton joined a British commercial bank at the tender age of sixteen and retired as a director of its investment bank after twenty-eight years of service. He was lucky to live in many countries to which access these days is barred or at least is deemed unwise.

He knows that living in a culture which is not your own is a remarkable privilege. He met many amazing characters, good and bad. Elements of some of them are included in this story and in the subsequent stories in this series.

Cover Design by James,
GoOnWrite.com

Also by Richard Sexton

Book 1 - 'Saved by the Bull'

Patrick is sent to the South Pacific by his employer, Royal Counties Bank. At the age of 21, this plunge into another culture is exciting.

Local criminals who work for *Al Sharika,* a secret and ancient organisation, notice the well-meaning Patrick because of a series of unfortunate events. They try to blackmail him into helping them launder money.

Can he win the heart of Dr Jessica, the doctor for the islands? Events beyond his control threaten his chances with her. His naïve good nature repeatedly lands him and others in danger but he is helped by Penny, a mysterious young woman who 'works for the Government'.

What will happen to Dr Jessica when he goes back to Britain and why is the British Secret Service interested in him?

Most of all, can he escape *Al Sharika*?

Book 2 - 'Saved from the Desert'

After Long Leave in the UK, Royal Counties Bank posts Patrick to Bahrain. He is quickly tracked by *Al Sharika* which found him in Vanuatu and they redouble efforts to compromise and blackmail him into assisting their funding.

He may have dodged their kidnap attempts but now he risks arrest by the Religious Police in Saudi Arabia.

How can he survive capture and get back to Bahrain?

Will he ever see his doctor girlfriend again?

Can Penny and his friends protect him?

Book 3 - 'Saved by the Gris-Gris'

Royal Counties Bank closes the Bahrain Branch. Patrick transfers to their Wall Street, New York office. His first investment banking success in New Orleans brings him into direct conflict with the America arm of the ancient organisation again.

Fraudulent trading patterns reveal *Al Sharika* activity, as Penny in MI-6 had predicted.

Now his fiancée, Dr Jessica, has landed a job in New York as well, so they are together at last, but for how long?

A chance meeting with a Voodoo priest in New Orleans may help him, but a Mafia godfather offers more practical assistance.

www.ingramcontent.com/pod-product-compliance
Lightning Source LLC
Chambersburg PA
CBHW060239030726
47493CB00024B/1380